EYE

OF THE

ARCHANGEL

ALSO BY FORREST DEVOE JR.

Into the Volcano

EYE

OF THE

ARCHANGEL

A Mallory and Morse
Novel of Espionage

FORREST DEVOE JR.

HarperCollins*Publishers*

HarperCollins books may be purchased for educational, business, or sales promotional use. For information, please write: Special Markets Department, HarperCollins Publishers, 10 East 53rd Street, New York, NY 10022.

FIRST EDITION

Designed by Sarah Maya Gubkin

Library of Congress Cataloging-in-Publication Data
   DeVoe, Forrest.
    Eye of the archangel : a Mallory and Morse novel of espionage / Forrest DeVoe Jr.—1st ed.
      p. cm.
    ISBN: 978-0-06-072380-4
    ISBN-10: 0-06-072380-7
    1. Americans—Foreign countries—Fiction. 2. Intelligence officers—Fiction.
   I. Title.
   PS3604.E887E94 2007
   813'.6—dc22

                              2006041249

07 08 09 10 11 ID/RRD 10 9 8 7 6 5 4 3 2 1

Eye

OF THE

Archangel

BOOK I

Monaco

PROLOGUE

Three Serpents

This is no place for an old man, thought the old man.

It was the dead black hours before a Finnish winter dawn, but Kost had been crawling through the dark for a very long time, and for him the blackness had become as varied and informative as midday sunlight. There was the weak, ghostly black of the snow beneath his belly and legs, which crested against his chin like waves against the prow of a ship. There was the complexly woven black of the surrounding trees and, behind them, the rich blue-black of the horizon. Toward the base of the trees ahead, the glittering black of the narrow asphalt road leading into Virtaniemi. A two-kilometer walk to the middle of town, if the crude, smeary map had been accurate. Two or two hundred; if he made it across the border, the rest was trivial. About ninety meters down the slope, the guardhouse at the Soviet-Finnish frontier was two bright windows hanging in air; between and around them, a nimbus of bleached-out, substanceless black—just the absence of

light upon a stunned eye. Right before his chilled nose was the base
of a cyclone fence, a ghostly black lattice, against which his old leather
work gloves were a furry, animal black. The wire snips in his hand,
freshly oiled, were a black as brilliant as chrome. He tightened them
and a link of wire fencing parted with a sharp clack that was almost like
a spark of light. It seemed to Kost that the sound must be audible for
miles, but as a scientist he knew this was unlikely.

The man in the snow was tall and thin. He wore a workman's canvas trousers and short leather jacket, and had pulled a coarse woolen
watch cap over a scholarly forehead and flowing white locks. Even so,
Walther Kost had an aristocratic air. He looked more like a concert
violinist than a rocket scientist—at any rate, that was what Der Führer
had once told him, under the impression that he was paying a compliment. Kost was sixty-one years old, just ten months older than this
wretched ruin of a century. He was far too old to be wriggling on his
numbed belly through the snow. Still, as he'd done so often in his life,
he was shooing away his dignity like an unwanted cat and making the
best of a bad bargain.

Dr. Kost had been forty-six when the Russians rolled into Berlin.
This had seemed quite old at the time, and he'd sat in his laboratory
drinking tree-bark tea and waiting for death with a kind of sour equa-
nimity. Von Braun had long since cleared out, no doubt to somewhere
advantageous. Von Braun could always be relied upon to take care
of von Braun. And the Russians would want him alive, or the Americans—Wernher was a valuable commodity, the man who'd built the
V-2. In contrast, Kost would strike the invaders as a minor researcher,
a tinkerer, of little account. Unless, of course, they knew about Archangel. And no one knew about Archangel but Hitler, Goebbels, and
two of Goebbels's most senior aides; even Göring hadn't been trusted
with the dossier.

But apparently the Russians knew. The soldiers who'd taken him
had been courteous and apologetic—handpicked men, even the least
of them speaking passable German. They'd packed up his workshop
with un-Russian efficiency, handcuffed him tenderly, and bundled him
off to a brand-new laboratory compound ringed by snowy mountains
and smelling of still-damp concrete and fresh paint. Some village in

northwestern Russia. Kost was never to know the name. The men who unpacked his equipment and drawings were scientists, not soldiers, and Kost was forced to admit they were competent. He was presented with new catalogues of Swiss and American laboratory supplies—he would have preferred German suppliers, of course, but these had been largely destroyed—and invited to order what he liked. And when the lab had been re-created, a Colonel Schevchenko with a flint-gray face and a straggling white mustache had poured him a cup of excellent coffee and asked how long it would take to complete Archangel.

"Years," Kost said.

"Your Führer seemed to think it could be deployed in time to defeat us."

"My Führer was a fool," Kost said.

This shocked Schevchenko. It was comical, the awe these Russians felt for the potty little Austrian with the candy-sweet breath who had so utterly disgraced Kost's homeland. The old colonel washed away the gaffe with a sip of coffee and said, "Have you everything you need to begin?"

"I was seventeen the first time I shot a Russian," Kost said. "A pity it wasn't you, Herr Colonel, but you'd have been too old for the front even then."

"Have you everything you need to begin?" Schevchenko said again.

"He got up and limped off holding his arse," Kost remembered. "A fat fellow. All I'd hit was fat. Better than nothing, I suppose. Later, I'm happy to say, I did better."

"Have you every—"

"I've no intention of beginning. I'm not afraid of death."

"We've no intention of killing you," Schevchenko said indulgently. "After all the trouble we've taken? No, you'll resume work on Archangel quite soon, resume wholeheartedly, and entirely of your own accord."

"Why?"

"You want to see it finished. How long have you been working on Archangel and its predecessors? Seven years?"

"Almost."

"You want to see it finished. You want it badly. How long will it take, do you think?"

"I don't know."

"You have the rest of your life," Schevchenko said.

The morning of the first day, Kost sat down before his waiting assistants, brewed a pot of his favorite Earl Grey in a Pyrex beaker, and sat drinking and looking out the window at the firs marching up the mountain. His assistants watched him, all in a row, like a shelf full of stuffed owls. Kost drank half a dozen pots of tea in complete silence, returned exhausted to his room at six, and pissed all night.

The next day he did the same. It was the most difficult day's work he'd ever done. The third day, he picked up the beaker and then set it down with a grunt of despair he could not quite stifle. The assistants wiggled hopefully in their seats. Furious, stonefaced, he went to the plan files for a quick look at his drawings.

"You've shoved them in every which way," he muttered. He began pulling them out one by one and sorting them into stacks on the floor.

When he'd arranged the drawings to his satisfaction, he began.

Three weeks later, Schevchenko paid him another visit. "You're sulking," the colonel said with disdain. "You're not working properly. The dullest of my first-year students could do better. What more do you need to begin properly?"

"Fresh air and exercise. A pair of skis," Kost said, with equal disdain.

To his astonishment, a new pair of steel-edged Raichles appeared on the foot of his bed ten days later, fitted with Kandahar bindings and smelling beautifully of wax. His minder was a vast slab of young Russian manhood in corporal's stripes who skied with the grace of a prima ballerina. More out of curiosity than anything else, Kost tried to elude him; the young corporal shadowed him without effort, and they swooped down the slope in unison like mating birds. When Kost swerved near the trees, he'd seen waiting, in the depths of the woods, motionless sentries in deep-forest camouflage, holding Brens at present arms.

For some reason the incident lightened his mood, and for two weeks he dawdled through his days almost cheerfully. Schevchenko came again.

"Have a chocolate. They're Lindt's."

"I don't eat sweets."

"You're rather a useless fellow, aren't you?"

Kost inclined his head.

"You're still a vigorous man," the colonel said. "You must miss your wife."

"May I go now?" Kost said in a rage.

That night when he entered his room, Kost found a girl in a deeply cut evening gown sitting in his bedside chair. She stood at once and strolled around the bed to meet him, swaying on preposterously high heels. The gown did not fit. Beneath her nylons, her calves were nicked here and there. She was probably unused to shaving her legs. She lay her palms on his chest and gave him a prostitute's companionable smile.

"I thought I'd at least be given a bed to myself," Kost said.

"They beat me if I don't please you good," she sighed in his ear. "They beat me terrible."

"Well, they'd better get on with it."

She chuckled and left him.

When he was ready to turn in the next night, he found a red-mouthed young private sitting in her place. Kost had not laughed in well over a year. He laughed then, and was still laughing when the boy snapped, "Thank God anyhow. You are too old man"—and slammed the door behind him.

There is no doggedness like Russian doggedness. The next night it was Schevchenko in the bedside chair, one leg elegantly crossed over the other. Six young and quite lovely women stood at the foot of Kost's bed, in size order, dressed, if that was the word, in meager cotton shifts that barely covered them from nipple to hip. There was a Mongol beauty with fistlike cheekbones who was a trifle taller than Kost; there was a sturdy black-haired peasant who barely reached his shoulder; there was a delicate, near-translucent redhead and two honey blondes, one slim, one plump, both with black pubic thatches visible through the thin fabric; there was a surprised-looking girl with a bosom of bar-baric size. "I suppose I can't blame you," Schevchenko said, "for being fastidious. Science itself is a matter of fastidiousness, don't you think? Being picky about what methods one employs, what explanations one accepts. The correct explanation is invariably the comeliest, the most symmetrical. Though its symmetry is not always readily apparent. Any one of these women is available to you, Dr. Kost, or all in turn. If none please you, others can be provided. Do you think any of them will serve to clear your head?"

"Clear my head," Kost murmured, and grimaced. "Succinctly put. You're wrong about science, you know. Sometimes science is damned untidy. Sometimes it has to be. Have them raise their shifts."

Schevchenko spoke a few words in Russian. All of the women looked uncomfortable and all complied at once, lifting their hems to their chins. Kost was no judge, but going by the look on their faces, he didn't think they could be prostitutes, even if someone had dressed them like whores in a military brothel. He walked down the row, laying a hand on the belly of each, except for the redhead, whom he passed by without a glance. He came back to the little peasant, felt her stom-ach again, and nodded. Schevchenko nodded in turn and the other women covered themselves with a look of relief and began filing out.

"See you soon, Kost," Schevchenko said, his hand on the door-knob. "Oh, and I think I should warn you. My patience—"

"—has limits," Kost said. "Yes, I know."

Schevchenko shook his head, smiling. "No, Herr Doktor. I warn you that my patience has no limits at *all*."

The colonel closed the door very gently.

No one had told the little peasant to lower her shift, and she was still standing motionless, displaying herself to Kost's back. Though the room was warm, her body had begun to goose-pimple and her brown nipples had tightened, though not, Kost assumed, in arousal. Kost ges-tured for her to cover herself. "Do you understand German? Don't speak, just nod or shake your head. I don't want to hear from you, now or ever. Do you speak German?"

She nodded.

"All right. I go to bed each night at a quarter to eleven. I'll want to see you here at that time, and not before. When I get up at a quarter to seven, you'll leave. In between, I don't want to be bothered. I'm a thin man and I get cold at night. I chose you because you were the warmest. If I want anything else from you, I'll let you know. Do you need to use the toilet?"

She shook her head.

"Then get in and start warming the bed."

In the bathroom, he brushed his teeth, changed into his pajamas, and stared at himself in the mirror. A gaunt, hard face with a stubborn little beak and large, close-set, unwavering eyes. The man in the mirror looked stern to Kost, and free of doubt. Kost envied him. Returning to the bedroom, he found the little peasant spread out beneath the blankets like a starfish, dutifully trying to warm as much bed as she could. As he approached, she pulled in her arms and legs and waited on her back on the far side of the bed. Kost climbed in beside her, turned her by the shoulders to face away from him, and put his arms around her. Her back was solid and hot against his ribs. A strong young woman. She'd already filled the bed with her female scent and warmed it almost down to the foot of the mattress, where her stubby legs didn't reach. He tugged her closer and she obediently wriggled backward and fit her buttocks into his lap and her head under his chin. It had been a long time since he'd touched a woman. He was curious to see whether the feel of her body stirred him; he found it did not. He was surprised to find himself comforted, and fell easily asleep.

Kost did nothing to clear his head, as Schevchenko had put it, until Sunday night when the week's work was done. That night he pulled back the covers and told her, "Turn around."

She got on all fours. Forgetting his instructions, she said, "You like this way?"

"I don't want," he said, lifting her shift, "to have to look at some pig of a KGB woman."

Still facing the headboard, she shrugged. He slipped a hand between her buttocks, massaged briskly until she seemed ready, or nearly, then worked himself inside. She moaned.

"That's not necessary," he said absently, and she stopped.

It took less than two minutes for him to empty himself into her, after which he rebuttoned his pajamas, lay down, and said, "They've provided a douche. It's in the cabinet by the sink. Go use it."

She turned a grinning face to him and began to laugh. When he stared, she pretended to button her lips shut, hopped out of bed, and strode jauntily into the bathroom. She was soon back and snoring beside him. Kost was too dumbfounded to complain.

Over the next few months, the work resumed in earnest. Kost discovered which of his assistants were valuable and which of them impeded the project. He found he could have these dismissed. Candidates were offered as replacements, their curricula vitae diligently translated into German, and he chose among them. Once a month, Schevchenko examined his plans and notebooks. The old colonel had been trained as a physicist, and many of Archangel's more purely mechanical aspects eluded him, but his insights were valuable in the matter of ballistics. After eighteen months they were ready to build a working prototype, which meant tooling and equipping a small factory. "We'll have to wait for spring to break ground, and I'd imagine we can expect construction to take until midsummer," Kost said. "And fabricating the first prototype will take six to eight months after that. And, you know, it won't work."

"The first one? You'd hardly expect it to," Schevchenko said. "Have your requisitions ready by Monday and I'll sign them. How's Irina working out?"

So that was her name.

"Let me know when you're bored," Schevchenko said. "There's no shortage of girls. That's the one thing we've no shortage of these days."

"I'm used to her," Kost said. "I wouldn't want to have to get used to another."

"Well, tell me if you change your mind. We can always add it to the requisitions."

Every night Irina arrived just as Kost was preparing for bed, wearing the same worn cotton shift, and slipped silently under the covers, holding her hem down with one fist to keep it from riding up to her middle. She never used his bathroom except on Sunday nights. Perhaps she'd been instructed not to. Perhaps she was shy. After the first few months, she began to arrive a bit early and lie across the foot of the mattress, warming it with her belly so that his feet wouldn't be cold when he climbed in. On Sundays she'd get into bed naked and wait, buttocks gleaming dully, her cheek pillowed on her arms and her shift neatly folded in the farthest corner of the floor.

The first time she had her monthlies, she stood beside the bed and pointed at her middle. Beneath her shift he saw the outlines of a pair of knickers, bulging slightly with the cloth wadded inside. "It's all right," he said.

"I can have them send another girl," she told him. Her voice was unexpectedly low and husky. She waited calmly to see if he'd rebuke her for speaking.

"It's all right. It's just a little blood. I've never understood why people fuss about a bit of blood."

His voice had been gentle, as if comforting a panicky child. She was neither panicky nor a child. He felt ridiculous.

"Get into bed," he said.

Kost had expected the first prototype to fail, but the way it finally failed was discouraging: utterly. They might as well have had a pair of old boots on the test stand. "This isn't a matter of adjustments and refinements," Schevchenko said. "We've been flat-out wrong about transmission, haven't we?"

"I've been wrong, yes," Kost said.

"How long until we're ready to start on Ar-2? I'm assuming we'll need a fair bit of new basic research first."

"At least two years' worth. The entire designator code will have to be scrapped. We may have to do without a designator completely. But it'll take another prototype to say for sure."

"I was afraid of that," Schevchenko said. "Well, get your requisitions in order."

By that time Kost had forgotten he was building a weapon for a gang of vile Communists. He barely recalled that he was building a weapon. All he knew was that he had been, for nearly a decade, trying to assemble a frail and cryptic edifice of numbers and compound arcs, of precision-ground optical glass and flickering diodes and foaming tanks of fluorine, of neatly interlocking natural laws and elegant sup-

positions, a vast and spectral edifice meant to stretch from the earth
to the stars, and that this edifice had collapsed again, collapsed thoroughly and shamefully, and that an unknown number of years lay between him and any hope of success. He did not embrace Irina that
night. He lay like a lead soldier along the edge of the mattress. At a
quarter of two she rose silently on one elbow and gazed at him through
the dark. It was an impertinence, but Kost could not find the words to
say so.

"What's the matter with you," he said. "Go to sleep."

She didn't move.

"You're like a cow staring through a fence," he said. "Go to
sleep."

"It was bad today?" she said.

"Someone around here's a goddamned security risk," he said. "And
I didn't say you could speak. Be quiet and sleep."

"There is no risk here," she said. "Everyone know. Everyone of the
base, they tell with, with only—" She gestured vaguely. "With the face.
Not with speaking. Everyone know it is bad today."

"Yes. It was bad."

"I am sorry."

She remained motionless on one elbow, her outline almost massive before him, like a little hill. He still couldn't find the words to tell
her to stop looking at him.

"That night," Irina began.

He waited. He knew what night she meant.

"You touch everybody in the belly. But you don't touch the red
girl."

She'd been wondering for two and a half years.

"No. I didn't touch the red girl."

"Why?"

"My wife," he found himself saying, "had red hair. Dark red hair
like that. A bit curlier."

"Your wife is in Germany?"

"My wife was a Dresdener," Kost said formally. "She was visiting
her family."

"The Americans," Irina whispered.

"Yes," he said. "The Americans."

She was silent for a few minutes more. Then she stretched out an arm and rested a small hand on the center of his chest. She let it lie there, rising and falling with his breath.

He gathered her close and, for the first time, kissed her hungrily on the mouth.

The failure of Ar-2 was no less thorough, but it was also magnificently informative, and therefore depressed Kost and Schevchenko hardly at all. Ar-3 was a qualified success, but far more disheartening in its way, since no one concerned could find the reason why it had not succeeded completely. Ar-4 and Ar-5 were built simultaneously; the former a step-by-step replication of Ar-3, the latter a radical simplification. Both failed absolutely and, worst of all, identically. Four months short of the completion of Ar-6, Schevchenko died. Kost set down his tools and spent two days in bed reading *Magister Ludi*, which had always been his favorite of Hesse's novels.

"He was your . . . *captor*," Irina told him, stroking his neck. She still spoke infrequently enough that her low voice remained unfamiliar.

"He was an intelligent man," Kost said, turning a page. "There's few enough of them about. We couldn't have gotten this far without him."

Kost was fifty-seven years old and his knees were getting tricky. He no longer took Irina from behind. Instead he lay between her strong short thighs and let her gentle his back. Often Sunday night went by without his being moved to embrace her. Sometimes he found he required tenderness in the middle of a distressing week. Once he forgot himself so far as to kiss her hair and murmur *darling*. Schevchenko's successor was a young artillery major named Burgin with a broad dull face and no training in the sciences. "Eleven years," Burgin said. "I suppose you want more chocolates. I suppose you want more of those Lindt's chocolate truffles old Schevchenko used to stuff you with."

"I don't eat sweets."

"I'll give you chocolates, old man, if I don't see some progress soon. I'll give you some fine Swiss chocolates. And what's this about six full-time assistants? Half a dozen of our best young men from the Academy! Maybe I can let you have four."

"Very good. But the work will take longer."

"I strongly recommend, old man, that the work not take longer than very strictly necessary."

"There's a pistol on your belt," Kost said. "Why don't you use it?"

"Think I won't?"

The young man's German was quite good, but he let the words drop from his mouth like spit, in a thick Muscovite accent.

"Yes, Herr Major, I think you won't. You have been instructed to bring Archangel to completion, not to kill the only man capable of completing it. You can be replaced, Herr Major. I can't. Next Monday my quarterly report will recommend that staffing and funding be maintained at the present levels. You can give me what you like, and take the consequences. A very good morning to you," Kost said, and turned away.

The sound of the shot spun Kost in a full circle, his hand by instinct flashing to his hip, as if he were still a soldier, as if he still wore a gun there. The first thing he saw was Burgin's outstretched pistol. It seemed abnormally shiny and large. Then a balding, earnest-looking engineer named Leonidov, sprawled at Kost's feet. There was a ragged red hole in the engineer's shining forehead.

For a moment the workroom was plunged into silence. Then, with a thin cry, a young physicist named Schuster leapt up and sprinted for the door.

Burgin swung the pistol negligently and pierced his heart with a single bullet through the left shoulder blade.

He holstered his gun.

"I believe there are tools by the generator shed," he said, addressing the silent group of assistants. "Are there shovels there? Good. You, go bring shovels. Two of them, and a pick if you find it." He turned back to Kost. "You made a mistake, old man. You made a little mess here, and you must learn to clean up your messes. But because you are a frail old man, and the ground is hard, I will help you."

"You shot Leonidov to make a point, I suppose," Kost said, his voice fairly level. "But why kill Schuster?"

"He ran away!" Burgin said, surprised at the question. "A Soviet does not run."

In the event, Kost was given four new assistants after all, and, through the mysteries of Soviet bureaucracy, three unasked-for skilled machinists. These stood idle. Kost himself began to grow as idle as Burgin had believed him to be. He sat in a sunny corner of the main workroom, noodling endlessly in a notebook. Now and then he'd gaze out at the slowly subsiding mound of earth sheltering Leonidov and Schuster. When his assistants asked for instructions, he grunted, "Later." The machinists were transferred away again, along with two more of his assistants, and then two more, and at last he and a lone assistant were left in a cavernous, half-empty workroom, playing chess and engaging in long aimless chats about the project which were nearly philosophical discussions. He no longer cleared his head with Irina on Sunday nights, or at all. He did not touch her. She took to strolling nude around his apartment, brushing back her masses of black hair, or gazing out the window with her forearms folded on the sill and her posterior aimed at him like a cannon. On his sixtieth birthday she lay naked on his coverlet, rump in the air, ostentatiously reading *Das Lied von Bernadette*.

"You won't improve your German with that slop," he said.

"Shall I ask them to send you another girl?"

"I must introduce you to Burgin someday. You'd see eye to eye. You both want to put me on a quota."

"Do you know what will happen if they decide they've no further use for you?"

"I know what will happen in any case. I will die here. I will die here with my work undone and you waggling your fat crupper about and asking inane questions."

During the last year Kost barely spoke. He seemed to have fallen into a long dream, and in that dream strange harsh shapes moved across his drawings like a scythe. He began crossing out great sections of his plans with a red china marker and sketching in something new, something almost stupidly simple, as the first bamboo tube packed with gunpowder had been simple. With his lone assistant and one junior machinist, he began to build Ar-7. He understood that his mind had somehow been cleared of errors and that the new prototype would succeed if tested. He also understood it never would be; the money and men were no longer his to deploy. Burgin was a colonel now, and scarcely bothered to come by and threaten him. Kost's few requisitions went unsigned. The roof of the workshop was riddled with leaks; they'd run out of buckets to set beneath them. Kost had been forgotten. He was merely whiling away the time before the execution he knew was inevitable, ambling among his templates and equations as one might wander through a formal garden. One night a small, stern woman entered his apartment, a handsome woman in her early thirties with her hair in a tight black bun, wearing a snow-flecked overcoat open over the uniform of a KGB captain. It took a moment for him to recognize Irina. *How good of them,* he thought, *to send her. How good that they sent her, instead of a stranger.* He'd never seen Irina fully dressed before and, remembering what lay beneath the drab serge, he found himself, absurdly, stirred. She lay her coat over a chair and said, "You've no more time, Kost. They'll be coming for you soon."

He nodded.

She began to unbutton her tunic. "They say you've a photographic memory," she said. "Is that true?"

"Your German's gotten so good," he said. She opened her tunic. Beneath her brassiere, her torso was crisscrossed with black lines. He said, "I don't understand."

She unhooked her brassiere. A web of black slashes traversed her breasts.

"They say you can recall an entire page of tolerances to three decimal places after reading it once. They say you can sketch any drawing in your files from memory." She stepped out of her knickers and lay naked across the bed, staring up at the ceiling, her strong young legs stretched out straight, her arms at her sides. "Here," Irina said, and pointed at her left eye. "We're here. This is north-northeast, along the part in my hair."

She had drawn, with a sharp eyebrow pencil, a map over her entire naked body, starting at the line of her uniform collar and extending to her toes. He saw a dotted line along her shoulder trace the fence he saw out the window each day; he saw the slope down which he'd skied every Saturday until he grew too stiff to unfasten his own bindings at the bottom. She'd indicated barbed-wire fences with tiny black crosses,

electrified fences with a child's lightning-bolt, and scattered a constellation of *W*s for *Wache* to indicate the guard posts. With two parallel
lines she'd paved the road to town, and marked the distance in kilometers with a tiny, laborious *6.4* she must have drawn upside down. The
town was a few cross-streets slashed across her soft belly, her deep na-
vel pocking the police station, and the railroad station was a roofed box
with a list of times penciled at her waist. The tracks plunged through
the central thicket of hair and reappeared on her hip as another border
town. Along her left leg she'd sketched low hills, an Army post, a river
frozen hard. On her left ankle she'd indicated, with a dotted line and
a *G*, the frontier. On her foot she'd written: *Virtaniemi*. Finland. He
raised his stunned eyes to hers. He was an old man, a homely and unfriendly man, he had never shown her a moment's kindness, she could
not possibly have gotten any pleasure from their couplings. The look
in her eyes frightened him. She had been a girl when they'd assigned
her to him; now he saw the first fine creases at the corners of her eyes
and faint arcs bracketing her mouth. He'd spent more nights with her
than he'd ever spent with his wife. He had no idea where she was from
or how she passed her days. "I don't even know your name," Kost said,
almost to himself.

"You know my name," she said. "Schevchenko told you."

"I want you to tell me."

"Irina," she said, the tears sliding down her cheeks. "I'm Irina."

She got up, went into the bathroom and, weeping softly, began to
wash.

And now Irina was—where? Better not to think. And he was an old
man on his belly on the snow. A runaway slave. He'd began his career
as a slave to Nazi thugs and continued it as a slave to Stalinist louts, but
it might come out all right for him after all. His life's work was tucked
into the old document case at his side, and he meant to complete it
as a free man in Cambridge, where Hofstaedter might—*must*—still
remember him.

The final strand of wire parted, and Kost lay the snips down. He
wouldn't need them anymore. He lifted away a neat oblong section of

fencing—just a fraction wider than his narrow frame—set it beside the wire snips, and carefully inched through the gap.

When his boots cleared the fence, he began wriggling more quickly down the snowy declivity that shielded him from the soldiers' view. In theory, he was already free and could have strolled whistling toward the trees. In practice, he'd be shot without compunction if he were spotted, Finnish soil or no. A few meters from the woods, the declivity swooped downward—in the spring rains, it would be a stream bed, foaming with runoff—but Kost did not risk getting to his feet until he was well past the first line of trees. Then, panting, his body one long ache, he limped toward the tangled blackness where he remembered seeing the road into town.

It was where he recalled it, thank God. He still had an engineer's eye. He could not help exulting a bit when his boots touched the pavement. He began to walk more briskly. On the other side of the gentle rise before him, he'd be shielded from the guardhouses, and free. How long since he'd been really free? Twenty years? Thirty? He looked up into the sky, as if that were where his freedom would first appear. The dark branches revolved above him as he walked, seeming to wave, to signal. There was nothing more childish than being frightened by dark trees, and nothing more basic. These seemed to be turning, watching, nodding somberly. One of them edged closer to the road. *Nerves,* Kost thought. *Imagination,* and a huge hand clamped across his mouth and he was lifted into the air, feet dangling, his chilled ribs creaking as a mighty forearm crushed him close. He felt the prick of a hypodermic.

Kost was too tired to be afraid, and it was not in his nature to stop thinking. *Not a soldier, obviously, not with a hypo, and it isn't poison, either. If they wanted me dead, a trench knife would be simpler. And the Soviets wouldn't need to be quiet, not so close to the fence. I'm wanted alive. By whom? Whose slave will I be now?* The black trees began weaving tighter around him.

The hand holding the hypodermic, he saw, wore an iron ring shaped like three entwined serpents. Each one gripped the next in its fangs.

Then, nothing.

1

Your Lucky Day

The South African sunlight grew thick with dust motes, angling through the tall windows, and these swirled like troubled water as the sentry fell through them and bounced to a stop at Laura Morse's feet. His eyes were closed and his mouth was open. He looked as if he were singing hymns. His pistol slid from its holster and clacked on the plank floor. *He should at least have been able to get his gun out,* Laura thought disapprovingly. *When they haven't been properly trained, it makes you feel like such a bully.* She dropped to one knee and touched a slim hand to the guard's throat to check his pulse. The gesture was not so different from the one she'd just used to disable him. They were seventy kilometers east of Johannesburg, and it was the beginning of May, the middle of South Africa's autumn, but it was stifling hot in the guardhouse and the air was close and filled with the bookish scent of old, heated wood.

A lean, gray-haired, gray-eyed man stepped through the door behind her, closed it, and went over to the microphone on the guard's desk. He flicked it off and glanced down at the fallen man. "You always make the boys cry," he murmured.

"Only when they take liberties," Laura said.

"Don't have to tell me that, hon," Jack Mallory said ruefully, and looked again at the guard on the floor, this time with a touch of fellow feeling. He and Laurie had been partners nearly as long as they'd been field operatives for the Consultancy, and once or twice he'd tried making a pass at her. He supposed he was lucky not to have gotten what the guard got. "Well, we're clear back there. We got the woods and the whole back lawn to ourselves." He pivoted easily on his heels, scanning the guardhouse and the sun-bleached slope outside—he might have been surveying the guests at a garden party—and began searching the small hexagonal room, sketching a knot in the air with one forefinger as he opened the first cabinet. In response, Laura took two short lengths of nylon rope from her jumpsuit and began binding the guard's hands and feet. Her narrow face was creased with concentration. She had never been good with knots.

Not quite forty seconds later, Mallory let out a pleased grunt and set a loose-leaf binder on the guard's desk. Inside it were a handful of mimeographed pages in acetate sleeves. Laura examined them from over Mallory's shoulder, staying well back from the windows so that anyone looking down the slope at the guardhouse would see a solitary armed man, as expected, and not a man and a thin, wheat-blonde young woman in a snug gray unitard. The first page was a typewritten schedule. They examined it and simultaneously checked their watches, but the unconscious sentry wasn't due to be relieved for nearly forty minutes. One way or the other, it would all be over by then. The next page was a circuit diagram of the big house up the hill, which Laura folded neatly and tucked into a pouch at her hip, and the third was the house's floor plan. Last was a map of the entire estate. Mallory detached this and set it next to the floor plan, and they studied it together, Laura with mounting dismay.

"They got the hillside pretty well covered up from any of these windows along here," Mallory remarked. "They might not have guys at all of 'em, but they ought to have a guy at at least one of 'em. Guess we'll use the tunnel, like we said. Thank God they got one, anyway. Been kind of embarrassing if Analysis got that one wrong."

"Can't we circle through the woods and do the south wing?" Laura said. Her voice was the usual Boston Brahmin monotone, and only someone who knew her as well as Mallory did would have heard the apprehension in it.

Mallory shook his head. "You saw those woods. Maybe in midsummer. Not now."

Laura nodded. *Perhaps,* she thought, *it'll be a big tunnel. Like a subway. If it's not some little rabbit warren, where you feel you've been buried alive . . .*

"It'll be fine," Mallory said, and patted her shoulder.

Moving together as if they'd rehearsed it, they took the guard by the shoulders and knees and shifted him to the edge of the little room. A hatch had been set into the center of the hexagonal floor. Mallory slipped a small high-powered flashlight from a pouch on his thigh, flicked it on, and drew his Browning. He positioned himself before the hatch and nodded to Laura; as she pulled it open, he swept the opening with flashlight and gun, then leapt lightly down. When entering strange and possibly booby-trapped tunnels, gentlemen always go first. Laura's muscles tightened as Mallory's feet struck the invisible earth below, but silence followed; no blast from a buried charge, no hiss from a tightening trip-wire. In a moment she heard him whisper, *"Clear."*

Then, *"Little snug."*

Her stomach grew chilly. She switched on her own flashlight, followed her partner through the hatch, and pulled it shut.

It was worse than Laura had feared. Whoever had built the access tunnels between the big house and its guard posts hadn't wanted to shift any more dirt than absolutely necessary. The tunnel was barely two feet wide, and the ceiling so low that it almost brushed her spine as she crawled forward on hands and knees. Damp, splintery planks held back the earth above and around them, soft and bowed with age, half-slimy to the touch. The air was thick with mildew. It was, she knew, a bad place for Jack. The Consultancy's most senior agent was noted for fearlessness, but there is no fearlessness among intelligent men, only the mastery of fear, and Laura knew Mallory had always been prey to a claustrophobia that made elevators unpleasant for him and subway rides a mild hardship. It was, for obvious reasons, a well-kept secret; only three or four people in the world knew about it. Jack had never let it interfere with the execution of his duties. There was, however, always a first time.

Taking on your partner's fears is a beginner's mistake, one of the first things they warn you about in Basic Ops, but just now Laura couldn't help herself. She felt the thickness of dirt above him and the immensity of the earth in which he was buried. She felt the panic of the snared animal. She had the sense that the mud around him might at any moment rush in to fill his nose and mouth, that he would never see sunlight again, never stand upright again, that he would lie forever in a fetid crack in the South African earth. She could see nothing of Jack but his narrow behind, silhouetted by the glow of his flashlight, and his rhythmically moving boots inches from her face. Twice the rhythm seemed to falter, and she fought to keep her own breath from catching. Finally, when she judged they were about halfway along—when they were directly beneath the center of the house's great back lawn—he whispered, "Gimme a minute, hon," and stopped.

The hands of Laura's watch were not luminous. A glowing wrist-watch makes a good target. But her eyes were acute and her watch's face was faintly lit by the flare of her and Jack's flashlights. She gazed helplessly as the second hand made its nervous, jerky way around the dial. Jack's breathing was not quick or ragged. His control was better than that. She hoped her own was as good. The two of them hunkered motionless, head to heels, straining to regulate their breathing, as the second hand made another circuit. She racked her brain for something to say, something to do.

At last she reached forward and, gently, took hold of Jack's ankle. The pulse was quick beneath her fingers.

Leave him alone, she said fiercely, silently. *Can't you see he's doing his best? Leave him alone. Just let him be.*

She was not a religious woman. Who was she talking to?

Nobody.

The second hand crept around another quarter of a circle, a tick at a time. Finally Jack stirred.

She took her hand from his leg, and he began to crawl again, as he had when he'd first entered the tunnel, doggedly, steadily, as if he were performing an unpleasant and not terribly interesting chore.

Whenever Gray briefed Laura and Jack for a run at one or the other of the Consultancy's various HQs, he was very fond of the phrase "without interest." The rest of the job was without interest. And thank God for that, Laura thought; she was almost as shaken as Jack must have been, and found herself moving like a sleepwalker, guided, as veteran agents must sometimes be, almost solely by reflex and training. Jack crawled fractionally faster as the scent of fresher air began to seep toward them. Then they were in the big house's cellar and he was standing, Browning drawn, flash off, taking in deep, silent gulps of air. She followed him up the stairs and reached the cellar door just in time to see him cradling a second sentry in his arms, one hand across the man's back as if they were tangoing, the other gripping the man's wooden-stocked RPK to keep it from clattering to the floor. There was a gray nub at the sentry's throat: the handle of the titanium throwing knife Jack always wore in a sheath at his nape. Then they'd split up and were moving through the house's ground floor in silence, Jack circling to the left with the sentry's assault rifle, she circling to the right with her Colt Commander. The furniture was in dustcovers and the rugs in rolls along the walls, but dirty wineglasses littered the inlaid tables. On the windowsills, artificial flowers stood in milk-glass vases, the petals formed of tiny glass beads threaded on wires. Above her head she could hear a lazy conversation in country Russian. Something about the proper way to stew a chicken. She rendezvoused with Jack at the foot of the grand staircase without having met a soul, and then stood watch over it with the heavy RPK in her arms as Jack eased silently up the marble steps. In a moment, she heard what she'd expected to hear: an exclamation and a dull thud from above, followed by a torrent of outraged Russian and Jack's clumsy, Texas-accented Russian laboring in reply. Then, in English, "Aw, Grigor, don't be a damn—"

A single shot.

She was halfway up the stairs before the report had died away, the RPK poised for a hip-shot and her forefinger tensed along the trigger guard, but she'd recognized the sound of Jack's Browning and wasn't really surprised when she reached the top and found him shambling down the corridor toward her, his pistol swinging at his side, a look of dejection on his face.

She lowered her gun and said, "You were a bit loud."

Her voice, as always, was light and cool.

"Sorry," Mallory said, holstering the pistol. A balding, heavily built man lay sprawled on the carpet by the hall table, breathing raggedly. Hired help. No one she knew. Mallory hunkered down beside him and began securing the man's hands and feet.

"Got it?" she said.

Mallory patted his breast pocket.

"Then we're about done here?"

"I guess." Mallory doubled the knot at the man's ankles and stood with a grunt.

Laura nodded toward the end of the hall, toward the room where Grigor Volkov presumably lay. "I suppose he wanted to go out like a hero."

"He wanted something," Mallory said glumly. "I don't think he got what he wanted." There was a telephone on the hall table. Mallory picked it up and began dialing the thirty-six-digit sequence that accessed the Consultancy's switchboard from a nonsecure phone.

Mallory could be, in his quiet way, a bit cocky after a successful mission, but never when there'd been a death. He was certainly not cocky now. Laura knew how the day's work looked to him: he'd killed two men in the course of a routine penetration and lost his nerve over a trifle in front of his partner. He would find a bar tonight, she knew. He would probably stay drunk for days. He would find—she grimaced inwardly—women. But he was out of danger. She was probably more relieved about that than he was. There was no sign of anything in Mallory's face but fatigue and dull patience as he dialed the long access code. He did not raise his eyes when he said, "Listen. You were good back there. Thanks."

"For what?" she said. "Guarding the stairs? There was nothing to do. If you'd left me a deck of cards, I could have played solitaire."

"For down there," Mallory said, staring at the spinning dial. "Back in the tunnel. I was having, you know, a bad time. And you saw me through."

"Did I?"

"You were a good partner, just like you always are. You took care of me."

"Thank you, Jack, but really, I didn't do anything."

"You took care of me," he said again.

"Well, if you say so."

"Ah, go to hell," he said wearily. "'Lo, Phil? Mallory. That's right, Phil, on an open line, but there's nobody around anymore to care. Uh-huh. Two. Big guy and one of his ladies-in-waiting. Slapped down two others, but they're all right. Mop-up'll have somebody to talk to. Anyway, we got Gray his film and everything's nice and peaceful now, so you can bring us on home. All right, what?"

"Home, eh?" said the tiny voice, chuckling.

"What's so goddamned funny, Phil?" Mallory said.

"Mallory, you know how you're always bitching about how long Gray keeps you waiting around between jobs?"

"Yeah?"

"Well, Mallory, I hope you're smiling. Because today is your lucky day."

2

Billion with a B

Jack Mallory's age was difficult to guess. His hair had been steel-gray since his early twenties and his body was boyishly lanky. A trained observer might have put his age, correctly, at thirty-five, but as he walked up Rue Favart at two o'clock the next morning, Mallory seemed to be sunk deep in middle age. His long legs moved leadenly, and the creases in his wind-whipped face had deepened. His shoulders stayed square through an act of will. He was obviously one American in Paris who wished to God he was back home in bed. Mallory was dressed, as usual, in neat dark clothes that seemed more expensive than they were, and he carried a battered overnight bag; he'd come straight from Orly without stopping at his hotel. He didn't even know what hotel they'd booked him into. The Crillon, probably. Logistics liked luxury and assumed his agents did, too. As he approached the Opéra-Comique, Mallory drew a key chain from his pocket and sorted through it with his thumb. He located a worn coppery key stamped with a Greek φ just as he reached the opera house's front door. The key in his hand opened the janitor's closet of the Silver Crest Diner on Lexington Avenue in Manhattan and the front doors of the Daisy Wright boutiques in New York, London, and Via della Spiga in Milan. It opened the doors of Moore's Fine Tobaccos in Cape Town and the Stamperia Ondine in Rome. It opened the No. 14 maintenance building in Berlin's Tiergarten and the Fundação Hector Bonaventura in Rio de Janeiro and a police call box in St. Stephen's Green in Dublin and the Happy Town International News and Periodical Store in Tokyo's Ginza. And it opened the front door of the Opéra-Comique de Paris. He put the key in the lock, turned it, and went inside.

The door clicked shut behind him and Mallory rattled it to make sure it was locked, his movements matter-of-fact. Anyone watching him would have assumed he had business inside the opera house, which he had, and that he was there legitimately, which he was not. He made his way through the darkened lobby as easily as if it were his own living room, stepped behind the second gilt column to the left, took hold of a gilt cherub's chubby face, and twisted it like the dial of a combination lock. There was a deep click behind the stonework and the whine of a buried electric motor as the face of the column swung away. Behind it was a tiny elevator, almost a dumbwaiter, open-faced in the European fashion. Mallory glowered at it a moment before stepping inside. It was an eleven-second trip to the little suite of offices above the Opéra's great dome. He knew how many seconds it took because he counted them off every goddamned time. When it reached the top, he stepped out of it with a touch of haste and frowned with annoyance at himself, then took a moment to look around and get oriented. Since he usually worked out of New York, he hadn't seen the Paris station for a couple of years. It didn't look like anything had changed.

HQ-P was, like all the Consultancy's stations, a warren of narrow, shabby, windowless rooms, painted and cleaned as infrequently as possible and furnished with a mixture of grubby castoffs and gleaming electronic hardware. This particular set of rooms was squeezed in between the Opéra-Comique's inner and outer domes. The rooms around the circumference were low-ceilinged enough that Mallory was almost obliged to stoop, but by the time he'd climbed a series of ramps and steps to the central chamber, the ceiling was an affair of curved girders twenty feet over his head. In the center of the chamber was a decrepit conference table, pierced through the middle by the heavy iron chain that supported the opera house's great chandelier. The chain came up through the floor, passed through a squarish hole chiseled out of the tabletop, and vanished into the arched dimness above them. If you followed it with your eyes up to the peak of the dome, it always seemed to be faintly swaying.

Laura Morse was sitting on one side of the chain, and a small, fattish, heavily scarred man sat on the other. Mallory padded across the felt-lined floor and dropped into the chair between them. "'Lo, Laurie," he said, nodding. "Gray."

"Good morning, Jack," Gray said.

The trench bisecting his left cheek gleamed in the low light. His glasses were smeary and skewed. Before him sat a stack of papers, the edges precisely aligned, as always, with the edges of the table.

"Hello, Jack," Laura said. "Nice flight?"

"Fine. Yours?"

She shrugged. "Cargo plane. It was fine, I suppose. Someone remembered to bring me a box lunch. But I'm glad they got you a commerical flight."

"I'm delicate," Mallory agreed.

"Thank you both for coming on such short notice," Gray said. "It's very helpful."

"Sure thing," Mallory said.

"You're looking a bit—"

"One-fifty-eight, last time I checked," Mallory said patiently. "Didn't always get time for meals in Johannesburg. If I get to spend any time in town, I'll try to fat up a little."

"I'd appreciate that, Jack. I believe you're more effective when you, ah, eat. I'd like to see you at a hundred and sixty pounds or better. Do try to remember."

Mallory nodded. It was not a suggestion. Gray did not make suggestions.

"Well," Gray said, and laced his plump, somewhat grimy fingers together. "I suppose the usual thing would be for us to have a full de-brief on the South African matter, but Laura tells me there's not much of substance to report. You were not instructed to liquidate Volkov, but neither were you instructed to let him perforate you without demur, and given the circumstances, your response seems reasonable. His death should do the firm no harm, so long as certain—"

"I talked to Reismann right after I called Phil. He's in."

"On what terms?"

"The same. He's not an ambitious guy. He mostly wants to not be shot. I offered to not shoot him."

"Very nice. The rest of Volkov's *apparat* is unlikely to survive him, and picking up the bits is unlikely to be a rewarding task. I've asked Analysis to compile a list of assets worth acquiring. She's fairly skepti-cal, and probably with good reason, but in any case that's not the sort of bookkeeping that need concern you. No, I believe your role in the Volkov affair is concluded. You've both done your usual nice profes-sional job, and of course I'm quite pleased to have the film in hand."

"Bring much?" Mallory asked, rubbing his eyes.

Gray had opened the Consultancy for business seven years before, in May of 1956. Though it counted the governments of several nations among its clients, it was not itself aligned with any nation or ideology. Instead, the Consultancy was perhaps the world's largest private covert services firm, and operated solely for profit—Gray's profit. Though it was hard to imagine what the scarred ex-commando spent it on. *He sure isn't spending it on clothes,* Mallory thought. *Or even on soap and water.*

"The Society were exceedingly grateful to be reunited with their property," Gray said. "There'll be a suitable performance bonus for both of you."

"Thanks," Mallory said.

"Thank you," Laura said tonelessly. She was a CIA field agent on long-term loan to the Consultancy, and her Consultancy pay went directly to the Agency, bonuses and all. Besides, though her family's celebrated lineage rather bored her—collateral descent from the in-ventor of Morse code and the rest of it—she was still enough of a Morse to find bonuses a bit vulgar.

"And now," Gray said, "to the matter at hand. What do you two know about Project Archangel?"

Mallory reached into his breast pocket and pulled out a wadded teletype, which he smoothed flat and examined. He'd been wrong about the Crillon. Otto'd booked him into the George V. "You know, Gray," Mallory said, tucking the teletype away, "I'd kind of like to get to bed."

"No doubt you would. What—"

"You always start every briefing with a question, Gray, and it's never a question anybody can answer. I've never heard of Project Archangel. Laurie's never heard of Project Archangel. Nobody's goddamned heard of Project Archangel. Why don't you just tell us what it is and why it can't wait till tomorrow?"

"Actually," Laura said, "I have heard a bit about Archangel. Not much. It was meant to be Hitler's big secret weapon that was going to win the war for him after all. But that's all I know, except that it had something to do with rockets and that von Braun's always claimed to know nothing about it. He claims, in fact, that it's a myth."

Mallory looked at Laura.

"Sorry," she said.

"Your information is quite correct, Laura, as far as it goes," Gray said. "Hitler initiated Archangel in the fall of 1943, based, according to legend, on a series of dreams in which a winged being with a blue face and a single shining eye flittered down from heaven and told him all his enemies' secrets. Archangel was meant to be a spy satellite, the very first. And judging from statements made by minor members of the Archangel team after the war, one possessed of power and precision that would be impressive even today. Of course, it was never completed. The project's lead scientist, one Walther Kost, was captured by the Russians in '45 and taken to the village of Kildinstroi, where he was convinced or coerced to continue his research under their auspices. Three years ago, Kost, who by that time had been working under Soviet control for some fifteen years, escaped somehow and went missing. Earlier this month, a German dealer in sensitive information named Arne Jespers began shopping around a sophisticated spy satellite to various governments and private political groups. He is asking the better part of half a billion dollars."

There was a pause.

"Billion with a *b*?" Mallory said.

"Yes."

Mallory frowned. "That's screwy. That's not a price. That's just a big pile of zeros. Has anybody ever paid that much for *anything*? Hell, what did the Manhattan Project cost?"

Laura was shaking her head. "No. I'm sorry, no. No spy satellite could be worth that. Not even if it could count the change in your back pocket. Unless, I don't know— Is Jespers competent?"

"Quite," Gray said.

"Then whatever Archangel is, it can't just be something that zips around the sky taking snapshots. Not at that price."

"No," Gray said.

"So you want us to find out what Archangel does," Mallory said.

"I want Archangel," Gray said. "I want you to bring it to me."

"I don't blame you," Mallory said. "If it's worth half a billion bucks, it must be a handy item to have. Do we know the thing's finished?"

"According to our sources, Jespers has been approaching buyers since third May at the latest. They believe he expects a sale by midsummer. At the price he's set, I'd be surprised if he were trying to sell a work in progress. It seems reasonable to suppose that he's successfully tested a working prototype, and perhaps even completed the satellite itself."

"Do we know the thing works?"

"Arne Jespers has amassed a very considerable fortune by, in part, knowing the precise value of his merchandise. And he's invited bids from persons to whom a prudent man would not knowingly sell faulty goods."

"What if this gadget isn't really Archangel?"

"I'd rather like to have it all the same."

"Fair enough. Where do we start?"

"With Jespers. You and Laura are to infiltrate his operation, find who's behind the satellite project, and bring this individual and his creation to New York. If it is impractical to rescue or suborn the satellite's creator—Kost, or whoever it proves to be—you are to bring as much of the project as you can: plans, notebooks, models, that sort of thing."

"Do we destroy what we can't bring?" Laurie asked.

"Our client is prepared to pay quite handsomely for proof of Archangel's complete and irreversible destruction, but not nearly as handsomely as they will pay for its delivery in good order. Destroy what you can't bring, and if you can bring nothing, destroy everything. But I do hope you'll do better than that."

Laurie said, "It sounds like if Kost or whoever won't come home with us, you want him dead."

"I'd prefer it."

"I'm not killing him," Laurie said. "Not without more information and a better reason than I've got so far. Not if his only crime is working for Jespers instead of your client. I've been seconded to this operation for a while, Gray, but I'm still bound by agency work rules. If Langley hasn't approved the target, it's not my target."

"Goodness, how you fuss, Laura."

"And Jack—"

"Jack will do whatever proves necessary at the time, and sulk about it afterward," Gray said. Mallory let out a bark of laughter and sat up a little straighter. "As for you, Laura, I know far better than to try to hire you as an assassin. Let's discuss ways and means of succeeding, shall we? And not fret just now about who might kill whom in the event of failure."

"All right."

"What do we know about Jespers?" Mallory said.

"Arne Jespers," Gray said, seeming, as he often did, to read from a three-by-five card hovering in midair, "is a fifty-two-year-old Berlin native of Danish descent who rose from petty black-marketeering in the American Zone to become a highly successful dealer in military and industrial secrets. This firm has had occasional dealings with him as both buyer and seller, but has never before met him as antagonist. He is not, by the way, a man to be lightly antagonized, though in view of—"

"Half a billion dollars," Mallory said.

"Just so. Professionally he is known as the Dane, and addressed as such by business associates and even subordinates. Only his intimates call him Jespers, and only his very closest intimates call him Arne. He is an uneducated but exceptionally intelligent man and, within certain narrow bounds, highly disciplined. That is to say, his goods are of irreproachable quality, his purchases and sales are rigorously structured, and his deals do not fall through. In other ways his discipline is rather spotty. Jespers is gregarious and pleasure-loving, and always travels with a large entourage of bodyguards, chefs, advisors on art and wine, masseuses, suppliers of various drugs, miscellaneous females, old friends, and new friends, some very new indeed. You are to join this entourage."

"As?" Laura said.

"New friends. And should Jespers be favorably impressed with you, Laura—and I can't imagine why he wouldn't be—you might permit him to imagine—"

"Yes," she said.

"Temper, Laura. We're not asking you to bed the fellow."

"Good. How do we reach him?"

"Jespers's chief passion is auto racing, and he seldom misses a Grand Prix. The season begins in Monaco a week from Sunday. Pre-race preparations begin Thursday. You'll arrive Wednesday. We have arranged a sort of laissez-passer that will enable you to mingle with Derek Reade's team, Naughton America, who have been told you are financial backers and will accordingly extend to you courtesies and facilities denied to the average race-goer. It should be a treat for you," Gray told Laura primly.

Laura owned a new silver 3.5-liter Jaguar and a vintage Lancia Gran Turismo in racing red, both of which she maintained herself. She was rumored to keep pictures of them in her purse, where another woman might keep pictures of her man or her children. It was just a rumor. Nobody was about to go through Laura Morse's purse. "Who are we?" she asked.

Gray took two file folders from the briefcase at his side and set one before Laura and the other before Jack. They unwound the string fasteners, shook out the sheets of neatly typed foolscap, and began to read. Gray said, "Jack will be Jack Carroll, ex-CIA man, ex-mercenary, and founder of Carroll Security Systems, an international consulting firm specializing in industrial and corporate security and counter-espionage. And, for select clients, in assembling small private armies. A datum Jespers is likely to find intriguing."

Mallory frowned. "Thing is, Jack Carroll exists. I've worked with his people. Most likely somebody like Jespers has, too."

"But I trust you didn't meet Carroll himself."

"No."

"Few people have. He's become a bit of a recluse since retiring from active fieldwork, and generally runs his business through inter-mediaries. Carroll has a number of reasons to want to remain in our good books and he is, naturally, extending his full cooperation in this venture. Anyone who calls CSS and asks for Jack Carroll will be told he is traveling. Any messages will be passed through Carroll's personal staff to you in the field. I'm told, in fact, that Carroll is rather tickled to have you impersonating him. It appears that in person he's rather homely."

"If I'm such a hermit, what am I doing in Monte Carlo?"

"You've tired of the solitary life and decided to kick up your heels and enjoy your money a bit. Travel, do yourself well at table, go about with pretty girls. And you're a racing fan as well, of course. Mad for it. You'll be swotting up on the sport over the next week. Laura, you're Lily Prentice, Carroll's bored and greedy girlfriend of the moment."

"So I see," Laura said, paging through her packet. "Lily Reese Ann Sturtevant Prentice. Beekman Place . . . Miss Porter's . . . Radcliffe . . . kicked out of Radcliffe . . . Gstaad . . . Palm Beach . . . Biarritz . . . Gstaad again . . . Gray, will you ever give me a cover who isn't some gruesome little rich girl?"

"Possibly."

"I hope mine isn't a real person as well. What a horror she'd be. Well, at least this time out I'm not another little prig. In fact, I seem to be something of a hussy. How many men have I slept with, exactly?"

"You can't remember."

"Do I love Jack? Like him?"

"Not at all. Neither of you would be averse to a little flutter."

"And what am I doing in Monaco? I mean, really doing, except for vamping Jespers while Jack talks racing with him."

"Running Jack's backup, as usual. Providing muscle, if necessary."

"This Prentice woman seems to live on the beach. I don't look like that."

"Just so. There's a cardboard box beside your chair. Would you mind fetching it out for us? Thank you."

Laura set a battered and much-reused corrugated carton on the table, stripped back the ragged piece of tape that sealed it, and reached inside. She lifted out two narrow, metal-clasped manila envelopes marked with initials. One she tucked into her purse, the other she handed to Mallory. These were their identity documents and plane tickets, and required no explanation. She pulled out two flat boxes of ammunition, glanced at them, and handed them both to Mallory: bullets for his Browning. "And none for me. Am I going unarmed?" she asked Gray.

"Miss Prentice doesn't carry a gun. She wouldn't risk her nails."

Frowning, Laura pulled a tiny band of elasticized pink cloth from the box and examined it. "What's this?"

"As you observed, Laura, you don't look much of a beach bunny. Otto will provide you with wardrobe, as usual, but in the meantime we've booked you for a series of sunlamp sessions at a beauty salon on Rue Aubert. It should require at least six days to get you properly dark. That's one of the reasons I wanted to brief you both as soon as possible. You're to wear that during the sessions."

"What is it?"

"It's the sort of bathing suit Miss Prentice wears. We want your tan lines to be correct."

"You want me to—" she said. "This little— There's no top to it."

"Miss Prentice summers on the Riviera."

After a moment, Laura dropped the bikini bottom back into the carton. She closed it, smoothed the tape shut across the flaps, and sat with her hands atop the box, gazing forlornly into space.

"One last item of business, and then I'll let you both get some well-deserved rest," Gray said. "You'll be assisted on this run by a recent recruit, a very promising young man named William Harmon. Paratrooper, ex-Marine, sound background and extraordinary test scores. Quite green, of course, but that's where you come in. I'd like you to do a bit of mentoring. See what use you can make of him, what sort of stuff he's made of. Knock a few rough edges off. He's been extensively trained in demolitions, covert comm, penetration, evasion, and martial arts," Gray said with a nod toward Laura, "but this is his first trip out with us and he'll need a good deal of oversight. However, I can assure you that in the case of any, ah, rough stuff, Mr. Harmon is a very helpful fellow to have about."

"Me, Laurie, and this Harmon guy," Mallory said slowly. "Lot of artillery for a deal like this."

"Yes. Well, it's only fair to tell you that you're not the first operatives I've put on this assignment."

"Who'd you use before?"

"Gary Holt."

The silence, for a few moments, was complete. None of the Consultancy's field agents had heard from Holt for a month. At this point, no one expected good news.

Grunting slightly, Gray bent and took another file folder from his briefcase and set it on the table between them. "Gary, as you both know, was a believer in the direct approach. In this case he decided to attempt a straight break-in at Jespers's Copenhagen flat. I'm afraid it was a misjudgment."

The first sheet in the folder was a coroner's report signed by the Consultancy's Dr. Chaudhury. Holt had died of cerebral edema following multiple blunt trauma; the list of broken bones and ruptured organs extended well onto a second page. "As I mentioned," Gray continued, "Jespers employs a large number of bodyguards, whom he seems to choose for, ah, physical impressiveness. Gary was beaten to death barehanded by an assailant of almost superhuman strength. And, judging by the width of the knuckle marks, of great size. The killer wore a ring on his left hand, which in some cases left fairly clear impressions. On the last page you'll find a reconstruction of the ring's design. It means nothing to Analysis. Does it suggest anything to you?"

It was a surgeon's sketch, precise and graceless, made with firm strokes of a blue ballpoint pen and the slight clumsiness that is inevitable when one draws with rubber-gloved hands. Mallory saw three stylized snakes, twisted together, each sinking its fangs into the next. He shook his head. Laura did the same. Holt had had a deep voice, Mallory recalled, and a booming laugh of which he was a bit over-fond. Mallory wished he'd liked him better. No one would have a chance to like him now. Mallory closed the folder, slid it back across the table to Gray, and stood, feeling himself pass all at once into the final stage of exhaustion. "We'll try to be a little carefuller than Gary was," he said dully. "Anything else? Laurie, where'd they put you, the George V?"

"Yes."

"Me too. Share a cab over there?"

"Thank you, Jack," Gray said. "I do think that's about all for now. Laura, could you spare me a few minutes before you go?"

"All right," Mallory said. "Meet you at the corner of Richelieu and Haussman, then."

Laura said, "Richelieu and Montmartre. It changes names at the big intersection."

"Richelieu and whatever the damn boulevard's called. I'll try to have a cab waiting."

"Thanks."

Gray and Laura waited until they heard the elevator open, close, and start downward. Then she turned to him, a sort of weary defiance in her slate-blue eyes, and something else as well, something Jack Mallory had never seen.

Gray said, "You're as bad as Jack tonight, Laura."

"I'm tired."

"Among other things, Laura. You're both in very bad form."

"I told you. Jack's upset about Volkov. It was a simple job and he didn't think it should have required two deaths. He thinks he must have been sloppy somewhere. And of course he had a bout in the tunnel—who wouldn't? It was awful down there. And, you know, in front of me, which couldn't have been fun. He was fine after a minute, and it didn't affect anything, but he's taking it all very personally."

"As are you. I wonder if I'm not making a mistake, having you pose as Jack's girl again. You will be sharing a room with him, and perhaps a bed. In public, he will be treating you as a romantic partner. In private, he is likely to pursue other women, either to advance the job or for simpler reasons. Given your feelings—"

"Never mind my feelings."

"Unfortunately, Laura, my position obliges me to mind everything. I cannot afford to have your personal turmoil cloud your judgment or blunt your nerve."

"It hasn't yet."

"In addition, there is the danger that Jack will belatedly come to realize—"

"Jack," Laura said wearily, "in the years I've known him, has made a total of three fairly crude passes at me. I've shut him down each time. As far as he's concerned, that can only mean one thing: that I must not feel the slightest . . . Actually," she said with a desolate little laugh, "I think his new theory is that I'm, you know. A lesbian. Believe me, Gray, Jack will never know unless I tell him."

"Well, you have been a very productive team, and you do bring, both of you, unusual qualifications to the job. It would be nice to use you together." Gray pursed his lips, then said, "I imagine the risk is worth taking."

"It'll be fine," Laura told him.

Much later, she remembered that those had been Mallory's last words. Right before he went down into the tunnel.

3

Just Because I Always
Wear a Smile

Mallory strode through the door of the Silver Crest Diner with a relaxed and lively step, spotted Laura in her booth beside the coatrack,
and pretended to do a small double take. As he walked over to the
table, he caught the middle-aged waitress's eye. She mimed holding
a coffee cup and gave Mallory an inquiring look. He gave her a smile
and a nod in return as he slid into the booth, then turned the smile
upon Laura. "Look at you," he said. "I almost didn't recognize you."

"It was that last sunlamp treatment that really put me over the
top," she said, smiling back. "I got a bit of a start the next time I looked
in the mirror."

"If this was Alabama," he agreed, "they wouldn't let you sit at
the table with me. Lord, look at how dark you are. It makes your
eyes awful pretty. Don't worry, Laurie, I'm not starting with you,"
he said, raising his hands slightly. "Just saying. You're like those

photo-negative-looking girls we used to have back home. You know, these girls on the beach all day with the dark skin and the light hair. 'Course, they were always on the nice part of the beach. Guys like me got run off whenever we tried to come around and visit."

"Quite right, too," Laura said. The waitress brought Mallory's coffee, gave Laura a warm-up, and departed with a meaningless waitress's wink. "You're looking well, Jack. Have a nice time in Paris?"

"Pretty good," he said, and took a sip. "Stuffed myself like a Christmas goose. If you've got to eat like that, I guess Paris is the town to do it in. Gray'd be pretty happy if he saw me now." Mallory patted his lean midsection as if it were a paunch. "I don't know when I've been such a size. You enjoy yourself?"

"Yes. It's too bad you had to come home early."

"Aw, it was all right. Couple things to clean up," Mallory said. In fact, in response to a brief, badly spelled telegram, he'd flown to London, where a Japan Airlines stewardess named Atsuko Shimura was, by good fortune, scheduled for a two-day layover. The Consultancy kept a flat for Mallory in Kensington, and the two of them had passed the time there very pleasantly, Atsuko diligently trying to feed him up on chicken parmigiana, which she always made quite well, and pork *katsudon,* which she made quite badly. She'd taught him twenty new words of Japanese and lectured him on the fall of the Habsburg dynasty, about which she'd been reading. Just now Mallory was full of goodwill toward all womankind. He glanced at the neck of Laurie's sweater set, recalled the bikini panties in the cardboard box, and tried to picture her dark all the way to the waist. *What a world,* he thought peacefully. "Paris was kind of wasted on me anyhow," he said. "All I did was hit the books. Ask me something about Grand Prix racing. Go on. Ask me any damn thing you like."

"All right. Who won at Nürburgring in '57?"

"Juan Fangio. Broke the lap record a few times over while he was at it, trying to catch up with Ferrari after a bad pit stop. His seat'd come loose. It got him another world championship. His, um, fourth?"

"Fifth. Who won the first Monaco Grand Prix?"

"Guy named Williams in a Bugatti."

"What was the last year in which grid position was determined by lot?"

"In '32; by '33 they started using practice times. Monaco again."

"What's the slowest corner at Brands Hatch?"

"Druid Hill Bend."

"The fastest at Monza?"

"The Vialone. But everybody calls it the Ascari, 'cause that's where Alberto Ascari died, in, ah, I'm not too sure."

"Well, I'm impressed," she said.

"Not as impressed as me," Mallory said. "You already know all this stuff? I knew you liked cars, but I didn't know you were such a scholar about it. They should've just had you tutor me."

"I wouldn't have minded," Laura said composedly. "Where's our baby Marine?"

"According to Phil, he's due along at 1530." They both glanced at their watches. Analysts and code clerks can reach their desks when they feel like it, but extreme punctuality is a requirement for all agents in the field, where the penalty for lateness can be death—one's own, or one's partner's.

"Why aren't we meeting in the office, by the way?" Laura asked.

The janitor's closet of the Silver Crest Diner was the back entrance to the Consultancy's New York HQ, which meandered underground from Lexington Avenue to the Daisy Wright boutique on Madison. Wright herself was an active desk agent running two key networks for Gray. The Silver Crest was staffed by a mix of Consultancy staff, retired spies, and civilians; the waitress who'd brought their coffee had been, in younger, svelter days, a notorious field operative specializing in the subornation of diplomats. She was happy to have retired, though she'd once told Mallory that the demands placed upon a field agent's memory and endurance were nothing compared to those placed upon a diner waitress. "We're not in the office," Mallory said, "'cause that place has been getting right up my nose. And I wanted a decent cup of coffee and maybe a piece of pie. I've gotten used to this eating thing. I guess we'll duck down there if we need to use the stapler or something. Here he comes." It was just under two minutes before the hour. A small good sign.

The man who'd stepped through the door was, Mallory guessed, about six-two, with a prizefighter's physique and the look of great cleanliness that certain handsome young people naturally possess. The dossier put William Harmon's age at twenty-two. Mallory thought he looked younger. He wore old, clean khakis, a dark blue polo shirt, and well-shined black oxfords, which Mallory thought didn't quite go. His skin was olive and as darkly tanned as Laurie's, and his curly black hair was cropped close. Mallory didn't much care for his intense black-brown eyes. Good field agents don't look intense. Harmon was pretending to scan the room for a good table, which was correct technique, anyway; when you're meeting someone, the last thing you want to do is advertise the fact. Mallory stood. "Hello, William," he said.

Harmon looked over with slight surprise that seemed genuine. "Hello," he said, walking up and shaking the hand Mallory offered. "Didn't expect to see you here. How've you been keeping?"

This, again, was proper tradecraft: never use a name aloud without a reason. Though a more experienced man might have noticed that Mallory—the lead operative on the job—hadn't bothered to be discreet and acted accordingly. "Pretty good," Mallory said. "Yourself?"

"Not bad. Just a little bit of a headache from all this sun. You know any place around here where I could pick up a bottle of aspirin?"

"That's right," Mallory said vaguely. "This is Laura Morse, and I guess you know who I am. Have a seat. You want some coffee? A Coke? Pie's pretty good here."

"Good to meet you, Miss Morse," Harmon said, shaking her hand.

He looked very unhappy.

"All right," Mallory said placatingly, and added, "There's a drugstore on the corner, but those pills won't do you any good," before Harmon could repeat the line about the bottle of aspirin.

"Sorry, sir," Harmon said with a quick smile that made Mallory think he might be all right after all. "If you read my dossier, I guess you know I'm sort of a stickler. When I got my prebriefing—"

"You got prebriefed by Otto," Mallory said. "And Otto was hav-

ing a little fun with you. We do use that the-red-peacock-flies-at-mid-
night-yes-but-its-feathers-are-blue stuff sometimes, but not often. It's
all right. You'll get used to Otto. We all have. What are you having?
Eat lunch yet? They don't make a bad burger here, and the coffee and
apple pie are pretty good."

"I'm fine, sir."

"Have a cup of coffee, at least," Mallory said, signaling the waitress. "Be a sport. And May," he called to her, "can I have a couple extra
forks with my pie? Just in case you change your mind," he said, turning
back to the boy. "What'd Otto tell you about the job?"

"Is it . . . ?" Harmon said, letting his eyes flick around the room.

"You can talk all you like," Mallory said. "We asked you to come by
at 0330 because this place is always pretty empty around now. There's
nobody in here who doesn't work for us, Billy, including the staff, except those two old folks way over at the front table. And unless we
holler, they won't learn much."

"A Novik 3750 would fit easily in that woman's purse, sir," Harmon
said. "And its effective range at maximum is seventy feet."

"A 3750 with pack at maximum," Laura said, "would run through
its battery charge in twenty minutes. They're meant for semiperma-
nent installation with a shielded AC line, and if you crank them up to
max without proper baffling, they pick up so much ambient and room
tone that they're pretty useless. But I'm glad they've been training you
to think technically."

"You need the training," Mallory agreed. "And then you need to
learn when to forget it."

"Thank you, sir," Harmon said. "And ma'am. That's the kind of
guidance I'm hoping to get on this trip."

"The *sir* and *ma'am*'s something else you can forget," Mallory said.
"I'm Jack and this is Laura."

Harmon nodded, as if committing *Jack* and *Laura* to memory.
"Thanks, Jack. Anyway, I'm sure I can use all the tips you and Laura
can spare me."

"Good," Laura said. "Here's one. Invest in some long-sleeved
shirts."

Harmon looked down at his round biceps, where the tattooed initials *GH* were half-visible beneath the elastic of his sleeve, enclosed in a ring of five-pointed stars. "You're right, ah, Laura. People remember tattoos. If I'd known I'd end up going into covert work, I'd never have gotten it," he said sheepishly.

"It's not just the tattoo," Laura said. "It's the muscles. You're obviously very fit, William, and that's not so good. Making it obvious, I mean. People remember someone strong and tough-looking just as much as they remember tattoos, and they wonder about it more. In general, good looks are a very mixed blessing in this business. Anything that gets you noticed puts you in danger. But on the other hand, you can often use attractiveness to draw targets close. Both Jack and I have had to learn, and so will you." Seeing the boy's discomfort, she quickly added, "What does *GH* stand for? An old girlfriend?"

"Good habits," Mallory said. "It's a Marine thing."

"That's right," Harmon said. "Good habits. The sort of habits you want to cultivate in a shooting war. Full mental and physical preparation for each mission. Full mental and physical readiness between missions. Proper care of weapons. Proper use of supplies. Proper communication: listen hard, execute precisely, report fully." He'd been touching a finger to the tabletop to mark each point; now he saw them watching his fingers and pressed his palms flat to the Formica. "And, you know, and so on." The waitress set coffee and a large slice of pie à la mode before him, put another slice in front of Mallory, winked again, and left. Harmon gazed at the pie in dismay.

Mallory forked up a big mouthful with a look of contentment. "You were doing damn well in the Marines," he said, swallowing and forking up another. "Why'd you want to quit?"

"Because of all the goddamn—beg pardon, Miss Morse—all the waiting around. I got sick of it. It wasn't what I joined up for."

"Well, I'm afraid you've booted it good, son," Mallory said. "'Cause you'll be doing plenty of waiting around with us."

"Well," Harmon said, disconcerted, "I'm ready to do whatever's necessary." He looked down at his pie and dutifully began to eat.

"Good. How much did Otto tell you about the job?"

Harmon swallowed and said, "I'd rather hear it from the two of you. But I think Mr. Roller was pretty thorough. I got a two-page CV for Jespers, which I've memorized, of course, and an abstract on, you know, the device, which was pretty skimpy, but I guess that's all that's known for sure. I got a list of major deals Jespers has done over the past ten years, so I could get an idea of what I suppose you could call his style of doing business. Oh, and a CV on Kost, including a lot of speculative stuff about what he might have done for the Soviets, but no really finished intelligence. There isn't any. You know, just a lot of let's-suppose from analysts. You know the kind of thing."

"Yes," Mallory said. "I believe I do."

If Harmon caught the irony in Mallory's voice, he didn't show it. "I've got to say, the analysis didn't seem very helpful. They pay these guys to dream up scenarios, so I don't understand why they always seem to make such conservative guesses. I mean, if you've got the facts, let's have the facts, and if you're listing possibilities, then let's list *all* of them. But I guess I'll get used to filling in the blanks for myself."

"Uh-huh."

"I didn't know how much planning you'd done, or whether I'd be involved in the strategic end, so I figured I'd better do a little procedure-mapping. I found four successful technology grabs in the dead files that seemed to have some relevance to this one and made notes of what seemed like their common features. And I've done a little reading on space-based surveillance. There's some pretty good published literature on the subject, if you're interested."

"Kind of you to offer, Billy," Mallory said.

This time Harmon didn't miss Mallory's tone. Laura suppressed a wince and took a sip of coffee. Jack was naturally polite with strangers, but he could make himself unpleasant when he had to, and she agreed that, just then, he had to. The boy was a show-off, and easy to rattle. Either quality could be lethal in the field. If William Harmon was going to pop like a balloon, much better to pop him now. The boy was flustered, but he made a plain attempt to compose himself and said:

"Jack, do you have any idea of the sort of things you might want me for on this run? Not the inside stuff, I know, getting close to Jespers. I know you and Laura have all that covered. But the kinds of backup work I might be called on to do? I've had, if you don't mind my saying so, a pretty broad training courtesy of the Marines. And my alma mater, too. Dartmouth. I was ROTC there. I've done the Navy SEAL deep-water core course. I suppose that might be some use in a harbor town. Advanced ropes, HALO jumping, covert comm. I've got a second-degree black belt in go-ju. Of course, nothing like you, Miss Morse. Laura," he said, momentarily bashful. "I never got to see you, back when you were competing, but I did see the films of you and Tiger Petacchi at the '55 world competition. I've never seen legwork like that, anywhere, or, of course, speed. I guess no one has. They talk about you a lot around my dojo."

"Well, maybe we can spar a bit sometime," Laura said.

"I'd like that, if it wouldn't be too big a waste of your time. I'd like that a lot. Anyway, as I was saying, Jack, there's a number of—"

"We get the idea, son. You been to school," Mallory said.

"Well— Yes, frankly. I have."

"And you got As in all your classes. And now you're ready to come around and show us what you've learned. Teach us how to run a secure meeting in our own HQ. Offer a few helpful hints about running successful grabs. Improve our minds with a little reading on space-based surveillance. That about right?"

Brought it on himself, Laura thought. She took a spare fork and cut herself a piece of Jack's apple pie. *He's dished it out for himself. Let's see how he takes it.*

"I'm sorry if I was out of line, Jack," Harmon said, his voice tight. "I tend to be a little over-eager when I get ideas. But I guess, when I joined this firm, I was hoping there'd be a little room for initiative."

"Initiative?" Mallory said. "*Initiative?* Billy, we got enough room for initiative in this firm to make you sicken and die. We go through a tank car full of initiative every goddamned day of the week. But we don't need any from you, son. Not now, and not for a while. We don't need you getting all pumped up full of initiative and improvising some heroics for yourself and getting yourself killed. We don't need you bringing down the job while you're at it. We just had a good man die on us, die ugly, because he showed a little too much initiative. Because he had a few too many ideas. Don't you know Gray gave you to us so we could slap the initiative out of you and make room for a little sense?"

"No, I didn't. May I ask a question? Why do you keep staring at me like that?"

"'Cause I'm trying to figure out what's eating you."

"I wasn't aware that—"

"Well, *get* aware of it," Mallory said, almost equably. "Something's eating you. You got a stick up your hind end taller'n you are. You kind of remind me of me at your age, and that's not a compliment."

"I—"

"Shut up a minute and listen. Billy, I'm from a piece-of-crap little oil town called Corpus Christi. Corpus Christi, Texas. You're from Jersey—Morristown, right? Well, I been to Morristown, and the nicest part of Corpus isn't half as nice as the crappiest part of Morristown. And we weren't from the nicest part. There were nine of us, eight once Dad cut out, and I was second-oldest. Third-oldest if you count my mom as one of the kids, which she pretty much was. And she had her hands full. She had to do what she could to get a little bit of money for the rent, cocktailing mostly, and my older brother was always running around trying to earn his Career Criminal merit badge, so that meant from the time I was about ten years old, I was the momma. And I wasn't much of a momma. I changed all the damn diapers I ever care to change before I was old enough to shave. I tried to get everybody into a tub once a week and keep the babies from wandering out naked and killing each other on the front stoop and maybe get some kind of meal on the table once a day or so where everybody was sitting together the way I heard you were supposed to do. And I was hustling around in circles just hoping there was some way I could get things tidied up to where everybody couldn't see at a glance that we were oilfield trash. And there wasn't, Billy. There really wasn't. I'd look around at the place—actually, there was a whole bunch of places, we left a trail of screwed landlords all over town—and every other Saturday morning there'd be some new joker in his undershirt in our kitchen, drinking our coffee and nursing his head and trying to act like he didn't wish us kids were all in hell, and my mom flat-out and hungover in the back room and not getting up until three in the afternoon, 'cause that's when cocktail waitresses get up. And it wasn't Ozzie and it wasn't Harriet, and that just ate me alive. So when I finally got out of Corpus and into the Army, I was the most hundred-and-ten-percent son of a bitch you might ever hope to avoid. I'd been waiting all my life to see things done right, and by God I was going to show everybody what doing it right meant. And now here you are, a nice boy from a nice house in a nice town and a nice school, and you're just as big a goddamn do-right as I was, with just as little sense as I had. And that's why I have to wonder, Billy, what's eating you? What's got you all crossed up?" Harmon was sitting dead-still by now, just staring at Mallory. Beside him, Laurie was doing the same, Laurie and her strange new suntan. Two handsome young people with clear eyes shining out of dark skin. There was something there. What was so damn fascinating about their eyes and skin? His own words came back to him: *If this was Alabama . . .*

"Billy? You got a little Negro in you, don't you?" Mallory said softly.

Laura scooped up another chunk of pie. *So that's what it is.*

"My grandmother," Harmon said, and for the first time looked his full age, and dangerous. "On my mother's side. Is that a problem for you?"

"I'm guessing it's a problem for you, son. It's making you try too hard. That's what it is I been trying to put a finger on. That's what's eating you. You wanna prove you're not some shiftless spade, just like I always wanted to show people I wasn't some dumb mick with a dirty neck. And that's why I worry you're going to go freelancing all over the landscape and get us all killed the minute we get you over to Monaco. Look, Billy. Nobody ever thought I was much of a white man back in Corpus, and I never thought much about it at all. I don't give a good sweet goddamn whether you're chocolate, vanilla, or butterscotch, but you got to ease up a little or this thing won't work."

"I'll bear that in mind, sir," Harmon said stonily.

Mallory sighed and looked at Laura.

She nodded, patted her lips with a napkin, and rose, thinking, *This won't be pleasant.*

"Well, it's been nice to meet you, William," she said, "but I think you and Jack had better take it from here. Good-bye, Jack. See you both at the ops meeting."

Mallory stared hard at Harmon as Laura's heels clacked away toward the door, and continued to stare as the door swung open with a faint squeak and let in a blat of traffic noise, and as it thumped shut again.

Then he said, "All right. What did they tell you about me?"

"What do you mean?" Harmon said.

"It's a simple goddamn question, Billy. Answer it. What did they tell you?"

"They said you'd be, that I'd be working—"

"Billy."

"They told me," Harmon said reluctantly, "that you're about the best operative the Consultancy has. They said, well. That you always take care of your partners."

"Billy, what did they tell you about me?"

"Well, that you're sometimes a little looser than Gray likes. They said you're the only lead who doesn't keep his own files. Gray has Analysis do it for you."

"Billy. What did they tell you about me?"

"They said you were a drunk," Harmon snapped.

Mallory stood.

"Come and find out," he said.

At three in the morning, the East Side of Manhattan is relatively quiet, except for the rumble of big trucks down Second Avenue. The bars and nightclubs have closed—the legal ones, in any case—and the bakers, milkmen, and trash collectors are still clinging to their last hour's sleep. At such an hour, if you weave down the sidewalk arm-in-arm with a companion, singing at the top of your lungs, you will be heard, and Harmon and Mallory could be heard from the Seventy-seventh Street Boat Basin in Central Park to the on-ramps for the Fifty-ninth Street Bridge, two deeply unmusical tenor voices making an ill-advised attempt at harmony:

Just because my hair is curly
Just because my teeth are pearly
Just because I always wear a smile . . .
That is why they call me Shine

The night doorman at Mallory's apartment building admitted them in a state of shock. He knew Mallory was a drinker; night doormen know everything. But he'd never seen him come home raucously drunk, and certainly never with a male companion. *Live and learn,* he thought as the two made their way across the lobby, the older one guiding the younger one by the shoulders, and disappeared into the elevator.

Inside the elevator, Harmon leaned against the mirrored back wall and touched his face with his fingers as if checking for bruises. "Oh God," he said. "Oh God. I can't go home like this. I'm staying with my parents in, in—"

"Morristown," Mallory said. "You're not going home, Billy. This is my place. I'll put you up tonight."

"I can't let them see me like this," Harmon said, beginning to laugh. "I've been staying with my folks. I can't go home. Mallory, why aren't you drunk?"

"'Hell makes you think I'm not drunk? 'Course I'm drunk. I'm damn drunk. If I'm not drunk, I just wasted a whole bunch of Gray's money. In you go," Mallory said, opening his apartment door. "Whoop, watch the table."

"Where are we?" Harmon said. "I'm so, I'm so goddamn . . . what's the word?"

"Drunk. Couch all right? Use it myself sometimes. It's not too bad." Mallory opened a closet and pulled out a neatly folded set of sheets, a blanket, and a pillow. He carried them to the sofa and began making it up as a bed, his movements practiced and economical. "Have a seat," he said over his shoulder.

Harmon obediently lowered himself into an armchair and sat there with his eyes closed, breathing deeply through his mouth. "*Just because I wear a smile,*" he sang softly, "*and dress up in the latest style.* I can't let them see me like this. Mallory, why aren't you drunk?"

"There you go. Got a spare toothbrush, if you need it. Still in the cellophane. Or would you rather leave it till tomorrow?"

"Tomorrow," Harmon said. "It's just that I always . . . You have no idea how my mom got treated. Just for marrying a white man. The kinds of things people said when she, when the two of them went out together. Mallory? You have no idea."

"Sure I do. You keep telling me." Mallory turned the covers back and patted the sofa, and Harmon walked carefully over and sat down on it. He looked appraisingly at his shoes, then tried to get hold of the laces. Mallory dropped to one knee, untied the young man's shoes, and slipped them from his feet. "There you go. Glass of water?"

"I don't want a glass of water. I'm tired of . . . swallowing," Harmon said, and began to laugh again. "Mallory, I swear to you. I'm better in the field. I'm not this big a pain in the ass in the field." He climbed under the covers. Mallory went to the kitchen and returned with a glass of water. "What's this?"

"Drink it. You'll have quite a head in the morning. Drink a couple glasses of water now and it'll help take the edge off. Breakfast is at eight, or just coffee if you can't get breakfast down. We got a big day tomorrow."

Harmon drank the water, blinked at the taste of it, and lay there holding the empty glass to his chest until Mallory took it away from him. There was no intensity in the boy's eyes now, just sadness and a sort of fogged-over intelligence. His mouth, Mallory saw, was fuller now, more Negro-looking. He'd stopped primming his lips together to make them seem thin. Mallory thought it was a much more promising face. "Now, you're gonna remember what we talked about tonight, right, Billy? You remember?"

"Yeah. But I can't pronounce it."

"No . . ." Mallory prompted.

"Aneep . . . Ineetch . . ."

"No initiative."

"Initiative. No initiative," Harmon said.

"Right. And no . . ."

"Freelancing."

"Right. No matter what color you are."

"No matter what color I am."

"And what are the new initials?"

"AJF."

"AJF," Mallory said. "Ask Jack first. You're okay, Billy. Gray wasn't wrong about you. One day you'll be teaching some other kid, just like I'm teaching you now. And when that day comes—"

"If I have to be up in five hours," Harmon said, "why don't you let me get some sleep?"

Laughing, Mallory slapped the boy's chest. "G'night," he said.

He turned out the light, walked almost steadily to his room, and went to bed.

4

Three-Sixty

"Aren't you the least bit curious?" Laura said.

"About what?" Mallory said. He was slouched in the passenger seat of Laurie's Jag, watching the sunlit countryside stream by.

"Well, Carroll's supposed to be quite a wealthy man, and a racing fanatic. So wouldn't you think Gray's gotten us something pretty nice to drive? I mean, gotten *you* something nice. I'm sure you'll be doing the driving in Monaco. Jack Carroll wouldn't let his girlfriends drive him around like this."

"I guess you're right."

"And you aren't curious what they're giving you?"

Mallory shrugged. "Find out soon enough. I guess it must be something extra, or Otto wouldn't need me to test-drive it. Probably one of these fidgety little foreign deals that have to be handled just so."

"You're an unnatural man. You don't appreciate the good things in life."

They were heading north on Route 17. Even after all the years he'd lived in New York, Mallory was always surprised at how much nice country there was upstate: the neatly groomed farms and spruce little villages, the rolling meadowland, the blunt cliffs of dynamited rock, rising and falling as the road cut through the hills. He really had to get out of the city more. "Uh-huh?" he said.

"Oh, go back to sleep."

"Good idea."

"Listen, what did you do to Billy the other night?"

"Took him out and got him drunk," Mallory said, eyes closed.

"So I gathered. He looked like death at the ops meeting. But I mean, what did you *say* to him?"

"I dunno, Laurie. We were drunk."

"He was like a different man at the meeting. None of that clever-schoolboy stuff, just—" Laura lifted a hand from the wheel and pointed two fingers straight ahead. "Focus. Good questions. Good grasp. You must have said something to him. You were certainly saying things at the diner. That was more than you usually talk in a month."

"Sorry. I rattled on some, didn't I? That kid gets under my skin."

"I didn't know all that about you growing up, Jack. I mean, I knew you didn't have much money but, you know, the rest. About you raising your brothers and sisters."

"I didn't raise 'em. Nobody raised any of us. I never told you because it isn't that interesting. I told Billy because he's one of these oh-poor-me types, and I wanted to remind him the world's full of oh-poor-me."

"Well, whatever you said to him must have been the right thing to say."

"I got him drunk, that's all. He had a stick up. I couldn't pry it loose, so I figured I'd try and dissolve it. I ought to get you drunk sometime. Do you good."

"Thanks. What do you think about the job?"

"It's all right. What do you mean?"

"It doesn't bother you to be hired as some sort of glorified bur-glar?"

"I'm not like you, Laurie. I'm not that moral of a person. Most days I'm just glad I got a paycheck."

"I mean, it's one thing to steal missile stuff from the Russians or Chinese. But Jespers's just an independent, sort of like the Consultancy. Who says he doesn't have as much right to this satellite as Gray's client? I suppose Gray tends to have a nicer class of client than Jespers. You *are* asleep."

"That's right."

"Well, wake up, because here we are. I can't believe you're not curious about what Otto's gotten for us."

"Back home, Laurie, I was what they call a West Texas queer. You know what a West Texas queer is?"

"No."

"A guy who likes girls better than cars."

She let out a grudging snort of laughter as they turned into the gravel parking lot.

In front of the Consultancy's upstate proving grounds stood the weathered plywood silhouette of a man in a racing suit, his helmet under his arm. He was twelve feet tall and peeling badly, and listed a bit to one side. To stabilize him, someone had attached his chest by guy-wires to four buried cinderblocks. He'd since pulled two of them out of the ground. In his hand was a wooden checkered flag, and around his middle a banner advertising classes for aspiring race-car drivers. If you called the phone number on the banner, you could sign up for them, and sometimes people did. They were very good lessons, since they were taught by a retired second-tier stock-car champion named Kearns, who trained all of the Consultancy's agents in high-speed evasion and pursuit.

Kearns had no students that day, paying or otherwise, and was at choir practice in a nearby Congregational church, where he sang with his youngest daughter. Mallory and Laura were greeted instead by Otto Roller, the Consultancy's director of logistics, who stood by the wooden man's knee and waved his clipboard as they pulled up.

"It is the lovely Laura," Otto announced as they got out of the car. He kissed her on both cheeks. "The lovely Laura who comes to brighten our lifes, in her nice silver car that makes such noise."

"Hello, Otto."

"'Lo, Otto," Mallory said.

"Hello, Jack," Otto said. "You're a terrible fellow that you don't come to see me. When are you coming to see me? We'll have a real drink-up."

"Sounds good," Mallory said.

"That's the last thing Jack needs," Laura said.

"It's only that he is not drinking the correct things," Otto explained. "What is bourbon? Bourbon cannot possibly do a man good. It is drunk in Kentucky, and where is Kentucky?"

"Where it's always been," Mallory said.

"Exactly," Otto said. "We'll have a drink-up, and I will give you a most excellent Côte de Beaune Montrachet or some of this nice Czech *weissebier* I have found, it will be your choice, and with it we will have calf's liver sauteed with scallions and lingonberries and some good new potatoes and afterward a good Stilton and some of my Calvados, and the health will be back in your cheeks. Look how terrible you look."

"I look just the way I always— All right. I'm not falling for that one twice."

"Why don't you appeal to this lovely girl for help? Why don't you have her rescue you? It is because you have no acumen."

"Otto, where's our car?"

"Yes, Otto," Laura said. "Where's our car?"

"I appeal to her constantly, because I have lots of acumen," Otto said. "But I am too fat. It is a great tragedy. It is ruining both our lifes. Come with me and I'll show you the car you're all so excited about. It's a good car. It will put the health in your cheeks."

Otto Roller was a burly, sixtyish Bavarian whose own cheeks seemed unimprovably full of health. He had a pink infant's face, a broad belly, and a gray walrus mustache that seemed to ripple with good fellowship. He wore, as usual, a garish Hawaiian shirt over baggy corduroy slacks. As the head of Logistics, he knew more about the Consultancy's inner workings than anyone except Gray, and was therefore at constant risk of kidnapping or assassination. In consequence, Otto's left trouser pocket always held a tiny .22 Beretta, a purse gun. He was the Consultancy's deadliest shot, and it was all the gun he needed, though sometimes he carried two to save himself the bother of reloading. Otto claimed to go armed solely out of cowardice. He enjoyed joking about his cowardice, which was imaginary, and his gluttony, which was quite real. He never joked about his drinking, though his drinking was intemperate enough to worry even Mallory. Mallory tended to drink when he was between assignments, but Otto drank all the time, and it was a mystery to the rest of the firm how he was able to get through the immense amounts of work he customarily did. "Most people are like model trains," Gray had once said, "with a lever you can turn to make them go faster or slower. Otto just has a switch that turns him on or off, and I've never seen it off. I'm afraid one of these days he'll simply go smash." It was the only time anyone had ever heard Gray say "I'm afraid" and seem to mean it.

Otto led them along a rut in a weedy field to the old barn that served the proving grounds as office and garage. A garage door had been installed in the wall facing away from the road. The door looked nearly as dilapidated as the barn, but you would have needed a bazooka to pierce it. Otto had once tested it himself with a .44 Python, leaving half a dozen bright pocks, which were currently in the process of filling with soft brown rust. Now he bent at the waist with surprising ease and rolled the door up with a flick of one powerful arm. Inside, beside a battered workbench, stood a dull-yellow car with a short trunk, a long hood, and wire-spoked wheels. It had a blunt, abrupt look, like a stonemason's wedge. "My God," Laura said. "A Via d'Oro."

"Yes," Otto said complacently. "It's a good car."

"It's probably," Laura said, "the fastest production car in the world. A Ferrari Via d'Oro. The body's hand-made of mallite and aircraft aluminum by Ghia—under Ghia's personal supervision—and the engine's a supercharged Ferrari Dino 246 with Lucas injection, retuned for the street. Colotti transmission with a Borg & Beck twin-plate diaphragm clutch, Chapman struts in back, and Girling discs all around. The seats are parachute silk over cotton batting, because leather and horsehair weigh too much. The top end is somewhere over two hundred, at least ten miles better than the Cobra AC. They've only made a hundred and twenty Vias, and you can't buy them, not anywhere. The entire production run was sold out through subscription two years before the first car was finished. Too many people sent deposits, so they had to have a lottery to pick the buyers. A Via d'Oro. Oh, Otto."

"You are unkind," Otto complained. "You already made for me my whole speech."

"All that sounds pretty good," Mallory said mildly. "How's it handle?"

"Very— Sorry," Laura said. "I've actually only just read about them. Go on, Otto."

"Very stiff," Otto agreed. "Very fussy. These are very soft tires on very hard shocks, you see, and they don't like to let go. So power slides, drift turns, all this must be done very nicely, because it digs in and digs in and then! Boom, away you go. So you must be alert. Are you alert?"

"Pretty much."

"You must be very alert. And touch it like a little sleeping infant when you start and stop, just the most delicate tiny pat on the pedal, because a little bit of gas and you are already too fast, and a little bit of brake and you have already stopped completely and your nose is through the windshield. It has too much power and too much brakes. It has too much everything. It is a very good car. When you come to Monaco, you must seem very comfortable with it, so now I want you to get in and become its friend. Here. You see the switch for the supercharger?"

"Thanks," Mallory said, taking the keys. "Yeah, I see it. There's not much else on the dash. C'mon, Laurie, get in. You can tell me what I'm doing wrong."

She climbed into the passenger seat at once and sat for a moment, running her eyes all over the cockpit, even twisting in her seat to examine the upholstery, before she remembered to say, "Oh, I will."

The car was new, but there was little of the typical new-car smell of vinyl or leather, just the smoky smell of the new Dunlop tires and the somehow furry garage-smell of old crankcase oil on concrete and the rotten-wood smell of the old rafters overhead. Then Mallory closed the door and there was no smell at all. The seat was hard as a church pew. It gripped him firmly around the hips. Mallory and Otto were much of a height, but Mallory's legs were longer, so he slid the seat back a notch, locked it into place, adjusted the mirrors, and let his hands linger for a moment on the smallish steering wheel. This was wrapped in perforated leather and dusted with talc. He snapped the rallye-style shoulder-and-lap harness closed across his torso and tugged it snug, then let his palm settle on the stick shift. Laura was already sitting buckled up in her seat, trying not to look impatient. The doors had no armrests; her hands were clasped in her lap.

First-rate drivers have an instinctive feel for a car. They inhabit it fully and feel the road beneath its tires as if walking barefoot. Mallory was not a first-rate driver, just a skilled one, but even he could see that this was a superb car, and he found himself wanting to be first-rate for it. He set a light foot on the gas and twisted the ignition key.

The barn filled with a thick roaring and the car gave itself a shake and lay trembling beneath him. Mallory lifted his foot from the gas and the trembling softened. A high idle. Very high. The Via d'Oro was probably a V-6, Mallory guessed; it ran a little rougher than American V-8s, but steady and somehow livelier, too. Otto was nodding, lips thrust out, a look of comic satisfaction on his face. He raised a hand and made a ring of thumb and forefinger, like a cartoon chef demonstrating approval of an entrée. Mallory let out the clutch, slipped into gear, and softly lay the sole of his foot against the gas pedal.

The car lunged forward. Mallory frowned, embarrassed, and eased back still farther.

"Oh dear," Laura said happily.

"She's a perky little thing," Mallory said as they rolled out of the garage.

"Drive the car," Laura said, beaming out at the track. "Just drive the car."

Otto walked alongside, keeping a proprietary hand on the driver's-side back fender as Mallory pulled out onto the track. Then he stepped away and waved his clipboard in farewell. "A slow lap first," he roared, "and then a few quick ones, and then you may try some"—he flourished the clipboard—"foolishness. And I will time you." He held up a stopwatch. "I will time you as if you were a champion."

The proving ground contained three tracks run together. One was a miniature Grand Prix circuit three-quarters of a mile long and loaded with tight corners and hairpins. Another was a flat oval with two long, wide straightaways, where Otto had set up a slalom course with rubber traffic cones. The straightaways were broad enough to practice the "foolishness" Otto had mentioned: the complex and specialized evasive maneuvers that every senior Consultancy field operative had to master and that few ever had occasion to use. At the rear of the grounds was a steeply banked oval track, which Otto had blocked off with a line of cones. There was no point in practicing on a banked track when they'd be driving on public roads.

Mallory swung onto the first course, noting the tightness of the steering—there seemed to be no play at all—and brought the speed up to 40 mph. The transmission felt like nothing he'd ever driven, a mixture of resistance and fluidity that recalled the action of his own Browning. Changes were crisp and distinct, and the engine each time moved from one pure note to another. It made him think of Kearns at choir practice. He slowed at the first bend and knew halfway through that this had been unneccessary; he'd eased up to 50 mph by the next bend and scarcely slowed at all at the third. The Via seemed to like it better that way. It was quite a car. Fifty seemed to cost it no more effort than idling. The first lap, Mallory saw with something like a pang, was already almost over. *Lord, this is nice,* Mallory thought. *This must be what driving's like for Laurie. When you drive something like this, you can see why she likes it so much.*

"What do you think?" she asked after he'd finished a few laps.

"It's all right," he replied. "Gonna see how she brakes now. I'll try not to put us out on the hood."

Like all good drivers, Mallory was sparing with the brake, preferring to use gas and gearbox to modulate speed. Now he tried to ease the car to a smooth stop. He'd developed enough of a feel for the car to avoid abruptness, but had to start and stop three times before he was braking smoothly enough to satisfy himself. He frowned for a moment, then drove across the short stretch of blacktop linking the Grand Prix–style course to the flat oval and brought the car up to 60 mph.

"Panic stop," he said, swinging from the first broad curve onto the straightaway. "Get braced."

Mallory crash-halted the car from 60, from 70, and from 80, several times at each speed, trying to get the wheels to disengage. The car was reluctant to do so. But when he succeeded, the skid was unusually straight. The Via was perfectly balanced, and, owing to the stiffness of the suspension, did very little nosing-in.

Engine, transmission, tires, suspension, and brakes, all exceptional. One last bit of hardware left to try. Mallory brought the car back up to 80 mph, swung hard through the far corner, and thumbed on the supercharger.

The Via, already speeding, leapt ahead like a racehorse leaving the starting gate, the rich roar of the engine rising to an enraged scream as it sucked air down through the NACA inlet in the hood and spat it into the Dino's six cylinders as flame. An octave above the scream of the engine, the supercharger's chain drive seemed to whistle. Mallory was at the next corner before he had a chance for a proper look at the speedometer, and had to use the brake more than he liked to manage the car onto the next straight.

"Now, that's just silly," he said. "Unless they're gonna put wings on this thing and let me fly it, what the hell'm I supposed to do with all that?"

Laura did not reply.

Mallory swooped a few times around the broad track, then eased back down to 40 and sent the Via through the slalom course, noting with approval bordering on awe how little rolling the car did and how fiercely it held the road. For the next few laps he tried bringing the car up faster and faster on the clear straightaway—96, 103, 124, letting it subside to 75 or so on the far turn, and then negotiating the traffic cones at ever-higher speeds. He gave up at 68 mph, an almost foolhardy speed for that sort of driving, when he flattened the third and fifth cones. "Lord, Jack," Laurie said. "You're a really good driver. I had no idea. I feel guilty, hogging the wheel all this time."

"Don't be guilty. Driving's just work to me. Happy to let somebody else do it. Every man ought to have a pretty girl to drive him around. All right now, let's try some foolishness."

Mallory tried to send the Via into a four-wheel drift. Here, for the first time, the little sportster balked. It was happy to turn and happy to drive straight ahead, but it had not been built for sliding all over the road, and for an ugly moment Mallory thought he was going to roll Otto's shiny new car and make everyone upset. He cut the wheel more sharply next and kept a more stubborn foot on the gas, and was rewarded with better results. But even after a few good drifts, it was a challenge to convince the car to spin into a one-eighty and come to rest facing the way it came—one of the key evasive maneuvers Kearns had taught him. When he finally got the wheels to disengage on the third try, the car spun out entirely and came to rest crookedly on the shoulder.

"Damn you anyhow," Mallory told the car.

"That's no way to talk," Laura said.

"You gonna tell me what I'm doing wrong?"

"You're not doing anything wrong."

"Must be."

"No. You just haven't— You just aren't approaching this with the proper attitude. Look. Imagine you're asking a girl to dance. The most beautiful girl. All right? Except, all the while, you're thinking that you're probably bothering her and she'd really rather you went away. What happens when you do something like that?"

"I try and not do that. But I get your point."

"Right. So this time, remember: the girl wants to dance with you."

Mallory grunted.

But the next one-eighty was more successful, and the one after that a textbook illustration. After that, he ran through the entire repertoire with relative ease: the Sidewinder, the Hot C, the Sliding Door, the Cutter. Mollified, Mallory headed back to the Grand Prix track and took the car for a few more high-speed laps through the thicket of hairpins. Then he coasted to a halt.

Otto, standing on the grassy median with his stopwatch and clipboard, bowed in Mallory's direction and began to walk over.

Mallory stepped from the car and waved Otto back. The engine was still grumbling richly. He set a hand on the roof and ducked his head into the open door.

"All right, Laurie," he said. "I know you're dying to."

Wordlessly, she got up from the car and almost trotted around to the driver's side.

Mallory settled into the passenger seat and buckled up as Laura set her feet experimentally against the pedals and hitched the seat an inch forward. She checked the mirrors and adjusted one. Her blouse was wrinkled beneath her shoulder harness, and she smoothed it down.

An instant later, Mallory found himself crushed back into his church-pew-hard seat.

There was nothing jerky about Laura's acceleration. It was a smooth forward surge like a big wave. But they'd hit 71 by the first corner and were cresting 75 as she wrung the car back onto the short straight and flicked on the supercharger.

After that, disconnected sensations of headlong speed and sudden changes of direction. Laura's first lap was faster than Mallory's last, and she only got quicker from there, sending him straining alternately against the strap over his left shoulder and the door at his right. Her touch on the gearshift seemed caressingly light, and her right hand appeared to have returned to the steering wheel almost before it had departed. "Pretty fast fingers," Mallory said. "You ever learn to cheat at cards, I think you could make a decent living."

"Tachyphrenia."

"How's that again?"

"Tachyphrenia. It's a neurological term. Tachyphrenics see time as passing very slowly, and have abnormally quick reaction times. I'm a bit tachyphrenic, most days, and I've learned to slip into a deeper state when I want."

"Like when you fight."

"Exactly. It's probably why I did so well. My style's always been reasonably good, you know, and my eye and so on, but when you get to the top you find other people whose technique's as good as mine, and sometimes better. But none of them were ever as quick as I am. That's why I like it when things go fast."

Her lips were slightly parted, and her eyes held a look of religious exaltation.

After the second lap, he stopped looking at the speedometer and simply hung on. On the third lap, she began to incorporate tight, fluid drifts into her passage down the straightaways and the lone chicane, returning to the racing line without apparent effort. It was the sort of maneuver he'd been trained to make at 60 miles per hour; Laura was doing it at better than 90. The snakelike darting of her right hand from stick to wheel, and the shuddering of the wheel in her thin hands, made an odd contrast with the almost daydreamy stillness of her face.

"I'm not making you nervous, am I, Jack?" she said.

"Naw," he said, eyes on the road ahead. "Just gimme a chance to make a good Act of Contrition."

Ignoring the flat oval circuit Otto had prepared for them, Laura skimmed between the traffic cones he'd used to block off the banked oval and barreled onto the first straightaway. She was no sooner on the course when she slapped the brakes and threw the car into a smooth, effortless-looking hundred-and-eighty-degree spin and, as soon as they'd come more or less to rest, trampled the gas and leapt down the track the way she'd come, heading for the first, steeply banked turn. Mallory decided to look at the speedometer again as they swept up the curve: 92. They were 50 degrees from the horizontal. He felt a voluptuous swooning sensation as centrifugal force drew the blood down into his legs. They left the turn faster than they'd entered and were doing 142 by the time she slowed for the next. "Kearns didn't teach you all this," Mallory said.

"I race," she told him. "I've been racing for years. When I can, you know, not as often as I like. I chipped in with two friends to buy an old Formula Vee racer and had it rebuilt. Formula Vee's like Formula One, but with Volkswagen engines and brakes. It's sort of like a farm league for F1. There's an amateurs' division. I had to do a bit of insisting to get them to let me enter. A lot of men," she said, hauling the Via through another eye-glazing turn, "don't think women have the upper-body strength for racing."

"Guess they must be mistaken."

"Yes."

"How d'you usually do?"

"Usually," Laura said, "I win. What a pity we don't have a really long straight. I've never been anywhere near two hundred miles an hour. Actually, if you don't mind, I'd like to try now. I probably won't be able to get much closer than one-sixty on a little track like this."

"Well," Mallory said philosophically, "as long as it's just one-sixty."

Laura accelerated into the looming turn and this time sent the Via up to the very top lip of the banked curve. Then she shot down into the straight like a pebble leaving a slingshot. They were in fourth gear now, and the entire car was singing like a tuning fork over the squalling of the Ferrari engine. The tachometer needle was wobbling near the red line, and the speedometer ticked steadily around the dial: 130, 140, 150. It nudged the 160 mark, brimmed over. Ahead of them, the banked curve looked like a wall. *We're done,* Mallory thought. *Gonna shoot right up over that thing and fly. Or punch a hole straight through.* But they were already decelerating hard, Laura downshifting madly, the howling brakes filling Mallory's ears. They fishtailed left and right and then straightened, shot up the wall-like curve again, and came down on the other side at a modest 78 miles an hour. Midway through the straight, Laura punched the brakes, cut the wheel, and sent the car into a three-sixty, spinning it through a complete revolution that left it standing still, facing down the track again, ready for another lap.

She sat silently behind the wheel. Mallory exhaled. He unbuckled his harness, got out, and strolled around the car on legs that seemed insubstantial, unreal. It was a mild spring day, the sun very bright. Mallory smelled sunlit concrete and unmowed grass, and, washing over it, the sharp, harsh scent of the heated engine, which had not yet begun to tick and cool. He half seated himself on the fender and looked out across the track, feeling the engine's heat rise from the hood at his back. Otto was coming across the grassy median to meet them, grinning and pretending to blow on his stopwatch to cool it down. Mallory looked back at Laura. She was still motionless in her seat, fingertips resting lightly on the wheel, nostrils flaring, eyes glowing. It took her a few moments more to come back from wherever she was and meet Mallory's gaze.

"That," she said at last in her usual drab tones, "was nice."

5

Ballerinas

Though the Grimaldi coat of arms shows two monks brandishing swords, the Grimaldis themselves are not notable for piety or martial vigor. Instead, they have earned a place in history through a centuries-long pursuit of the main chance. A shrewd old Ligurian shipping family, they came to Monaco in 1297 after being exiled from Genoa following a dust-up between the Ghibellines and the Guelphs. Until the French Revolution, they lived there quite comfortably by levying taxes on wine, lemons, tobacco, port traffic, and playing cards. After the revolution, they did what the Grimaldis do best: they adapted.

Charles III opened Monaco's first casino in 1865 in hopes of extricating himself from bankruptcy. To build it, the prince appointed the architect of Paris Opéra, who nestled the new Palais de Chance among jacarandas, fig trees, and pineapple palms, surrounded it with fountains and terraced gardens, and crowned it with a verdigris dome visible all over town. Beside it the prince placed the Hôtel de Paris, so that the gamblers would have a place to sleep, and the Café de Paris, so that they'd have a place to eat. Charles III called the new neighborhood Monte Carlo, in honor of Charles III, and it was such a success that he abolished taxation in Monaco five years later.

After that, Monaco went from strength to strength. The new railroad opened in 1886 and brought herds of pleasure-loving aristocrats to fill the chemin-de-fer tables of the *salons privés* and to tuck into caviar and pink champagne on the roof of Le Grille. Edward VII was a regular at the Café de Paris, where Escoffier invented the flaming crêpes suzette for him. According to legend, it was named after one of Edward's fiery, unroyal companions. Diaghilev brought his Ballets Russes to the Salle Garnier and, after losing her last hundred thousand francs at the Casino, Sarah Bernhardt attempted suicide at the Hôtel de Paris. She did no lasting harm to herself, and certainly not to the hotel's reputation. By the 1950s, Monte Carlo was a pleasure quarter of unrivaled glamour and a business of unrivaled profitability, and Aristotle Onassis had wangled control of it. He kept a suite at the Paris for his friend Winston Churchill, complete with a gilt bronze hook for the cage of Churchill's pet parrot. The hotel's wine cellar is the world's deepest, and one morning Lord Beaverbrook raided it for a bottle of 1815 cognac, which he and Churchill polished off before breakfast.

The combination of balmy breezes, raffish glamour, and a complete absence of income tax was so attractive to the world's well-to-do that, the previous year, President de Gaulle had sealed Monaco's borders to halt an influx of prosperous French citizens bent on resettlement. This had had no lasting effect. As of 1963, Monaco was the smallest, richest place on earth: less than three-quarters of a square mile in extent but boasting the world's highest per-capita income, and eighty percent of its residents were affluent immigrants. It was a glittering and lavishly storied haven for the famous, the infamous, the titled, and the rich: bankers and oil sheiks, starlets and countesses, heirs and heiresses, professional gamblers and professional houseguests, and an endless procession of wealthy, purse-minded retirees turning their wizened faces up to the sun. Presiding over it all was the current Grimaldi, His Serene Highness Prince Rainier III, scion of what was now the world's

oldest reigning royal family, with his new movie-star wife and his re-
newed control of the legendary Casino, which he had just successfully
wrested back from Aristotle Onassis.

"How do you like the place?" Laura asked on their first night.

"It isn't Corpus Christi," Mallory muttered. He closed his empty
suitcase with a clack, boosted it onto the top shelf of the closet, and
looked sourly around the pink-and-gold bedroom. It was a big room,
showoff-big, and there was a bigger one through the arched doorway,
a sort of living-room deal with a wet bar and a Buick-sized TV and a
bunch of antique furniture that made him worry about breaking things.
Everything he saw had little gold curlicues along the edges, like a rash.
And out the window, as far as he could see, was just a whole lot more of
the same. "This place isn't Corpus," Mallory said. "And that's the one
good thing you can say about it."

The average Grand Prix—if one can speak of any Grand Prix as being average—is staged on a purpose-built course deep in the country,
which has been laid out for the convenience of the drivers and teams.
A spacious paddock is set aside for the motor homes that serve the
drivers as quarters and the teams as headquarters, and for the trans-
porters that ferry the cars from track to track. Beside the paddock lie
the garages, where the cars are set up for the race. The garages abut
the pit lane, where the cars are serviced during the race, and both ends
of the pit lane open out onto the track.

But in this, as in so many respects, Monaco is different from other
Grand Prix. Since it is an old-fashioned round-the-houses circuit and
laid out in the heart of a busy city, there is scarcely any room for pits
or paddocks. Instead of sleeping in motor homes, the drivers usually
put up in hotels (the Metropole is a favorite), unless they are part of
the growing minority that make their homes in Monaco year-round.
(Successful Formula One drivers are rich men with a tenuous sense
of national identity, and the advantages of a principal residence in a
pleasant and tax-free spot are as plain to them as to any French ren-
tier.) Since the paddocks have no room for proper garages, the teams

commandeer commercial garages all over town from the Wednesday before a race weekend to the Monday following. The garage owners are well compensated for the inconvenience, and the prestige of housing a Grand Prix team for one week each year has a certain commercial value during the other fifty-one. Team Naughton had set up its base in a waterfront garage on the Avenue de Port. It was the one place in Monaco where Mallory felt at home.

He'd spent the morning there, sitting on a pile of tires, talking to Harry Burch, an anvil-jawed Yorkshireman with a look of dyspeptic zeal. Burch had greeted Mallory by saying, "What is it? 'Fraid we're a bit busy just now. Who're you?"

"Jack—" Mallory had said.

"Right, Ken told me a man named Carroll'd be hanging about. Said you'd given us a packet and I was to be nice to you. Wish I was rich enough to piss my money away on racing. Damn-fool sport. Who are you?" he said to Laura. "There was supposed to be a Miss Prentice."

"Yes," she said.

"We're a bit busy right now," he said, shaking her hand. "Hope you won't be in the way. Not much here for a girl to see in any case. Don't much care for women in my pit. They chatter. They think cars are racehorses and try to make pets of them. Sometimes they try to make pets of my drivers."

"Who are *you*?" Laura said.

"Me?" Burch said, surprised. "I'm the ringmaster of this circus. Harry Burch. Team manager."

"Do you insult everyone you meet, Mr. Burch?"

"What a bloody stupid thing to say. I'm far too busy to insult anyone. Got a team to run. I suppose you think I should twitter about waggling my eyebrows and kissing hands. Want your hand kissed?"

"Not by you."

"Now who's being insulting? Never mind. You'll be all right, Miss Prentice, as long as you stay out of the way and don't pet things."

"I'll try not to."

"Yeah, it's pretty nice," Mallory told Burch.

"Nice?" Burch said, affronted. "*Nice?* What's nice?"

"Like you said. Being rich enough to piss away money on your damn-fool team."

Burch let out a shout of laughter. "Well, long as you know that's what you're doing. It *is* a damn-fool sport. Costs a packet. Bunch of freaks, too. Here comes our chief mechanic, all in a tizzy. Look at that stupid bastard. Somebody told him Italians are supposed to be excitable. Emilio Rossi. Hello, Millie, meet Jack Carroll. He's giving us money."

Emilio Rossi did not look excitable. He had a long hound's face, pouchy brown eyes, and an air of bottomless weariness. He clasped Mallory's hand in both of his and squeezed it passionately, ignoring him. "Harry, you must speak with Derek," he told Burch, still gripping Mallory's hand. "Because we are all dying of this hard rubber."

"Driver picks the tires, Millie."

"You must speak with him. I have some beautiful new green-spot R6s that wear so nicely but can give us just a little bit of adhesion so the car doesn't fly away into the sea. But, no, the tire must be hard like a coin, and overinflate, and with these torsion bars! Like my arm! There is no adhesion. I must keep him on the road, and with what?"

"It's Derek's job to keep the car on the road. Your job's to keep Derek happy."

"He will spend the whole race sideways."

"He likes being sideways. Good at it. Give him more camber if you're worried."

"He won't permit this. He doesn't want the tire to wear. He thinks my men cannot change a tire." Rossi abruptly realized he was standing beside a beautiful young woman and took Laura's hand in his. "Dear lady," he said, then returned to Burch. "You won't speak with him?"

"What do I ever do," Burch said, "but speak with you stupid bastards? All right, Millie, send him over."

As little as he cared for Monaco, Mallory had to admit he was having a good time. He'd escaped, for a few hours, the Hôtel de Paris. His belly was full; he and Laura had just shared the team's lunch of sandwiches from a nearby bistro. The Monegasques made the best sandwiches in the world, and Mallory didn't know why they frittered away their time on stuff like last night's dinner, where you had to guess what was on your plate and what the hell they'd poured over it. He was, for the moment, safe from people trying to speak French to him. His French was damn near as bad as his Russian. Billy Harmon wasn't due in until evening, so that was one worry he didn't have yet. He was surrounded by people who worked for a living. Such people are a minority in Monaco. He was wearing old dungarees and a windbreaker and sitting comfortably on a stack of tires. Someone had scrounged up a café chair for Laura, who, on Otto's instructions, was wearing an orange-and-purple Marimekko dress and too much jewelry. On her own initiative, she was wearing a look of thinly veiled boredom and distaste. Once again Mallory was impressed with Laura's acting ability; he knew she was in heaven.

The doors of the garage had been thrown wide, and the scent of the Mediterranean two blocks away made an odd and pleasant mix with the gluey smell of crankcase oil. Towers of stacked tires rose to the ceiling, and cables and hoses lay neatly coiled, all in patterns as strict and mysterious as a Navajo sand painting. An array of long toolboxes and toolracks had been deployed along the walls and workbenches, scratched and dinged but still brightly enameled in the team colors of gold and midnight blue. A banner along one wall read NAUGHTON USA. Beneath it, the body of a racing car sat without its wheels on an iron framework, looking like the fuselage of a tiny, wingless fighter jet, its savage oval mouth rimmed with gold. Around it stood sawhorses bearing sections of hull and twisting lengths of exhaust pipe, and around all this moved purposeful jumpsuited figures, heads bowed over this bit of machinery or that, intent as surgeons. Emilio Rossi threaded his way between them and tapped one on the shoulder. The man lifted his head, and Mallory recognized Derek Reade.

Reade's picture had been in the briefing packets, but neither Mallory nor Laura had needed it; his picture was also in the papers on a regular basis. The accompanying write-ups generally referred to his "movie-star good looks" and to the fact that, at thirty-one, he'd been through two divorces and a party to two more. Reade was a short, wiry, black-haired man with a strong nose and a finely made mouth hovering on the verge of a smirk. A dark comma of hair fell over one eye. Mallory wanted to tell him to go buy a comb. He strolled over, wiping his oily fingers on a rag; Mallory thought of the chief mechanic's hands, which had been spotless. The driver smiled and inclined his head toward Laura. "Hullo," he said with a faint Mayfair accent. "I'm Derek Reade. Nice to meet you." Turning his eyes from Laura to Mallory with visible regret, he again said, "Hullo."

"Derek, this is Jack Carroll and Somebody Prentice," Burch said. "Couple of Ken's money people. Don't let 'em waste your time. Derek, why don't you stop picking on Millie? He broke his heart getting you those R6s. Why don't you try 'em?"

"I see Harry's given you a good old Team Naughton welcome," Reade said to Laura, smiling. He saved a bit of smile for Mallory, then turned back to Burch. "I knew Millie'd come running to you. I'm perfectly willing to try his damned tires, but I'd like to try my own setup first. Can't you tell him I've driven this track before?"

"Not with the new mill, Derek. Not with this sort of power. Your style might be a bit fine and large for the Lola on a pinchy little track like this." Burch turned to Mallory. "Derek likes his oversteer. Likes to let the tail break away and swing round the outside when he's entering a corner. Halfway through the curve, he's already pointed into the next straight and ready to get on the throttle. Does it better than anyone but Moss. Some days he's better than Moss. Thinks he's Moss, in fact. He's a vain little bastard and he doesn't mind his elders. Derek, try the R6s, all right? Costs you nothing. Do your own setup in the afternoon. Make everybody happy."

"Outgunned again," Reade said amiably. "All right."

"Apologize to Millie. Silly bastard sweats blood for you."

"Like hell," Reade said, just as amiably. "'Fraid I'll have to run, Mr. Carroll. Miss Prentice. But perhaps you'd like to stop by the Sporting Club tonight? They're having a do for the teams. Harry can fix it up for you. All right, Harry?"

Reade nodded and headed back to the car, walking as gracefully as a matador.

"Thinks I'm a bloody social secretary," Burch said. "Vain little git. Thinks he can drive Monaco like it was Indianapolis. You've heard all that lot about the Race of a Thousand Corners. Literally true. Hundred laps, ten corners a lap, maybe thirty-six hundred gear changes in all. Hell on the gearbox. Hell on the tires. Worst circuit in the calendar. High stone curbs, no gravel traps, not many runoff areas, scarcely any room to overtake, scarcely any room to drive straight on. No margin anywhere, and Reade wants to go skating about like Sonja Henie. He'll do it, too. Might even win. Stupid bastard's the smartest driver in the series."

"Uh-huh?" Mallory said.

"Best I've seen," Burch said firmly. "Best road sense, best nerve, best touch, best brains. Wonder why a boy like him, who could get a drive with any team in the world, signed on with a little piss-pot one-car outfit like ours? When Ferrari, Daimler, Cooper are all begging for him? Because he's smart. He knows the works teams have lost their edge. It's the new independents like Ken Naughton who've the new ideas. On Sunday there won't be a sweeter car on the grid than ours, and little Derek knows it. We finished in the points last season. This year we've a shot at the championship. A couple more good years and Naughton will be a dynasty. And Derek'll own it, the way nobody but old Enzo owns Ferrari. See what I mean about smart?"

"So what's the problem?" Mallory said.

"Problem? 'Makes you think there's a problem?" Burch said suspiciously.

"I dunno. What makes you think so?"

Burch frowned ferociously, then scratched his nose. "No problem, I suppose. He's no worse than any of the rest of 'em. They're like goddamn ballerinas, these drivers, a bunch of show dogs. When you come right down to it, they've all got something wrong with 'em. Reade, now, he thinks the ladies fancy him."

"The ladies seem to agree."

"Thinks the ladies fancy him," Burch said darkly. "Goes twittering about with this one and that. They get him drinking. Silly bastard can't drink, but he likes to be a great fellow with the ladies, so I'll see him show up at a test session green as pickles, head in his hands, boo-hoo. Wasted day. Someday he'll do that in a race and I'll wash my hands of him. Told him so. But they're all ballerinas, one way or another. See that young fellow over there by the tires, taking it all in, not a word out of him? Long chin, straw-colored hair, bony? Our reserve driver, Mark Coney. You know what those are, Miss Prentice? Fellow you pay to hang about just in case your driver can't drive. Fine young fellow. Head on his shoulders, no temperament, no nerves, beautiful control, outbrake anybody, never fussed in traffic. No chatter. Drive a lap and he's got the track, *got* it, every last little wrinkle. Know what his problem is?"

"What?"

"Rain. Useless in it. Goes to bits. See, Mark's a boy who likes to stick tight to his line, but when it's wet you've got to splosh in there and slug it out. Different every lap. Got to improvise. That's not Mark's style. He'll play it safe until he finds his wet line and can drive it just so, and by then the race's lost. Not a coward, mind, but can't bear to look clumsy. Very fussy for an American. Treat to walk the track with him, though. Doesn't miss a thing. Teaches Reade sometimes. Listen, you two aren't bad for rich buggers. Why don't you come along?"

"Glad to," Mallory said. "Come along where?"

"*Tomorrow*," Burch said impatiently. "First thing. Walk the track. Do it every year. Refresh the old memory, see what bits and pieces have changed. Do it Wednesday morning, most weekends, but we got in late. You're all right, for rich buggers. You don't chatter. Can't bear people who chatter. Come along with us. What do you say?" Before Mallory could respond, Burch's face hardened. He'd caught sight of something over Mallory's shoulder. "*Bloody* hell," he whispered. "Don't look round. Too late, here they come. And it was shaping for a nice day, too."

Mallory turned and saw a very large young man in a plaid sports jacket and a bright yellow shirt, who'd just entered the garage and was glancing around it as if he'd seen better garages in his day. He had thick reddish hair, slicked back with stickum, and the kind of overdeveloped physique that comes with daily exercise with barbells. The jacket, Mallory judged, was bespoke. The tailor had been directed to cut it far too snug, from plaid tweed that was far too loud. Mallory was particular about clothes, and he agreed that the young tough's were ugly enough to spoil anyone's day, but he still couldn't see why Burch was quite so upset. Then he noticed the faint bulge of a shoulder holster under the tough's left arm and, at the same moment, saw two men following behind him. One was thickset and middle-aged, with quiet, composed eyes. The other was Arne Jespers.

"Mr. Burch," Jespers cried. "I've come to visit you."

"Do a bolt if I were you," Burch muttered to Mallory. "Nasty bit of goods. But we've got to be nice to him."

"He giving you money, too?"

"Worse. Gives a bundle to the club. Automobile Club de Monaco. They underwrite the race. So all the teams are lumbered with him. Arne Jespers. Knows a fair bit about cars, I must admit. Hello, Jespers," Burch said, raising his voice. "Hope you're well. I was just telling this fellow we're busy. Look about if you like. Got to get back to my car. Nice to have seen you."

Arne Jespers was slight and slack-looking, with a large, much-broken nose and lively, protuberant eyes. His fingers were dark with nicotine, and he let a cigarette drop from them and carefully crushed it out with his heel before entering the garage. He received Burch's snub with an air of high good humor that seemed to be habitual. The bodyguard in the plaid, though, was outraged. He glared after Burch as if ready to knock him down, then looked back at Jespers for permission. Nothing, Mallory thought, was sorrier than a bodyguard spoiling for a fight. Jespers wore gold-rimmed spectacles, and as he entered the garage he took them off and polished them on his shirt, beaming around nearsightedly as if he couldn't wait for his glasses to be clean to start seeing all there was to see. Then he put the spectacles back on his nose and beamed around again. The photos, Mallory decided, didn't do him justice. Jespers was homely, even homelier than his pictures, but had an air of childlike vitality that made him extraordinarily magnetic.

Like his young bodyguard, he was expensively dressed. But Jespers's clothes were somber, and would have been elegant had they not been rumpled—one of his shirttails had come undone while he was polishing his glasses—and copiously smeared with cigarette ash. He nodded at Mallory and grinned delightedly at Laura, giving her a little bow. "*Bonjour*," he cooed to her, "*bonjour*," and reviewed her face, torso, and legs, his face alight with a sort of grandfatherly lechery. He gave Mallory a bow as well, then turned his attention to the wheelless car. This he favored with a look nearly as lecherous as the one he'd given Laura.

His companion wasn't so quick to turn away. The man was short, no more than five-foot-six, but massive through the torso and arms. He had the blandly attentive manner of a chief engineer visiting a construction site, and his gray suit was nondescript, like the clothes of all good professionals. He was a professional, of course. Mallory guessed he was Jespers's head of security. The boy in plaid would report to him. Probably a new recruit being broken in by the boss. The man's deep-set, considering eyes swept Mallory once and tagged him as a fellow pro; swept him again to say: *You're not an immediate threat. And I'd appreciate your keeping it that way.* His eyes flicked to Laura, but Laura was bored, sulky Lily Prentice, and he didn't look at her long. Then he turned and joined Jespers by the car.

Mallory strolled over to Laura, who was staring down at her nails as if making sure they were all there. "Hey there, Lil. Having a good time?"

"Not bad," Laura replied, her voice scarcely louder than her breath. She and Mallory had grown skilled at reading each other's lips.

"What do you think of Jespers?"

"Interesting. The kind that clowns. *Very* wide awake. I'm sort of looking forward to talking to him. I must say I'm less impressed with the Trainee."

"Trainee?"

"Junior goon in the plaid jacket. I assume the short man in gray is showing him the ropes, but I doubt he's a very apt pupil. He's already strolled by twice trying to look up my skirt. Unfortunately for him, they teach you how to sit at Miss Porter's."

"Poor guy. Didn't you actually go to Miss Porter's?"

"Yes. Any instructions?"

"Getting bored?"

"Why, are you going to make things more interesting?"

"You know, that's not a bad idea," Mallory said.

He turned on his heel and strolled over to the group gathered by the stern of the dismantled racer, where Derek Reade was discoursing to Jespers about some detail of the gearbox. The man in the gray suit was leaning against the back wall. The kid Laura called the Trainee was standing by the car's nose, eyeing Reade. Mallory brushed by the Trainee just close enough to be rude, and then stood beside Jespers, again, just a trifle closer than was polite. He was certainly close enough to make a bodyguard nervous. The Trainee lumbered forward, closed his hand on Mallory's shoulder, and hauled him back.

In any case, that was the Trainee's plan. But when Mallory stepped back, it was with the speed and ease of a *tanguero*, and the young man suddenly found himself staggering off-balance. Rattled, he responded as if to an attack, doubling a big fist and driving it forward. It connected with empty air. An instant later, the flat of Mallory's left elbow slammed into his temple.

Then the Trainee was on his back on the oily floor, his plaid jacket flung wide to reveal a new-looking calfskin shoulder holster. The holster was empty. The gun was in Mallory's hand. He held it casually by the barrel and gazed down at the Trainee as if meditating on the world's folly.

Mallory raised his eyes to Jespers. Without looking away from him, he checked the gun's safety with a thumb and then tossed it to the man in gray, who caught it one-handed without taking his eyes from Mallory.

"He one of yours?" Mallory asked Jespers in German, indicating the fallen man. "You ought to train him. If he were one of my boys, he'd know you never put your hands on a man you're not sure you can kill."

"Fighting?" Burch gasped, coming forward at a canter. "Fighting in my pit? And *guns*?"

"One gun," Mallory said mildly.

"Guns!" Burch said in a fury. "Right. Out. *Out*. All of you lot, out right now. Go on, hop it."

"Mr. Burch," Jespers said, spreading nicotine-stained fingers as if in benediction. "A thousand apologies. *Ten* thousand. We will leave, we will leave immediately, we will leave in *shame*. But please don't expel this gentleman here, who has acted very, ah, correctly in a quite awkward situation." He turned to Mallory. "A thousand apologies, my good sir," he repeated in German. "I'm afraid my young employee here is a bit overzealous."

"Hell, don't apologize to me," Mallory replied in German. "He's the one on the floor."

"'Matter with you," Burch said, eyes glittering with rage. "Didn't you hear me? I said *out*."

"Oh, come off it, Harry," Reade said, laughing. "No harm done. Well, hardly any," he added, looking down at the Trainee. "A bit of excitement's not a bad thing after all this fussing about. Tell me," he asked Mallory, "where'd you learn that sort of shrugging business you did just now, that put him down and got you his gun? It seems rather a useful trick to know."

"Does, actually. Treat to see," Burch said, abruptly forgetting his rage. "Mind, you'll all still have to go. I suppose. Disgraceful thing. Can't we at least move this big fellow someplace? He's in the way."

"Dunno where I learned it," Mallory told Reade. "Just one of those things you pick up. You could say I'm in the business. I run a place called Carroll Security."

"Carroll?" Jespers said, and switched back to English. "*Jack* Carroll? Why, I know you, Mr. Carroll. I know you by *repute*. You have furnished some very fine men for a few of my little businesses. Why, you must shake my hand now, Mr. Carroll! You must shake my hand and tell me that you forgive me!"

"Sure thing," Mallory said, shaking hands. "Mr. . . . ?"

"My name is Arne Jespers. And you are Mr. Jack Carroll! The mysterious man no one meets, and I have met him! And he speaks quite excellent German—as if I was home! You have spent some time in Berlin, Mr. Carroll, don't say you haven't."

"Three years. Had a damn good time, too," Mallory said truthfully.

"The Army, I suppose?"

"'Fraid so."

Jespers waved a hand. "Please, no awkwardness. We were on the same side."

"We were?"

"The *victorious* side," Jespers said, spectacles gleaming. "I am always on the side of the victors. It is much pleasanter." He looked down at the Trainee, who was beginning to stir and look muzzily around.

"Now here is a young man who must decide which side he is on." Jespers's look of lively good humor had not altered, and it did not alter as he gave the Trainee a swift, savage kick in the shoulder. The young man scrambled to his feet, looking at Jespers with dazed dismay. Then his eyes found the man in gray, and his expression became one of pure terror. "You enjoyed your nap, little man?" Jespers inquired. "You are quite refreshed? Clearheaded? Ready to perform more tricks for the grown-ups?"

"Dane, I—" the young man said.

"No. No, it's not necessary for you to speak now, little man. It will not be necessary, I think, for some time. No, don't look for your gun, either. The grown-ups have taken charge of it. Perhaps you could instead do for me a small favor? Perhaps you could go back home? Hm? And wait there? Do you suppose that you might do that for me?"

The young man almost spoke, but caught himself and nodded instead. He was fumbling one-handed at the back of his jacket to see how badly it was stained, all the while gaping at the man in gray. Then he mastered himself, dropped his arms to his sides, and turned. He left the garage doing a fair imitation of a man walking normally, not marching, not stumbling, and vanished around the corner.

"And now you have met our Howard," Jespers said. "Our *How*-ie. Isn't Howie a superb name for him? Isn't he a perfect Howie? I am afraid that Howie is still what one might call unripe fruit. But we will *ripen* him. We will ripen him *thoroughly*. I will go now, Mr. Burch, and please do accept my apologies for such disruption. But Mr. Carroll, *you* must assure me that this is not to be our last meeting. You must offer me a chance to correct this bad first impression."

"Be here till Monday," Mallory said affably. "Me and Lil are at the Paris. Come by for a drink."

"The Hôtel de Paris? Oh, that will never do. Such an awful stuffy unfriendly place, how can one enjoy oneself there? No, I cannot permit this. Now, I have myself just a small little villa down the road in Cap Ferrat, just a little house, very convenient for the races, and there is a pool. And you must both come and be my guests there for the week, you and your beautiful lady, and let us make you comfortable. Please say that you will? Beautiful lady," he called to Laura, "won't you come? Won't you be merciful? We will be your servants for the week. We will be your servants our entire *lives*."

"All right," Laura said, laughing. "You don't mind, do you, Jack?"

"Happy to," Mallory said.

"Then it's settled, and I am reprieved. But forgive me once more," Jespers cried, "I was forgetting. Mr. Carroll, beautiful lady, I would like you to meet our invaluable Mr. Kendrick. Mr. Kendrick, Mr. Jack Carroll."

The man in the gray suit hadn't left off gazing at Mallory since he'd entered the garage. Now he nodded and extended his hand. Close up, Kendrick's shoulders and arms seemed outlandishly thick. Though Mallory's own hands were large, his vanished in Kendrick's as if he were a small boy shaking hands with his father. The man in gray had the hands of a giant. Instinctively, Mallory checked the fingers for rings—for a single ring composed of three entwined serpents. There was none.

But Kendrick saw Mallory looking. And, for the first time, he smiled.

6

A Few Marks
Between Friends

"You've got a funny way of introducing yourself," Laura said.

They were spinning along the coast highway toward Cap Ferrat, the sun sparkling on the waves to their left, the Alpes Maritimes rising to their right, the Via growling contentedly beneath them. Mallory was at the wheel. He smiled faintly but did not respond.

"How did you know Jespers would take it that way?" she said.

Mallory shrugged. "I didn't. I was just trying to get something going. You know, you find a loose thread and you tug it a little. I guess I did think Jespers might be the kind of guy that likes to be entertained. And that he wouldn't much mind what happened to Howie." Mallory shook his head. "Howie. We oughta give him to Billy. We oughta give 'em each other."

"That's unfair. I think Billy's going to be fine."

"He's a hot dog," Mallory said. "What did Burch call 'em? A show dog. He gets right straight under my skin. I wish to God we weren't babysitting him this trip. Do you remember where that kid went to get the sandwiches?"

"What kid? You mean, for lunch at the garage? I didn't notice."

"Those were good sandwiches," Mallory said musingly. "If I can just get a supply of those sandwiches, I at least won't starve before we get home."

The Côte d'Azur can be blazing hot in May, but the day was fine and mild, and the wind fresh. The slopes above them glowed with fields of poppy and lavender, and the beaches beside them gleamed with tanned flesh, like another expensive cash crop. As the Alps turned they revealed, and then hid again, tiny labyrinthine towns clinging to the crags, with arched and stepped streets surrounded by medieval ramparts and crowned by openwork wrought-iron bell towers. The fields were dotted here and there with farmhouses of fieldstone smoothed with plaster. Their north walls were blank and windowless to repel the blast of the mistral. Everywhere they saw the terra-cotta tiled roofs that in Monaco itself were giving way to lumpish, sand-colored concrete apartment blocks. It was barely ten kilometers to Cap Ferrat, and soon they'd turned onto the little peninsula and were motoring past a succession of vast houses surrounded by stone walls and sturdy steel gates. "Think I ought to stop and ask directions?" Mallory said.

Laura looked momentarily puzzled, then smiled. "That's right. In theory, you don't know where Jespers lives. He *was* pretty sketchy about the directions. You're an unnatural man, Jack. You'd rather have me drive, and you don't mind asking for directions. Well, if we see anybody . . ."

"Too late. Here it comes up on the left, I think. Lord, it's a big 'un."

"And the gate," Laura observed, "is open."

"And the gate is open," Mallory said. "You were right, Lil. He's an interesting guy."

The gate was open, but not unguarded. When they pulled inside, they found their way blocked by another hulking young man, this one seated in a folding lawn chair in the middle of the driveway, a parasol cocked over his shoulder and a Sten gun in his lap. Rising without undue haste, he strolled over and asked in bad French who they were, his manner neither polite nor rude.

"I'm Jack Carroll," Mallory said in English. "And this is the beautiful lady. Your boss told you to expect a beautiful lady?"

The guard considered this. "I will park your car," he said at length. A vaguely Scandinavian accent.

"You won't," Mallory said. "You'll show me where to park it, and you'll use that walkie-talkie to tell your boss to break out the beer and onion dip. And keep that Sten away from the paint job, if you don't mind."

The guard looked at them lugubriously, then gestured in a circle. "You may park your car," he said. "That tree has good shade."

He turned his back on them, picked up his lawn chair, and carried it out of the way as Mallory eased past.

"Are you quite sure Jack Carroll's supposed to be that rude?" Laura said.

"Just trying to take care of your baby, hon. What would you've done if I'd let that goon park the Via?"

"Fainted with fear. I think we park on the lawn. It looks like that's what the lawn's for."

"Guy's supposed to have a private nine-hole golf course out back. Hope he treats the grass better than this. Lord, tell me the front door's not open, too."

"He can't be this careless. He must be making a point of some kind."

"What's that dingus on the door? A wreath?"

"Carline thistles," Laura said. "The Provençals nail them to the door for good luck."

"Yeah, I remember now. It was in the packet. Sounds like kind of a peasant thing, though, isn't it? You wouldn't expect it on a house like this."

"No, you wouldn't. I count four so far."

"Including the lawn-chair guy?"

"No."

"Then it's five. Guy past the little gazebo back there. Just let go his gun and brought up his walkie-talkie. See him?"

"Well, I suppose with that much muscle around, Jespers feels he doesn't need to lock the doors."

"Another show dog," Mallory grumbled as he killed the ignition and set the hand brake. "Everybody's a goddamn show dog but you. And you drive too fast."

They stepped out of the little yellow car into the shade of a linden tree, and Mallory opened the trunk. Inside was a single Louis Vuitton suitcase, conspicuously new. It was one of a matched set of eight. Both Jack Mallory and Laura Morse liked to travel light, and so, as it happened, did Jack Carroll. But Lily Prentice always traveled with enough changes of costume to outfit a production of *Parsifal*, and the other seven suitcases, plus two old-time steamer trunks, would be arriving from the Paris later in the day. Mallory picked up the suitcase and closed the sportster's trunk, and he and Laura walked across the ragged lawn to the front door. The button of an electric doorbell had been set crookedly into the pink stucco wall beside it, with screws that looked new; Mallory pressed it and heard only a gritty clicking. "Hello?" he said and rapped on the half-open door with his free hand. "Anybody home?"

He looked at Laura, then shrugged and opened the door.

The villa's foyer was two stories tall and littered with shipping crates and corrugated cardboard cartons, some open and apparently empty. Between the crates and boxes stood a few spindly gilt French-looking antique chairs. Somebody had set an unplugged circular saw atop one of them, the blades digging into the velvet upholstery. The frescoed ceiling above them was a riot of putti scattering flowers and of lavishly proportioned nymphs pointing at clouds. All around them was the smell of warm, dusty velvet and cool stone and, more insistently, of marijuana smoke. "Started the party without us," Mallory said.

"Seven," Laura observed softly.

On an elevated gallery above them were two more immense young men in bulging sports jackets. One stood at parade rest in a corner and the other leisurely walked along the balustrade, a compact assault rifle in his hands, one eye on the couple in the doorway. Neither made any move to acknowledge their guests.

"Seven and counting," Mallory confirmed. "Hello," he called up.

The guard with the assault rifle kept walking. The other looked down at Mallory as if still waiting for him to speak.

"These folks haven't been to Miss Porter's," Mallory told Laura.

They walked unimpeded beneath the gallery and into a vast glass-roofed patio. Its gleaming mosaic floor was patterned with mauve tulips and golden serpents. On this were stacked even more crates, along with miscellaneous items of antique and ultramodern furniture, a ragged row of folding metal chairs, a BMW motorcycle with side-car—muddy tire tracks traversed the tiles—a rack of dumbbells, and a couple of weight-lifting benches. In the center of all this stood a brocade settee, and upon it lay a young woman, reading a copy of *Photoplay*. "Hello," Mallory said again. She didn't seem to hear.

She was an enormous girl. Mallory guessed she'd be over six feet if she stood up, though she gave no signs of standing anytime soon. She was dressed in an old kimono and seemed to have just gotten out of bed: her heavy chestnut hair was disordered and her white feet were bare. Her arms and legs were thick but gracefully made. She'd taken no great pains to keep her kimono fastened in front, and she'd hiked up one marmoreal knee, displaying a triangle of lacy red cloth. She was almost ferally beautiful: a square jaw; a dark, ripe mouth; a tiny, perfect nose; and smooth, high cheekbones crowding against tiny, almond-shaped eyes. The eyes were set unusually high: she had little in the way of forehead. She raised a glowing marijuana cigarette to her lips and inhaled deeply, and then scratched lazily at her bare calf and turned the page, regarding the photos of grinning starlets with solemnity. Around her was a nimbus of oyster-colored smoke. "*Bonjour*," Mallory said loudly, and she raised her eyes and regarded him.

"*Bonjour, mademoiselle*," Mallory said. "*Pardonnez-nous pour vous . . .*"

"*Déranger*," Laurie said.

"*Déranger*," Mallory said. "*Nous sommes des invités de Monsieur Jespers qui sont, ah, qui sont juste arrivé. Savez-vous où il peut être trouvé?*"

She did not respond; she did not move. She did not even breathe. Marijuana addicts, Mallory knew, learned to hold the smoke in their lungs endlessly in order to enhance its effect. She'd just taken a puff, and probably didn't want to waste it. He placidly returned her gaze. Thirty seconds ticked by, and then forty-five, and then, with a hiss, she released two pale jets through her tiny nostrils. At last she lifted her sleek head, parted her lips, and bawled, *"HOWIE!"*

Eastern Europe, Mallory guessed, from the sound of it. They had some big girls there.

Mallory's ears were acute, and in a moment he heard the flush of a distant toilet, and then heels clacking along a hallway. Then Howie appeared, walking briskly.

"Good afternoon, Mr. Carroll," he said. "And Miss . . . ?"

"Prentice," Laura said.

"Good afternoon, Miss Prentice. I'm Howard. I'm very sorry to have kept you both waiting. I was called away."

"Hello, son. Didn't expect to see you again so soon," Mallory said. "No hard feelings, I hope?"

"It was my fault, Mr. Carroll," Howie said a bit mechanically. "You acted quite properly. In fact, Mr. Jespers instructed me to apologize for my rudeness, and to—" The boy jibbed momentarily, then recovered. "To see to your comfort here—personally. May I take your bag?"

"That's all right, son."

"Mr. Jespers instructed me to take your bag," Howie said.

The young woman on the settee chuckled richly and gave herself a stretch, writhing slowly and languidly like an immense cat, the movie magazine clenched in one smooth fist, the glowing cigarette in the other. When she was finished, her kimono was half-undone and most of one young breast was in view. On an ordinary woman it would have been a large breast. On that stupendous torso it seemed dainty. She noticed it, casually tucked it away, and returned to her reading. Mallory saw that Howie was careful not to look at her.

"All right," Mallory said, handing over the suitcase. "Here you go."

"Thank you, sir," Howie said. "Will you come this way?"

"You might want to change that jacket," Mallory told him. "It's a little scuffed up in back."

"Mr. Jespers instructed me not to. He'd like me to wear this for the next thirty days as a—" Howie swallowed. "As a reminder. Would you watch your step on the stairs, please? Some of the treads are loose."

As they climbed to the second floor, Laura and Mallory could see that the villa was furnished, if *furnished* was the word, in a fantastic hodge-podge of styles. Louis Quatorze demilune cabinets jostled redwood patio furniture, and the sturdy local oak chairs were gathered around chrome-and-glass tables of the latest design, which in turn were covered with dirty checked tablecloths littered with empty beer cans. Gray steel industrial shelving had been set up along one wall, and on it stood *terre rouge* flowerpots, T'ang dynasty vases, plastic scale models of German fighter planes, pornographic bronze statuettes of coupling Indian gods and goddesses, smirking porcelain shepherdesses, and what Mallory could have sworn was a bowling trophy. In one corner sat a case of Mouton Rothschild '54. Beside it, a crate of Coca-Cola. The soda was half gone, but no one had gotten around to the champagne yet. To Mallory, who scarcely knew what he was looking at, the place looked like a junk shop. To Laura, who could guess what the furnishings were worth, it looked the same.

Howie led them around a corner, knocked experimentally on a door, and opened it. The bedroom inside was luxurious, but a set of luggage already stood at the foot of the bed.

"Sorry," he said. "I thought that one was free."

He led them across the hall and tried another door. This time, they found a half-dressed young woman applying eyeliner at a makeup table. She gave them a look of unexcited expectancy, like a receptionist. "Sorry," Howie told Laura and Mallory again; the girl didn't seem to expect an apology. "They tend to move around a lot. Don't worry, we'll find you a nice one. A nice room," he clarified.

The third bedroom was unoccupied, and Howie set the suitcase on the bed and opened the drapes. It was a lovely room, with a canopied bed tasseled in saffron, a set of tall windows looking out over the back garden, and a small stone balcony. Surprisingly enough, it was clean and in perfect order. "All right, you're in luck," Howie said. "The other two in this wing haven't got their own bathrooms yet. I'll just let the place air out a little." He opened the windows and let in the Cap Ferrat breeze. "Mr. Jespers is waiting for you. Would you like to freshen up a little, or should I take you in to see him now?"

"Lil?" Mallory said.

"I'll have a *bath*," Laura announced, as if she'd been wondering for days when someone would have the common decency to let her take a bath. "Run along and say hello for me, Jackie. Find out when dinner is."

Jackie, Mallory thought. *That's pretty good.*

He let Howie close the door of the room behind them and then followed the broad plaid back down the hall and across the gallery to the opposite wing. Laura, he guessed, wanted a chance to sweep the room for bugs and surveillance devices. Those sorts of things bothered her. Most likely she also wanted to give Mallory a chance to buddy up with Jespers one-on-one, and she probably wanted a little privacy to do her daily kata, the solitary, stylized exercises that kept her fighting skills honed to such an extraordinary level. She might even find time for a bath. She'd certainly remember to dampen the tub and towels and the ends of her hair. As they passed the patio, Mallory looked down and saw the brocade settee was empty. All that remained was a rising corona of smoke. Wherever the big girl was, she'd remembered to take her magazine.

The other wing had another long row of bedrooms, with saxophone music wafting from one of them and what sounded like the noise of a marital spat from another. At the end, a door opened onto a solarium full of yellow sunlight and broad-leafed plants.

As the bodyguard stepped over the threshold, Arne Jespers sprang forward and slapped him furiously across the face.

"Pig!" Jespers shrieked, and slapped him again. "Pig turd! Abandoned my guests, did you? Left them to wander about lost, did you? *You were not to leave that door! You were not to leave that door until they arrived!* You were to *welcome* them, and instead? Hm? Instead? Don't *speak!*" he shouted, kicking Howie in the shin. *"Don't speak or I'll have you killed!* Out, out of my *sight!* Don't let me see your stupid pig-snout today!"

Howie fled.

Jespers watched him trundling hastily down the hallway. Abruptly he began to laugh.

"Such a welcome!" he said to Mallory. "Oh, such a welcome—what can I say? I have already, ah, *exhausted* my right to apologize! Mr. Carroll, I am afraid you will have to take us as we are!"

"'S all right by me," Mallory said equably, shaking Jespers's proffered hand and following him into the room. "Don't mind finding my own way. I like a chance to snoop around. Hello again," he said. The enormous young woman was reclining on a sofa by the far wall, still reading her *Photoplay*. It was hard to imagine her getting up and walking there. Maybe she'd been carried in a sedan chair.

"You've met Milena?" Jespers inquired. "My beautiful Milena Swierczy? I am sure she has introduced herself. Her manners are even better than Howie's. Milena, *liebchen*, meet Mr. Jack Carroll." She glowered at him briefly and returned to her movie magazine. "Ah, Milena likes you. She likes you, or she would have thrown something. But where is your beautiful lady, whose name I should by this time know?"

"Lily Prentice. She's having a bath."

"She is displeased by this rude reception?"

"Probably. She displeases easy."

"And so I am disgraced once more. Well, all I can do is give you a drink. So I shall give you one." Jespers turned to a silver wine bucket, hauled out a bottle embedded in a massive block of ice, poured a few fingers of the clear liquor into a gilt teacup, and handed it to Mallory. "Aquavit. Have you had it? It is quite—*invigorating*. We will toast your arrival and your patience," he said, refreshing the contents of his own teacup. "What can I say? As always, I am in a state of disorganization. One *cannot* get good staff. This is apparently impossible."

"Never easy," Mallory agreed.

"And so one hires Howies, the Howies of the world, and beats them. And hopes that they will improve."

"Surprised you didn't break a hand on him."

"He *is* a big strong fellow, isn't he?" Jespers said, looking cheerier.

"You seem to specialize in 'em."

"Ah, but it's very nice to hire big strong fellows. If you are in a business like mine, where people are often becoming annoyed with you and wishing you harm, you want to have big strong fellows about with guns, many big strong fellows, to discourage this."

"If they got guns, what do they need to be big strong fellows for?"

"To inspire *fear*," Jespers said. "And *amusement*."

"Amusement?"

"Yes, it's very good to have people think you're a funny chap. 'Oh, that Jespers, what a peculiar man, all those muscle-boy fellows about, I'm afraid there is something *unwholesome* there! I must be very careful with a peculiar man like that!' You see? It causes people to tread warily, and when people are too careful, they make mistakes, and from these one can profit. Also, I like strength. It's very nice. I don't want to be a strong man myself, because that's hard work and I detest to work, but I like to have strength around, to *look* at it, to *gaze*. I even like a strong lady friend. Isn't she a beast?" he said, stroking Milena's mighty haunch. She cuffed his hand away. "Someday she'll tire of me and snap my neck, and that will be that. Even my ladies obstruct me. Oh, what am I to do?" he crooned, sounding perfectly happy. "Mr. Carroll, can you tell me what I am to do?"

"Doubt it."

"Without my Mr. Kendrick I would lose hope. I would *despair*. But your problems must be quite similar, Mr. Carroll. You don't have many people wishing you harm?"

"Nope. Everybody likes me."

"But surely, in your profession . . . Let us be candid. You are not simply a man who provides bodyguards and burglar alarms."

"I provide a hell of a lot of bodyguards and burglar alarms, Mr. Jespers. And it's a damn good business."

"But in addition you, ah, *consult* on other projects. And after you have done, let us say, a project for government X concerning rebel group Y . . ."

"Or for rebel group Y concerning government X. I'm not fussy. But those guys don't hate me. Not X, not Y."

"No?"

"Nope. If I do a good job, they want to hire me themselves. See, that's one thing that's kind of sweet about this business. When I was in the Army, the guys on the other side hated us. When I was CIA, same thing. But all I am is a hired hand now, and nobody hates a hired hand. They can see we work hard for our money. They see we mostly get a good outcome. They don't hate us. They ask us for a business card." Jespers laughed. "I'm not joking, Mr. Jespers. I hand out business cards in the field. I do it all the time. Here, want one?"

"Thank you."

"Aw, now I'm kind of sorry I did that. I'm just illustrating a point. I'm your guest, Mr. Jespers, and I'd hate you to think I was hustling you for work. Or for more work, since you say you're already using my guys."

"Houston, Berlin, Hong Kong, São Paulo," Jespers read, holding the card close to his nose. "You have four offices?"

"Four main offices and seven branch offices. And I don't know how many little field offices. It changes. I got people to keep count for me."

"You run quite a large business, wouldn't you say?"

"We do all right. We're not General Motors."

"How large a business, exactly?"

"Large as it needs to be. We got our regular staff and then a bunch of what I guess you'd call temporary help. And we know always where to get more. Probably a lot of the same places you get your guys. Anyway, we can take on some pretty big jobs."

"But how large in actual numbers? Of staff? Of major projects?"

"We're doing pretty well these days, knock wood."

"You are not going to answer my question, are you, Mr. Carroll?"

Mallory grinned. "Would you answer questions like that if I put 'em to you?"

"Kendrick would be very vexed," Jespers admitted. "But at the same time— See here. Since I use your firm's services from time to time, I assume you have informed yourself about my métier."

"Sure. Information."

"Yes. And it is, as you might put it, a damn good business. But it is seasonal, fearfully *seasonal*. At any given time, there are only so many things *really* worth knowing—that are on the market, of course, that can be bought and sold. So I have begun to look around a bit, to branch out. And there are *such* opportunities! Here, you see this?" He picked a glass jug from a side table and removed the metal stopper. "Have a sniff of this, if you don't mind."

It was a light, musky perfume with a hint of honeyed fruit—over a quart of it. Mallory didn't wear cologne or care for scent, but he had to admit this one was agreeable. "Nice."

"A new fragrance from a *parfumerie* whose name I should perhaps not, ah, *divulge* at this early point. When it is placed on sale next spring it will be priced at one hundred and eighty dollars the fluid ounce. Perhaps you know that— Oh dear." Jespers, trying to pour a drop of perfume onto his wrist, had slopped it down his arm and all over the floor. The room blossomed with scent. He began futilely trying to brush the stuff from his shirt, but did not stop speaking. Judging by the state of his clothes, he was a man accustomed to spilling things. "Perhaps you know that Grasse, just down the coast, is the center of the world's perfume industry? Yes. It's quite fascinating. They use an *Arab* steam distillation process. It was invented by the court scientists of the Caliphate. A ton of jasmine flowers is required for a single liter of jasmine essence. This is why you see such vast, such *enormous* fields of jasmine in this area, of lavender, jonquil, roses, herbs. You see trucks loaded quite to the top with flower blossoms, all heading for the stills! It's quite splendid, and highly profitable for a fellow with a bit of capital. But I am continually defeated by this fearful disorganization." He gave up trying to brush off the spilled perfume and sat thoughtfully smelling his hand.

"Seems like you make things work all right."

"I stumble along, Mr. Carroll. I *flounder*. But if I had an organization, a proper organization like yours, I could make things work all right indeed."

"Well, I don't mind discussing it a little, if you like. You know, the business end of my firm. It's not a secret, Mr. Jespers."

"But you must not call me Mr. Jespers! I cannot permit this any longer. You must call me Arne."

"Happy to, Arne. Call me Jack. I never much liked being mistered."

"Jack," Jespers said. "*Jack*. How excellent. Do you golf, Jack?"

"Golf? Some."

"Will you golf with me, Jack? I have a little course out back, a little terrible course I had installed, but it is not so bad, really, and this way I can get some exercise. Come now, we will golf. We will golf *vigorously*. We will clear the, ah, cobwebs from our minds and think great, useful thoughts, and you will teach me. I will be your student."

"I don't mind."

"You know, you are an intriguing fellow, Jack. I am really quite pleased that we've met."

"Me, too."

"I am convinced that this visit of yours—yours and the lovely Miss Prentice's, of course—that this visit will be quite remarkable, quite *memorable*."

"Hope so," Mallory said.

Mallory knew the world was full of men who talked business while golfing, but he never thought he'd be one of them. In fact, he figured the whole idea of becoming a spy was that no one ever expected you to do either. Still, he'd caddied a couple of summers as a kid in Corpus and could play moderately well, and he was prepared to answer questions all day on how you hired hired guns.

But Jespers wasn't much interested in the guns end of the business. His questions were a lot more basic. What was a purchase order? What was a sales report? What did payroll departments do? What did office managers do? How did one fire people? Jespers had never fired anyone. If they made enough mistakes, he killed them, or let them think he was going to, in which case they ran off and stopped posing problems. Did that seem correct to Jack?

Jespers's private course was immaculately barbered, but showed few signs of use, and Mallory was not surprised when his host began complaining of the heat on the second hole. By the third hole, his attention was plainly wandering, and when Mallory sank an eighteen-foot putt on the fifth, Jespers mopped his brow theatrically and declared they'd both exercised quite enough for a warm day. The mammoth young caddies wheeled their bags away—the clubs Jespers had loaned him were easily the nicest Mallory had ever handled—and Mallory followed Jespers into the house for an entirely unnecessary shower. He wasn't sorry to quit. Jespers was an embarrassingly bad golfer, though only Mallory seemed to be embarrassed about it.

The shower itself was interesting. Mallory had expected to return to his room, but instead Jespers led him to a country-club-style locker room with a tiled enclosure where a party of ten could have showered together. They were met there by two young women in bathing suits and rubber sandals, who helped them out of their clothes, handed them bars of soap, escorted them into the showers, adjusted the water for them, and diligently scrubbed their backs. Mallory's attendant was a tiny snub-nosed blonde who had to rise on tiptoes to lather his neck. Jespers's was the young brunette Howie had surprised at her makeup table. She smiled at Mallory when he entered the locker room. It was a receptionist's smile. Mallory assumed that either of the women was available to guests of the house, which was one reason they didn't much interest him, but there was nothing seductive about their routine. It seemed like business as usual.

"I guess you don't like being alone much, huh?" Mallory said. "Even to shower."

"It's much jollier to have company," Jespers said. "Don't you find it so?" He closed his eyes and held still so the brunette could fit his spectacles back on his nose.

"It's nice, I guess. Not sure I really care for being washed. Too much like being in the hospital."

"You've spent a bit of time in hospitals, haven't you, Jack? How scarred you are. I thought you said everyone liked you."

"Uh-huh. But that doesn't matter much, does it? If they got a job to do."

Jespers laughed. "Very true. I give you my word, Jack: if we should ever fall out, which I must admit would sadden me very greatly, I promise I will never scar you."

"Just kill me, huh?"

Jespers nodded gravely. "I promise," he said.

The men let themselves be dried with a series of vast white towels—Jespers blissfully, Mallory bemusedly—and wrapped about the waist with two more. Then they padded down a narrow back hallway and emerged into brilliant sunlight. They were in a courtyard that had once housed one of the lush semiformal gardens for which Cap Ferrat is known, crammed with peach trees and royal palms. Jespers had dug a pit in the center of it and installed a blue swimming pool with a broad concrete apron.

On the far side of the pool was another array of weight-lifters' apparatus, and a couple of profusely muscled young men were busy there, rhythmically boosting huge barbells into the air and hauling on creaking pulleys. On the near side of the pool stood two empty massage tables and, around them, a muddle of chaises longues. Milena lay on one of them, and Laura on another. They were on opposite sides of the courtyard and did not appear to have struck up a friendship.

"Hello, ladies," Jespers sang. "I hope you are well. We have exercised. We have *cleared* the cobwebs from our brains. Milena, dumpling, how nice, I see you've gotten dressed. And you, Miss Prentice—the opposite."

Laura Morse wore sunglasses, silver high-heeled pumps, and a frown. If you looked closely, you could see she was also wearing a leopard-print bikini. The bikini had room for maybe a dozen spots, Mallory guessed, and revealed a razor-edge of pale, untanned flesh all the way around the waistband, and made him briefly and acutely sorry he'd never gotten anywhere with its owner. "Miss Prentice, you really mustn't look quite so *good* like this," Jespers continued. "Or you will cause me to say things to which your very dangerous boyfriend will object."

"You're a charming man," Laura said in her drabbest voice, and took a sip of her drink. "Did you have a nice time, Jack?"

"They wash him," Milena said suddenly. Her voice was deep and melodious. "Arne has girls for washing, and they wash your boyfriend." She showed Laura a mouthful of white teeth.

"I hope they got him behind the ears," Laura said.

"They did," Mallory said.

Jespers flopped down with a grunt on one of the massage tables and gestured to Mallory to do the same. He was certainly an unpleasant sight in a bath towel: spindly, flabby, with narrow, asymmetrical shoulders and a deflated-looking paunch. It was hard to believe he was only fifty-two. He seemed an old man. "Come," he said, squirming on his belly to get comfortable. "We have exercised, and now we will rest and let the girls soothe our weary muscles. *Soooothe*," he said again, dissatisfied with his pronunciation. "Where are those girls? They should be here. I am going to fire them. *Girls?*" he called.

He rapped out a few words to the young men in what must have been Danish. They stopped exercising at once, and one of them raised two fingers to his lips and let out a piercing whistle.

A door opened at the far end of the courtyard, and two women entered, walking in step, both dressed in crimson silk robes. They were young, pale blonde, long-legged, slender to the point of thinness, and identical in every way: the same long, fine noses; the same full, sulky mouths; the same vacant green eyes beneath thick golden brows; the same small, high breasts. They sashayed around the pool to a spot in front of the massage tables, undid their robes and, still in unison, let them slip to the ground. Beneath the robes, they were naked and gleaming with oil. They stood motionless for a moment, as if waiting for applause.

"Jack, may I present the Twins," Jespers said. "Kirsten and Kristen Skarsgaard."

"Shouldn't they be in school?" Mallory said.

"Their combined age is thirty-five," Jespers explained. "Thirty-five is too old for school. Come, girls. You mustn't keep our guest waiting."

The Twins bent gracefully at the waist, took bottles of oil from their robes, and approached the massage tables. The one who'd assigned herself to Mallory raised one long leg balletically high, set her toes on the corner of his table, and, with a smooth, agile lunge, was all at once standing atop it. At Jespers's table, her sister had just done the same. Still moving in concert with her sister, the girl pivoted and settled down astride Mallory, her loins light and slick against his back. Assuming it was expected of him, Mallory gave Laura a quick, uneasy look. She was staring fixedly at the sky. Good. Probably wasn't acting, but correct all the same. He flicked his eyes around the patio, this time from an instinctive dislike of being pinned down, and saw that Kendrick had appeared in a second-floor window and was watching him.

Mallory stared back. The girl sprinkled oil across his shoulders, took hold of them, and began to knead.

Jespers sighed. "Ah, isn't this nice?"

"Uh-huh," Mallory said, watching Kendrick.

"They are very good girls. This kind of staff, I must admit I have never had a difficulty in hiring good staff of this kind. In this business I first began, you know."

"Business?" Mallory's voice was taut. Kirsten, or maybe Kristen, was digging hard thumbs into the base of his neck.

"Of *procuring*. Isn't that how it is put? Of procuring women. There is a splendid American word, *pimp*. I was a pimp."

"Uh-huh?"

"You seem surprised. Yes, I know, it is supposed to be the handsome fellows who become pimps, but I had my own way of going about things. I was never afraid, from a very young small age, to ask a woman, 'Why don't you go with me? You went with this one, so why not with me?' And sometimes, you know, the girl will go with you simply because she can't think of an answer!"

"Jack knows that," Laura remarked.

"I do," Mallory said. It was a little hard to concentrate. His Twin was sliding up and down his back, thumping at his ribs with the edges of her stiffened palms.

"Isn't it strange? Of course, I was also good with a knife—oh, not *very* good," Jespers said modestly, "but fairly good, and I had killed men and was considered *dangerous*, and when I found something good to steal, I *also* had money. So even though I was an awful-looking little chap I got girls. And sometimes I would get a girl for a friend, you know? 'You went with me, why don't you do me this favor and go with my friend?' And after a little while I find, to my quite pleasant surprise, that people are paying me money and I am a pimp. But I was never a good pimp. I liked my merchandise too much! You can't be a pimp, Jack, if you are too fond of your inventory."

"Is that right," Mallory said.

"You've broken Jack's heart," Laura said. She turned her back to them, picked up a paperback crime novel, and began to read.

"That is your girl?" Mallory's Twin inquired, her lips close to his ear.

"Yep."

She grunted and wrenched harder at his upper arms.

Jespers said, "But then this most wonderful thing happened, this marvelous news. Germany lost the war. It could *not* have been better. While we were fighting the war, I was a young fellow in the black market, and I suppose business was all right. But now, oh my, everything is in a muddle, and business becomes very *good*. From all my years of supplying persons with girls and gasoline and nice things to eat, I found I was in a position to learn all sorts of useful stuff. And what I learned from the Russians, say, I could now sell to the Americans, and what I learned from the Americans, I could sell to the Russians, and the British, also, were buying everything just so as not to be left out. So I had finally found my métier. I had been a bad thief and a bad pimp, and maybe not so wonderful as a black-market fellow, but this business of information, this *suited* me. Because I had a knack for learning things and deciding if they were true."

"It's a nice knack to have," Mallory said. The girl atop him spun on the small of his back, as if he were a pommel horse, and began working on his legs. "I never cared for that part of the intelligence game. Always made me jumpy, trying to sort out the liars from the fellows who've got something good. Especially when, most of the time, the liars're a lot more convincing."

"How very true that is. But here I have an advantage, a very *peculiar* advantage that perhaps you've heard about. This," Jespers said, and tapped his large, misshapen nose. "I have a really abnormally *precise* sense of smell. I am like a dog, actually. For instance, I can often tell who is in the room with me without looking, just as a dog can."

"Yeah? You could smell I was here if you couldn't see me?"

"Oh, quite decidedly. You have a very distinctive smell, Jack. A very dry, rather *wolfish* smell. But more importantly, I can smell fear, just as dogs do. I simply cannot tell you how useful it is to know when you are dealing with a frightened man. Men who sell false information, you see, are often frightened. At least, when they attempt to sell some to me. Oh, my nose is useful in all sorts of situations," Jespers said, chuckling. "It lets me know when a woman is, ah, kindly disposed in a physical way. For example, Jack, to me it's quite clear that at this moment the Twins find you quite *agreeable*."

"You are disgusting old man," announced the Twin atop Mallory.

"*Mmmph*," Mallory said. She had dexterously set her knees between his shoulder blades and eased her weight onto him. His spine crackled softly. Kendrick was still at the upstairs window, arms folded. Mallory wished he was elsewhere, or at least on his feet, with his arms free.

Perhaps Jespers smelled his discomfiture, for he abruptly said, "So there you have it, and I have bored you quite enough with the story of my little businesses. But it all began with procure . . . *ment*? Procur*ing*? How does one say it?"

"Pimping," Mallory said.

"*Pimping*," Jespers said with relish. "And now I am living this very pleasant life in such pleasant places as this, and can go and watch motorcars going fast, which, as I grow too old and weary for all this sexual stuff, is becoming my favorite thing. What do you think of the race, Jack? I know you're an admirer of Derek Reade."

"He's all right."

"Yes? I believe Derek Reade to be overrated."

"What, does he smell like he's gonna lose or something?"

"If only one could smell such things. You think he'll win this Sunday?"

"Hell, no one ever knows that. Might cook his gearbox and retire in ten laps. But if he finishes, yeah, I guess he'll do all right. Be in the points, anyway."

"Do you know, I doubt this. I believe Derek Reade is too *emotional* a driver. In race after race one sees it. He will declare a sort of duel with a single other driver, he will form an obsession, a *mania* for this opponent, and thus fail to take into account the entire field. And so he will win his duel and lose the race."

"He's won enough of 'em."

"He can be skittish in slower traffic."

"Yep. But he wins enough of 'em."

"I believe your patriotism blinds you to this man's very real weaknesses."

"Reade's a Brit," Mallory pointed out. Kendrick had disappeared from the window. Mallory wished he knew where he was.

"And so is Kenneth Naughton, I know, but they race for America. Your America. Do you know, I predict that Team Naughton will finish *quite* out of the money. You should listen to my prediction, Jack. Remember, I have a very long history of winding up on the side of the victors."

"Guess we'll see. Season's just beginning. Will you be at Silverstone?"

"Most unfortunately not. I must hurry back home after this race to supervise a project of mine, one of my tiresome little bits of business that let me lie beside this nice pool with pretty girls. It's a shame, really. However, we should have a nice race on Sunday. A nice, *interesting* race."

"All right, Arne. How much?"

"I beg your pardon?"

"How much?" Mallory said pleasantly. "You been trying to finesse me into betting on this race. You probably think you know something about it I don't. Maybe you do. Maybe not. Anyway, how much?"

"Jack, I assure you—" Jespers said, laughing.

"I got a nose myself sometimes, Arne, and you smell like a man who's bluffing. I think Naughton'll finish in the money. How much you want to bet?"

"Oh dear. Shall we say fifty thousand?"

"Marks?"

"Dollars."

There was a brief pause.

"Fifty thousand dollars," Jespers said merrily, "that the American team will finish *out* of the money. Not first, not second, not third."

"You said 'finish.' If something happens to keep Naughton from finishing—"

"Of course," Jespers said. "In such a case, the bet becomes invalid.

Jack, I like you more and more. Your utter lack of trust is most refreshing."

"You make him tense again," the girl atop Jespers warned. "After Kirsten work so hard to relax him."

"No, he is relax," Kirsten reported, testing Mallory's muscles. "He must be *very* rich," she said approvingly. With that, she gave Laura an unfriendly look and slapped Mallory across the shoulders, and Kirsten and Kristen rose together. Leaping lightly down from the massage tables, they bent and gathered up their robes.

"All right," Mallory said, rolling onto one hip and rubbing his neck. "I don't mind. Fifty for me if Naughton takes third or better. Fifty for you if they take fourth or worse. Nothing for anybody if they don't finish."

"Done," Jespers said. "I'm pleased you're a sporting man. I would have guessed as much. And now we will drink to our wager. Did you like your massage?"

"The girls are good," Mallory said politely. "But, tell the truth, when it comes to a rubdown I'd rather have somebody like one of your boys over there. Somebody who can put a little oomph into it. Women just don't have the muscle."

Abruptly, Milena sat up.

"Oh dear," Jespers said merrily. "You've made a mistake, Jack. And *such* a mistake! You've made Milena angry."

When she rose, Mallory saw he'd been wrong in imagining Milena was a six-footer. She was more like seven feet tall. Her gracefully sloping shoulders were as broad as his, and thicker, and beneath her smooth white skin lay the muscles of a lioness. A rope of plaited hair hung down her back, over a yard long and thick as a girl's arm. Without being the least bit fat, she was the biggest thing he'd ever seen in skirts, and, as Jespers had said, Mallory had gotten her riled. Broad hips majestically swaying, she walked slowly over to his table like a wrestler entering the ring until she was standing directly before him, thick arms akimbo.

She said, "I don't think I hear so good what you say, little man. About how a woman is weak. Say it again."

Mallory sat up and amiably returned her gaze. Even sitting on the table's edge, he had to tip his head back to do it. "Well, what I said was, I'd rather get a rubdown from a man, because men're stronger. I believe my exact words were 'Women just don't have the muscle.'"

Milena took her hands from her hips and slipped them under Mallory's arms. Effortlessly, almost tenderly, as if she were lifting her newborn baby from its crib, she hoisted him into the air until he and she were face-to-face. Mallory was five-feet-eleven, but his toes dangled nearly a foot from the floor. He kept hold of his towel with one hand so it wouldn't unwind.

"Again," the huge girl whispered, her lips nearly brushing his. "Maybe this time I hear you better. Again, little man. What did you say?"

Mallory smiled pleasantly and said, "I forget."

7

Up on the Wall

Though you wouldn't have thought it to look at her, Laura Morse liked to eat, and the food at Jespers's table was superb. But that evening she chewed listlessly and left half of each course untouched. *It's a good thing Lily Prentice is such a pouty little brat,* she thought, prodding her *loup grillé au fenouil* with a fork. *If our cover depended on my smiling tonight, we'd be dead.*

The long table was covered with sticky vinyl tablecloths and stained Delft lace, upon which stood the splintered cases of Mouton Roth-schild and Coca-Cola, pyramids of full and empty beer cans, and heaps of oily, half-empty dishes leaking sauce. She and Jack were among two dozen guests, none of whom she'd personally have chosen as table-mates. There were stammering cocaine addicts and slowly blinking morphine addicts, giggling underage prostitutes eating breakfast cereal and an elderly man in a Boy Scout uniform, two dour and swarthy gentlemen sporting unfamiliar military decorations, a scattering of epicene youngsters in overtight Carnaby Street suits and flame-bright ties, and a couple of obvious members of Jespers's former profession. The food, course after course of it, was served by the omnipresent musclemen. The one who'd first met them at the front gate had just slopped gravy on her arm, and she was trying to wipe it off with a paper napkin printed with clowns' faces and toy drums.

The Twins had come to the table nearly as nude as they'd been that afternoon and were making a run at Jack, turning their gleaming shoulders this way and that, peering at him bright-eyed, and chattering to each other in Danish. The huge Polish girl was glowering at him like an owl at a field mouse. She was wearing an indescribable fringed orange dress and seemed to nurture schemes of her own. The hi-fi was blaring Mantovani, someone was experimenting with bongos in a corner, and everyone was roaring at the tops of their lungs, the voices echoing from the frescoed ceiling. And Jespers was telling Jack, in zestful detail, how he'd once tortured an ex-partner to death.

"Oh, he was a stubborn fellow," Jespers said. "Fortunately, there was a metal shop in the back of his factory, and here there were all sorts of useful mechanisms."

None of this should have bothered her, not even those girls and Jack, not if she was working. But that was precisely the problem. Since they'd arrived in Monaco, Laura Morse had had nothing to do. Jack was making excellent progress with Jespers, but no thanks to her. The wager might be mad, but Gray was good for it, and in any case there was nothing she could do to affect its outcome. There was no backup team for her to lead, no attempts upon Jack's life for her to quash, no covert comm for her to manage. There was nothing for Laura to do but work on her tan and sip sugary drinks and wait for Jack to figure out a use for her. Inaction is the most difficult challenge for any agent of direct and aggressive habits. In particular, it is the bane of those working backup. Flying bullets enliven one—at least, one with the temperament to be in the field—and hardship focuses the mind and stiffens the will. Far more troublesome are the ennui and petulance that stem from simply not being needed. At such times, when his senses are heightened and his skills are unused, the small unpleasantnesses of an agent's surroundings can seem unbearable: a persistent drip, a cloud of flies, the whine of a transistor radio. Or drug-addled clamor, naked floozies, and squalid displays of wealth. Gray had questioned her fitness for this mission, had doubted she was professional enough to rise above her feelings for Jack, and she was fiercely determined to prove him wrong, but there were moments during this interminable dinner when she wondered if she would.

"A machine for cutting steel rod," Jespers was saying, "*nipping it off,* and threading a hole. And I notice it has just room for a man's finger." He poked a forefinger into the opposite fist to demonstrate, sprinkling drops of oyster purée onto his jacket. He set down his fork and began brushing at his jacket, saying, "There was a clearance of eighteen millimeters, just sufficient for one knuckle. Very good. So, we get started."

"Soup," said the goon at her elbow, and sloshed a scarlet broth into the bowl before her.

One of the Twins leaned over and stared at Laura's feet. "Your shoe is silver," she reported.

"Yes," Laura said. They were silver and vulgarly high, with elaborate silver lamé rosettes.

"That is a pretty shoe. I wish I have a shoe like that. You like her shoe, Jack?"

"They're all right," Mallory said.

"You're welcome to these," Laura told her. "They hurt."

"They look like they hurt," Mallory said. "You look good in 'em, though. So what finally worked the trick?" he asked Jespers. "I assume you finally got him to talk."

"It has a little flower," the Twin announced. "A little flower of *cloth*. I will get a shoe like that." She looked meaningfully at Jespers.

"Yes, yes," Jespers said. "Well, I did, and it's a—"

"Jack buy the shoe for *his* girl," the Twin said pointedly. "Maybe he buy for us also."

"Don't buy them shoes, Jack, I warn you," Jespers said. "If you feed a stray cat, it never leaves. As I was saying, he did talk, and it's a funny thing. After we finished his left hand—you could scarcely call it a hand anymore—he was still insisting he didn't know, and I must say I was half-convinced. My assistant was ready to do the other one, but here I had a thought. I had a thought, and so instead I said, 'Go and bring Emil'—his son, Holger's ten-year-old son. 'Bring Emil.' Very well. In comes Emil in his little nightshirt. 'Oh, Papa,' he cries. It was quite touching. Holger was trying to hide his hand, what remained of it, crying, 'It's all right, Emil! It's all right!' 'Hello, Emil,' I said to the boy. 'It's your Uncle Arne come to visit. Now, where were we?'"

Milena was chewing steadily at a dish of calf's brains with shelled peas, openmouthed, elbows on the table. All evening she'd been gazing sullenly at Jack. Now she reached out a long arm, grasped a ladle, and dished a heap of sweetbreads onto his plate, her movements deliberate. "Eat," she said.

"Thanks," Mallory said.

"You should eat. You are thin," she said.

"Well, so's she." Mallory nodded at Laura.

Milena shrugged and went on chewing.

"Don't make personal remarks, *liebchen*," Jespers said. "But it's true that you're just poking at your food, Miss Prentice, just picking and poking. I'm afraid I have spoiled your appetite with my awful story." He sounded amused.

"I'm on a diet," Laura said.

"Do you ever go to Copenhagen?" the second Twin asked Mallory. "It is good there if you like pretty girl."

"Don't bother the man," Milena said.

The Twins shrank back and regarded her with plain hatred. "We can talk," the first one said defiantly. "Jack likes talking us."

"Jack is polite. He doesn't want to be bother by skinny little girls. You are shaking your little *cycki* at him, but he has already seen everything and he does not care."

Jespers spluttered with laughter. "Careful, Jack. You've aroused some *primitive* passions among my girls! And I can't say which of them is the most dangerous."

"I can," Mallory said. "So, he talked?"

"Oh yes, straight away. It's a funny thing. He would have let us chop him to bits, but he couldn't stand to have his child see. The certificates were in an ordinary safety deposit box down at our bank, and he told us where to find the key. But the joke was on us! Because when we got there, Emil had already been, and the whole kit and caboodle was quite gone, and no one has heard of Emil since. A resourceful boy. I wonder what became of him. He must be your age by now."

"How about Holger?"

"Oh, he died. We tried to make a proper tourniquet, but we must not have had the *technique*. It was all very clumsy and stupid, I'm afraid. I was quite a stupid young man. But we must not continue my awful story. We must discuss something pleasanter."

"All right," Mallory said. "Why don't we talk about Archangel?"

There was a loud clack, and for a moment Laura thought she'd dropped her fork. But her training, thank God, hadn't permitted her to do any such thing; one of the musclemen had let a serving spoon fall onto a tray. He was staring at Jack with astonishment; in fact, all the bodyguards were regarding Mallory with either incredulity or dawning anger. Jespers himself had gone quite motionless, and silence spread out from him like ripples from tossed stone until at last the entire riotous room was quiet. Even Kendrick, who'd been silent all night, seemed to take on an extra measure of stillness. He gazed at Mallory, a faint smile on his lips, a soup spoon poised in one gigantic hand.

"What an extraordinary question," Jespers said at last, with no trace of his usual jolliness.

"I say something wrong?" Mallory said placidly. "Thought you'd like talking about it. It's not a secret, is it? The satellite? Lord, Arne, you start shopping some gadget around and asking half a billion, it's not going to stay quiet too long. 'Course, I know it might not be Archangel, your gizmo, but it's a natural thing to wonder, isn't it?"

"Perhaps. You feel a particular interest in this subject?"

"I always feel a particular interest in five hundred million smacks. Wouldn't mind cutting myself a slice."

"You wouldn't mind this, eh?" Jespers said.

"Nope. Why don't you tell me about your satellite, and I'll see if there's any little service my boys and I can provide to get in on the action. Aw, what're you doing now, trying to smell whether I need killing?"

Slowly, Jespers smiled, showing a stained set of dentures. The eyes behind the gold spectacles lit again with merriment. "Yes, Jack. That is just what I'm doing."

"What do you think?" Mallory said, and took a mouthful of fish.

"I haven't decided," Jespers said.

"How about Kendrick over there? What does he think?"

"He hasn't decided," Jespers said. Kendrick smiled and spooned up a bit of soup. "But after all—why not? Why shouldn't you hear? Yes, Jack. It's true. The satellite in question is in fact the legendary Archangel. It has been missing for eighteen years, and I have found it. And I propose to sell it for a very *agreeable* sum."

With that, the silence broke, and the guests went back to their conversations. They were used to Jespers selling things for agreeable sums.

"How'd you get it?" Mallory asked over the hubbub.

"I built it."

"Who taught you to do that? I heard the Russians had Archangel's head guy. Fellow named Koch."

"Kost. Walther Kost. Yes, I discovered three or four years ago that Kost was being held in a research compound outside of Kildinstroi, near Murmansk, that he had been developing the device for the Soviets since the war, and that he had nearly completed a successful prototype. I was able to locate the KGB captain responsible for him and to determine that she had, with typical Soviet slovenliness, fallen in love with her charge. I have my own people in the KGB, of course, and she was a lonely and, I must say, somewhat over*sexed* young lady. It was not difficult for my agent to, ah, per*suade* her that her lover's life was in imminent danger and *instill* in her the desire to help. They devised an escape route, which she communicated to the professor by the very congenial method of drawing it on her bosom. Kost was not a young man, but he was an ex-commando, a tough and able fellow, and I was confident he would not waste this nice opportunity. Once he crossed the Finnish border, he was under the jurisdiction of no nation, and so I had him picked up and put under mine. And there you are. He doesn't like me, of course, but he didn't like the Soviets either, except for his little KGB concubine, and it is difficult for a man to stop working when he has a lifelong habit of doing so."

"What happened to the KGB girl?"

"Oh, it wasn't desirable that she hang about asking my agent questions. We dropped a few hints of her complicity in the right quarters and she was carted off to the Lubyanka. She killed herself in her cell a few weeks later. Tore her uniform into strips, I'm told, wove a rope, and hanged herself."

"You're a charming man," Laura told Jespers for the second time. It was not, she thought, necessary to conceal her revulsion, just to inject a note of helplessness into it. Jespers bowed slightly. *It would be a pleasure,* she thought. *I hope I never get to liking that sort of thing, but in your case, it would be a pleasure.*

"Sounds all right," Mallory said slowly. "I guess you might be telling the truth."

"You guess—!" Jespers said in astonishment. "Jack, you really are the most extraordinary—"

"But the thing that bothers me is, if all you're talking about is twenty-year-old spy technology—"

"Jack," Jespers said very quietly.

Mallory found it advisable to stop.

"I think it would be profitable to continue this conversation . . . privately," Jespers said. "Don't you agree?"

"Yep," Mallory said. "'Fact I do. Lil? You excuse us?"

"No. No, we've talked enough business for tonight. *Now,*" Jespers said, with an abrupt return to his usual geniality, "I can offer you what my man assures me is a quite *exceptional* Armagnac. And maybe a little cheese?"

"I'm pretty stuffed, thanks," Mallory said. "Armagnac sounds all right, though."

"I'm tired," Laura said, pushing her chair back. "I'm going upstairs. I'm going for a walk or something. Jackie?" She looked at Mallory.

"I guess I'll stick around awhile," Mallory said.

Milena poked his shoulder, rocking him to the side. "Have you seen the garden?" she demanded. She glared at the Twins, who stared sulkily at their plates.

"Yep," Mallory said. "We were all there this afternoon, remember?"

"Well, good night," Laura said, and turned to go.

Milena rose to her full height and tossed her napkin on the floor. She took hold of Mallory's arm.

"The garden is pretty," she told him. "Come. I will show you the garden."

The wind through the Via's windows was almost cool on Laura's face, cool and blessedly clean. Her wheat-blonde hair streamed out into the Provençal night. The roar of the little car's engine seemed to move through her like rushing water through a streambed, cleansing her. She took a breath and let it out. She was beginning to feel better. The job was what mattered, and the job seemed to be going damned well. Jack had taken a fair-sized risk at dinner, but, as far as she could see, it had paid off. A man in Jack Carroll's position would quite likely have heard of Archangel, and would certainly be interested in it if so; it made sense that the best way to camouflage their interest was to proclaim it, albeit in strictly commercial terms. Of course, Jespers might be shrewd enough to have seen through the gambit—to have sniffed out, so to speak, Jack's motives. In which case, the best thing would be to stick tight to Jack and stand ready to counter any attempt at liquidation. But Jack was the lead operative, and he'd plainly dismissed her for the night. Maybe he and Jespers wanted to talk alone after all. Or maybe that big girl—

Laura looked out to sea and deliberately cleared her mind.

The black Mediterranean gleamed like molten tar. A ghostly surf glided up the black beach and back again. The lights of Monaco were coming into view. In the dark of the evening, the new high-rise buildings, whose rows of concrete balconies ordinarily gave them the look of immense cheese graters, were almost lovely: vertical arrays of glowing lights. Up ahead she saw the Port de Monaco, the black water glimmering with the reflections of the long white yachts. When she got to the Place d'Armes, she turned up the Rue Grimaldi, found a parking spot, and locked the car. There was one sane, clean place in this wretched hive of ugly wealth, and she was going there.

It's not unheard of for a team to sneak a peek at a rival's cars, and not beyond the bounds of possibility that an unscrupulous competitor might try to nobble one, and so Team Naughton had stationed a husky dockworker on a café chair in front of their makeshift paddock, with instructions to remain there until dawn. He was a serious young man who did not take his responsibilities lightly. As Laura Morse slipped through the garage's back door, which she'd silently jimmied in less than a minute, she could see him through the panes in the garage's front door, steadfastly patrolling the pavement. She relocked the back door and walked steadily out into Team Naughton's pit. She'd had all morning to memorize the layout, including the coiled hoses and stacks of oil cans, and she moved with fluid ease until she was standing beside the fierce, missile-like car that would be Derek Reade's mount on Sunday. She stood there silently as her eyes adjusted, as if standing beside the bed of a sleeping lover. The chromed carburetor intakes came into focus first, and the shining edge of the windshield. And then, bit by bit, the car gathered itself out of the darkness until she could see the neatly braided cables, the complex exhaust manifold, the bolts that held gearbox to engine block. The wishbones and torsion bars appeared, taut and hard as a thoroughbred's fetlocks, and finally the gently zigzagging grooves in the tires. It was a beautiful car. There was a strictness to the shapes which seemed almost moral, and Laura stood there and drank in the sight like clear water.

No veteran agent is ever unaware of the passage of time, and Laura knew exactly how long she'd been standing there—not quite twenty minutes—when she heard a familiar Yorkshire accent outside. There was no need to look around for hiding places; true to her training, she'd located several as soon as she'd entered the garage, and she knew she had plenty of time to reach any of them. But she chose not to hide. Skulking behind a rack of tools was the opposite of what she'd come to the garage to do. When the lights came on, she blinked and looked around to see Harry Burch standing by the front door, one hand still poised at the light switch, a scandalized look on his face.

"What are you doing in my pit, Miss Prentice?" he said.

"Hello, Mr. Burch," she said. "I'm sorry. I know I shouldn't be here."

"What are you doing in my pit, Miss Prentice?" he repeated. "How the hell'd you get in here? Antoine's not supposed to let anyone in."

"Oh, I sort of sneaked in," she said vaguely. "I've always been good at sneaking, even as a girl," she added truthfully.

"Miss Prentice. What . . . are you doing . . . in my *pit*?"

"I've been admiring your wishbones," she said at random. "They're about as steep as I've seen. I guess your roll center's pretty low."

Burch looked at her blankly.

"Below the pavement, as it happens," he said at last. "One of Ken's specialties. Suits Reade's technique."

Keep him talking, Laura thought. *The longer you keep him talking, the longer before he throws you out.* She dreaded being sent back to the horrible Vandal encampment of Jespers's villa. She dreaded having to sit in her room with a paperback novel and wait for Milena to get done with Jack so the Twins could have their turn. She dreaded being exiled from the soothing scent of oily concrete, from the purity and calm of the beautifully engineered little car, from a place where everything made sense. "You must get a lot of negative camber as you move toward full bump," she continued. "You're not worried about scrub?"

"Ah . . . no. We're sprung pretty stiff."

"Dampers inboard, I see. I'm sure that's slipperier, but where do you put your limit stops?"

"We do without 'em. They bounce back."

"No limit stops? Reade won't thank you for that when he's up on the wall at Monza."

"Now that, Miss Prentice, is where you make your error," he said. "Look in the cockpit a moment, will you please? See that T-shaped handle down to your right? That's a bit of fiddle we worked up. Adjustable dampers. Custom job from the Armstrong people. Reade can stiffen 'em or soften 'em up just as he likes, depending on the weather, the surface, how much juice she's carrying. Twelve settings, and number twelve is quite hard enough for Monza. We swap out the dampers on the faster circuits, anyway."

"That *is* nice," Laura said. "It makes so much sense, too."

"I'm glad you think so, Miss Prentice."

"Well, I'm sure what you've just told me is in confidence, so thank you for trusting me. I promise you it'll go no further."

"Suit yourself," Burch said, suddenly glum. "It'll get about anyway. Next season, half the grid'll have adjustable dampers. Everything gets about. We all watch each other like, like . . ."

"Fashionable women at a party."

"That's just what it is, Miss Prentice. You've hit it exactly. Fashion. Look at the grid. Three years ago only the fancy buggers, if you'll pardon me, had engines in the rear. Now we've all got 'em. A couple seasons ago it was all wire wheels. Now it's all alloy."

"Last year it was space-frame. This year, monocoque," Laura agreed.

"Exactly. V-6, V-8. Pirellis, Dunlops. Hemlines up, hemlines down. Fashion. Here now," Burch said. "You're a surprise, Miss Prentice, you truly are. You're not such a silly bitch as you pretend, now, are you?"

"Oh, I'm a silly enough bitch all right," Laura said with a touch of bitterness. "But I like cars."

Burch stood there in the shadows, fists in his pockets, anvil chin thrust out, staring at her. Laura was, all at once, very weary.

Quietly she said, "I was feeling a bit low. Jack's off . . . somewhere, and I thought, well, I thought if I had a look at the car, it would make me feel better. So I did. And it has. And that's what I'm doing in your pit, Mr. Burch."

Burch kept staring.

Then he said, "Come have a drink."

Mallory wondered what time it was, and how soon he could decently go back to his own room. Not that he hadn't had a good time, in a way, but . . . The big girl was letting out a sleepy, contented hum like a dynamo. It made the bed tremble. Maybe she was asleep. Scary to think of her making that noise all night. He lifted her leg-sized arm from across his chest, and the hum took on a note of inquiry. She shook the arm free and gripped his thigh with one hand. Mallory gave up. He lay there, breathing carefully and gingerly feeling his bruised ribs.

"Darling," she said, or something like it.

He grunted.

"You are happy?" she said.

He replied, "Well, yeah, it was fun. But, you know . . ."

"Yes?"

"Back home we got this old story. About an Indian princess who fell in love with a grizzly bear."

"Yes?"

"Well, that's sort of how I feel right about now."

"You feel like bear?"

"I feel like princess," Mallory said.

She considered this. "You make joke?"

"I guess," Mallory said.

"Don't make any more of them," she said.

The Cap Ferrat dawn was just breaking, and neither Kirsten nor Kristen were early risers, but they'd both been busy for well over an hour. They'd pinched and poked and slapped each other awake by four o'clock. At 4:20, they'd been in the chef's bedroom, making small threats and large promises. Now they were in the courtyard by the pool, setting a breakfast table with three chairs and piling it high with good things to eat. There was a tiered silver platter of *tartes au citron* dusted with confectioners' sugar. There were a beribboned wicker basket of Marseilles figs and half a dozen Cavaillon melons on ice. There was an earthenware bowl of chili-and-garlic rouille ringed by wedges of coarse bread, a chafing dish filled with black truffles in honey, and another filled with spiced scrambled eggs. There was a chilled magnum of Veuve Clicquot Grande Dame, glass pitchers of fresh-squeezed orange juice, and a big pot of fresh black coffee. The pièce de résistance, though, was their own favorite, which they had Jespers air-freight in from the United States twice each month: Baby Ruth bars, a five-kilo pile of them, fresh from the kitchen freezer. Everyone knew Americans liked to stuff themselves. Even the thin, handsome Jack had eaten respectably at dinner. And the previous evening, they'd interrogated Howie and learned that Jack would be leaving the house by six—some mad-foreigner thing about taking a walk with the race-car people. The American bitch was off sulking somewhere. The Polish cow never rose before noon. The Twins were lightly clad in silk skirts and flowered bikini tops, their hair artfully disarrayed, their lips gleaming. They were ready. They bustled around the table, fussing and poking at the heaps of food, and then disposed themselves becomingly upon two of the three chairs and waited. At a quarter past five, they heard a step on the flagstones.

They turned to find Jack entering the courtyard with a meditative air. He was flanked by a glowering, tousled Milena, her big braid swinging behind her like a panther's tail, and an immaculate, tautly smiling Lily Prentice.

When Jespers appeared with his newspaper half an hour later, he found the five of them breakfasting together in silence, their knees jostling under the table. The Twins looked crushed, Milena looked murderous, and Jack looked carefully blank. Only the Prentice woman seemed icily composed. Jespers began to laugh.

"You're just like me, Jack!" he cried. "Just like me. You would make a very bad pimp. Or perhaps a very good one . . ."

8

Walking the Track

It was just as well that Harry Burch did not play poker. When Mallory and Laura arrived at the garage that morning, he greeted Laura with a look of such thunderous discretion, a look that so plainly advertised that her secret was safe with him, that everyone on the team wondered what in hell the two of them could have been up to. *She must've snuck off last night to talk cars with him,* Mallory thought. *Not a bad idea. Can't hurt to be friends with the team manager, and we sure seem to be friends with this one.* Burch beamed at Laura, his face red and shiny, as if he'd just finished Christmas dinner. He gazed keen-eyed upon Mallory like a watchful father-in-law. "You listen to this young lady," he said. "Don't you sell her short. Imagine she could teach you a thing or two."

"Always could," Mallory said.

The team manager had brought two thermoses of coffee; one strengthened with brandy and one not. The second was for Derek

Reade and Mark Coney, who'd be driving later in the morning. Burch ceremoniously poured out a mugful for everyone and handed them around himself. Reade and Coney drank theirs while studying a clipboard together. They looked like choirboys sharing a hymnal. Burch had purchased cream and sugar especially for Laura and was disappointed to find that she took hers black.

As a special treat, he had Mallory sit in the racer's cockpit. Built for the smaller Reade, the cockpit was coffin-tight; Laura watched her partner carefully and was impressed by his self-command. He chatted amiably while wedged inside and joked about his waistline while wriggling free, and no one could have guessed how trying the experience was for him unless they'd learned, like Laura, to gauge a man's pulse rate by the flickering of his carotid arteries. Jack's hit 1:30 or so while behind the wheel, and when he was standing beside the car again there was a faint sheen of sweat at his hairline which had nothing to do with the summer weather. They exchanged glances, Jack's ruefully amused, hers, she hoped, neutral. *Goddamn them,* she thought irrationally. *Sticking him in there. As if he didn't have enough to worry about.*

When they'd finished their coffee, they set down their mugs and stepped through the big garage door into empty streets rich with the early-morning scent of fresh bread. They crossed in front of the Théâtre de Variétés and were on the track.

"There you are," Reade said to Coney before they'd gone a yard. "Some things in life you can always depend on." The two drivers laughed, and Reade turned to Laura and explained, "See that little hump just ahead of the finish line? Been there forever. We can all count on getting a bit airborne there every lap. Been onto old Chiron for years about smoothing it out, but I guess it's meant to be a local landmark. Don't mind it myself. Wakes you up if things've gotten boring."

Coney smiled shyly. "Yeah, Derek always drives a real boring race," he said.

He had a sleepy Californian accent, but Laura thought there was nothing sleepy about his eyes, which had already returned to the track.

"What we're doing here, Miss Prentice," Derek said, "is reac-quainting ourselves with the track, the subtleties of it. What you might call the grace notes. Where the road's paved slick, where it's rough, where the camber's helping you hold it on a corner, where it's sloping off the wrong way. How they've got the barriers, which ones're hard Armco, which are soft straw bales, how deep they've got the gravel in the traps—whether you can drive across if you need to, or if you'll sink right in. Not that there're many traps in Monaco. Where our corner-ing and braking points might be, you know, little landmarks we can use to tell when it's time to turn or get on the brake. It can be anything. A postbox, a crosswalk, a word on an advertising banner."

"Go on and let 'em lecture you, Miss Prentice," Burch said. "Makes 'em feel like big men."

"I'm very anxious to hear," Laura said. "I imagine it's a great help to you, Mr. Reade—"

"Call me Derek."

"Thank you," Laura said without undue warmth, "Derek. It must help that you live here. You must know the circuit intimately."

Intimately, Laura saw at once, was the wrong word to use with a man like Reade. He took it as encouragement. Not that his sort needed much of that.

"Mmm, but it's different every time, isn't it?" he said languidly, and managed to inject a wealth of suggestion into the phrase. "And they're different streets when you're racing 'em. All the things that strike you as landmarks when you're walking or driving about in a passenger car, all those are just a blur at a hundred and sixty miles per. It's a different city. Besides, you're scooting along so low to the pavement that little things you mightn't notice on a stroll really jump up and stick you in the eye."

"Sometimes literally," Burch said, and laughed heartily at his own joke.

"Mmm," Reade said.

I hope he isn't going to keep mm'ing like that, Laura thought.

"Now, here we're coming up to the Virage Sainte Dévote," Reade said, "the first corner. It's always a mess. Narrow, bumpy as hell, flops you all about. You've got a lot of different cambers, you see, from the different streets crossing. It'd be an ugly corner in the rain, with all those streams of water shooting this way and that down the hill. That's another thing we look for, hollow places that'd be underwater when it rains, flat or smooth spots that'd take a film of water, how the drainage lies and so forth."

"There hasn't been a wet race in Monaco since '36," Coney said.

"Good thing, too, eh, Mark?" Reade said, and laughed. There was something not entirely kind about Reade's laugh. "Mark doesn't care for the wet."

"I guess it's something I need to keep working on," Coney said.

"It's nasty stuff, rain," Reade said soothingly. "If you're not the lead driver, you can't see where you're going. Everything's lost in the spray. Water pours into your helmet, and, ah, it's a bit uncomfortable. You see, a driver'll sweat off three kilos or so during a race, so before we start we always chug-a-lug down the water. Well, if you drive a cold race, you don't sweat as much and it, ah." He gestured at his sinewy midsection. "Builds up," he said and grinned at Laura.

"I understand," she said.

"It's damned changeable, too, lap to lap. Puddles don't stay put the way tarmac does, you see. But Mark here'll get the hang of it someday soon, and then we'd all better watch out," he said. "He's a damned fine technical driver. Stronger than me."

"Miss Prentice knows better than that," Coney said quietly.

"Please call me Lily," Laura said, with far more warmth than she'd shown Reade.

"First names all around, then," Reade said, with the air of a man who knew quite well that he hadn't been invited to first-name Laura, but who wasn't going to hold a little thing like that against her.

They'd reached the Sainte Dévote corner and were passing through the shadow of the great church. Coney prodded a manhole cover with one foot and then stood on it, trying to rock it with his full weight. Reade joined him, and for a moment the two were oblivious to anything but the clanking disk of iron under their feet.

"I'll get on 'em," Burch told them. "Disgraceful. It'll be right by Sunday, I promise you. Have a word with those lazy buggers."

"Smoother than last year, anyhow," Coney remarked to Reade.

"They've laid down a nice thick layer of asphalt along the florist's there, see? Right over to the travel agency."

"They've simplified it," Reade agreed. "But I don't care for all this paint on the crosswalks. A bit slippy." He returned his attention to Laura. "I'm damned serious," he said, and abruptly sounded it. "When it's just a matter of taking a car to its limits, there isn't a stronger driver than Mark in the series. He's got better technique than I do, tighter control, nicer judgment. Put him on an empty track in a quick car and he'll deliver better times than I do six days out of seven. True. Only problem is, races aren't run on empty tracks. You can't just go out there and try to win. You've got to make the other fellow lose. You've got to rattle him, to see where he's weak and stick him there. It's a tactical sport, Lily, and quite as mean as boxing. And Mark hasn't a mean bone in his body, have you, Mark? Well, he's young yet, and new to the Grand Prix. That's his only problem. He still hasn't had that taste of blood yet."

Though this couldn't have been the first time he'd heard the speech, Coney was listening carefully.

So were Mallory and Laura. *Finds himself irresistible,* she thought, *and imagines I do, too. I'll bet Jack thinks this is funny as hell.*

A talker, Mallory thought. *And I just went and bought fifty grand's worth of him. Well, anyway, it'll be fun watching him try and make Laurie.*

They began walking up the Montée du Beau Rivage toward the Hôtel de Paris, between a double row of palms glinting dustily in the rising sun.

"We're coming up on the Casino corner," Reade said. "It's a tricky one. You've got to brake before you can see what you're braking for, and then there's a dogleg between the Casino and the hotel with a lot of iffy surface. But I'm rather fond of Casino Square. It gives you a lot of scope to, ah, express yourself."

"How about it, Burch?" Mallory said. "Do you want Reade out there expressing himself?"

"It's what he's paid for," Burch said shortly.

"It can't be handled too gingerly," Reade continued. "You've really got to attack it. But if you hit it right, you're nicely set up for a real flying exit from the square, where the road slopes down quick toward

the Mirabeau hairpin and you can do a bit of overtaking. I like," Reade
told Laura, "overtaking."

"Do you," she said.

"Mmm. It's sort of a specialty of mine. So much of this business
is technical, you know, and so much of it is just hanging on, endurance—racing's quite *physically* demanding. But overtaking, now, that
introduces an element that's a bit more . . . personal. You're not just
testing the car and the circuit. You're testing the fellow in front. It's a
bit of a seduction, actually. You're feeling your way, getting to know
your opponent, learning his rhythms, his limits, seeing how far you can
push, keeping your touch light but never quite letting up, never letting
him get used to you but never letting him forget you, either. And when
you've picked just the right spot at just the right time and applied just
the right amount of pressure—and neither of you knows *quiiite* when
that'll be until it's already happening—there's a moment when he sees
he'll have to open up and let you through. When he accepts it. A moment of . . . surrender."

Oh dear, Laura thought.

From behind them, they heard an anxious, American-accented
"Excuse me?"

They turned to see a tall young man with dark olive skin and close-
cropped black curls, whose long-sleeved shirt could not quite conceal
his prizefighter's physique. There was a rucksack on his shoulder and
a map in his hand. Plainly he was one of those earnest young Americans who traverse France on foot every summer in search of culture
on the cheap. Each year, a few stray into Monaco under the misappre-
hension that it is part of France. Gamblers or not, they usually take a
financial beating before they can find their way out again. "I'm sorry,"
the young man said to Laura and Mallory. "You American? You look
American."

Burch and Reade began walking again. Coney paused, as if a call
had been issued for an American and he felt he ought to stick around
and make sure they didn't need an extra one.

"American enough," Mallory said. "What can I do for you?"

"I guess I'm kind of turned around," the young man said. "Do you,
do either of you know where the Hôtel Lucien is supposed to be? I

think it's supposed to be on Boulevard du Jardin Exotique." He made heavy weather of the French names.

"Not that I know of," Mallory said. "See your map a minute?"

"Sure."

It was a standard tourist map, available in the lobby of any of the town's hotels. On the cover was the crest of the local tourist information office; inside, it was divided into a coordinate grid, the lines of which were labeled with scarlet numerals along the edges. The young traveler unfolded it, his movements awkward and overeager, and handed it over. Mallory took hold of it.

When he did, his right thumb landed on the little scarlet 2. He held it there for a moment, remarking, "Looks like it oughta be a nice day today."

Laura heard this last comment and invisibly rejoiced. Whatever else Jack had been doing the previous night, he'd been working. And *today* was good news in itself.

"Hope so," the young tourist said quietly.

"Here's where we are, see? And here's where you're going. So it's first left, third right, round the square, first right. And there you are."

"Got it. Thanks."

"If you don't mind a suggestion? There's a pretty good little place to eat right around your hotel. Called Le Something Sportif or Something du Sport, you know, like that. Solid food, and pretty cheap for Monaco. Right around, ah, *here*." As he pointed out the intersection with a lifted forefinger, Mallory's thumb came to rest midway between 4 and 5.

"I'll try to make it over there," the young man said, nodding. "Thanks for the tip. Thanks a lot, both of you. You've been awful kind."

"Good luck," Mallory said, returning the map.

The young man folded it deftly, as though he'd momentarily forgotten to be clumsy, stowed it in his rucksack, and strode off.

"Come on, Lily," Burch called. "Jack. We're waiting."

So are we, Mallory thought.

In a town full of ornate and discreet hotels, the Hôtel Hermitage was unquestionably the most ornate and most discreet, and Jespers had chosen it without hesitation as the venue for his meeting. Nor had the Hermitage let him down. They'd assigned him a private conference room whose existence was unknown even to the hotel's most devoted guests. Tucked under the hotel's cupid-encrusted eaves, it was spacious, softly lit, and soberly appointed. On one side, it overlooked the hotel's glass-domed Jardin d'Iver, where the Monegasque sun filtered down through an immense stained-glass sunflower and illumined lush ferns and wrought-iron balconies. On the other side, it commanded a view of the Avenue d'Ostende and the harbor. The room boasted an annex containing a private kitchen, where the pathologically fussy or intensely security-minded could have their own chefs prepare their own food, and a small, marble-paneled, temperature-controlled wine cellar, whose contents had taken nearly a century to assemble. Set into the center of the leather-lined conference table was a sunken brass humidor with room for three dozen cigars, which could be raised into position with the touch of a switch.

It was a room made for lavish hospitality, but Jespers, uncharacteristically, was not in a hospitable mood. The kitchen was unused, the wine cellar locked, the humidor empty. The men seated around the table were drinking mineral water and had been forbidden to smoke. This meeting had been forced upon Arne Jespers, and he saw no reason to pretend he was happy about it.

He stood at the window, looking out across the harbor at the crag called the Tête de Chien, his hands lightly clasped before him. Behind him, three men were seated around the table, each as far as possible from the other two and all staring at Jespers's narrow back. Around the perimeter of the room, three phalanxes of bodyguards sat in straight chairs against the oyster-gray walls, each group clustered behind one of the three men and carefully watching the two others. In the farthest corner of the room, Kendrick stood at parade rest, watching the entire room without appearing to pay much attention to anything at all, dressed in a brown suit as nondescript as his gray one. He was the only man there who seemed relaxed.

In spite of the warmth of the day, the windows were shut. Through their double panes came an endless, snarling, metallic roar, like a pack of steel hounds on the hunt: twenty-one Grand Prix teams at practice. Each driver was pressing his car to the limits, each trying to better his best lap time. For each of the twenty-one teams was competing for one of sixteen starting places when the race began in two days' time.

The Russian spoke first.

He was an obvious senior *apparatchik*: face and cheeks blotched from good living, eyes wary and hard. His thickly tufted eyebrows were grayish white. He had survived for a very long time. His dark blue suit was expensive but fit his thick body like a carton, the lapels oddly truncated, the shoulders too heavily padded. It was one of the mysteries of life, Jespers thought, that even the wealthiest Soviet official could never seem to find a decent tailor. "I would not like to think," the Russian said in effortless English, "that we have reached an impasse."

Jespers did not turn around. "Let me reassure you, Sergei. If you have reached an impasse, you have reached it quite alone."

"Forgive me if I disagree," said the man to his left. "I believe that I, too, am quite close to what my *colleague*"—the word dripped icicles—"describes so accurately as an impasse."

The second man was tall and almost offensively fit; even his narrow, rawboned face seemed to have been shaped by strenuous calisthenics. His dull blond hair was cut short and beginning to gray. His cheap suit fit him perfectly, and had the air of a uniform. His aspect was emphatically Prussian, which made it all the more surprising that his English, though flawless, was delivered with the soft Argentine accent of the born *porteño*. "Two of us consider ourselves quite nearly at an impasse, and perhaps three." Here he looked placidly at the slight Southeast Asian seated across from him, whose expression did not alter. "And if your three potential bidders are at an impasse, Mr. Jespers, then so, it follows, are you."

"Am I, Ernst?" Jespers said. "You know, I think I don't agree. I think the world is full of potential bidders. But it is not really so full of Archangels."

Jespers's back was still turned to the room. On impulse, he opened the window—it swung easily on well-oiled hinges—and leaned moodily on the sill as the hornet-swarming din of the F1 pack washed over him. It was an excellent place to watch the practice. The cars shot around the Sainte Dévote corner and flew up the avenue below him toward Virage Massenet, where they disappeared into Casino Square. Their polished fuselages flashed in the sun, and now and then one emitted a brief spray of sparks as it bottomed out after a dip or a short journey across the curbs. The noise they made was rather Wagnerian from this height, stirring rather than actually painful, as it would be out on the pavement. Every few seconds one of the snarling voices was briefly muted as it disappeared into the tunnel that ran along the waterfront, then let out a blare as it shot back into the sunshine at 160 miles per hour, heading pell-mell toward Virage Tabac. "Maybe all three of you have come to an impasse," Jespers allowed. "But you have come to it without me. I am precisely here where I have always been, offering an item such as I have never before offered, such as I may never be in a position to offer again. I ask nothing but money—"

"Absurd amounts of money," the Russian said.

"In exchange for absurd amounts of power," Jespers replied.

"To be acquired by means of a mechanism you will not describe," the German said.

"For the most excellent of reasons," Jespers said, turning at last to face his inquisitors. "Gentlemen. We are not children, we are not novices. We are experienced men. Two of you"—here he inclined his head toward the Russian and the German—"have had dealings with me before this, dealings that have been as profitable for you as they have been for myself. The third"—and here he turned to the silent Oriental—"has come to me only after satisfying himself through the most exacting and exhausting and rigorous investigations that I am a man who has never been known to deal in bad faith, a man who is *entirely* without dissatisfied customers."

"A man," said the Oriental softly, "who has buried nearly half a dozen of his business partners between 1928 and the present day."

He was slight and apparently young, and spoke in a voice devoid of both accent and emotion. He wore an incongruously festive flowered shirt over khaki trousers. His bodyguards were also dressed as tourists on holiday, their brightly colored clothes an odd contrast with their stone-still faces and military posture. He had folded his small hands before him on the table when he'd first sat down, over an hour ago, and had scarcely shifted them since.

"Five, to be precise," he continued. "Of course, our researches may be incomplete."

Jespers smiled upon the little man with a sudden access of his accustomed geniality. "How thorough you are, Mr. Xiong!" he said delightedly. "I myself believe the number to be five, though my memory, I very much fear, is not what it should be these days."

"And yet you require our trust, and apparently expect it."

"Mr. Xiong," Jespers said. "I do not offer you, any of you, a partnership. I offer you a piece of merchandise. Some of my former partners have, I quite admit, a few reasons to complain about me, even if only from the next world. But my customers have none. As I am sure your nice thorough researches have confirmed."

"You are correct, Mr. Jespers. Your relations with your past and present clients are as you portray them. But moral character is not such a complicated thing as you imagine. A man is either a betrayer or he is not. You are a betrayer. It is true that you have never yet betrayed a client, Mr. Jespers, but also it is true that you have never had such weighty reasons to betray one."

"Nor such weighty reasons to deal honorably," Jespers said impatiently. "Gentlemen, you have no real grounds for all this—"

There was a shriek of tortured tires, distant but compelling as the cry of a child in a far room, and then the cannon-like report of a high-speed impact. Then tiny, excited voices and the siren of the safety car, pulling out onto the track to slow the other drivers.

"You see?" Jespers said. "Your childish fears are causing me to miss all this excitement." He turned his back on his guests again and peered out the window. "Yes, down at Tabac. It would appear that Cooper has suffered a reverse. And their driver, I fear, even more so." The yellow flag was out over the pit wall, striped with red to indicate oil on the track. The marshals were converging from all over the circuit, the rushed clopping of their footsteps almost inaudible. Old Chiron the race director was hurrying in a stately way along the harborfront. The unfortunate driver had been thrown clear and lay like an abandoned rag doll ten yards from the smoking wreckage of his car, his racing suit splotched with red and black and his limbs hideously disarranged. As Jespers watched, the motionless form disappeared in a gathering crowd of marshals and onlookers. The yachts in the harbor continued to gleam, opulent and white. Their occupants were beginning to gather on deck. One was peering at the wreck with binoculars. It would be nice, Jespers thought, to have a pair of binoculars just now. He turned back to his guests, who had neither moved nor evinced any particular interest in the commotion outside. "Life is short, gentlemen," he said. "Far too short to cause any unnecessary unpleasantnesses."

"I trust that is not a threat," said the German with the *porteño* accent. "There is no one in this room whom a sensible man would threaten."

"Absolutely no one at all," Jespers agreed. "Gentlemen. I have indulged you long enough. I have agreed to an entirely unnecessary meeting. I have permitted you to attend it armed and with your"—he waved scornfully—"retinues. I have, because of certain infantile political prejudices which two of you hold so very dear, excluded Americans from the qualifying process, in spite of the wealth of that nation—and this is a kind of interference I have never before permitted. I have submitted to your insulting and unimaginative questions. I am tired and I am becoming irritable and I will not answer any more of them. As I have said quite clearly and often, I am prepared in four days' time to produce Archangel itself and to demonstrate its special capabilities to your complete satisfaction. Until that time I shall make no explanations and provide no descriptions, for reasons that should be quite obvious. For all we know, there is an enterprising young man on the roof at this moment as we *speak*, with, say, a parabolic microphone and earphones, recording every word for his masters, and this would be an unpleasant, an *unfortunate* thing for all of us. I am inviting you, *welcoming* you, armed and *with* your retinues, to my operations center, where we will be properly secure—"

"And at your mercy," the Russian said.

"You are at my mercy *now*, Sergei. Monaco is one of my strongholds, and I have certain standing arrangements here. If I wished it, not one of you would leave this city alive. The situation will be no different at my compound. You will each pay one million dollars in earnest money for the privilege of admission. This sum will be non-refundable. You will observe Archangel in action and be permitted to explore its capabilities fully; you will be permitted to interview its creator. And then you will have thirty-six hours to prepare your bids and present a satisfactory proposal for payment. And this is all I shall say today. Gentlemen?"

There was a silence—not a long silence, but a deep one.

And then Xiong the Oriental unfolded his steepled hands and set them on the table.

"I am satisfied," he said, his voice no more animated than before, and rose.

His bodyguards rose with him. One opened the door, and a second stationed himself at the opening, hand hovering near his hip. When the door opened without event, the second guard left, followed by Xiong himself, and then by the rest.

The German called Ernst gazed after them, then looked back at Jespers and nodded curtly. He, too, rose and made for the door. His legs were long, and he reached it nearly at the same time as Xiong's last bodyguards; he paused to let them pass. His own bodyguards followed, and then the table was empty but for the fat Russian.

"Sergei?" Jespers said. His usual good humor was returning.

The Russian smiled abruptly. It was the smile of a small boy who believes he can wangle an extra cookie. "Dane," he said. "You know how it is. We old fellows, we don't like to be left behind, do we?"

The two men laughed, and the Russian rose with a grunt. He stepped up to Jespers, fondly patted his cheek, then waddled to the door. "Not even a little glass of cognac," he said in German as he went, tugging down his suit jacket, "but I forgive you, Dane. The big deal has made you jumpy. Come to the Tip-Top tonight. We'll have some girls."

"I'm tired of girls," Jespers said. "I'm getting too old for all this nonsense."

"I am twice your age, Dane, and I am not too old," the Russian said, his hand on the doorknob. "And when I am dead and turned into dirt, I want someone to sprinkle a pinch of me on some nice young lady."

Flanked by his minders, he departed.

Jespers turned back to the window and, for a minute or so, watched the speeding cars outside. The wreck had been lifted away by crane. The driver had been spirited off by ambulance. The puddles of oil had been mopped up and the pavement scrubbed clean. The remaining twenty drivers were again pressing their cars and selves to the limit, as if nothing unusual had happened. For, in the pitiless world of the Grand Prix, nothing unusual had. Kendrick walked leisurely from his corner, hitched up his trousers, and seated himself on the corner of the table behind Jespers. He sat there a moment, legs swinging.

He said, "I guess that wasn't a complete waste of time. Pretty close, though."

"Exceedingly close," Jespers said, eyes on the speeding cars. "But this is what it is to be a salesman. You must let them waste your time. They must always waste your time, and you can never waste theirs, and in this way they come to feel important and in a good mood for giving you money."

"I don't think anyone's ever in the mood to give away this kind of money," Kendrick observed. His voice was flat and quiet, and all one could say about it was that it was American.

Larry Kendrick was born in a farm town outside of Decatur, Illinois. Until he was sent to Okinawa at nineteen, he'd thought the best thing in the world was football. But once in the Pacific theater, he decided that soldiering was better than any kid's game, with the added advantage that you were never too short to turn pro. When the shooting stopped, Kendrick headed for North Africa, and from there moved on to spend a few years supporting various minor insurgencies in and around Colombia. He was an oddity among mercenaries—a shrewd, quiet, relaxed man in a world of brawling hotheads—and his reputation soon won him a place in the highly profitable world of gray-market personal security. When Arne Jespers had met him, Kendrick had been running a private Army of two hundred men for a Milanese rubber manufacturer with a number of surprising side businesses. The Dane had lured him away by the simple expedient of adding a zero to his annual salary. He'd been with Jespers for six years now, and they'd been through a few bumpy rides together. And Kendrick had a notion that they'd stepped on board another.

He said, "Got a minute, Dane?"

Jespers turned. "One minute," he said, holding up a finger. "And then we will go and watch the practice."

Kendrick nodded. "Did some checking on Carroll and the girl."

"Yes? In this you exceeded your instructions." Jespers's voice was a bit chilly.

"Dunno about that, Dane," Kendrick said. "My instructions are to keep you alive. And until you tell me to stop, that's what I'm do-ing. There's not much on the girl, but then, there wouldn't be. What we got seems all right. Carroll's a lot meatier, and he reads like Car-roll, all right, reads like him six ways from Sunday. We always got two-three people in CSS, you know, just on general principles, and we've checked with them, and walked it back a few other ways, and there's only two people in the world he could be. Jack Carroll—"

"Or?"

"Or somebody Jack Carroll personally hired to impersonate Jack Carroll. If he's a ringer, he's a ringer working with the real Carroll's full and direct cooperation."

"And why should a man do such an extraordinary and tiresome thing as have himself impersonated?"

"I couldn't begin to tell you, Dane. But I don't like him. He acts right and talks right and handles himself right, but he feels wrong. He's just off, like milk when it's starting to go. I don't like it when I'm deal-ing with one of the few guys in the world you can't really check up on, who's managed to go back and scrub his own record so there's not so much as a family snapshot or yearbook photo or goddamned parking ticket around. Carroll did that—everybody knows he did that about eight-nine years back, before he was anybody really worth watching, and it cost him plenty. His outfit's one of the few private firms that could do the job for any amount of money. And now he shows up in your backyard, a man who hasn't taken a vacation or left Texas except on highly secret business since the spring of 1954, and says, Here I am,

I just decided to get me a girlfriend and go see the sights. I don't like it. I don't like it when patterns get broken."

"I begin to suspect that we're having two wastes of time this afternoon."

"Carroll and Prentice were staying at the Paris," Kendrick said.

"As they themselves informed us, Mr. Kendrick."

"They made their reservations eleven days ago."

Jespers was still. Monaco's Hôtel de Paris is one of the world's most exclusive and desirable hotels, and to reserve a suite for the week of the Grand Prix one must typically book a year ahead. The best rooms are booked several years in advance.

Kendrick said, "A Mr. and Mrs. Harold Merritt Clarkson Jr. of Diamond Head, Hawaii, were paid ten thousand American dollars, cash money, to cancel their reservation for the Empress Eugénie Suite and accept in exchange a single room at the Savignac in Cap Ferrat. They were told that, by so doing, they would be aiding the national security of the *Yew*-nited States of America, and sworn to the deepest, darkest, inky-blackest secrecy. And the fella they dealt with is a low-level operative—we've got the initials *KR*, but no name—of Carroll Security Systems."

Jespers did not reply.

"Now. Carroll's a man who's got the money to gratify some whims. And if he had a sudden notion that he'd like to go see the Monaco Grand Prix, and see it from a big suite in the best hotel in town, I guess this is pretty much how he'd do it."

Jespers remained silent.

"But I don't like it," Kendrick said.

"Where is Jack now?" Jespers said.

Kendrick nodded. "I've had him shadowed since he left the place this morning," he confirmed. "Aside from Prentice and Team Naughton, he's spoken, just in passing, to exactly three people. There was a waitress at Oscar's, who's good-looking enough that I guess it's not too suspicious he'd give her the time of day. She's still at Oscar's, working out her shift. Hasn't even taken a break to pee. There was a big spade tourist with a rucksack who asked Carroll for directions. We trailed him to the Lucien and confirmed he's staying there. We haven't seen him leave, but hell, it's a hotel, and he could've double-doored my man easy enough. And there was one of those damn toy-soldier *carabinieri*, you know, with the ribbons and the little white cap. My man couldn't get close enough to pick up the discussion. And this guy left his post an hour and ten minutes later and went home, supposedly with a stomach bug. Anyway, he lives in a rooming house with just one way in and out, and he's still there, all right."

"Where is Jack now?" Jespers repeated.

"We lost him," Kendrick said, and smiled broadly. "About an hour ago, after the team'd gone back to work and he and Prentice were window-shopping on Grimaldi, he looked around, gave my man a big old grin, and all of a sudden yanked the girl into a taxi. Had the driver cut an illegal U and off they went. When the cab pulled up in front of the Paris, it was empty. I guess if I was on vacation and some clown started tailing me, I might maybe have done the same thing."

Jespers seemed to be absently studying the figures in the carpet.

"Actually," Kendrick said, "There's three possibilities on this guy, not two. One is, he's clean. Another is, Carroll hired him as a double. But he could also be working for some other outfit—CIA, Vickers & Frost, the Consultancy, MI6—who's somehow managed to get the real Carroll to play along. Carroll doesn't stooge much, so it's not very likely, but it's not impossible either."

Jespers looked up at Kendrick and very softly said, "I like Jack. I believe him to be my friend."

"And that's why I plan to keep watching him," Kendrick said. "Want me to quit?"

Jespers considered, and then smiled without pleasure and said, "We are missing the practice."

They turned and left the room without another word.

Up on the roof of the Hôtel Hermitage, the enterprising young man in the earphones remained motionless for nearly five minutes after the click of the closing door. Then he reached into his tourist's rucksack and switched off a miniature tape recorder. Moving deliberately and without haste, he detached a limpet microphone from under the ornate eaves—a parabolic mike isn't much use against a closed double-paned window—coiled it neatly, and stowed it, along with the headphones, beside the tape recorder. He arranged the rucksack carefully so that a casual search inside would reveal nothing but folded clothes. He was dressed in a workman's coverall and was carrying a large box of unnecessary tools, and was ready to explain his presence on the roof in serviceable French to any interested passerby, but he still scanned all the windows within view before rising to his feet and moving toward the access door. Despite what Jack Mallory might think, Billy Harmon was not always a show dog.

"You were right," Harmon told Mallory. "The food's good here."

The Bistro Sporty was one of the many Monegasque businesses that had adopted Americanized names following Rainier's marriage to Grace Kelly. It was dark, plain, and just large enough that, at the quiet hour of eight minutes to five—Harmon had arrived promptly at four-thirty, as per Mallory's silent instructions—three spies could enjoy a secluded table out of earshot of the proprietors and the handful of other customers. Billy had ordered a *croque madame* and a Stella Artois, and was making short work of both. The tight olive skin over his jaws rippled as he chewed. *He even eats earnestly,* Laura thought, and sipped her Zinfandel.

"Actually, I didn't have any idea whether the food was good here or not," Mallory admitted. "I just wanted you to meet us here 'cause it's the right distance from everything else. But I'll admit that sandwich looks all right."

Harmon nodded and swallowed. "Excuse my eating while I talk, but I really haven't had much time for meals since I got in."

"You've accomplished an amazing amount," Laura said.

"Thank you. I appreciate your saying that, Lily, I really do," Harmon said. Mallory was careful not to smile. It was proper tradecraft, sticking to work names like that, but it was also something Mallory himself wasn't bothering with. If anyone from Jespers's *apparat* got wind of this meeting, they were all blown and probably dead, even if they addressed each other as Number One and Number Two. "Anyway," Harmon continued, "I thought he was pretty cute, our guy. I don't see that he gave 'em a thing on the project, or us, either. Unless you can see something I missed, of course. Do you want a dupe of the tape?"

"Too risky," Mallory said. "And it sounds like you're telling us everything that matters. You trust your memory?"

"Pretty much."

"Then so do I. Get the tape in tomorrow's New York pouch. It's always better to have empty hands."

"Which pouch?"

"Pet shop. What do you think of Jespers?"

"Overall?"

"Yeah."

"I think he's having a good time. I think he's the kind of guy who has a good time, and that's what makes him dangerous."

"I believe you're right," Mallory said.

"A guy who's enjoying himself, enjoying his work, a guy like that doesn't hesitate or press too hard or any of that. He just—" Harmon extended a big arm and rippled it, surprisingly, like a hula dancer. "He just flows. I think that's why he seems to get on with the Russian. Because the Russian's enjoying himself, too."

"I think you nailed it, Billy. Got any good guesses on Archangel?"

"No."

"Laurie, how about you? You're the analyst, or used to be."

She shook her head. "Nothing on Archangel, but this should get us good IDs on the bidders."

Harmon swallowed and wiped his fingers. "Well, actually, Lily, I did a little preliminary work on that. Got a secure line going to Analysis back at my hotel and had a quick chat with Miss Schorr. The Russian she said you'd both know."

"Sounds like Sergei Melnikov," Mallory said. "GRU. Runs their weapons research bureau or something like that. Don't know him, but we sort of got friends in common."

"Superior Secretary of the Sub-Directorate for Strategic Technological Research," Harmon said. "He's not a technical guy, though I guess he's probably learned on the job. What he is is a smooth operator, an old Kremlin hack who's been slick enough and tough enough to grab a fat job and hang on to it for the last nine years. He's in charge of buying or stealing military secrets for the Soviet Army, and from what she says, he's a pretty smart shopper."

Mallory said, "And he's got money to spend. I'd've been kind of surprised if he wasn't at the meeting. Go on."

"The guy named Ernst is most likely Ernst Halprin, a member of the Supreme Executive of La Hermanidad de Ultima Thule. Know 'em?"

Mallory shook his head and looked at Laura. She said, "A sort of South American Nazi fan club, as I recall. They were hoping Hitler would get around to conquering them, too. When he died, they went paramilitary. They're based in— Was it Rio?"

"Caracas," Harmon said. "It used to be sort of a social club for wealthy right-wing South Americans. In '45 they were taken over by a few fugitive SS officers and began stockpiling weapons and recruiting mercenaries. Their goal is to reunify Germany and establish a Fourth Reich there with the help of a great deal of Venezuelan oil money." He took a sip of his beer. "Thirsty. The Oriental guy's a little surprising. He's a pretty good bet to be Lae Xiong, Associate Director of External Security for the Pathet Lao. I guess you know what he wants."

"Something to impress the French, I guess," Mallory said. "Seems kind of like hunting squirrels with bear shot, though. And where the hell would the Pathet Lao get that kind of money? Not from Hanoi. Moscow wouldn't bid against itself. And China's still backing what's-his-name."

"Phouma. Analysis says all she can think is that the Pathet Lao are fronting for some clandestine extranational consortium with interests in that area. Anyhow, that's what I got. Actually, she already knew Melnikov was bidding, which is how I knew to go to the Hermitage— Analysis knew he was staying there. How'd you know the meeting was today at two, Jack?"

"Asked," Mallory said.

"It's sometimes the best way," Laura said.

"I guess it's good to know about Halprin and Xiong, too, right?"

Harmon said. "Melnikov's probably riding too high to turn, and the other two seem too ideological. But maybe you can get an angle on one of them. And we know to watch out for Kendrick."

"Well, we already sort of knew that. He's been giving me the stink-eye from the first time we met. I kind of assumed he'd be doing some checking up—he'd be kind of a slob if he didn't. Nice to know our cover's held up so far. Listen, Billy, you've done a hell of a job. You really have, and Laurie and I are damn happy about it."

"Thanks, Jack. I hope I'll do as well when the action starts."

Like all first-rate field operatives, Laura Morse and Jack Mallory were almost completely free of involuntary facial expressions, and Harmon knew it. So when the two of them raised their eyebrows at once, he knew they'd done so deliberately, for his benefit.

A moment before, he'd been close to preening. Now he deflated. "Ah— Did I say something?" he said.

"I don't know how to break this to you, son," Mallory said.

"The action's started, Billy," Laura said. "This is the action."

"Well, you know what I mean," Harmon said.

"Yeah, we do," Mallory said. "And I'll say it again. The action's started, and started damn well."

"I guess some jobs are quieter than others," Harmon said.

"This isn't quiet, Billy. This is regular. You're wondering when the shooting starts, the shooting and the blowing up munitions dumps and the, what's the word, hairsbreadth escapes. Well, hopefully never. All that stuff goes on, Billy, goes on a hell of a lot more often than Laurie and me would like, but that's because usually somebody screwed something up. Billy, spying isn't soldiering. It isn't war. You're not here to kill the bad guys and win the day for freedom. You're here to get your hands on some intel, and the best possible outcome is when the folks you've penetrated don't even notice you did it."

"Well, I don't know what to say," Harmon said slowly. "I didn't sign on to bug hotel rooms. I didn't sign on to be a stenographer or a, you know, some kind of reference librarian."

"I wouldn't describe the job quite that way, Billy. But it's not usually supposed to be action-packed. Tell you what: Why don't you let this thing play out a little before you decide it's too boring to bother with? It might start holding your interest after all."

"All right," Harmon said, smiling stiffly.

"It's all right, huh?"

"Yeah," Harmon said. Then he smiled for real. "It's all right. AJF."

"AJF?" Laura said.

"Ask Jack first," Harmon explained. "It's my new number-one rule that Jack gave me. I'm sorry, Jack. I guess I got a little attack of initiative there for a minute, but I'm better now. You won't have any trouble with me this trip, I promise you."

"Good to hear."

"Ask Jack first," Laura said musingly.

"Yeah," Harmon said. "Like the man says. Anyway, what are my orders?"

"No orders just yet," Mallory said. "You're going to start doing what we're doing. Taking a vacation. We haven't got any work for you 'cause we don't have any ourselves. We're letting things develop. When our man moves, we're hoping we'll go with him, and you'll have to find a way to follow. Get Logistics to help. It's what they're there for. And when we're in his compound, whatever the hell that is, you might wind up seeing more of your kind of action than you ever dreamed of. Meanwhile, go get yourself a drink or something. You've earned it. And we'll be getting back to the, ah . . ."

"Whorehouse," Laura said.

"Laurie doesn't like it there," Mallory said, grinning. "Can't say it's my idea of heaven, either, but it keeps you entertained. All right now, scoot. You'll be getting our signal soon. And I'll say it again: You've done damn fine work."

"Thanks, Jack," Harmon said. "And I'll make sure I— Well, thanks."

When Harmon was gone, the two senior agents fell silent. Then Mallory said, "What do you think . . . Lily?"

"Don't make fun of him," Laura said. "Even you started out by the book."

"Point taken. You worried?"

"I thought he did an excellent job."

"I asked if you were worried."

"You mean, about his nerves?"

"Naw, I think they're all right."

"Or his training?"

"I guess that's okay, too."

"Or about whether he's got any God. Damn. Sense?"

"All right," Mallory said. "We're both worried."

9

Gone

In the four years Anders Becher had been driving for Cooper, he'd developed a reputation for dogged, methodical racing, and he'd been no less methodical than usual when he crashed that afternoon. He'd been just lifting off, neither early nor late, on the straight leading into Virage Tabac when the Renault in front had shed a defective mounting bolt, which had bounced along the Quai des États-Unis, the jagged end of the snapped shaft twinkling in the sun, and been sucked up into his right front brake drum. The wheel had locked at 148 miles per hour, and Becher's Cooper had entered Tabac upside down and rebounded off the Armco barriers and back into traffic. Only the deft work of the Lotus behind him had averted general calamity. Becher was a thirty-two-year-old native of Geneva, a solemn, quiet man with emphatic black brows. He'd married a black-browed woman from Ulm and fathered three black-browed children: a boy aged eight, a girl aged six, and another boy aged five, who liked to draw his father in a rocket-shaped car with flames shooting out the back. At twenty-eight minutes to 4:00, Becher was admitted to Nice's Hôpital St-Roche with a ruptured liver, multiple fractures of the ribs and right arm, and a right leg almost severed at midthigh. At a quarter past 4:00, preparations were begun to amputate it. Nineteen minutes later, Derek Reade turned in a lap time of 1:34.6 and was awarded pole position at the twenty-first Monaco Grand Prix.

Laura, Mallory, and Jespers were having an aperitif by the pool when the news came through. Jespers tut-tutted over Becher and shook Mallory's hand over Reade.

"This is very jolly, that your man has done so well," he said. "It makes Sunday nice and exciting. Well, I think we will finish our drinks now and then we will take a drive into town, where I have made arrangements, if you don't mind, for viewing the race with a little more convenience."

"Lil and me've got tickets for the grandstand," Mallory said. "I figured we already had it pretty well arranged."

"Oh, but you're forgetting what a lazy fellow I am, Jack, and how I like to be comfortable all the time. I've subleased a little flat in town on the Boulevard Albert, overlooking the finish line. So tonight we can stay there and tomorrow morning we can simply *roll* out of bed and sit comfortably on the balcony with a nice drink and maybe something to eat and watch the race in high *style*. And I am hoping you will both do me the favor, the *honor* to join me. In fact, it will be quite awkward if you do not, since I have already had your bags packed and sent there."

"Oh?" Laura said. "I hope you haven't creased my dresses."

Her ill humor was genuine, though she privately felt that the dresses Logistics had given her could only be improved by a little creasing.

Mallory said, "You sublet . . . Lord, Arne, how the hell'd you find somebody willing to leave town for Race Week?"

"Oh, they are not leaving," Jespers said cheerily. "They are watching from the grandstands and living in a very nice hotel in Menton, and with the money I have paid them to go and stay there for a night they can now buy a nice little cottage somewhere. I like little cottages, don't you? With a garden full of begonias and maybe a cat. It's a very happy outcome for everyone." Howie appeared at the door with a suitcase. "Ah, here is your bag that you came with, Jack. It has your gun in it, so I didn't send it away. I am afraid you would consider me a very rude host if I sent your gun away. I had Howie clean and reload it for you, and you may take it with you when we drive to town. Drink up, now, and we shall have a small dinner when we reach the flat. Roast duck. And roast *potatoes*."

"Sounds like you've got it planned," Mallory said.

"Yes," Laura said. "It does."

When they walked out onto the front lawn, the scene recalled a cross between a high-toned Army repple-depple and a circus caravan: crates of wine and wheels of cheese stood on the lawn beside two live ducks that had been tied to the base of a concrete urn and were quacking disconsolately, while a young bodyguard wheeled a motorcycle up a one-by-six plank into the bed of a truck, and a half-dressed young woman wandered by yawning, holding a flowered pillowcase full of clothes. A long Bentley had pulled up, and three of the cocaine addicts were arguing in very rapid Italian about who would sit where. Laura and Mallory wandered through the melee, tucked their suitcase into the trunk of the Via, and drove off almost unnoticed.

"You took all that very meekly," Laura said when they were on the road.

"Guess so," Mallory said. "Thought about arguing, but I was afraid he'd sic Milena on me. Besides."

"Besides what?"

"Besides, I like roast duck. It's the closest thing France's got to barbecue."

The address was a huge new apartment building on the corner of Rue Suffren-Reymond, the sort of up-to-date structure that had always looked to Laura like a cell block wrapped in marble. The apartment Jespers had sublet was equally charmless. It was immense and labyrinthine, and Laura guessed someone had created it by knocking together two three-bedroom flats. Whoever it was had furnished it in very expensive bad taste. Bits of red-blond Danish modern elbowed their way past dark, ornate chests in black oak. Jagged bronze lamps teetered on little chrome-and-ivory tables. On the walls hung lumpy abstract canvases that seemed to have been painted in oatmeal, marmalade, and soot. She found she'd been given a room to herself. Doubtless, after last night, this was Jespers's idea of tact. Her trunks had been lined up beside her room's single bed. The paperback Nero Wolfe she'd been reading had been, she presumed, tucked away in one of them, but there was no way to tell which. She gazed at the row of trunks bleakly, gave up, and wandered out to explore.

The apartment did have one virtue: a long terrace, ugly in itself, which commanded a glorious view of the harbor, the finish line, the mouth of the tunnel, and four of the circuit's most dramatic corners. She slipped through a set of sliding glass doors and leaned on the dank cement balustrade. A faint breeze puffed at her face and was gone, leaving behind the mixed scents of scorched rubber, auto exhaust, and the ocean. She thought about the young Swiss driver who had crashed. He was rumored to be losing a leg. Probably he was on an operating table at that moment. Though she hadn't spent as much time in them as Jack, she was tolerably well acquainted with hospitals and ORs, with the lights that were somehow both bright and dingy, with the ineffable subtle coldness of the air and the feeling of lying helpless in the hands of strangers. Becher was a name without a face to her. He was not a leading driver, and she was only sketchily familiar with his career. And yet she felt a kinship with him, the kinship that exists between all professionals who earn their pay by putting their lives in jeopardy. The race was over for Becher, and presumably his career with it. She wondered what one-legged ex–Grand Prix drivers did. She hoped he'd salted a bit of prize money away. She had no idea what it was like to be short of money, any more than she knew what it was like to be short a leg, but she doubted it was agreeable. She hoped he had a nice wife, someone to take care of him. The day had turned cloudy. A low gray sky pressed down on the glistening yachts and, beyond the little twin lighthouses, on the flat gray sea. Laura Morse was a woman who enjoyed her own company and was used to working solo, but all at once she found herself piercingly lonely. She wished she were sitting down with Jack somewhere, discussing tactics and evaluating odds. She wished she had a job of work to do. She wanted someone to attack her, to attack Jack, to pull out a gun and start shooting; she wanted a threat to neutralize, an enemy to vanquish. Failing that, she wanted to be home, on her own living-room sofa, with a cup of strong tea and a good book. An old paperback crime novel, say, like the well-thumbed Nero Wolfe that was locked away somewhere in one of those god-damned trunks.

A movement caught her eye, and she turned just in time to see Jack and Jespers disappearing into a study, holding cigars. Jack hadn't seemed to see her, though she'd been standing silhouetted against the late-afternoon sun, well within the range of his quite acute peripheral vision.

The door closed behind them with a click.

In the kitchen, one of the ducks let out a piteous screech and was abruptly silent.

Laura walked back to her room and lay down on her single bed. The bedside clock read twenty minutes to five. *Five minutes,* she thought, then, *The hell with it.* She rolled onto her left hip and closed her eyes.

Like all of the Consultancy's field agents, Laura Morse had been trained to take advantage of fleeting opportunities for sleep, and so sleep came quickly for her, as it always did. But it brought little rest. She seemed to be navigating through shifting planes of dim gray light. It was an exhausting process that required her to remain silent and to hold still for long periods while somewhere a hidden mechanism let out a series of deafening roars. Though she couldn't see it, she knew what the mechanism looked like: a sort of inverted chandelier that gave off great heat, like a steam engine, and spun dizzyingly fast. It was bad news that it was spinning so fast. It meant that she'd failed to control her breathing. She was making stupid mistakes. She was letting herself get rattled, like an amateur. She found a winding path along the waterfront, and the scent of the ocean gave her courage. *As long as you can still find your way to the sea,* she thought, *things can't be as bad as all that.* And soon the machine was spinning more and more slowly, and then it was coasting to a halt, and then it was still, the orange flames dimming, the barbed brass arms cooling, and then she rolled onto her back and found herself awake. For a while she lay motionless, breathing deeply. Her throat and belly seemed cool and sensitive. It was as if someone had been lying naked beside her, skin to skin, and he had just gotten up from the bed. She was naked now herself. She scanned the row of absurd, hulking trunks, then swung her feet to the floor, rose, and walked barefoot around them. Behind the trunks lay a corner of her own apartment back in Newton, with an old brass standing lamp, a curtained window, and a claw-footed paisley sofa that had been in her family for three generations, moving from one side of town to the other every thirty years. Jack was sitting on the sofa. He was naked, too, and reading an immense book. The corners of its pages were attached to metal rings, which in turn were attached to the binding by a system of cloth straps. You pulled on the rings to turn the pages. It was a manual of regulations for Formula One racing, issued by the Federation Internationale de l'Automobile on the Place de la Concorde, and Jack was deeply engrossed in it. She sat down beside him and, without looking up from his reading, he raised an arm so that she could snuggle under it and against his ribs. It was a familiar sensation, snuggling against his ribs. She had been doing it for years. She belonged there. It was not clear whether they were married or simply had been lovers for a very long time; she could not recall whether they had been lying in bed after making love or simply taking an afternoon nap together. He let his hand fall, cupped her shoulder in his palm, and murmured, "What's the matter, hon? Couldn't you sleep?" It seemed a kind thing to say. It seemed the kindest thing anyone had ever said to her. Tears came to her eyes, and as she blinked them back, she caught sight of a sluggish movement in the other room. Through the doorway, she saw that she was still lying alone in her single bed in Monte Carlo. Or, anyway, that someone was lying in her bed—someone thin, blonde, young, nude. Someone whose face was averted and could not be seen. *It might not even be me,* she thought. *It could be anyone. It could be anyone without a face.*

She jerked awake and then, with a panicky grunt, sat up.

The bedside clock read a quarter to six. She rubbed her hands over her face, as if to make certain it was still there. She felt real tears in her eyes. She was in her rumpled single bed in Monte Carlo, dressed in slacks and a sweat-dampened sleeveless jersey, beside that row of huge absurd trunks she was still too exhausted to open.

She rose quickly, as one does when one is afraid of relapsing into a nightmare, and stood panting lightly, her hands on her hips, willing herself calm. She couldn't have said which disturbed her more: the moment of vertigo when she'd seemed to stand outside herself as if watching a stranger sleep, or the lost sweetness of being Jack's woman—a thoughtful Jack, a bookish Jack, a Jack who, she fully recognized, did not happen to exist. She touched the skin beneath her eyes. *Like a lovesick teenager,* she thought. *A hysterical little girl. What the hell, Morse, do you call this? Harmon might have some excuse for getting into a swivet on this trip. He hasn't had much experience. You have. Shape up, Morse. Shape up, or admit you're no longer fit for the job.* She slipped the jersey over her head, unhooked her damp brassiere, and stepped out of her slacks and panties. She found a wicker laundry hamper in the corner and dropped her clothes inside. A quick cold shower was always a good way to reset one's gyroscope. So was a good look in the mirror: the sight of panic or distress on one's own face had a useful distancing effect. She stepped into the tiny bathroom adjoining her room and closed the door.

Leaning with her palms on the sink, she studied her reflection. Field agents, like actors, must know for professional reasons precisely how they look to others, and Laura felt she had a fairly clear idea of her appearance. The face that met her gaze was narrow, delicately made, and unusually beautiful. The slate-blue eyes were slightly close-set over the high cheekbones; the long nose was as fine as the spout of a Limoges teapot, though infinitely straighter; the mouth was wide but dainty and, without lipstick, quite pale. It was, she knew, a forbidding rather than an inviting beauty. Laura Morse looked humorless to most people; humorless, sexless, and joyless. Ronnie Fellowes of London Station had dubbed her La Remorse. The long, slim body that was so glamorous in clothes looked frail and meager without them. It had aroused, along with desire, fiercely protective feelings in the few men she'd taken to bed. She pretended to be amused by this, but the truth was that she greatly enjoyed being treated as if she needed protecting.

Perhaps she depended on it. She'd had few lovers, and had permitted none of them to touch her often, not because sex did not move her, but because it moved her too much. She was feeling a bit better now. She no longer felt quite so much like a doomed figure in a tragic drama. She was feeling more like a scrawny, naked twenty-nine-year-old with a mild headache and a preposterous suntan. Dear God, was that tan awful. It looked as if she'd applied blackface to her entire body for some sort of pornographic minstrel show. Her girlish breasts gleamed darkly, seeming even smaller and sharper. She was sure that her un-tanned buttocks, if she could see them, would be glaring like a pair of floodlamps. The air was heavy, humid. It seemed to cling to her. The dream clung to her as well, and the sense of a world that was double, tricky, wrong. She splashed cool water on her face to rinse the dream away, but she couldn't dispel the idea that there had been some signifi-cance in it: the thick book of Grand Prix regulations, the faceless figure on the bed, the shuddering of the hidden machine. Her body was still taut and lively with arousal, with the imagined passage of Jack's hands, with the hardness of his scarred ribs against her breasts. Her nipples were painfully stiff. She was sure that if Arne Jespers were with her, he'd have something to say about the way she smelled. She tried laugh-ing at the thought and almost succeeded. Shaking her head, she pulled a towel from the rack and dried her face, and as she did so, began to be aware of a commotion somewhere outside. She did not hear it yet; it was too distant to be properly heard; it was something she merely sensed. And then she did hear it: the rumbling of agitated male voices. She dropped the towel, walked briskly from the bathroom, yanked open a trunk at random, and began dressing with astonishing speed in the first clothes that came to hand: a pair of peach bikini bottoms—she couldn't see where they'd packed her panties—a lacy black brassiere, a beige sundress that was not suitable for evening and through which, she was vaguely aware, the black bra would probably be visible. She slipped on a pair of canvas deck shoes; they didn't go, either, but she'd be able to move fast in them. She was just putting on her lipstick when Mallory's footsteps approached the door. Then two firm raps.

"Come in," she said.

His face was grim as he stepped inside. "Grab your purse."

It was already in her hand.

"Reade," she said.

It was not a question. She was wide awake now.

Mallory nodded. He said, "Gone."

Mallory had seen Laurie, he considered, more ways than most men ever got to see most women. He'd seen her after twenty hours of interrogation in a dockside cargo container in Lisbon, and he'd seen her lying face-down in an Arkansas soy field, waiting for execution at the hands of a psychotic Okie gunrunner. He'd seen her after three straight days and nights of wakefulness in the German Hospital in Istanbul. He'd seen her ready to perish of hypothermia in the winter waters of Japan's North Sea, and he'd seen her with a Russian 7.65 bullet between her ribs and a fine froth of blood on her lips. (Gray, who had a fair bit of capital riding, in part, on Laurie's good looks, had spent a fair bit more to have the scar erased by Swedish cosmetic surgeons, though if you knew where to look you could see it even through her new suntan—a small, ragged oval under one breast, with the faint dead gleam of shark hide.) Mallory had seen Laurie freshly escaped from a Stasi holding pen, muttering and staggering through a fabric warehouse near the Karl-Marx-Allee with a skinful of sodium pentothal and both eyes swollen almost shut, but he wasn't sure he'd ever seen her like she was that night in Monte Carlo—absentminded, just plain not paying attention to the job—and he wondered what in the hell was wrong with her.

In the beginning, she'd seemed fine. Burch was telling them how he'd last seen Reade that afternoon in a scrum of jostling reporters. Reade was getting the kind of attention any driver receives when he gets pole at a Grand Prix, and especially at Monaco, where overtaking is rare and grid position is critical. Burch had been getting a fair amount of attention himself, and then there had been the photos: the two of them pretending to examine a stopwatch together, or taking turns pointing at the pit board. And there had been, as Burch pointed out, ladies around, dear sweet God had there been ladies, like a school of bloody piranhas, and finally Burch had said, right, had told the lot of 'em, right, that's enough, that'll do, and sent Reade off to the Naughton caravan for a debriefing and a bit of a natter with the rest of the team. He'd seen the vain little git plow off away through the crowd of bints, and he'd seen the caravan's door open and close, but when he'd gone inside, Reade hadn't been there. In fact, him plowing through that crowd of bints, that was the last anyone had seen of him. "I wash my hands of him," Burch said. "I wash my hands. He must be out there. I'll find the little bastard and drag him in by the scruff, I'll *murder* him. I couldn't go out there. I couldn't face 'em. All laughing at me. Can't manage his bloody driver. Make a bloody fool of us. Make us all a mockery. You wouldn't mind having a look, Jack, would you, a quick look round? Quick hunt round the bars? Must be with some woman. Must be. I'll kill him. I'll murder the little git. Be very grateful to you, Jack. See what you can do, can't you?"

This had been precisely what Mallory had had in mind, and Laura had seemed all right while he and she were deciding whether to bring Harmon in. They figured they'd better leave him be. A call to the Lucien would be insecure, and their contact protocol was tight but sort of time-consuming. Best not to risk it for anything but an operational necessity. Certainly not for something as goofy as a damn-fool bet, especially since there was always the possibility that Reade's disappearance had been staged to finesse them into prematurely activating—and perhaps compromising—their local network. It would have been a fairly basic ploy, maybe too basic for Kendrick, but there was no sense in taking the chance.

No, Laura had been okay up until then. In fact, he wasn't quite sure when she'd started to get that look—that blank, blackjacked look, like a sulky teenage girl who's tired of listening to the grown-ups talk. On any other woman's face, that look would have bored Mallory. On Laurie's face, it shocked him. They'd started their hunt at the Chatham, of course. It was a neat, near-shabby all-day bar set along the climb to Casino Square, run by a couple named Rose and Jean-Louis Bernard. Its regulars called it Rosie's, and it had long been Monaco's central gathering place for those who loved racing. The walls were lined with photos of the drivers and mechanics who drank there, and the winners of past Monaco Grand Prix, and with plaques and thumbtacked postcards addressed to Rosie or Jean-Louis, postmarked from all over Europe and Asia and signed with legendary names. Rosie wasn't at the bar, but her husband was, with his broad, bristling mustache and his little-boy haircut. Mallory had stopped in on his first night in Monaco, and Jean-Louis had taken a shine to him. "Your man," he had told Laurie, "does not talk. He is not a man who talks in bars. Your man is a man. Do you understand me?" Laurie had said that she did.

Tonight, Jean-Louis was scandalized at the thought that a driver of Reade's stature would be in his bar the night before the first race of the season. "We all know that Derek can be a bit . . ." He raised his palm and wobbled it. "Where a young woman is concerned. And there is so often a young woman concerned. But tonight? I would not serve him, Jack. How could I? May my hand drop off my wrist if I would serve him. I would give him a glass of warm milk and beg him to go to bed. Probably he is home in bed at this moment. Jack, he is a driver! I am sure you are mistaken."

"To be mistaken, Jean-Louis," Mallory said, "would be a big happiness to me." He paused to marshal his French. "But I fear . . . If it is possible that you have a word with the regulars, who might know where he goes, a very small quiet word . . ." By this point, Laurie, whose French was flawless, would ordinarily have leapt in to rescue him. Tonight she seemed to be thinking of something else.

"Of course quiet," Jean-Louis assured them.

Mallory looked around. Laurie was gazing at the photos of drivers and their cars. "We will inquire of those who are in the bar a little, if it is good with you," he said, speaking as much to her as to Jean-Louis.

Laura looked at Mallory as if trying to remember where she'd seen him before.

One of the regulars thought they might have seen Reade at the Tip-Top, so off they went. It was packed when they got there, and they split up to work it separately. When Laurie reappeared at his side after ten minutes, Mallory was struck again by that odd faraway look in her eyes. "Oscar's," she said drably, though perhaps no more drably than usual.

"You okay?" he asked.

She said, "Fine."

At Oscar's, a Newport yacht broker thought he might have seen Reade leaving the Beau Rivage, and at that august institution they met a Dominican jute-planter's daughter who could have sworn she'd seen him sitting just inside the entrance of a plush little bar off the Boulevard de Suisse, and from there they were sent to other, lesser-known bars, farther from the harbor, and from there to a series of hotel suites in Monte Carlo and La Condamine. Sometimes they were met with polite bafflement, sometimes with incredulity at the thought that a leading driver would be engaged in a pub crawl on the eve of a major race, and sometimes they were told they'd just missed him: by an hour, by a couple of hours, by ten minutes. And each time, it was Mallory who made the inquiries, while Laura stood at his elbow and seemed to be waiting politely for him to be finished.

The streets grew steadily louder and more difficult to navigate. It was the night of the Poseurs' Grand Prix. The Saturday evening before each year's race, it had become a tradition for well-to-do tourists to parade through Casino Square in their expensive sports cars. There were Maseratis, Ferraris, Fiats, Triumphs, Shelby Cobras, Aston-Martins, MGs, Lancias, Jaguars, and a low-slung, knifelike something called a Lamborghini, which had been introduced earlier that year and was known to burn up roads, gasoline, and money with equal profligacy. The cars crept along at a walking pace, their drivers and passengers waving out the windows as if to cheering crowds. One gentleman was seated on the rear deck of a red Corvette Stingray convertible, dressed in what seemed to be his idea of a driver's costume: a silk scarf, swimmer's goggles, and a Green Bay Packers' helmet. He was blowing kisses to the female passersby. It was a pretty mixed crowd on the pavement: Brazilian gamblers with tense smiles and ruby stickpins, Arab oil sheiks in snowy head scarves and sumptuous Savile Row suits, a smattering of third-tier stars and starlets—down the coast, the Cannes Film Festival had just ended—and a fair number of young women who possessed the physical qualifications to be starlets but whose likely occupation was somewhat humbler. There was a lot of carefully tanned skin on display, and a lot of beautifully trimmed gray mustaches. Mallory guessed most everybody had a pretty decent glow on, though it was all fairly prim by Texas standards. A couple had stepped over the iron fence surrounding the lawn in front of the Paris and were decorously necking between the diamond-shaped flower beds. Along the curving row of boutiques on Massenet, among the motor-themed window displays, a lone drunk crouched beside a revolving watch in an illumined glass display case, trying to tell the time as it spun by. The night was unseasonably cool and damp, and Mallory couldn't help noticing that the air was thick with gathering rain.

They got the tip they were looking for on a yacht out in the harbor, where many of the evening's most exclusive parties were held. They didn't have an invitation, but that was all right. Women with Laurie's looks seldom needed one. She was still off in the clouds someplace, though every now and again she'd seem to look Mallory over, head to toe, as if she'd never seen him before. By now, Mallory was worried. Laurie still had that dead, inward-turned, almost sullen look. She made him think of a high school kid at a sock hop who wants to ask a girl to dance and doesn't have the guts to do anything but stand around looking bored. If he hadn't known her better, he'd have thought she was trying to work her nerve up to do or say something she was scared of, but that didn't make sense—he'd never met anyone whose nerve needed less working up than Laurie's. The damp air put a halo around the harborside lights. They were like bright, spreading stains. The black water below them looked clear and clean, and Mallory wanted to bathe his face in it. They threaded their way between a few dancers on the stern deck and climbed down three steps into the main cabin. Everyone there seemed very young. "Reade?" said a jovial bald man a bit older than the others. He shook his head, either admiringly or pityingly, it was hard to tell. "Old Reade. I guess you'd better talk to Becky over there about old Reade."

Becky proved to be a dour-looking girl in a backless dress, sitting on the lap of a fat, amiable young man in a shimmering shantung suit. Judging by the cut of her frock, she was not fond of foundation garments. Judging by the way she sat, she hadn't been to Miss Porter's. Her shining brunette hair spilled over one hazel eye. Through the other, she regarded Mallory without favor. "He's a bastard," she said. "Who're you, anyway?"

"My name's Jack."

"He's a smirky short little bastard anyway. He's a pervert. I don' wanna talk to you."

The fat man smiled. "You want to talk to everyone, Becky," he said, stroking her hip. "It's why we love you so."

"You're all bastard perverts," she said, squirming away from his hand and almost overbalancing. He steadied her with his forearm. "What's wrong with me, anyway?"

"Not a thing that I can see, hon," Mallory said. "He must just be a pervert, like you say. Know where he went?"

"He liked me," she said. "He came in with them, but he was liking me. But I guess he liked them better."

"Liked who, hon?"

"Both of 'em," she said.

"What a rotten little ponce, boy," the young man said without heat. "I was all starstruck when he came in, but *really*. I guess I'd be pretty sick along about now if I were a Naughton fan. You're slipping again, sweetie," he said, and adjusted Becky's shoulder strap. "You ought to make up your mind to either keep this dress on or take it off."

"Sure," she said. "That's what you're all hoping."

"Derek doesn't have much good sense, hon," Mallory said. "That's why his friends need to look after him. Who was with him, Becky?"

"They *both* were," she said impatiently. "And he liked me anyway. But then he liked them better again. Blondes. What's so great about being a blonde?"

"Nothing," Laura said. It was the first thing she'd said for half an hour.

"Nothing," the girl agreed. "It's just that if a guy comes in here, comes in here and acts like he likes—"

Laura took hold of the girl's face and brought her own close to it. The blankness of her slate-blue gaze did not alter. "Becky," she said, her voice quiet but so clear that it cut through the din of the party. "We know the Twins were here with Derek Reade. We know they took him away again. Tell us where they took him. Now."

"Sally Lou's," the girl said, her voice abruptly distinct. The hazel eye was huge and terrified.

"Thank you, Becky," Laura said, and stood upright again.

Becky's face crumpled. She reached up and touched Laura's hair.

"Pretty," she whispered, "you're all so pretty," and twin tears slid down her cheeks.

The bald man provided Sally Lou's address with a brief laugh and no surprise whatsoever. Mallory knew what the place would be like before he got there. It would be on a quiet, prosperous residential street. The neighborhood would be almost but not quite perfectly nice, and the house would be the nicest-looking thing in it. It would be "legendary," it would be a "meeting place for artists and statesmen," it would be mentioned, in fact, in the racier guidebooks, and a certain percentage of its business would come from middle-class couples who thought they were adventurous and who'd sit chastely in the anteroom and have a few astonishingly expensive drinks with Sally Lou. Sally Lou's real name, of course, would be Sophie-Louisa or Soledad or Song Li, and she wouldn't be American any more than she'd be a native of wherever she happened to do business. She'd just think an American name gave the place a cosmopolitan air. It would be the one vulgar thing about her. She would be polished, warmly welcoming, coldly intelligent, and possessed of either startling ugliness or "the remains of a once-great beauty," and be dressed with enviable chic and just a fraction too much impeccably applied makeup, and her clientele would love to tell each other what a lady she was and what a lovely voice she had. Mallory had been taken to places like this in a dozen cities in Europe and Asia and every damn one of them was the same. In the event, the place was pretty much what Mallory expected, except that Sally Lou's makeup was actually pretty sparing and her voice was sort of harsh. She was a petite, dark, finely made woman in her sixties whose back had already begun to hunch. She looked up at Mallory with the greatest sorrow. "If only I could assist you," she said with a faint Central European accent. "But unfortunately I am unacquainted with your friend."

They were speaking English. Mallory figured Sally Lou was way too busy to have to fool with his French.

"I understand, ma'am," Mallory said. "I know your guests expect a little discretion from you—sort of rely on it. In fact, I guess we're sort of relying on it, too."

"I don't understand," she said, not sounding particularly puzzled.

"It would be pretty unpleasant, wouldn't it? If Reade were to show up here the night before the race. 'Specially if he'd gotten himself to where he was in no shape to drive tomorrow. That'd be pretty bad for the team and, I've got to say, not too good for the house, either. Wouldn't you think?"

"I appreciate your concern," she said coolly, "for the reputation of this establishment."

"So I was thinking," Mallory continued, "that if Reade were to wind up here tonight somehow—not saying he's here, you know, just saying that he might sooner or later be by—then you and me would have a common interest in handling the thing nice and quiet. Maybe we could discuss it a little? Just in case?"

At the word *discuss*, Sally Lou's eyes brightened.

Mallory folded his hands on the polished walnut table between them, and Sally Lou pressed them sympathetically in hers. When she did so, they crackled softly.

She withdrew her own hands and composedly counted the roll of bills in them. With each bill, Sally Lou's face grew softer. By the time she'd counted off the last, her expression was tender, and she gently tidied the edges of the stack of francs, tucked it into her purse, and closed it with a click.

"It is as you say, Mr. Carroll," she said, her eyes large and tragic. "You are a man of understanding, a polished young man, and it grieves me to say that we do in fact have business to discuss. Would you both please come with me?"

The front room of Sally Lou's looked like somebody's rich great-aunt's parlor, and the girls in it were fashionably dressed. Their dresses might have been on the skimpy side, and they might have shared Becky's views on underwear—though they sat a lot more like ladies—but if you squinted, you might just be able to pretend you were at a party somewhere. The back room, though, was decorated like a minia-ture nightclub, and the girls wore nothing but earrings and high heels. Some of them were posing on a sort of little runway, so guys could make their selection, and some were dancing with other guys, old-fashioned dancing to ballroom music coming from a concealed speaker some-where, and in the middle of the room was the biggest bathtub Mallory ever saw, full of girls who'd shucked off their shoes and wore nothing now but soap bubbles and gooseflesh. They were pretending to scrub each other with loofahs and rinsing each other off with silver pitchers and running their hands up and down their own legs as if straightening the stockings they weren't wearing. They were being damn careful to keep their hairdos dry. They looked as if they thought they were missing something good on TV.

It was all pretty dismal, all right, and Mallory expected Laurie to keep her eyes front and center, the way she'd done at Jespers's place, but what she was doing instead was staring. She was just plain staring around the room, still sort of absentminded, but sad, too, at the big girls and little girls and pale girls and dark girls and top-heavy girls and bottom-heavy girls and skinny, leggy, Laurie-shaped girls. Not for the first time, Mallory wondered whether Laurie favored women. Maybe that's why she was such a damn sourpuss. He personally didn't mind much what people got up to in bed, but it struck him that a girl who could only fall for other girls was in for a rocky time of it. When you came right down to it, what did he actually know about Laurie? He knew how she handled herself in the field, all right, but what did he know about her life, about what she liked and didn't, what she did when she wasn't working, what was actually on her mind? The three of them stepped into a small, open-front elevator in the rear and rose to the third floor. They were all wedged in together. Sally Lou smelled like a powder sachet and Laurie gave off a surprising amount of heat. They stepped out onto a wide, thickly carpeted corridor set with brass-handled doors on either sides. The doors were old and thick, and you couldn't hear much through them. The little you could hear didn't seem to be helping Laurie's mood. Sally Lou unlocked the second door from the end and inclined her head like a funeral director, and he and Laurie went inside.

The bed in the center of the room was an enormous, lace-curtained four-poster, and the man who lay in the center seemed smaller than ever. Derek Reade was not smirking now. His face was slack and pale, the strong nose bloodless. He looked not asleep but dead. His shirt was missing and his trousers were undone; one shoe dangled half-unlaced from his stocking toes. Laurie moved unhesitatingly to the bed, lay three fingers against his throat, and then lowered her nose to within an inch of his open lips. She rose with a wry face and sat on the edge of the mattress.

"Chloral-based, I'd say," she offered. "Maybe a touch of scopolamine."

"A mickey," Mallory said.

"A very strong one. His pulse is steady but way down, and his temperature's pretty low. He'll be out another eight hours at least, and I doubt he'll be on his feet before teatime."

"And rain's coming on."

"And rain's coming on," she agreed.

"A mickey. In this house. I am desolated," Sally Lou said, and seemed to mean it. "I am entirely to blame. I should have known those two little ones were rotten. Mr. Reade came in with two little blonde girls, perfect, lovely, as alike as two shiny new centimes. I knew that they were rotten but I was greedy, and I have received my—retribution. Mademoiselle, monsieur, I am at your disposal. My nephew, a very large, sturdy fellow, is in the kitchen; I can summon another, equally strong, in five minutes. The gentleman would, for them, be a trivial burden. There is a back staircase, and I can provide a closed car with a trustworthy driver. My friends in the Deuxième Bureau inform me that the house phones may be used with reasonable confidence. If you can aid us in resolving this matter with discretion, I promise you the friendship of the house, and the gratitude of"—her eyes flicked delicately between the two of them—"of all who work here."

"We'll try and not let you down," Mallory said. "Could you leave us alone here for a minute?"

"Certainly," Sally Lou said, and bowed herself out the door.

When the lock had clicked behind her, Mallory turned to Laurie. "Well," she said dully, "this doesn't seem as complicated as all that. Or am I—"

"Forget about Reade a minute."

"All right."

"Reade's not going anywhere. I'm not worried about Reade right now. I'm worried about you. Listen, hon, what's up? What the hell's wrong with you tonight?"

"With me? I wasn't—"

"You been stumbling along like somebody sandbagged you. You been acting like you're drunk or half-asleep. I know all the waiting around's been hard on you, but this isn't just that. Something's on your mind and you're not telling me what and you're doing a piss-poor job of hiding it. All right, then," Mallory said. "I'm still lead on this job, and we're still working by my rules. And I say you don't get to keep secrets on this run. So I'll ask you again: What's on your mind?"

Laurie gazed steadily into his eyes. He was aware, again, of the heat of her slender body.

"All right, Jack," she said softly. "I'll tell you."

10

Kendrick Insists

Arne Jespers had been an insomniac all his life. It was not, he considered, an unpleasant affliction. He required little sleep, and rather enjoyed being awake while others were snoring; he liked seeing and hearing and thinking things no one else was around to share. He thought most clearly and fluently in the small hours. There was less around to distract one. He was, he knew, a very easily, a very *readily* distracted man. As a small child he'd spied on his parents during the night, and when they died he'd spied on the other children in the orphanage, and in this way he had often been able to acquire useful bits of knowledge that would improve his situation when daylight came. He'd learned to steal in the quiet hours of sleeplessness. He'd gotten some of his favorite things that way, and learned to hide them. Sleeplessness had been a treasure house for Arne Jespers. The private wakeful hours were like secret late-night treats sneaked from the cupboard, just for him, and in fact these days he sometimes crept down to the kitchen in the hours before dawn, one of his fine new kitchens with all the appliances, and made himself a nice sandwich.

Tonight he'd made a nice *big* sandwich, a highly *miscellaneous* sandwich, a sandwich that would probably horrify his chefs. Herring in wine sauce, big round disks of raw onion, gobs of chutney, slices of Emmenthaler cheese, some sauerkraut, some slivers of cold roast duck, a few chunks of cold sausage from breakfast, all on two thick slabs of pumpernickel. It was a gross sandwich, a disgusting sandwich—and he was enjoying it thoroughly, wandering the halls as he munched, leaving dribbles of sauerkraut juice behind him. The only thing the sandwich lacked was bacon. Perhaps he'd wake someone up and have them fry some bacon. He stepped through the sliding glass doors and leaned his elbows on the balcony railing, looking at the yachts in the harbor as he ate, dropping bits of sausage and onion into the Boulevard Albert below. He was very happy. Tomorrow was the first Grand Prix of the season. It was the best day of the year, a day better than Christmas—his childhood Christmases hadn't really been so good—and he'd found a way to make it still better: it would be a Grand Prix that would bring him fifty thousand American dollars. For his nostrils were full of the fragrance of oncoming rain.

Oncoming rain, and—he sniffed deeply—something else. Something pleasant, something *luscious*. What? Not the cheese, the nice stinky cheese; not the Bermuda onion, that clean, sharp, almost sweaty onion; not the rich, sweet duck; not the freshly paved roadway below; not the rope, tar, brass polish, damp canvas, and diesel fuel of the harborfront; not the lovely cool sea with the lovely expensive boats on it, winking sleepily in the moonlight, all white and long and shiny; but something in between the sweetness of the duck and the salt of the sea, something . . .

He stopped chewing and listened. The flat was carpeted everywhere. It was that kind of place, that ugly, modern, *deluxe* sort of place. But he could hear the faintest, the very faintest rhythmic creaking down the hallway, as if of tiny leather straps, flexing. And then a delicate clack-clack on the kitchen linoleum. And the scrape of a bottle along a counter, the ping of crystal . . . He swallowed the last of the sandwich, wiped his fingers on his shirt, and moved, in utter silence, back through the glass doors.

No one in the library, no one in the dining room, and then he rounded the corner and caught sight of her. She was wandering unsteadily down the shadowed hall that led to the guest bedrooms, her back to him: a darkly tanned young woman, wheat-blonde and almost too thin, holding two champagne flutes and a bottle and dressed, quite charmingly, in nothing at all but earrings and high heels. The shoes bore silver lamé rosettes. Their straps creaked faintly as she walked. Her white buttocks shone in the dimness like dear little lamps. *Ah,* Jespers thought fondly, *the young aristocrat. She's grown weary of her coldness. She and Jack have mended their quarrel. If I spoke right now—if I offered politely to chill her champagne—how delicious to see her jump, to spin round, her hair flying, to see the look on her face . . . But actually, no. It's nicer like this. It makes a nicer memory. How lovely she is. How drunk she is. Well, let the young people be happy.* He savored the universal scent of female arousal as she disappeared into Mallory's room. *Even dead drunk she walks like a lady,* he thought wistfully. *What a lucky fellow Jack is.*

Mallory woke to the sound of revving engines. He guessed it was about 5:30 a.m. Three hours of sleep, round about. It would have to do. He listened harder and didn't hear rain. He felt it, though, hanging in the air, waiting. He looked down at the slender, silent figure at his side. She'd gotten the sheet twisted around her head and was hidden from about the fourth rib up. In the darkness, her suntan was almost black against the white sheets. He stroked a palm over the finely modeled ribs of her back and the delicate ridge of her spine, over her perfect little white heinie and the shadowy cleft between. She made an indistinct meowing noise and, catlike, pressed her tail end against his hand. He found he was ready to take her again, just as she was, asleep and half wrapped in the sheet, but that probably wasn't a good idea. She'd be awake then, and he wasn't sure either of them was really ready for the conversation they'd have when they were awake. He wasn't usually bashful about mornings after, but this one seemed a little complicated.

He took a long last look at the unwrapped half of her and thought of those long, patrician legs locked shuddering around his back. The world, he thought, was a pretty remarkable place. He swung his feet to the floor and padded to the bathroom, all without making a sound. It was one of those times covert-services training comes in handy.

In the bathroom he pressed a towel against the nozzle of the faucet and then turned it on slowly. When enough warm water had soaked into the towel, he turned off the tap, scrubbed the towel over his face and torso, and slipped it into the hamper. He dried himself with a clean one and put on a lick of deodorant. Hopefully he'd find time for a shower later on. Back in the bedroom, he dressed quickly and noiselessly in tan slacks and a yellow polo shirt. He chose them from the two dresser drawers he knew would open silently. He put his wallet and keys in his pocket, slipped on a pair of moccasins, and took another last look at the woman on the bed. Gingerly, he drew the sheet down over her hindquarters and most of those legs. There wasn't enough sheet to cover all of them. Then he eased out of the room.

He closed the door quietly behind him and listened. Silence from inside. Silence all through the enormous apartment. But from down the hall, out on the terrace, Jespers's voice, speaking too quietly to be understood.

Jespers was the last man in the world Mallory wanted to see right now.

He turned and walked deliberately toward the voice.

Out on the long concrete balcony he found Jespers sitting with Kendrick on a couple of webbed nylon chairs, American-style mugs of coffee in their hands. Between them stood a small glass table bearing a long loaf of bread with a serrated knife stuck in it, a smeared block of butter, a couple of jars of jam, a pot of coffee, and one empty mug. "Good morning, Jack," Jespers said.

"Morning," Mallory said.

"You are up admirably early. I'm afraid you've had a trying night. Here, have a little coffee. We are both sitting here being wakeful. Come and be wakeful with us."

Kendrick nodded in a fairly neighborly way, filled the last mug, and passed it over. Mallory only had Harmon's word for it that the man could talk at all. He reached out one of those massive arms, snagged a chair between two fingers, and drew it close with a grating noise. Mallory nodded and sat.

They sipped their coffee and looked out to sea.

"Your friend is still sleeping?" Jespers said.

"She had a long night, too," Mallory said.

"Indeed. And so we shall let her sleep." Jespers smiled sadly. "You found our poor Derek?"

"We found him."

"I am afraid you placed your trust in a rather frail vessel."

"Looks like I did."

"You will notice that I do not insult you by suggesting you trusted *me*. I am sure you are too astute to have done any such thing."

"I haven't given much thought to whether you're trustworthy, Arne."

"And now?"

"I can still think of more interesting things to worry about."

"You're not having any bread and jam. It's very good."

"It looks good," Mallory said. He bent, cut a thick slice, and began to butter it.

"If you wish, I will release you from the terms of our wager."

"Coffee's still nice and hot," Mallory said, buttering. "How'd you like the rest of it in your lap?"

Kendrick smiled faintly. Jespers looked down at his slacks. They were dotted with crumbs and stains, some old, some fresh. He regarded them with surprise and began trying to brush them away. "You would ruin my outfit," he said.

Mallory bit into the buttered bread. It was good. It felt good to eat. He wondered why he ever wasted his time on liquor when bread and butter were so good. He took a spoon and dabbled on a little orange marmalade.

Almost shyly, Jespers said, "The wager, you still agree to it?"

"Yeah," Mallory said, his mouth full. He wondered whether he was just being pigheaded. He didn't think so. He didn't much care.

"Mr. Coney is a gifted young man," Jespers said musingly. "And it has not yet begun to rain. All kinds of things are quite possible. Perhaps you'll take my money after all, and that shall be a good lesson to me. I'm hungry. I'm too hungry for bread and jam. Mr. Kendrick, go wake a cook and have him make us some omelettes." Kendrick took a last swallow of coffee and stood. "Have breakfast with us, Jack."

Mallory took a swallow himself and set his mug down. "No thanks, Arne," he said. "Think I'll go down and see how Naughton's getting on. They'll have something to eat at the garage." He began to rise.

Kendrick's touch was so gentle that, for an instant, Mallory was almost unaware of it. Then he felt an immense weight on his shoulders, bearing him inexorably downward, and then he was sitting again, unable to stand, unable to so much as shift in his chair. Kendrick's hands were like warm stone: hard, weighty, immovable.

"Please," Kendrick said pleasantly. "I insist."

11

The Winner's Circle

It was just about ten in the morning when Coney pulled into the pit after his last warm-up lap and let the big Lola-Climax V-8 shudder and die. He eased himself up out of the cockpit, took the chief mechanic's steadying arm, and stood. He unstrapped his helmet and pulled down the white balaclava that hid his long face. In his pale eyes was the same quiet, unsleepy look as always. It was almost exactly four hours to race time. He gave himself a stretch. Grand Prix drivers are all, of necessity, physically powerful men, but not all of them look it, and Mark Coney was slender and not much taller than Reade. Clasping his hands behind his back, he cracked his shoulders. "Feels good," he said.

"How's the car?" Emilio Rossi said.

"Good," Coney repeated. "She feels strong."

"It's good?" Rossi said.

"Yeah. You guys did nice work." Moving deliberately, Coney pulled off his gloves, nudged back the cuff of his racing suit, and took off his heavy steel watch. He handed them to Rossi. He did the same with his wedding band, and, last of all, reached into his collar and unfastened a silver Saint Christopher's medal. Before racing, Grand Prix drivers remove their watches and jewelry. If you wreck and catch fire, wearing metal can worsen your burns. It was Coney's habit not to take off his watch, ring, and medal until he'd completed his last practice lap. As with most drivers, it was hard to tell where habit left off and superstition began. Behind Rossi stood the rest of the team, going quietly about their business and trying, he knew, to seem confident. He did not look at them, or up at the darkening gray sky.

"You know, Mark, this is your car now," Rossi said. "It must run the way you like it. The setup must please you."

"I think she's all right," Coney said slowly. "You and Derek have been working all week to get her just so. She feels pretty good to me. Rather not start fooling with her now."

Rossi nodded. "But just the same, Mark, there is a decision we must make."

"Uh-huh," Coney agreed.

It was, he knew, the same decision every team in the lineup was weighing: wet tires or dry? Wets are soft and deeply grooved. Used on dry pavement, they wear quickly and overheat dangerously. Dry-weather tires grip poorly in the rain. Some teams would change between one and the other three or four times over the next four hours while waiting for the race to begin, based on nothing but hunches and the slightest flickering of the sky. There were tiny splats of rain here and there on the tarmac, and a cool breeze that might either bring more or blow the hints of drizzle away. Guessing wrong could cost a team the race. The crew were waiting silently now. Burch was standing against the back wall. Coney knew Burch wanted to talk to him. For some reason, he dreaded it.

He finally looked up at the sky. The clouds seemed hard as quartz.

Not today, he thought. *Not today of all days. I don't ask You for much. But please, just not today.*

———————

The hell of it, Burch thought, *is that he's such a good bloody kid. That's what stings, all right. But there's no sense fooling ourselves. You can hear it spatting down, a little here, a little there. You can feel it getting ready. It's coming.* Burch was resting a palm against a tall stack of tires, the way a farmer might set a meditative hand on the flank of a cow. They were wets, and he was fidgeting his thumb along the grooves. He wasn't worried about whether to put them on. He knew in his bones the rain was coming, and he knew the boy was sensible and would make the right choice. No, tires were the least of his worries right now. He had a race to win and, he knew, only one way to do it. One desperate, dangerous, scarcely legal way. He'd been up half the night working it out, and he wasn't cherishing the thought of telling the poor bloody youngster about it.

I guess it's come to that after all, he thought. *Well, it's a mad stunt, but worth a try, if Coney's game for it. Hell of a thing to ask a man. But the boy's got the guts for it. If anyone does. Well, I guess I'd better go and talk to him.*

You are like an old woman, Perriand told himself as he settled his stocky frame more comfortably into his Ferrari. *Seeking signs, seeking portents. You are worse than an old woman who writes down her dreams in a book. You are as bad as a gambler.* Laurent Perriand lived near the Casino and held gamblers in low regard. He had just edged his car onto the starting grid for the last time and was waiting for the flag. Sixth position. Not as high as he would have liked. He had been racing poorly in practice, racing stupidly. Well, now he was here. The grid this year was offset pairs instead of the old three-two-three formation. It was far more sensible. This way a man was not so hemmed in. The weather was threatening, but for him this was not a source of concern. He was a good wet-weather driver. Rain would be unpleasant but advantageous. It was not the weather that oppressed him, but his own foolishness: this morning he'd awoken with his sheets flat across him, as if they had covered a corpse, instead of in a heap in one corner as they usually were, and this had upset him. Upset about sheets! And then, two hours later, on his first warm-up lap, he had seen a girl, the most beautiful young girl in pale lipstick, sitting alone on the balcony of Oscar's, watching the cars, and she had seemed to give him a look of great sadness. And on the next lap she had looked away. Well, one always thinks the look on a woman's face means something. It meant nothing. It meant that he, Perriand, was a fool. He had been full of superstitions since he had come to race for Ferrari. It was the effect of associating with Italians.

There was Moss over to the right, in third position. *A devious one,* Perriand thought admiringly. If you pressed him too hard in the wet, he would pretend to skid at the entrance to a corner, he would do it convincingly, artistically, and so you would lift off, thinking, *Ah, there's a slippery bit.* And so for the next ten laps all the drivers would go out of their way, would spoil their lines, to avoid a slippery bit that did not exist. And Moss would go sailing through. Moss always repaid study. The breeze had whipped up a little chop in the harbor. Over the loud-speakers, the announcer was admiring his own voice. Up ahead was Tabac, where poor Becher had been brought low. They said he was do-ing well. Doing well for a poor cripple, they meant. The barrier along the corner was hung with a long advertising banner that read *"c'est shell que j'aime c'est shell que j'aime c'est shell que j'aime."* And then a row of inane colored hearts.

Every balcony in sight was crowded. There were people dangling their legs off the rooftops, people clinging to the rock face of the Tête de Chien. Out in the harbor, the rich ones were on the decks of their yachts, watching through binoculars. Perhaps they hoped for another Becher. *Vultures,* he thought with a stab of hatred. And then he put it away. He put it away with the woman's face, with Becher's leg, with the chill at the base of his stomach that overtook him the morning of every race and did not ease until he took his place on the starting grid, with the colored hearts, with the flat sheets, with the thousand tiny marching prancing jeering troubles of an ordinary life. One had to put it away, to compose oneself. All this nonsense had no place here in the car. He had come to race. It was time to race. He put it all away.

———————

Not even a bit of sun in the sky, thought Nigel Baines, squinting skyward from the top row of the grandstand. *Not the tiniest little cheese-
paring bit.* You pay for a holiday and you want a bit of sun, or you
wonder whether you were a fool to come. Not that he hadn't considered staying home this year anyway. It wasn't the same, Monaco without Fiona. Her lovely round bum should have been on the seat next to
his. They should have done the race together, like they'd done for the
past six years, but she'd given him the push, had moved on to greener
pastures, you might say, told him what to do with his warehouseman's
job and his drunken mates and his useless little car and his grandstand
tickets. And he wasn't the smooth sort who could pick up a new bird
on a moment's notice. Not that you'd find another girl who understood
racing as well as Fiona. He hadn't even had the heart to sell her ticket,
and God knows he could have used the money. It was beginning to
rain, too. A good thing he'd brought his mackintosh. At least it wasn't
broiling hot, for once. Funny how everyone still smelled of suntan lotion like always. Force of habit, must be. Well, Monaco was still Monaco, the best bloody race in the calendar, and Fiona or no Fiona and
rain or no rain he was bloody well going to enjoy it. It was almost
two. Hopefully old Chiron would get things started on time. Nigel
checked his sack of sandwiches. He always brought his own makings.
The French had funny bread.

   HRH had done his tour round the circuit in the Rolls, wig-wag-
ging to everybody, didn't seem to enjoy it much. And now there he was
in the royal box, old Rainier, looking more like a banker than a prince.
He'd watch the first few laps and then leave. Couldn't stick the noise.
Be back in time to present the trophies. Best seat in the house, lovely
big awning to keep the rain off, and he walks right out of the Monaco
Grand Prix. It wasn't natural. But Nigel supposed royals were more
delicate than you or me. And then, if your bird was Grace Kelly, you
might be a bit eager to get back off alone with her. He imagined Grace
Kelly in the empty seat beside him. Princess Grace in a wet mackin-

tosh. Wet mac and suntan lotion. Easy, boy. A bit skinny for his taste, anyway. A bird should have something to sit down on.

There was that Coney fellow at the head of the grid. Lonely place. They were all lonely places, but still, there was an awful lot of pressure on the young fellow. Made a bit of a name for himself on oval tracks in America. But Indianapolis wasn't the Grand Prix, and here he was in his first Grand Prix with no proper time to prepare. And they said he was bad in the wet, too.

No telling, though. Anything could happen. Anything always could. That was the beauty of the sport.

Here came old Chiron with his flag and his old forehead crimpled up like always.

And now here . . . we . . . *go*.

And *ooooooh*, dear me, poor clumsy Coney. Overeager. Lifted off the clutch too soon and stalled it. Beginner's mistake. Got her started up again quick, give him that—Lord, the boy was quick. But still far too slow to miss the regular old traffic jam you always had on the first corner. There he went, finally wriggling his way out of Sainte Dévote in fourth place. Never seen pole position pissed away so quick. And it wasn't even properly raining yet. Well, he'd have to see. Pack hadn't properly sorted itself out yet. Track still green, tires not up to proper running temperature. Looked bad for Team Naughton, but no one had really shown the kind of race they were going to run. Too early. The huge DUBONNET banner over his head gave itself a shake in the misty breeze, and suddenly Nigel felt a rush of happiness. Hell with Fiona. Hell with everything. He had the best damn seat he'd ever had. He was surrounded by people who loved racing as much as he did. He was at the bloody Monaco Grand Prix. He took a breath of rubber, petrol, and suntan lotion. It was the most beautiful bloody smell in the world.

Anyway, Mallory thought, *it was sure enough loud.* He'd read Monaco was the loudest race in the calendar. It was the echoes that did it, apparently. The harborfront was faced with massive concrete buildings, more of them every year, and the noise bounced off them like it would off canyon walls. He leaned forward and set down his glass. He noted, from the corner of his eye, the way Kendrick tracked his movements from the corner of his. The noise probably bounced off old Kendrick pretty good, too. The remains of breakfast had been cleared away and replaced with a covered dish of chicken salad, a heated chafing dish full of toast, and a silver bowl of grapes. Beside it stood a bottle of Hennessy XO to ward off the damp. Mallory and Jespers were drinking it out of juice glasses. Kendrick was still on coffee.

It was pretty exciting, Mallory had to admit. Probably would have been even if you didn't have fifty grand on it, though he'd never been much interested in racing as a rule. When he'd seen it on some bar's TV, it had always looked kind of tedious. The cars all looked the same. They kept going around the same corners, mostly single-file. When one of them passed, you couldn't see how they'd done it, or why they hadn't done it before. You knew they were going fast, but from way up where the camera was, it just didn't look that way. And here in Monaco, narrow and twisty as it was, sometimes they just *weren't* going that fast: a lot of the time, they were doing sixty or seventy, no faster than you'd go on the freeway. Of course, you wouldn't be doing sixty through three hairpin curves in a row, like you did at Virage Mirabeau. But once you knew a little about what they were doing out there, about the game of feints and bluffs between attacking and defending drivers, about the dozen things that made the tough corners tough, about the calculations of risk each driver had to make and remake, two or three of them every second, just to take one single smooth-looking lap around the track, it started to be pretty damn interesting after all, and the cars stopped looking all alike and started to take on personalities. And when two of them disappeared up the Montée in the middle of a duel, you swore under your breath a little until they reappeared out the mouth of the tunnel and you could see how things stood between them again. And when they shot out that tunnel at 150 or 160, leaving clouds of spray, jockeying all the way while grinding down to fourth gear in the few seconds it took to reach that tight hard left at Tabac—sweet goddamn that was a sight, whether you knew anything about racing or not. And, of course, when it was the Naughton car you were watching . . . His palms were a little wet. He was even a little achy from tightening up every time the car took a corner and urging it forward with his shoulders every time it had a little clear road ahead.

He tried to keep an eye on the pit board, the way he'd read a team's serious fans were supposed to do, but you couldn't see it too good from this angle. So he was a little surprised when Naughton took its first pit stop. It gave you sort of a sinking feeling—*Oh Lord, why're you stopping* now? Rossi was standing at the front of the pit with that paddle they called the lollipop, showing where the car's nose ought to be when it stopped, and the car shot down the pit lane and into its place like a bullet snapping into a chamber. It had barely come to a halt when they jammed a sort of wheeled trolley under the nose and another under the tail and popped the whole car into the air with a single jerk on both handles while two men jumped onto each wheel, one to grab it and the other to undo the lugs. They had the tires off in about the time it took his eyes to focus on them. Had 'em off and sprang away with 'em just as eight more guys sprang forward with fresh ones and did just the same thing in reverse. The pit floor was marked with tape like a stage gotten ready for a play. Everybody knew where to stand and when to jump. By the time the new tires were on, the second of two men had emptied a big can of fuel into the car's tanks and they'd given the driver some water, and Burch was down on one knee beside the cockpit, talking intently. From where Mallory sat, all you could see of the driver was the back of a midnight blue helmet with a gold visor. You couldn't see inside. Mallory wished you could.

"Perhaps poor Mr. Coney is asking to be let out," Jespers said. "Such a very trying race he's been having. Still, he seems to have got over his stage fright a bit. In fact I must say that your young Mr. Coney impresses me greatly. I admire that he is working so valiantly to overcome his bad start and"—a broad display of stained dentures—"to make our little wager so stimulating."

Mallory smiled mirthlessly. Rossi flipped up the paddle, and the little car shot away, this time—maybe it was his imagination—moving with a little more confidence.

"Our young friend back there is sleeping through all this excitement," Jespers said. "You don't think she'll be angry at us, that we haven't awoken her?"

"She's all right," Mallory said.

"Have some chicken salad, Mr. Carroll," Kendrick said. "You need feeding up."

He nudged the bowl nearer and poured Mallory another tot of brandy. The brandy bottle looked almost miniature in his hand. One of those miniature bottles the airlines hand out to make you feel better about being far away from home.

Every year at the beginning of the Grand Prix season, ten thousand Italians pour across the border into Monaco to cheer for Ferrari, and every year for the last four years Donatella Necchi had come with them and returned to Rome when the race was done a slightly richer woman. And some of her clients were gentlemen, and more than one had bought her a seat beside him in the grandstand, in appreciation for the delights she had shown him and because it is a pleasure to sit in the sun with a woman who is not starved nor flimsy but made as God intended a woman to be made, and because some men have open natures and generous hearts and a sense of what is fitting, but it was also true that some men are louts and beasts and pigs and mongrel dogs bereft of civility and just now Donatella was unfortunately beneath one of them.

She had gone with him willingly to the Hôtel Mirabeau even though the race was about to start, for the view from the Mirabeau's balcony is magnificent, but *there* was the window, and *here* they were on the bed, with the lights out and the curtains half-drawn. It was an outrage. Beyond those curtains was the Grand Prix of Monaco. Beyond those curtains, Mollino was driving. It was true that Donatella would have loved the Grand Prix even had Mollino, may God always forbid such calamities, never been born, but he had been born—a Friulian like Donatella—and taken his place as the greatest driver of the age, and now embodied all that was excellent about the Grand Prix: nerve, panache, finesse wed to near-brutality. They all squawked about the *sprezzatura* of Reade, all the silly little girls and boys, but Reade was tactically weak and unsteady in traffic and not fit to change Mollino's oil. His only trick was to oversteer. Even she, Donatella, did not waggle her rear end about as much as he.

Just now she was waggling her rear end quite vigorously, in hopes of concluding the matter with this sow sometime before the entire race was finished, but although this made the sow louder, it did not, alas, make him quicker. Over his snorts and sighs she heard the rain pattering down. She listened to the droning of the field outside as she might have listened to an aria: how they downshifted from fourth down to second between Casino Square and the hotel where she, Donatella, was pinned under this gross pig, then hard right beneath that very balcony, if only she could see it, and then, in a passage of great drama and beauty, steeply downhill while downshifting to bottom gear at the entrance to the tight tight Station hairpin with its vicious negative camber, that had defeated so many good men, then almost at once savagely left onto the Promenade and one's first view of the sea. The sea! Donatella did not like being on top—why should the woman do all the work?—but just then she wished she were atop this cretin, this mule, this gruesome pumpkin, so that she might occasionally bounce high enough to obtain a quick glimpse of the track.

What sort of man would rather poke a fat girl in a dark room than see Mollino drive? *"Oooh, caro,"* she moaned, and dug her nails painfully into his spine, but the miserable donkey did not notice. He was hairless, like some loathsome sea creature, and pink, and stank of sweet cologne, and you could tell he was vain of his strength. With every thrust, Donatella's back hitched farther up the mattress. Her head was already crammed sideways against the headboard. The sound of the pack was fading, the minutes were ticking by. *Oh, finish,* she thought, *you calf, you sow, you squid, won't you ever be finished?*

He was in his own bedroom, alone. Derek Reade could tell that much without opening his eyes. Someone had taken him back to his own flat on Grimaldi. He lay there, eyes closed, head hammering, and listened. Outside, the thunder of sixty-four tires circled him, growing louder and fainter and louder again until it rattled the windows. Outside was the angry, endless drone, rising and falling, of sixteen high-performance engines pressed to their limits. He opened his eyes a slit. He was very sick. His skin was cold and raw. His gut felt like a snowbank the dogs have pissed on. Somebody had closed his shutters carefully, but a few bits of weak afternoon sunlight still speared through the cracks. They burned at his eyes. There was a clock by the bed. He was afraid to look at it. Instead he listened to the rising and falling thunder of the racing pack. And, over the noise of the cars, just barely audible, the gentle patter of rain.

It should have been poison, he thought, and closed his eyes again.

By now Nigel was well soaked, right through his mackintosh, but he didn't care. A race like this was worth any amount of soaking. Moss was driving superbly, and Perriand and Ginther were well worth the watching, but as far as he was concerned, the whole show this year was Team Naughton. It was an astonishing thing, how young Coney was rallying. It was as if he was teaching himself the business of Formula One racing while you watched. The first few laps, he'd barely gotten the car round the track, as if he'd never driven the course before, or as if maybe the Lola mill was too much power for him. And of course he'd dropped from pole to fourth to eighth and been damn lucky not to fall further. And then he'd taken hold of things. That's what it was: he'd just bloody grabbed hold. He started working his way back as if he was teaching himself how. Teaching himself how to defend, you might say, shaking off one challenge after another, so that soon he wasn't being overtaken anymore, and now he was seeming to figure out how to overtake. It was like one of those nature films where you see a flower grow and blossom out in two shakes. It gave a fellow hope. It gave every fellow who was sort of a duffer in life the idea that no matter how far back in the running he'd gotten, the race wasn't over yet, and he could still just take hold of things and make 'em work irregardless. The field had thinned out by nearly half. *Bloody place eats transmissions. Got to be tough,* Nigel thought happily. The backmarkers swooped by and headed up the Montée du Beau Rivage in a cloud of spray. "Like a bleeding water ballet," he told his neighbor gleefully, and the man, who did not speak English, grinned and thumped Nigel on the thigh.

During a race, a Grand Prix driver's pulse goes as high as two hundred a minute. It was one of those things Perriand wished to the good God that they wouldn't tell you. But they told you anyway, and now, when you were trying to concentrate, you lost a precious fifth of a second wondering if your own pulse was at two hundred yet. It probably was. The rain was strong now, and Perriand had to fight to keep his chilled feet on the wet pedals. His body was soaked inside his racing suit, his eyes were wet with effort. The g-force on the tighter corners threw his tears against the inside of his visor. But he was content. After a week of stupidity and clumsiness, he was at last racing as he was meant to race. He'd been pressing Ginther hard for four laps now, filling his mirrors, as the English say, resisting all attempts to diffuse his own momentum, and now he felt the crisis was approaching and that he would prevail. Ginther had closed the door on him twice now, but the second time with notably less conviction. The third time he would yield. They were both in the tunnel, in sixth gear; it was one of the few brief moments when one could open the throttle fully. The tunnel's lights shot past overhead like a curving stream of tracer bullets, and then daylight exploded around him—even on a wet gray day, every lap, it was like an explosion—and he was downshifting toward Tabac, knowing that this would be the crucial moment. Up ahead was that banner: *"c'est shell que j'aime c'est shell que j'aime."* He was in the entrance to the corner, at his braking point, and now he waited a precisely controlled fraction of a second to apply the brake, by his boldness forcing Ginther outside of his line, and then he saw that he was not holding. He had misjudged the depth of the water. He was—he slammed against the row of colored hearts, seeing his right front wheel snap free, and then he had rebounded into Ginther's back right wheel and was mounting it, and then he was flying. Perriand skimmed across the track and along the straw bales by the water's edge, watching his spinning front wheel precede him into the harbor. He was going in. He got ready to lift his hands from the wheel so that the kick of the wheel at impact would not break his arms. He was flying lazily, gracefully, toward the deck of a beautiful white yacht, a girl in a flowered dress was watching him approach with binoculars, he stared into their double mouths, and her own red mouth opening below them. *"It's Shell I love."* He was not flying but falling. *"I love."* He saw the row of heavy iron capstans at the water's edge. He was going there.

Perriand lifted his hands from the wheel, but he knew it would not make any difference. Nothing would ever make any difference again.

Oh dear God, Nigel thought as the Ferrari struck the row of iron bollards and dissolved into a rolling mass of red flame, and the red flame dissolved into white, a white clot of churning molten light plunging into the water, *oh dear sweet oh my God*. He felt sick. *My God.* He felt sick and guilty. You always hoped to see a bit of action, though you never admitted to yourself what that might be, and then it happened and—*Oh God*. The water that had been thrown into the air by the crash was still showering down on the harbor and the harborside track. The nearby yachts were slewing and shuffling against their moorings. The line of hay bales was smoldering. Behind them, smoke and steam poured out of the water from a sunken glaring core of flame. *He can't be alive in that. You can barely stand to look at it. The poor, poor bugger,* Nigel thought, and took a mournful bite of his sandwich.

"Dear, dear," Jespers said, leaning forward against the balcony wall. "I can't see," he complained. He rested his chin on the railing.

Kendrick's deep-set eyes had merely flickered to the towering spray of water and then, true to his training, were back on Mallory. Someone had trained Kendrick right. They'd trained him right long ago, and it had stuck. The man in gray said nothing, but the eyes that watched Mallory were darker now, and the wide mouth was grim.

Mallory was silent as well. Then he said, "Where's that brandy, Kendrick?"

Done, thank the Lord Jesus Christ, the young sow was finally done, and Donatella was free. She was finally free, and there was half a race yet to watch, and she would do no more business until it was over. It was a pity the sow had lacked the simple civility to let a poor working woman linger on his balcony, but he was a pig and a manatee and would burn in hell covered in bubbling sores and shrieking for mercy and it was better to be free. She sloshed along through the thickening rain, elbowing her way through crowds and peering around the backs of strangers. Why were there no gentlemen to stand aside and let a lady see the race? When had the accursed Monegascos grown so tall? She was mad to know what she had missed: who had crashed—that ghastly sound!—and how it was for Mollino. Poor Mollino who had run half his race without Donatella to cheer him on. It was not possible that he had crashed. God is not so cruel.

Even in her highest heels, Donatella was not much more than one hundred sixty centimeters, and so she was halfway down the Montée du Beau Rivage before she found a place along the barriers where she might command a decent view. On a straight, of course, which was not her preference, but with a passable view of Dévote off to the right and, if you craned your head, Massenet off to the left. The only trick was to get up on the stone base of a lightpost. In slacks and sandals, she would have bounded up like a goat, short and round as she was, but in a skintight rayon dress and stiletto heels, the matter was not so simple. At her first attempt, she merely scraped the side of her shoe down the side of the stone. Off came the buckle. She swore bountifully. She hitched up her dress—someone behind her cheered and she cursed him—and tried again. This time she was able to plant her foot properly. But then her hands slipped from the dripping post and sent her flying backward into the belly of a young man just coming out of the Hôtel Hermitage.

She spun and glared at him. He was in the way. He was tall, and tall men were despicable: they blocked one's view. He was too shabby, in his absurd rubber poncho, to be staying at the Hermitage; he had obviously stepped inside to deal with a necessity. And instead of excusing himself for his clumsiness, he was looking her up and down and laughing. In his ridiculous child's yellow waterproof, he was laughing at Donatella.

"Hello, dearie," Nigel said. "How about it?"

"Go 'way," Donatella snapped. "I will tell your wife."

"Haven't one," he said affably, "but that's all right. Nice to have seen you." He turned.

"I am a lady, you mule."

Donatella's dress was cut low in front, hitched up at the bottom, and translucent with rain. "Well, anyway," Nigel said over his shoulder, "I can see you're not a gentleman."

"*Vaffanculo,*" she said. Then, "Wait. How does Mollino race?"

Nigel paused. "Horse," he said firmly, "de combat. Wrapped it up on lap twenty-six trying to outbrake Clark on Sahnt Devotay. Cracked an axle. Bye-bye."

She let out an inarticulate cry.

"Oh, *he's* all right," he said comfortingly, "but poor bloody Perriand wasn't so lucky."

"He is the fire there?"

"Yerse, poor bugger's the fire there."

"Dead?"

"I should think so. Where have you been? It's been a hell of a race. Nearly brought out the red fl—"

They fell silent as the pack roared by again.

"Mollino retired and poor Perriand dead," Donatella said bitterly, gazing after them. "And there goes that *froccio* Reade, happy like a bird."

"That's not Reade, dearie. He's horse de combat too. Some bint slipped him a mickey last night at Sally Lou's. The Coney kid's driving."

"But Mark Coney cannot race in the wet!"

"You'd think not, wouldn't you? But in fact the young fellow's pulled himself together and is having a bloody good drive. Slow to get away, mind you, and very raggedy for the first dozen laps, but he's found his rhythm, all right, and he's been moving right up. Overtook

Lotus on Upper Mirabeau, sneaked past Ferrari on Gasworks, and now he's back up to fourth and pressing BRM hard for third. I've never seen him attack like that. Been right on Ginther's pace for half a dozen laps. Lovely to see, really. Well, can't stand here jawing all day. Nice to have seen you."

Donatella nodded brusquely, kicked off her shoes, and prepared for another assault on the lightpost, eyes gleaming, dark lips parted, wet legs straddled. Nigel took a last look at her well-filled skirts and on impulse said, "You know, I've an extra ticket for the stands."

She spun and clutched his arm. "Take me with you!" she cried.

"Take . . . ?"

"Take me with you to the stands! Let me sit with you!"

"I—" Nigel said.

Donatella began to shake him back and forth. Small as she was, she shook him easily. "Let me *sit* with you. Let me *sit* with you. Time *passes*, we are *missing* the *race*! You can have me after, all night, up and down, any way you like, for no money, but *nell' interesse del Dio*, you stupid *Englishman*, take me *with* you!"

"All right," Nigel said, recovering. "I don't mind if I do."

He whipped the mackintosh from his shoulders and draped it around hers with what he privately thought was something of an air. Snatching up her shoes, she gripped him around the waist.

"*Hurry*," she cried, and hustled him toward the grandstands.

On lap ninety-five, Jespers had his sommelier bring out champagne, and since then he'd been twisting the bottle through the ice in a preoccupied manner, his protuberant eyes on the race, but when the front of the pack burst from the tunnel on the final lap, he stopped twisting and simply sat there, gripping the bottle. The front two were Stirling Moss and Richie Ginther. It was a good day for BRM. Both cars had solid leads, which was not a surprise; they had dominated for a dozen laps. The few seconds while the three men waited for the third car seemed very long, and then Naughton's gold-rimmed mouth shot into view, a sea-green Lotus a fraction behind it and crowding in from the right. The two cars remained wheel-to-wheel into Tabac, trailing billows of spray, and did not break formation down the Quai Albert and into the Gasworks hairpin. Lotus made a desperate final attempt at the entrance to Gasworks and was rebuffed, and the two cars crested the bump at the finish line with Naughton a quarter of a length ahead.

On the balcony, Jespers and Mallory let out their breaths together, and then Jespers turned to Mallory, one nicotine-stained hand extended and a glint of delight returning to his eyes. In the harbor, the big yachts were sounding their horns, bringing forth deep, chest-fluttering tones. The crowds were roaring, klaxons were honking all over the city. Mallory permitted himself a small smile as he shook Jespers's hand, which was cold from the neck of the bottle. He felt good. Goddamn did he feel good. "Well, Jack, I must say," Jespers shouted over the mingled din, "this race I have seen, I believe it is after all worth fifty thousand dollars to have seen it. I shall never forget it. It is quite excellent, what your young Mr. Coney has been able to accomplish. I congratulate you both, I *salute* you. To secure third place after Moss and Ginther, in such conditions, after such a start, this is something to be quite proud of. I must say— Jack, I will go so far as to say that it has moved me."

Mallory smiled again, without much warmth. The band was playing "God Save the Queen" in honor of the British victor. Moss was out of his car and limping toward the steps of the royal box, helmet under his arm. Rainier and Princess Grace were waiting on the top step, their eyes somber. Moss's wet, grimy face was somber as well. The remains of Perriand's Ferrari were still being winched from the harbor. No one would feel much like celebrating tonight. Still, the crowd surrounding the Naughton Lola-Climax had an air of relief mingled with quiet triumph. They pressed close around the blue-and-gold car and to the slender figure in the muddy racing suit, they reached out helping hands. The driver took hold of one of them and clambered exhaustedly from the cockpit. Then, as Mallory, Kendrick, and Jespers watched, she unstrapped her dripping helmet, pulled down her balaclava, and shook out her long, wheat-blonde hair.

Jespers sprang trembling to his feet. His eyes bulged as if he were being throttled, his dentures glittered. Spinning on his heel, he stalked down the hall to Mallory's room and flung open the door. In the bed lay a mass of pale blonde hair, two long brown legs, and, in between, a tangle of white sheets. He ripped them away. The girl underneath rolled over and revealed a pair of vacant green eyes, blinking sleepily beneath thick golden brows.

"Which?" he said, choking.

"Kirsten," she murmured. "Go 'way, old man. I want to sleep."

She fumbled around for the sheet. Not finding it, she hugged the pillow closer and closed her eyes.

Jespers's rages never lasted long. By the time he got back to the balcony, he had begun to chuckle. Down by the royal box, Laura was holding her silver bowl and sedately accepting congratulations. Flashbulbs flickered. The starlet provided to kiss the winners gazed at her in consternation.

"She is full of surprises, your Miss Prentice," Jespers said.

"She is," Mallory said. "Surprised me pretty good last night when she told me about this stunt. I knew she had something on her mind, but I'd never of guessed it was this."

"A resourceful and talented young lady."

"She's all of that," Mallory agreed.

"Well," Jespers said, "this is something of a quandary. You see what a quandary I am in? One solution to this awkwardness, Jack, is, I think, to offer you a job. To *recruit* you, to invite you to work with me, because a man who is so resourceful like this and can make such a fool of Arne Jespers is not a common man, and I should take advantage."

"Uh-huh?"

"On the other hand, it would be neater and, I must say, also quite satisfying simply to kill you."

Mallory glanced to his right. Kendrick stood beside him, a silenced pistol in one vast hand. He held it so that it could not be seen from the street. The handsome, square-jawed face was empty of expression. He might have been holding a cigarette lighter. Mallory looked back at Jespers.

"I already got a job," Mallory said. "I already got fifty grand, too, but it's always nice to get another helping. You can send the check to my office and make it payable to CSS Special Projects. As for the rest of it, let me know what you decide." He nodded at Kendrick's pistol. "Silencer's kind of a waste, if you want my opinion. In all this racket, no one'd hear it if he used a bazooka."

Jespers sank into his chair. He was gazing deep into Mallory's eyes, as if he were childish enough to believe one could see the truth there.

"You have some idea of the scope of my operations, Jack," he said slowly. "You know that they are quite extensive and quite profitable. Permit me to suggest that you have not actually grasped their full extent. I believe that no one besides Mr. Kendrick and myself does fully grasp this—the power my organization wields, the wealth it commands—and all this in spite of their state of disorganization, of *slip-shoddiness*. Of, sometimes, *chaos*. Can you imagine what astounding things might be possible if this *apparat* had the advantage of a resourceful and disciplined brain such as yours, to help me"—Jespers made a fist and squeezed it hard—"*mold* it? To forge it as one forges steel? Perhaps I expressed myself poorly, Jack. I did not mean to offer you a salaried job. You are a consultant. I offer you a contract, of a kind that you will be familar with, one yielding fees on a contingency basis. A quarterly percentage for as long as you are acting on my behalf. The figure I propose, Jack, is five percent."

"Of what?"

"Of gross receipts. Five percent of all the monies I take in from our various operations. Which, on the one project we have already discussed, would amount to . . ."

"Twenty-five million dollars," Kendrick said neutrally. "Give or take. That'd be Mr. Carroll's cut on Archangel alone, if we get the kind of price we're expecting."

Mallory said, "Sounds like fun, Arne."

"Yes?"

"Sounds like a whole lot of fun. And a damn sight more fun than being shot, if you were serious about that and not just smarting off." Jespers showed a thin edge of dirty teeth. "Yeah, I guess I'm interested, but I think there's a couple questions that we need to get answered before we shake on it. First off, how do I know I can trust you?"

"You cannot know this. You must calculate the odds and take your chances."

"Fair enough. Second thing, how do you know you can trust me?"

"A more interesting question, and I can answer this. Do you know why I am going to trust you?" Jespers said. "Because you're an intelligent man. And an intelligent man, if he were sitting before me, smiling so charmingly, at his ease, legs crossed just so, plotting betrayal, plotting to betray Arne Jespers, such a man would be very afraid. And if you were afraid, I would smell it. And you are not afraid."

"Well, all right then," Mallory said mildly.

Kendrick tucked the pistol away, pulled the champagne from the ice bucket, and began untwisting the wire around the cork. The wine foamed free, and he filled three flutes with it. Jespers raised his. "To our—our partnership. Yes, I feel I can call it this. Our partnership." Mallory was still watching Kendrick; the short man remained impassive. "But even more important—to the surprising, the astonishing Miss Lily Prentice, and her gallant victory."

"To Lily," Mallory said.

They drank. Mallory had never cared for champagne. He supposed this stuff was the good kind. Anyway, just now it tasted pretty goddamn sweet. Jespers smiled into his glass, swirling the last of his champagne in circles.

"Someday, Jack," he said meditatively, "perhaps we'll find out what you're afraid of."

BOOK II

Mont
Saint-Sévérin

1

Where the Angel Lives

Mallory knew some folks with private planes, and he knew some air-lines with jets, but he'd never met anybody with a private jet before, and he wished he wasn't blindfolded so he could enjoy the ride. It was a nice enough blindfold, as blindfolds went. Some kind of dark silk. He appreciated the caviar, too—not the taste, which was just plain salty to him, but the thoughtfulness of it. What he mostly liked, though, was the bottle of Jack Daniel's they'd put by his elbow, with a nice heavy rocks glass that didn't slide around and a covered bucket of ice set into some kind of cabinet beside his seat. Though Mallory would have preferred George Dickel, this was still pretty good for the middle of Europe. Arne Jespers might not be all that nice of a person, but Mallory thought he was a pretty decent host.

Beside him, Laurie let out the faintest little ladylike rasp and was silent again. She never snored unless she was exhausted. She was all in. She'd had something to say about his drinking whiskey with beluga caviar when they got on the plane—apparently it was pretty fancy caviar—but her heart hadn't been in it, and she'd gone to sleep right afterward. Being blindfolded didn't give her that uncomfortable, closed-in feeling like it did him.

At one point, Jespers had come over to sit by the two of them: Mallory had heard his shuffling step, and then the creak of the leather cushions, and then he had the idea that Jespers was watching Laurie sleep.

"A remarkable young woman," Jespers had murmured.

"Uh-huh."

"I must admit that I entirely underestimated Miss Prentice. Of course, the rich are often as serious about their hobbies as we working men are about our professions, but I should never have guessed that this quite ornamental young lady was such an accomplished amateur driver. Formula Vee, did you say?"

"You trying to tell me Kendrick wasn't onto the Formula Vee people as soon as the office opened this morning?" Mallory said.

"Her record was quite impressive," Jespers admitted.

Documents had worked from midnight Saturday to Sunday evening, diddling the files of the Formula Vee Racing Drivers' Association of America so that the greater part of Laura Morse's victories would be credited to one Lily Prentice in case anyone called to ask. Mallory made a mental note to buy Florrie Davis some flowers when he got home. Always assuming he got home.

"I should have known that a man like yourself would choose for his companion a woman of exceptional, of *uncommon* gifts," Jespers said. "I underestimated you both. It is a good lesson to me. How lovely and young she looks, how weary. Well, we shall not disturb her. If anyone has earned the right to sleep, it is she."

Mallory had wholeheartedly agreed.

"I do apologize for the blindfolds," Jespers said.

"They're a little surprising. Thought I was your partner, Arne. Don't you trust me?"

From behind Jespers came Kendrick's soft, flat voice. "Mr. Jespers is too busy a man to distrust people, Mr. Carroll. He's given that job to me."

"A short probationary period," Jespers said. "I'm sure you can see why we might require one."

"Uh-huh. Where's my fifty?"

"In your special projects account in Geneva. We wired it. Perhaps you'll wish to call your office when we arrive and confirm?"

"Perhaps I will," Mallory said.

"Well, I shall leave the two of you in peace now, before I awake the weary Miss Prentice with my chattering," Jespers said.

"Thanks," Laurie said distinctly. "I appreciate it."

The thing about jet flight was, it really didn't feel like anything. It felt like sitting still in a little room while a big dynamo whined steadily outside. It didn't feel like flying until they began to descend. It was a steep descent, and Mallory reached out to steady the Jack Daniel's, but it was gone. Kendrick must have taken it. By now Mallory could identify everyone else in the plane by their footsteps. Only Kendrick was completely silent unless he decided to talk. When they began to descend, Laurie stirred beside him and said, "Hm." She was awake again. It took her no time to come to full consciousness from even the deepest sleep. The plane banked hard to the right, and then harder the other way—Mallory thought of the twin hairpin curves of Upper and Lower Mirabeau—and then, with a little bump and shriek, they were down and braking fiercely, engines squalling in reverse. It had been a short flight, less than two hours. They were still in Western Europe somewhere.

The plane had no sooner coasted to a halt when Kendrick was beside them. "We're here. Would you stand up, please, both of you, and take a step forward?"

They unbuckled themselves and obediently stood. Kendrick said, "I'm behind you now, Mr. Carroll, with a coat. Would you extend your arms?"

"We brought coats, Kendrick," Mallory said.

"They're not warm enough." He felt heavy fur sleeves slip over his arms, and then a weighty collar settled on his shoulders. He rubbed a hand over his sleeve. Mink or sable. Fur, anyhow, and not rabbit. "And now, Miss—"

"I'll put her coat on, thanks. Give it here."

Kendrick complied, and Mallory settled the coat over Laurie's shoulders. Mallory heard the hatch open. The warm cabin began to fill with freezing air. "Would you take Miss Prentice's hand, please?"

Her palm was cool and hard, as always. Kendrick took hold of Mallory's elbow. Mallory willed himself not to resist.

"Thanks," Kendrick said. "Now step this way. And left, and now—right. All right, you're at the top of the stairs. Seven steps down, narrow and steep. Handrail to the left. Little slick at the bottom. There you go."

As he heard Laurie's right shoe strike the icy tarmac, Mallory withdrew his hand from hers and whipped off his blindfold. "Enough kid's games," he said. He put his hand to the back of Laurie's head, undid her blindfold, and, blinking in the glare, handed them both to Kendrick.

"Too bad," Kendrick said, pocketing them. "I play a mean game of pin the tail on the donkey."

They were somewhere in the Alps—whether Swiss, Italian, or French, Mallory couldn't say—on a tiny airstrip carved into the valley between two massive peaks. One peak was low, blunt, and very close. The other toppled jaggedly into the bright blue sky about a quarter-mile distant. Judging by the air, they were already quite high above sea level. Snowy firs grew to the very edge of the airstrip. The plane's shining white wingtips barely cleared the branches. The jet fit into the narrow strip like a violin into its case. "Lord," Mallory said. "Now I'm glad you had us blindfolded while we were landing."

"First time this thing touched down with me on board, I damn near wet myself," Kendrick agreed. "Now I don't even notice. We use retired carrier pilots, Mr. Carroll. They're used to getting it right on the first try. This way, please."

The wind bit at their faces as they moved out of the lee of the plane. Jespers had fallen silent. He was staring up at the more distant peak. The clownishness had gone out of his homely face; the merriment had left his protuberant eyes. Mallory followed his gaze and saw, near the top of the far peak, a fortresslike cluster of ancient stone buildings clinging to the snowy rock. It was at these that Jespers gazed, a slight, aging man wrapped in a bulky sable coat, standing alone and unspeaking on an icy strip of concrete.

Beside the airstrip was the terminus of a cable car. There was a small concrete platform for boarding the gondola, with a corrugated-steel roof. Beneath this was the steel bull wheel that drove the cable. The wheel was immense—at least fifteen feet in diameter—and painted bright orange, with spokes thick as a man's leg. The lower half of it disappeared into a deep slot in the concrete deck. There were warning black and yellow stripes all around the edge. The gondola itself was a flattened ovoid like a melon seed, lacquered a deep scarlet. A row of tinted windows wrapped around its circumference.

"There's our ride," Kendrick said, nodding.

Inside, the gondola was upholstered in white leather, and well-heated. Mallory touched the window with a knuckle; it was electrically warmed to prevent fogging. When they were comfortably seated, Kendrick swung the door shut with a deep thump, and the car set off. automatically.

The acceleration was smooth and carefully calibrated; the car took off at little more than a brisk walking pace but increased steadily in speed as it rode the cable up through the surrounding firs, and was soon gliding above the snowy treetops at an impressive clip.

"Very cozy, just the four of us," Mallory said. "Handy that there's a seat for you, Kendrick. What do you think I'm gonna do if you leave me alone with your boss for a minute? Push him out the window?"

"They don't open," Laura observed.

"Don't lean too hard, Carroll," Kendrick said easily. "I might just be hired help here, but Mr. Jespers lets me do what I need to do, if I decide I need to do it."

"This is the difficulty with young men," Jespers said, still gazing out the window. "When a pretty girl is present, they squabble. We are not on vacation now, gentlemen. We are at work. We are going to the office. I have chosen you both and I expect you to work harmoniously together. If you cannot do so, I will know I have chosen in error. And as I told you in Monaco, Jack, I don't fire people."

The car was still rising and accelerating, silently except for the deep, soft thrum of the speeding cable. In the distance, Mallory saw a tiny scarlet pip descending the hillside: the other car, rushing down to meet them. He looked down: they were at least a hundred feet over the wooded slopes below.

"We are now approaching my operations center," Jespers said in a somewhat lighter tone. "A deconsecrated *monastery*. Isn't that fine? It provides us a lot of very useful privacy for our, ah, work. It had already been somewhat renovated by the previous owner, a wealthy manufacturer of soap flakes called Symmes, who had planned to make it a nice retirement home for himself up in the mountains with pretty scenery to look at, but Mr. Symmes was unfortunately prone to melancholy and flung himself from a balcony shortly after settling in. Into a crevasse he went, and his body has never been found. Apparently the huge mountains surrounding him gave him *thoughts*, thoughts of his own insignificance. This kind of thought I am, perhaps, too coarse a man to think of, and so except for the cold, which I don't like so very much, this place suits me very well. I purchased it six years ago on quite favorable terms from Symmes's executor, whom I knew in a business way, and since then I have made certain improvements. That steel-roofed building down the slope is our new seven-hundred-and-fifty-kilowatt power plant, a good modern oil-fired generator that we needed for our various projects. And just on that ledge by the little bare rock face is a nice new turbine helicopter, because maybe sometimes we might need to go someplace quickly without waiting for my plane to arrive. The only other access to the compound is this funicular which I had installed. I'm very proud of my funicular. Isn't it fast? Of course, one can *climb* up from the village, but this requires that one be very fit and takes many hours. Yes, here we are relatively safe from surprises, I must say."

The second gondola was increasing rapidly in size from a scarlet dot to a scarlet marble to a scarlet ball, and then abruptly it swelled up to become the twin of the car in which they rode, and shot past half a dozen yards away. Their gondola wobbled slightly as the shock wave struck it—the other car wobbled as well—and then the other car was shrinking into the distance as it swept downhill toward the airstrip. It had been empty. They'd passed the halfway point, and now the mountain began to rise again to meet them.

"We're moving, all right," Mallory said. "What's that big glass deal, Arne, up there behind that sort of turret? Funny place for a greenhouse. Funny size, too."

"Your eyes are very good, Jack."

"Uh-huh. What is it?"

"More improvements," Jespers said. "It was quite challenging, all the construction. Everything had to be brought up from the village with a tractor, or even on men's backs."

"What kind of improvements?"

"Things we needed for our work. There is the village, way down the slope, just a little village. Can you see it? Let your eye follow the train tracks from the viaduct. See?"

"What's the village called?"

"Oh, it's very difficult to pronounce."

"Like trying to get a girl's bra off back in seventh grade." Mallory sighed.

"I'm sure you were a great success with seventh-grader's brassieres," Laura said. "What's up there?"

She was pointing to the jagged split peak towering over the old monastery. Against the glaring sky, it seemed dark as the blade of an iron spear.

"Ah, an angel lives up there," Jespers said. "An angel to watch over us."

"Uh-huh," Mallory said.

"What an unsatisfactory audience you are, Jack. Nothing entertains you."

"I'm not here to be entertained, Arne. I'm here to earn my five percent."

The mention of money seemed to cheer Jespers. "You must permit me to tell you things my own way, Jack, in my own time. You are far too serious. Miss Lily, dear beautiful woman who takes my money, do you never grow tired that Jack is so serious all the time?"

"No, I'm serious, too. My Lord, here we are already. That *was* fast."

"You are impressed!" Jespers cried. "I have impressed a pretty woman. Now I am happy again."

They stepped out onto a stone terrace, recently swept of snow and surrounded by vertiginous drops on three sides. Before them was what seemed like the monastery's front door. The door, Mallory guessed, was another improvement: it was forged steel with a narrow slot at eye level, the slot filled with layer upon greenish layer of wire-reinforced safety glass. It looked like the back door of an armored car. There was no doorknob he could see, but as they approached it, the door swung smoothly open with a soft pneumatic hiss, and Mallory saw one of the musclemen inside, dressed in a parka and holding a grease gun chest-high. He thought back to the open door of the Cap Ferrat villa, with its broken buzzer. Jespers hadn't been joking. Cap Ferrat was for play. This place was for work.

Before them hung a pair of heavy velvet curtains, which the guard deftly parted with his free arm, the grease gun still poised for rapid one-handed firing. Jespers led the way through; Mallory followed Laura. They found themselves in a narrow, winding stone corridor lit by a row of slitlike vertical windows to their left. Up ahead, they could smell a wood fire burning. Rounding a corner, they saw a huge hearth, the kind with two narrow stone benches inside it, and in be-tween them, a broad, twisted iron grate on which a pyramid of thick logs blazed. Before the fireplace was a worn brocade couch. Upon the couch lay Milena. She was still lightly dressed, as if she were insen-sible to cold, and still reading the same movie magazine. Beside her on the brocade cushions lay her massive chestnut braid, like a sleeping python. "Dumpling," Jespers said, "here you are, looking so cozy. Did you have a nice flight this morning? Everyone treated you properly?"

Jespers did not seem to expect a reply. In any case, he didn't get one. Ignoring him, Milena favored Mallory with a look of dull hunger. "Hello, Jack," she said softly. Then her tiny eyes flicked to Laurie and took on a gleam of pure malevolence.

She's not right, Mallory thought, feeling a chill that had nothing to do with the moaning wind outside. *That girl's not just a little unusual on the outside. There's something wrong upstairs, too.*

"'Lo, Milena," he said.

"This way, if you would," Jespers said.

They followed the corridor until it debouched into a great hall with curving walls and a stone floor. Branching stone columns supported the complexly arched ceiling. Flickering iron sconces fixed to the columns provided the only light. At the far end, an arched doorway opened onto a stone balcony dusted with snow. Beyond the snowy balcony lay a jagged rock face, seeming only inches away in the clear mountain air. A raised gallery ran along the right side. Beneath the gallery, the black mouth of a corridor.

"*Sss-sss-ssssss,*" went Jespers softly, and Mallory almost jumped. He'd seemed to be hissing directly into Mallory's ear, though he was striding toward the balcony up ahead.

"A whispering gallery," Laura said quietly, her voice seeming to come from everywhere at once.

"The finest outside of Saint Paul's," Jespers whispered triumphantly. "Isn't it fun? These monks were such interesting chaps."

"You installed electric light everywhere else so far," she remarked. "But not here."

"Indeed not. We couldn't risk spoiling the acoustics. Besides, these old oil lamps are far more picturesque. And now I will show you where I keep my toys."

As they passed the mouth of the corridor beneath the raised gallery, Mallory saw the faint horizontal beams of a row of electric eyes, set six inches apart and stretching from the floor to the ceiling, closing off the tunnel so that not even a house cat could slip through.

Beyond the barrier of electric-eye beams, a narrow stone staircase ascended into the dimness.

Without turning around, Jespers seemed to know where Mallory's eyes had strayed. "Patience, Jack. All in good time. Come into the chapel with me."

Mallory only had Jespers's word for it that the stone room had once been a chapel. There were stained-glass windows, all right, weird-looking ones full of faces and hands poking out of clouds, but the pews had been removed and the altar was hidden by a vast collection of—well, a vast collection. The only time he'd seen anything like it was when a young mezzo-soprano had taken him into the property room of the Vienna State Opera House. At the time, he'd been paying closer attention to the girl than to her surroundings, but even then he'd been struck by the towering, dizzying jumble of weapons, idols, bits of architecture, the half-dismantled coaches, locomotives, sailing ships. The difference was, all those things had been fake and these looked to be pretty much real. "Symmes was something of a collector," Jespers said, "of all kinds of oddball stuff, and he used this place as his storeroom. Have you ever seen such a mess? That big oak box over there with all the straps and hatches is an Edwardian portable lavatory. It was used by a rather *pampered* hunter in the African bush. One sits inside with one's head poking out the top. And here are I-don't-know-how-many child's toy wagons from America, the wooden ones over here and the metal ones, where are the metal ones? Over there some-place. A hundred and fifty years old, some of them, but some of them are brand-new things he'd buy in hardware stores and so on. I suppose he liked the looks of them. And here on the wall is his collection of cer-emonial, ah, *knives*, scimitars and daggers—no, forgive me, I am in-correct. The daggers and whatnot are my own. I'd forgotten. Well, old Symmes is dead, so it's all mine now, anyway, and here, if you please, is an actual Egyptian sarcophagus. How they got it up the mountain I couldn't tell you. I'm told the lid alone weighs over a ton. It was meant for quite a young man, a young prince, something of an *adolescent*, you see, and so it's not really very roomy inside." Mallory looked at the massive stone lid, smoothly carved into the form of a swollen, armless figure with a flowing headdress and a tranquil, round-cheeked face. It looked like over a ton, all right. It was laid crookedly across the even more massive body of the casket, revealing one end of the deep stone slot meant for the body. The slot was narrow. It would've been a pretty tight fit for any decent-sized teenager. Mallory felt a little suffocated just thinking about it.

"Nice cheerful stuff," he said, looking away.

"Symmes used to move all the junk around with this," Jespers said, picking his way through the clutter to the corner, where a yellow fork-lift stood at the ready. He clambered into the driver's seat and turned the steering wheel back and forth, as if driving. He tapped the horn button with his fist. When it didn't make a noise, he said, "*Toot-toot.* Will you look at all this stuff? This fellow Symmes was such a mad old pig."

"Sounds like your kind of guy," Laura said.

"I felt quite at home here at once," Jespers said happily.

"Well, this is interesting, Arne," Mallory said. "Or anyway, it'd be interesting if I was on vacation. But like you said, I'm not. I'm glad you got a nice sarcophagus here, even if it's not really very roomy, and an Edwardian crapper, and a whispering gallery and the rest of it, but I was sort of wondering when you'd get around to telling me about Archangel. Because you been doing the big striptease for me since Cap Ferrat, but I've got to say you still haven't shown me much of what I paid my two bits to see."

Jespers listened to this speech with exaggerated surprise, then turned to Laura as if appealing for help. "You know, Miss Prentice, don't you find it curious that a young man, who believes that life goes on forever, is always most upset when he feels his time is being wasted? Whereas old fellows like me, who know how very short life is, and how precious, we old fellows are far more patient? I find this so very interesting. Beautiful lady, would you mind very much if I discussed for a few minutes a little bit of business with your impatient young man? Mr. Kendrick, could you show Miss Prentice to her quarters? You will, I hope, find them reasonably comfortable."

"I guess I've been dismissed," Laura said.

"We've both been dismissed, Miss Prentice," Kendrick said after a fractional pause. "Would you come this way, please?"

The two men were silent as Laura's footsteps died away; even on the flagstones, Kendrick's step was almost inaudible. Then Jespers climbed down from the forklift.

"Come," he said again.

They walked wordlessly through the whispering gallery, the sounds of their footsteps flying up around them like startled birds, and to the balcony at the end. Heavy sliding glass doors had been installed across it. Jespers touched a button and these slid silently back, letting in a mass of frigid air and a few swirling flecks of snow, and then the two men stepped out onto the narrow balcony. The doors eased shut behind them. Mallory saw that the rock face before them, which earlier had seemed to be only a few inches away, was perhaps thirty yards off. He could not see the bottom of the ravine below them. It was beginning to fill with blue dusk as the afternoon waned. The rock face above them glowed gold and saffron in the low sun. Mallory fastened his fur coat and stuck his hands deep in the pockets; Jespers hugged himself. The parapet around them was no more than hip-high, and Jespers stood well back by the doors. "I like to come out here and think," Jespers said. "I like to come out here and make myself brave, because I don't like heights so much, so being here is a good exercise. You are standing very close to the edge, Jack. Being up high, this doesn't bother you?"

"No, I like it."

"Why?"

Mallory considered. "It's clean."

"You're making me quite nervous. Symmes is still down there somewhere, you know. The snow is deep, no one knows how deep, and there are hidden caves and fissures and so on. It was not possible to search for his body. Perhaps in a hundred years he will appear at the bottom of the mountain. In the spring. It's very pretty out here, don't you think? Also, here you have privacy."

"What's the matter, think Kendrick's eavesdropping on you?"

"That man oppresses me." Jespers sighed.

"He oppresses me pretty good, too. What's your beef with him?"

"There is no poetry in his soul."

"If you're looking for poetry, Arne, I think you kind of booted it. There's none in mine either."

"Oh, forgive me, Jack, but here I must disagree with you. You are a spy, Jack, and a spy is always a poet. It is why he chooses such a ridiculous profession. Mr. Kendrick is a soldier. He imagines that the affairs of this organization can be conducted as the Army conducts a campaign. At his chosen field, security, he is quite excellent, quite without rivals, but he does not understand the life of the entrepreneur, who lives by—*improvisation*. And so there is continually this conflict between us."

"So you sicced us on each other, and now I can have this conflict with him instead."

"Now, Jack, I must—"

"I never much liked dogfights back home, Arne, and I never much liked the guys who liked 'em. You brought me in over him and rubbed his nose in it. You let him know you thought I could do things for you that he couldn't. You must've let Kendrick get too strong around here, and now he's cramping your style. So you slung us both into the dog pit. If I win, your problem's solved for the moment, and if he wins, maybe scrapping with me'll soothe him down a little. And if neither of us wins, you can go on playing us off against each other."

"I have made you my *partner*, Jack," Jespers said, sounding hurt.

"You haven't done a goddamn thing but blow in my ear. You promised me five percent of your gross. You could've promised me five hundred percent, too. I haven't seen any money, and you haven't risked any information, either. You haven't told me a goddamn thing I couldn't have learned in twenty minutes by picking up the phone."

"Is this what you thought yesterday when I made my offer, Jack?"

"Yeah."

Jespers shrugged. "Then we understood each other from the beginning, and I can't see why you are so upset."

Mallory let out a bark of laughter. Jespers stared off at the shadowed rock face and continued in a somewhat wounded tone: "You are in the monastery of Mont Saint-Séverin, Jack, in the Swiss Alps, perhaps two hours from Davos. This is my European operations center. Behind the electric-eye beams in the whispering gallery is a series of rooms with stone-and-rubble walls between one and a quarter and four meters thick. These are the most solidly built rooms in this exceedingly solidly built monastery. Three hundred years ago, the monks used them to store the tiles they manufactured, glazed tiles with pictures of little frowning saints and pretty blue cornflowers, which were quite highly prized all over Europe. I have used these rooms to store Walther Kost and his workshop. I have used them to store Archangel. Kost completed a working prototype nearly five weeks ago. It performs flawlessly on the workbench. All that remains is to test it from space. We have purchased, quite legitimately, a British Strongbow 9-A solid-fuel booster rocket designed for small scientific satellites. The launchpad is in the cleft peak above us."

"'Where the Angel lives.'"

"Yes. The large glass structure that you saw from the funicular, this is our control center. In perhaps one hour I will fly back to Monaco to collect three potential buyers and escort them to this compound, representatives of the GRU, the Pathet Lao, and a Venezuelan group called the Brotherhood of Ultima Thule. I will bring them here late tonight. On Wednesday at dawn we will all meet in the control center, you and I and the bidders, and witness Archangel's launch. Does this satisfy your curiosity, Jack?"

"No. What's Archangel?"

"An extraordinarily powerful spy satellite."

"Not for half a billion bucks, Arne. What's Archangel?"

"An extraordinarily powerful spy satellite. You will meet Dr. Kost tomorrow, and he will explain its special capabilities."

Mallory shook his head. "You haven't let me into the kitchen with the big folks yet, Arne. I'm still down in the dog pit with Kendrick."

"Your teeth are quite sharp, Jack," Jespers said, gazing up at the sunlit peak. "I am sure you will manage."

The room Jespers had given them was large and circular and located in one of the smaller turrets Mallory had seen from the cable car. Two tall, narrow windows pierced the walls, one facing north, the other east; they had been enlarged recently, it seemed, and fitted with hinged triple-glazed panes. The sills were nearly four feet deep. A quarter of the room had been enclosed with opaque black glass walls and converted into a gleaming modern bathroom. A miscellany of overlapping rugs covered the stone floor: sheepskin, pony skin, and several mismatched Persians. A fire burned brightly in the hearth at the foot of the bed, and electric baseboard heaters lined the room's stone walls. For all Mallory knew, it was the only warm place in the monastery. When he stepped through the door, Laura was reclining on the enormous bed, reading her battered Nero Wolfe. "Have a nice chat, dear?" she said.

She pointed to the bedside table, the corner of the fireplace, and the open door of the bathroom.

"I dunno what kind of chat we had," Mallory said, shrugging off his fur coat and dumping it on a chair. "He's pretty cute. Lord, I'm bushed."

He flicked a finger across his throat.

Laura closed the book, rose, and drew a small pair of pliers from her purse. The pliers' tips were long and curved. After a few minutes of silent work, she presented Mallory with three diminutive listening devices, one of them smeared with fireplace soot and one beaded with water.

Mallory set them in a row on his palm and examined them. "Look at these pretty little things," he said.

He dropped them on the floor and, as Laura winced, smashed each one in turn with his heel.

"The man of action," she said.

At the desk, Mallory found an envelope. "Engraved stationery," he said, not bothering to lower his voice. "See? Like a damn hotel."

"They misspelled Mont Saint-Sévérin," Laura observed at his shoulder.

Mallory swept the fragments into the envelope, sealed the flap, and glanced around the room. He went to the door, opened it, and gave a sharp whistle. A guard strolled around the corner, gun at his side, finger along the trigger guard, an inquiring look on his face. Mallory tossed the envelope at him and he caught it left-handed.

"Give that to Arne," Mallory said, and closed the door on the man's impassive stare. "Dumb ass caught it," he muttered. "What's Kendrick teaching these people?"

"He'll bring it to Kendrick," Laura said. "Is it wise to tweak Kendrick's nose?"

She spoke inaudibly, her face turned to Mallory so he could read her lips. Bugs or no bugs, it's always best to act as though an enemy has an ear pressed to one's door.

"That old boy's nose is permanently tweaked," Mallory said equally inaudibly. "And Arne needs to know I'm worth my pay, which means I don't lie down and let myself be bugged without letting somebody hear about it. Anyway, I don't want to have to fool with this kind of crap the whole time I'm here. Where'd you put the rig? Here we are." He reached under the bed, pulled out a flat metal box like a miniature stereo tuner, and began disconnecting the leads and tucking away two wire-fine antennae. "Thanks for doing the sweeping."

"That thing makes it a pleasure. I was done in about forty-five seconds. It's nice using a proper setup, not one of these little gimmicky ones that's tricked out to look like a hair dryer or something."

"That's the beauty of this cover," Mallory said, grinning. "It's like running naked. If somebody goes through your luggage and says, 'Hey, what's all this spy stuff?' You just say, 'Oh, that's my spy stuff. I'm a spy, and I never go anywhere without it.' Hon, did we bring a limpet mike?"

"Yes."

"And some phones with a mini-bump and about twenty feet of cord?"

"Yes, somewhere. Mm, I see what you mean. Well, I'll dig it out."

"Thanks."

"Did he drop the veil?"

"Lifted a corner, I guess. They launch the gadget Wednesday morning. Commercial booster, bought legal. Launchpad's where you'd think it was, Kost's where you'd think he was, bidders're who Billy said they were. Arne's bringing 'em in late tonight. In theory, tomorrow Kost'll tell me himself why this dingus is so wonderful."

"But Jespers didn't."

"But Jespers didn't." Mallory dropped with a sigh into an armchair and stared out the window. "Kendrick has no poetry in his soul."

"Jespers told you that?"

"He did."

"Well then, your little talk wasn't a waste."

"On the way back, I tried to walk down a side hall and see what I could see. Guy out there headed me off. He said Mr. Kendrick wanted me to have an escort until I knew the place better. I said, 'What kind of escort?' He said, 'The kind that escorts you back to your room.'" Mallory shook his head. "Smart-mouth punk. And then he goes catching whatever you take a mind to throw at him."

"Did you think we'd get the run of the place?"

"Jespers is screwy enough for anything."

"There's whiskey in that cabinet. I don't know if it's anything you'd like."

"If it's whiskey, I'll like it. Thanks." He rose with a grunt and poured himself a drink.

"Thirty-six hours isn't much time," Laura said.

"It's plenty of time to do something stupid. I dunno whether it's enough time to do something smart." He took a sip and lifted his chin toward the darkening view out the window. "What do you think of that?"

"The west face? I don't like it."

"How much do you not like it?"

She shrugged. "It's not something I'd do for fun."

"No."

"When am I going up?" she said.

"Dunno. Maybe never. How about the chopper?"

"It's a Sikorsky S-61 Sea King. Five blades, twin turbines, amphibious—for what that's worth in the middle of the Alps—and, as of last year, the world's fastest. Something like three hundred thirty, three hundred forty kilometers an hour. I've never seen a civilian one before. Do I have a key?"

"Maybe. Let's say no."

"Well, hot-wiring it could be ticklish, or it could be easy. I'd hate for us not to have a fallback. As for flying the thing, I couldn't do it well, not without practice, but a helicopter's a helicopter and I imagine I could put this one down on a potato field somewhere without killing us all. A big bird like that's more forgiving than a little one, and it goes higher faster. Which is good. We'd want to get up out of range of the Alpine thermals as quickly as possible. They're murder."

"So are ack-ack rounds."

"Well, yes. Do they *have* anti-aircraft guns?"

"They got everything else. Probably not, though. You better try and rest up tonight. You still look pretty beat. How're you feeling?"

"I hurt. Lord, do I hurt. That was the hardest physical work I've ever had to do. I hate to admit it, but I actually didn't quite have the muscle for the job. I was overextended the entire time. I used a lot of lung sutras, which helped, but if I hadn't been taught how to block pain, I'd never have gotten through it. Ow. Let go of me. What are you doing back there? *Ow*," she said blissfully.

"Hold still, or this'll hurt."

"It already hurts." Mallory had set down his drink and was behind her, his long fingers enveloping her narrow back, stretching out each long, sore muscle in turn, and letting it go. Each time, he seemed to release a stream of warm honey into her veins. He set a sinewy forearm across her collarbones, pressed the knuckles of his free hand against her back, and rippled them. Her spine crackled softly. "Ah. *Hah*. Where did you learn to do that?"

"My mom was a waitress. You know that. She'd come back from a double shift all beat down and crimped up from standing all that while, and I learned how to work the kinks out again. It made her easier to live with. Didn't I ever tell you that? Surprised it didn't give me a what-you-call. A complex."

"It probably did. There must be some explanation for you."

"She was never exactly a mom to us anyway. She was only sixteen years older than me. Not even. She was more like some dimwit big sister who was always in trouble. Pretty legs, though." He was kneading his way down her arms to her fingertips.

"You'd better stay away from my legs, Jack," Laura said sincerely.

Her back and arms felt as if they were glowing.

"Don't worry, I don't want to get kicked over the next Alp. There you go. Feel any better?"

"My God, I feel wonderful. Thank you."

Mallory flopped back into the armchair and took another swallow of his drink. Laura remained standing, eyes closed, savoring the new ease in her back, neck, and arms. "Are we really going to try a grab before launch?" she said, inaudible again. She opened her eyes to see Mallory's response.

"Well, it's hard to see how we could grab it after, unless we got somebody standing on a cloud with a butterfly net."

"Easier to just demo it, of course, but we weren't to do that except as a last resort. In which case we'd still need to deal with Kost and the plans anyway."

"Standing on a cloud . . ." Mallory said, rubbing his face.

"Jack?"

"I dunno. Nothing. You know, Laurie, I was awful proud of you yesterday."

"Well, thanks."

"Don't goddamn well-thanks me like I just passed you the salt," Mallory said irritably. "You got us through the door. Jespers wouldn't take me so seriously if I hadn't won fifty grand off him. You came up with the play and set it up with Burch and executed it pretty near solo. It was impossible and you did it anyway. I was damn proud. He was congratulating me on having you for my girl and I was all puffed up like it was true."

"Well," Laura said, "I'm afraid I don't know what to say to that except thank you." She picked up her book and resettled herself on the bed. Her voice was as cool and impassive as always.

By the time Mallory looked around at her, her face was cool and impassive as well.

Dinner was brought to them on trays: covered earthenware bowls of rabbit cassoulet with Toulouse sausage and baby onions, and a silver dish of steamed asparagus. Afterward, they took turns changing in the bathroom, Mallory into an old pair of striped flannel pajamas and Laura into a prim cotton nightgown. It was her own. She'd had a look at Lily Prentice's nightgowns and did not propose to wear any of them while sharing a bed with Jack Mallory. They brushed their teeth side by side at the sink. The toothpaste foam was white against her dark face. Her eyes were still dark and haggard. *Jack's girl,* she thought, rinsing. *Ha.* She spat and dabbed her mouth dry.

She was already in bed when Mallory stepped from the bathroom holding a towel and looking from one window to the other.

"Good idea," she said sleepily. "We don't want slush on the rugs. Um, I don't know. The north one?"

Mallory spread the towel out beneath the north window and got into bed beside her. "'Night," he said, stretching out with his hands behind his head.

"Good night," she said, turning on her left hip, away from him.

He put out the light.

At three in the morning, they awoke together. The north window of their room had gone dark. They listened, motionless, to a series of faint clicks and scrapes, and then to a soft grinding noise as the window swung slowly open. A current of cold air curled through the warmth and touched their faces. Laura slipped noiselessly out of the bed and stood beside it, waiting. As they watched, the blackness in the window resolved itself into a towering figure, broad-shouldered and bullet-headed, bearing a silenced gun in one gloved hand, who eased himself down from the stone sill and stepped quietly to the floor.

Mallory rolled over and switched on the bedside lamp and the massive figure paused, blinking in the glare.

"Not bad," Mallory said. "You're even a little early."

"I told you," Billy Harmon said. "I don't like waiting around."

2

Understood

The limpet mike was fixed to the inside of the door, the cord trailing across the jumble of rugs to an amplifier the size of a pack of cigarettes, and from there to a pair of earphones. Laura Morse held one of the earphones to her ear. She listened carefully for a full minute, then nodded fractionally.

"All right," Mallory said to Harmon, "how did you work it?"

Harmon had pulled off his gloves and laid them neatly on the rug beside his gun, and was now chafing his chilled fingers together, crouching on the towel Mallory had spread beneath the window. "Little nippy out there," he said. "Is that . . . ?"

Laurie had taken a small polished steel flask of brandy from the bedside table and nudged it across the rug toward Harmon with her free hand. He took a swallow and shivered.

"Thanks," he said, wiping the neck carefully on his cuff and capping it again. "Ah. Well, I tailed you to the airport by car—how'd I do, by the way?"

"Good," Mallory said. "Laurie thought she might've seen an aqua Renault just before we turned off N7, but she wasn't sure. Was that you?"

"Yeah," Harmon said dispiritedly.

"You did very well," Laura said. "I was looking for you and, as Jack said, I still wasn't sure. Go on. What did you do at Nice, pick up our registry number with field glasses?"

"Yes, and then I got on to Jim Landry at the big dish in Geneva. I didn't know you were headed to Switzerland—they were just the biggest tracking station I could think of. That we've got an in with, anyway. Once we had compass bearings, we made an educated guess, and I was in the air on a Greek military jet fifty minutes after you took off. Patched Landry's signal through to the onboard C-Reg on a mirror line, so we knew when you started making your descent, and then the pilot managed to sweet-talk air traffic on a freight strip outside of Davos. Listen, why's the Greek Air Force so nice to us?"

"I'd guess their government owes Gray money. What happened then?"

"After that, it was just a matter of being lucky and making good trains. Had a look at the schedules and a map, and it seemed like it'd work out faster and maybe cleaner than renting a car. Stavrinos sends his best, by the way. He says he's got a fresh deck waiting for you, still in the cellophane, any time you want to come around and try and win your money back."

"It'll wait a long time. Where are you bivouacked?"

"About two hundred—"

Laura lifted a slim finger and Harmon fell silent.

Lip-reading was not one of the boy's many talents, not yet; his voice had been soft but audible. It was unlikely but not impossible that he'd be audible in the hall outside. They did not intend to run the risk. The three spies sat motionless as Laura listened over the earphones to a guard's quiet footsteps as they approached their door and then dwindled into the distance again.

When they'd faded into silence, she nodded, and Harmon resumed: "Maybe two hundred yards down the slope to the south-south-west, in a capsule tent dug into the snow. Middle of a stand of firs. I'm hid pretty good there. When the mouth of the tent's closed, you can stand right on top of it and still miss it. Warm, too. Really nice stuff. Special issue?"

Laura shook her head. "Off the rack. You can buy pretty good things in a mountaineering equipment store, if you're willing to spend. How are conditions?"

"We're lucky. The snow's deep light powder and there's a good steady wind, maybe twelve knots. If it stays this cold, I'd guess any footprints or ski tracks we make should be gone in about six to eight minutes."

"Good. What does eight minutes buy us?"

"Plenty. Perimeter guard goes around two by two, both with submachine guns, and they're not regular—your guy Kendrick's too much of a pro for that. But the shortest interval's eleven minutes. I watched all evening to check. They're not sleepwalking, either. They spend a lot more time on the slopes with blind brows than they do on the clear ones where you can see all the way down. Of course, I've got no idea what kind of rota they've got for the inside guards."

"They just wander around smarting off to the guests," Mallory said. "What you got there?"

"A map of the monastery," Harmon said. He was unable to keep a note of pride from his voice.

"Son of a bitch. Son of a sweet blue bitch, how'd you get that?"

"Most of these little villages have a guy who's sort of the town archivist, the guy who knows all the stories. This one runs the tavern by the guesthouse. He's also the mayor, and he's got a whole little library on the Order of Saint Séverin, including some nice maps of the old monastery. He let me sketch a couple. I told him I was a student from the University of Maryland doing his master's on Alpine ecclesiastical architecture."

"What if he wanted to talk about Alpine ecclesiastical architecture?"

"He did. My French got very bad."

"You got a little fancy there, Billy. A story like that can be checked. Jespers might have the mayor on salary."

"He won't check," Harmon said. "People are damn lazy."

Mallory frowned, then said, "Where does the mayor think you're staying tonight?"

"He thinks I took the 1621 train back to Davos."

"In a small town, Billy, people always know who gets on the train."

"That's why I got on the train, Jack. Picked a nice soft snowbank and rolled off into it when we slowed for the first curve out of town. Then I hiked the long way around and climbed back up through the woods."

"Well, all right then."

"You did a terrific job, Billy," Laura said.

"Yeah, you did, actually. Just make sure you don't get too terrific. A couple of times, you got close. Give that map here. All right. Here we are, and here's the places we've had a chance to check out. And here's where Jespers says Kost is, behind an electric-eye fence you haven't got the equipment to cross. That's supposed to be where they built Archangel. But that's just what Jespers says, and he's got no special reason to be honest. I want you to check and see if Kost's really there. You don't need to see the man himself—he'll be in bed. Just look for some sign that somebody's using the place to build space doodads."

"Then what?"

"Then nothing, Billy. Then exactly nothing. You go back to your tent and wait for our signal. Look, this area where Kost's supposed to be is One. Over here's Two, and this is Three, and that's all the possibilities I can think of. Just give us one, two, or three short pulses on the reserve channel when you get back to your tent, wait exactly five seconds, then repeat. Then you're done for the night. *All* done. We don't want you to spring Kost, or talk to him, or even unlock the back door so we can sneak in later. Just verify and scram. Is that understood?"

"Understood," Harmon said.

"It had better be."

"I guess you're one of these grizzled veterans," Harmon said, holstering his gun and getting ready to go. "One of these grizzled, battle-scarred old-timers who hides his heart of gold under a crusty exterior."

"Don't bet on it," Mallory said.

When Harmon pulled himself up onto the roof, the moon was bright. He didn't mind. He'd spent half the afternoon and all of the evening on his belly in the little capsule tent, sighting up the hill with high-powered glasses, and by now he knew the shape of the monastery as well as he knew the shape of his childhood bedroom. In particular, he knew where the windows and sightlines were. In a bright moon like this, Harmon knew he'd stick out like a beetle on a wedding cake if anyone looked his way, but to look his way, you'd have to be high enough to see over the peak of the roof before him. To look his way, you'd need wings. The moon wasn't a problem. He was fine.

He rested his tensed muscles and let himself take pleasure in his firmly planted feet, and in the memory of an impeccable ropeless climb up seventy feet of near-vertical fitted-stone wall, using nothing but the strength and skill of his highly trained fingers and toes. There is always a measure of happiness in doing what one does well, and Harmon was a superlative free climber. Completing the climb without tools took a little of the sting out of his soul. He hadn't enjoyed having Jack trim him down. It had hit him especially hard because he'd really thought he'd been performing pretty solidly. Well, Jack was just doing it to toughen him up, he guessed. It was childish to mind it. He was going to forget all about it now and get back to work.

Harmon flexed his fingers, shook the last tension from them, and gazed out across the complex of roofs. He could see little from where he clung to the monastery's slate shingles, but he wasn't looking with his eyes. He had always scored in the top percentiles of any standard-ized test he'd taken, including the highly specialized ones adminis-tered by the Consultancy's Intake Section, and he scored particularly high on Visualization and Visual Memory. In his mind, Harmon had crafted a miniature Monastery of Saint-Séverin. He'd worked at it for hours, adding a touch here and a detail there, and now it was as clear

to him as if he were turning it in his fingers. There was the window
he needed to access the wing Jack had called One, directly across the
bulk of the compound. There were the exposed areas of roof—those
under the visual command of a window or balcony—that he'd have to
avoid. There were the snow-heavy areas as well, and the ones that had
a shaggy look, as if the slates were loose, and the steeper roofs that
were probably more trouble than they were worth, and the lower roofs
that would take him out of his way. He revolved the little monastery in
his mind, plotting his path. It would have been tempting to use the balconies; a number of them were connected by external terraces, so that
you could walk unseen from one to the other. But the snow on the terraces wasn't light powder that blew clean. It had thawed with the heat
of the monastery and frozen again, and any footprints he left in that
snow would be unmistakable when daylight came. The balconies were
closed off with motor-driven glass doors, too, which were probably
harder to gimmick than the windows. And maybe they were wired to
a central desk, so an operator could tell each time one opened. That's
the way Harmon would have done it, anyway. So the balconies only
looked easy. The roof was best.

Once he'd plotted the path in his mind, it took Billy Harmon
slightly less than three minutes to cross the complex of roofs, sometimes crawling sinuously on all fours like a cat, sometimes muscling
himself over a ledge or rooftree, and sometimes strolling as casually
as he might have strolled along a sidewalk. At no time did he rush. At
no time did he stop moving. When he reached the far edge of the final
roof and cautiously hung his head over the edge, he noted with satisfaction that he was almost directly above the window he'd sought—no
more than seven or eight feet off. The roof's edge was crenellated here,
and he took hold of one of the squarish stone teeth and found it solid.
Unzipping a pouch at his hip, he drew out a coil of yarn-thin braided
nylon-and-teflon rope. Working rapidly, he fastened a loop around the
base of the crenellation, anchoring it with a titanium piton, then ran
his fingers through the other contents of the pouch, found them in
order, and withdrew a doctor's stethoscope. The chromed steel tubes
had been spray-painted matte black so that they wouldn't gleam. He
hung the stethoscope around his neck, as doctors do, and zipped his

hip pouch closed. He hooked a steel carabiner through the harness at his waist, tugged it to see that it was well seated, snapped the rope into it, and saw the rope was moving freely. He gripped the rope. Moving with a lightness surprising in someone his size, he swung himself unhesitatingly out into the void.

Six seconds later Harmon was suspended beside the window, his toes lightly braced against the wall, his gloved hands gripping the rope. He'd descended almost as quickly as a falling man, but with perfect control. The window was lit. No sense putting things off; he eased over and peered around the stone ledge. Nothing but a view of blank, brightly lit sheet-rock wall. The wall looked new. He fixed the rope into the harness at his waist, tugged it, and saw there was no play. He slowly released the grip of his left hand until he was being supported solely by the harness. When both hands were free, he flexed them, then nudged up the edge of his woolen cap, plugged the earpieces of the stethoscope into his ears, and set the business end against the glass. For ninety seconds by his watch, he listened. Nothing. Not a thing. Anyone in there was asleep. It was a damn shame. He'd have to go inside to find out anything.

He slipped the stethoscope into his hip pouch, checked the contents again by touch, and withdrew a small, blunt-ended retractable knife like a box-cutter and a small T-shape of black-anodized aluminum that looked a bit like a safety razor. He set them on the window ledge. Beside them he put a small squeeze bottle of silicone lubricant and a chamois. Then he went to work.

The window yielded easily and silently; its fittings were identical to the one in Jack and Laura's room, and Harmon worked without hesitating. He was less worried about getting the window open than about the cold air he'd let into the warm hallway when he did. He'd been well aware of the icy currents he'd let loose across Jack and Laura's bed. There wasn't much to do about it except to try and move fast and hope his back and shoulders shut out the worst of the draft. Harmon tucked away the tools he'd used to breach the window, brought out a rag, and carefully wiped down the sides and soles of his boots. He did not intend to leave wet footprints. If he was going to die tonight, it wouldn't be for something as dumb as that. He touched the gun at his waist and checked to see his hip pouch was zipped. *All right,* he thought. He eased the window open and squeezed himself through.

The window was deep-set enough to be like a small tunnel, and Harmon took his time wriggling through. When he stepped to the floor on the other side, he found himself in a short, brightly lit hallway running parallel to the outer wall. To his right, the hallway bent sharply to the left. Around the corner he could just see the edge of a closed door. It was a new door, painted dark cream, and looked somehow domestic. Sleeping quarters, maybe. To his left, the hallway bent sharply to the right. A heavy wooden door was set into the thick stone outer wall, and, around that corner, he could see nothing but a wash of bright light. It might lead to, or even be, part of the workshop. He'd take a quick look in that direction, he decided.

He heard a wooden chair scrape along a floor.

Damn. Ninety seconds on the stethoscope hadn't been enough. Sometimes the manual was wrong. He heard a slight grunt, as of a weary man rising from his desk. It came from no more than ten feet away. Then footsteps, coming closer. Harmon glanced at the darkened corner on the other side. He had just enough time to slip silently around it. Jack had told him—

Harmon felt a surge of irrational defiance at the thought of running and hiding because of what Jack had told him.

It lasted perhaps three-quarters of a second. Then sanity returned, three-quarters of a second too late. A tall, thin man with flowing white hair, dressed in dark slacks and a dark turtleneck sweater, stepped around the corner, holding a notebook in one hand and rummaging in his pocket with the other. Harmon knew the face from his briefing packet: Kost. The old man's eyes were weary but intent, and he seemed to be holding himself stiffly upright against a weight of fatigue. When he caught sight of Harmon, he stopped.

Harmon had his gun down by his leg and was holding one gloved finger up against his own lips.

For a moment, the two men regarded each other.

Harmon took the finger from his lips, touched it to his ear, and then made a circular gesture to indicate their surroundings, concluding with the universal palm-raised sign of inquiry. The old man stared.

There was something Harmon didn't like about the man's stare. It seemed to express not joy at the sight of a rescuer, not fear of a possible assailant, but simple and unhurried calculation.

At last the old man said in a conversational tone: "We are alone here. And there are no listening devices in this apartment. I would not tolerate them."

Harmon understood only *no* and *listening*. His German was too sketchy for a conversation. And it was time, unfortunately, to talk. He said, *"Parlez-vous français, Herr Doktor?"*

"I prefer English," Kost said in English. "Who are you?"

"It doesn't matter. You're Kost."

"Yes."

Improvising, Harmon said, "How soon can you be ready to go?"

For the moment, it seemed imperative to conceal the fact that he'd blundered into this meeting and had no idea what he was doing. Harmon would worry about death later. Right now, he feared only looking like a fool.

"Go?"

"Yes. How soon?"

"This is rather sudden. My work—" Kost said, then stopped. "Very well. I am at your disposal."

Harmon hesitated. The man seemed curiously uneager.

He said, "We're not going now, Kost. We'll want you to bring your notebooks along. We'll want you to bring Archangel."

"Of course," Kost said wearily. "You say 'we.' May I ask who is this 'we'?"

"Not yet. Can you be ready this time tomorrow?"

"Am I to exchange one set of captors for another without asking who or why?"

"You won't be a captive if you make it to the other end. You'll be a free man."

"Ah. A free man. And Archangel?"

"Is the price of your ticket."

"Yes." Kost pondered once more, then appeared to reach a decision. "Well, this time tomorrow I will be in the control center, preparing for the launch. I shall be surrounded by assistants and technicians. And, of course, guards."

"Of course. When do you get up on Wednesday?"

"I hoped to sleep until one a.m."

"We'll try to come by at a quarter to one. If we can't swing that, we'll try again after the launch. Where do you sleep?"

"Here. Behind that door."

"Alone?"

"Yes," Kost said with a touch of irony.

"That closet over there's your plan file?"

"Yes."

"Show me."

Kost took a long steel key from his pocket and opened the door. Perhaps the closet had once been used to store wine. Perhaps it had always been used for precious manuscripts. The door was of heavy wooden planks joined with thick, ancient pegs; only the glittering lock was new. The closet was no more than a deep notch in the massive outer walls, made of the same dark gray stone as the rest of the monastery. It had been fitted from floor to ceiling with steel shelves. The shelves were stacked neatly with rolled diazo prints and battered clothbound notebooks. Kost set the notebook he'd been holding on a stack of similar notebooks and neatened the stack with a forefinger.

"How many copies of that key?" Harmon asked.

"One other. It is kept by a Mr. Kendrick. This copy never leaves my person."

"Leave it on your desk tonight. Hide it, but not too well. And before you turn in, rearrange that closet so you've got all the major, mission-critical intel on the fourth shelf down. So that anyone who grabs the contents of that shelf has enough to reconstruct Archangel, even if they haven't got access to the prototype itself. Clear?"

"You make it quite clear," Kost said.

"All right, Kost," Harmon said. "Except for those two items, go about your business tonight and tomorrow as if we hadn't spoken. Try to get some sleep. Either way, you've got a big day ahead of you. Good luck. I'll let myself out."

Kost nodded, and Harmon set a gloved hand on the window ledge and swung himself dexterously up, thinking, *Jesus. Did I actually just say "I'll let myself out"?*

Harmon was clumsier wriggling out through the window than he'd been wriggling in. Once he'd gotten hold of the rope outside and was dangling beside the window again, he took a moment to compose himself. *It's not blown yet,* he told himself. *Please. Let the operation not be blown yet. We'd have had to make contact with Kost eventually. Jack'll know how to get things back on track again. Stupid. Jesus, so stupid.* He began to climb again, smoothly and carefully. He had to get word to Jack somehow. Had to let him know— He'd send four pulses on the transceiver, then wait for Jack's query. *He'll skin me alive. He's got every right to skin me alive. All right, enough of that. Enough. Let's get back to the tent without waking the neighborhood.*

It took a full three minutes for Harmon to clamber back up the monastery wall. This would have been a respectable rate for most experienced climbers, but it was painfully slow for Billy Harmon. His confidence and pleasure in his skill were gone. He wanted nothing more than to be back in his tent with the flap zipped shut. He wanted to go home and hide his face. As he reached the row of stone crenellations, he called himself to order again and tried to summon up his mental map of the roofs. Hopefully, the moon wasn't too bright just then. He looked up to check and saw a hand reaching down toward his, an enormous ungloved hand wearing a gleaming ring. It clamped around his forearm, and then he was being drawn up effortlessly into the air. And then he was flying.

Harmon smashed into the chilly slates with an impact that nearly knocked him cold. He felt an electric pain branching out within his shoulder like a bolt of lightning. The slates were cold against his cheek.

"I fell," he said aloud. His voice sounded strange. The gigantic black figure was moving toward him, walking easily up the steep slope of the roof. *Jesus, so big—*

He couldn't think. He couldn't *think*, he—

He saw a big leg lashing out.

It was his own leg, launched with a twist of his own sinewy back and the strength of his good left arm. A reverse leg-scythe, slashing directly at the shadow's chest. Harmon's body was not waiting for Harmon's stunned mind to clear. It had executed the kick the Manchurians call the Ox Horn, executed it perfectly, with savage force and startling speed.

But his opponent was no longer there to be kicked. He was flickering backward, as if he really were a shadow, and Harmon's boot merely brushed a fold of cloth and was swinging free again through the air. *Goddamn, fast* . . .

He used the momentum to roll to his feet. Spinning into a Horse Stance, he found the shadow already upon him again. He bit back the pain in his shoulder, feinted toward the figure's groin, then hooked both fists upward in a double heart-blow.

They met forearms like stone; Harmon screamed thinly through his teeth as a thumb and two knuckles gave way. He was in too close. One of the vast hands swooped out—he saw the ring dully gleaming again—and hooked Harmon's neck forward. He felt himself flipping over a big hip and then flying again.

When he smashed into the roof this time, he barely felt it.

And then all he knew was a methodical cannonade of blows from feet and knees and hands, of the big fist descending again and again, the twisted iron ring glinting coolly in the bits of moonlight. He felt his ribs crumpling. He felt his thighs snap, one after the other. He felt his nose and cheekbones collapse. His screams choked off as his throat filled with blood. He coughed up the blood and his throat began to fill again. He did not remember why he was on the roof. He did not know why he was being hurt. The pain was demolishing everything, even itself, as the roar of a hurricane will eventually drown itself out and become silence. All Harmon knew was that he'd forgotten something, forgotten the most important thing of all. *"Jack,"* he mumbled through pulped lips. There was something he needed to remember. *Ask,* he thought. If he could just remember . . . He whispered, *"Ask."*

The immense dark fist was rising again into the dark sky. Billy Harmon watched it rise.

"Ask . . . Jack . . . first . . ." he whispered raggedly.

It descended.

———

Then it was still on the roof, still and almost dark. Nothing moved, nothing made a sound, except the thickly humming wind.

And then the moon worked its way free of the clouds once more.

It cast a leaden light over the broken contours of Harmon's corpse. It lit each of the splintered black slates of the ancient roof. And it shed a silvery sheen over Milena's smooth Slavic cheekbones and the broad slopes of her shoulders. Milena smiled faintly, peacefully, as she looked down on the shattered carcass at her feet. The habitual sullenness was gone from her face. Her tiny eyes were almost gentle.

Then she slipped the twined-serpents ring from her finger, licked it clean of blood, and tucked it away in her breast pocket, next to her heart.

3

Hullabaloo

At 3:27 a.m. Laura Morse closed the window behind Billy Harmon, exchanged nods with him through the glass, and climbed back in bed beside Jack Mallory. She turned onto her left side. Silently, she wished the boy well. She wished him a clear head, good judgment, and sound memory. She wished him calm and self-possession. She wished him the thing all field agents need most: luck. Then she took a few cleansing breaths, as her sensei had years ago taught her, and went to sleep.

Almost exactly two hours later, she woke again with the knowledge that Mallory had not slept. She turned and found him lying with his hands behind his neck, staring at the ceiling.

"Did I sleep through it?" she murmured.

He shook his head, still staring upward.

For a moment, she was silent. Then she said, "Any number of things could have delayed him. He could still be doing recon. If so, he'll be back in his tent soon, before it's light."

Mallory didn't reply.

She said, "Maybe we'll find out more this morning."

He said, "I hope to God we don't."

Shortly before six, they heard two sharp raps on their door, and Kendrick stepped into the room, two of Jespers's mountainous armed guards behind him. He said, "On your feet, Carroll. You're needed."

Laura made a sleepy, petulant noise and burrowed further into the covers. Mallory blinked as if freshly woken. He cleared his throat and said, "Do you always—"

Kendrick said, "It's not a good morning for wisecracks."

Mallory believed him.

He swung his feet to the floor and rose, saying, "Be back in a little while, hon."

"We'll need Miss Prentice, too," Kendrick said.

"Like hell," Mallory said.

"Why is that man here, Jackie," Laura whimpered. "Make him go."

"Mr. Jespers asked to see both of you," Kendrick said. "You can argue with him when you get there."

Mallory had hauled on slacks over his pajama bottoms and was pulling socks from a drawer. "Don't look," Laura said, sitting up. "I need a shower. I'm never any good until I shower and do my face. Why do we have to get up so *early*?"

"Shoes and a coat, Miss Prentice. That's all you need."

"Well, then I'm not going with you."

"Hush," Mallory said, not looking at her. "You can make yourself pretty after we've got this sorted out." He was pulling on his shoes.

"You don't look like you've slept well, Mr. Carroll," Kendrick said.

"I never sleep well in strange beds," Mallory said, doing up his shoelaces.

Laura got out of the bed and blinked ill-temperedly around the room. In the chilly predawn light, Mallory noticed that the prim cotton nightgown was actually pretty threadbare by now and not near as modest as Laura probably thought. Kendrick smiled at her. "How about you, Miss Prentice?" he said. "How do you do in strange beds?"

Mallory stopped tying his laces. "It's not a good morning for wisecracks, Kendrick," he said.

There was something in his voice that rendered Kendrick silent.

Laura stuffed her bare feet into high-heeled shoes, yanked the heavy fur coat over her nightgown, and stood hugging herself angrily. "This'll probably all be something really stupid," she said.

"Yeah," Mallory said softly. "I believe it will."

Kendrick led them through the monastery to the whispering gallery, Laura's heels echoing, the two guards bringing up the rear. At the mouth of the tunnel, he inserted two keys into a wall plate and turned them simultaneously in opposite directions. The pale electric-eye beams vanished, and he led them up the stairs. The door at the top was closed with a combination lock. Kendrick blocked their view with his broad back as he dialed in the code. Inside was a broad, bright room like an engineering office, lit with rows of suspended fluorescent lights and lined with wooden drafting tables. The walls were hung with neat arrays of long maple French curves like those used by naval architects, and with cork bulletin boards. The cork boards were empty of drawings and the room was empty of people. At the far end, a heavy wooden door was set into the stone wall, locked with a gleaming new lock. Mallory, who'd burgled a fair number of offices in his day, thought, *That's where they got the plans, all right.*

A door on the left-hand wall stood open. Beyond it lay a windowless conference room, bare and utilitarian. On the wooden table lay a long bundle wrapped in a canvas tarp and secured with rope. In the far corner, Walther Kost sat in a straight-backed chair, his hands on his knees, staring straight ahead. His lean face was pale and set. Beside the long bundle stood Arne Jespers, looking thoughtful.

"Good morning, Jack, Miss Prentice," he said. "I apologize for this rude awakening, but I am afraid there is a matter we must discuss without delay. Our compound has been penetrated. We have had a visitor. Fortunately, we were able to put a stop to this fellow before he reached the control center or launchpad, but he was able to gain access somehow to Dr. Kost's workshop, and to speak to Dr. Kost." The ropes at the far end of the bundle had been unknotted. Jespers pulled back the canvas. "Do you know him?"

Mallory stepped closer, aware of Kendrick's eyes on him. It was easy to hold his face and voice steady. He was way past alarm, and this was pretty much what he'd expected since four that morning. "His own mother wouldn't know him," Mallory said. "Naw, I don't know him. Now, goddamn it, don't bring Lily here. She doesn't need to see—"

"Miss Prentice? Is this man known to you?"

Laura's body jerked back and her slim hands flew up to her face. "Oh God," she whispered between them, "it's awful."

"Do you—"

"It's awful, so awful. Why did you make me *look* at it?" she said thinly, and clutched her face harder. Her voice was a sort of meow, distorted by grief and horror. It was not, Mallory knew, all acting. It was pretty much the kind of noise he felt like making himself. "Take it away. Why did you *make* me? Let me go. Let me *go*."

"Get her out of here," Mallory said, still gazing at the remains of Harmon's face. Or anyhow, at the front of the boy's head; there wasn't much face left. He felt an enormous weight of sadness gathering inside him, a sadness thick as nausea. He prayed it would last a little bit longer. He could use it as a kind of ballast. He prayed it would stay like it was a little while before it turned to rage and began to rise. It was too early to let himself get angry. The job was sunk if he did that, and he and Laurie were dead. His voice was mild as he said, "Get her goddamn out of here. Now."

Jespers nodded.

"Avery," Kendrick said. One of the guards stepped forward. "Take her to her room and keep her there."

"Jack," she said, "what's *happening*?"

"Go back to bed, hon," Mallory said. "This doesn't concern you. I'll be back in a while. Go on, now."

When the door closed behind them, he looked up at Kendrick and said, "Looks like we've got work to do."

"Well, I'm glad you pointed that out," Kendrick said. "I appreciate it. Now that you mention it, I guess we do. 'Start with, you can answer a few of my questions."

"All right."

"We found a capsule tent in the woods where the kid must have holed up. Not much there. Train tickets from Davos. Ammo, film, water, dry rations, a piss pot, and this little item." Kendrick drew a sealed plastic bag from his jacket pocket. Inside was a black metal tablet, set with tiny steel knobs and a small, circular grille. "Know what this is?"

"Sure. An LTC. A compact ultralow transceiver."

"That's right, Mr. Carroll. Now, if I was to search your room—"

"I should've seen this coming," Mallory said wearily. "If you searched my room, Kendrick, you'd find mine. A nicer one than that."

"Always travel with an ultralow?"

"I do. Sometimes I want to call the office without using the house phone. Sometimes I don't trust my hosts. The kid was in my line of work, Kendrick, but that doesn't mean he was mine. Maybe he's yours."

"I work for Mr. Jespers, Carroll."

"So do I, and you've had longer to case the joint than I have."

"This is unproductive," Jespers said. "I don't want any more of this. You can give us no information on this boy, Jack?"

"I don't know him, Arne. It's the last time I'm going to say it."

"All right, Jack."

Mallory was angry by now, but he had a good grip on it and it wasn't a problem. He could use it now. He could harden himself up with it and be able to tend to business with Billy lying there next to him. He said, "It's not all right. It's not the least little bit all right. I'm not too concerned about anything Kendrick's likely to think, Arne, but I've got in the neighborhood of twenty-five million riding on this deal and just now it's looking a little shaky. When I agreed to come in, I thought you had some security."

"We do," Kendrick said. "That's why junior's on the table and the satellite's still neat and tight."

"How do we know he was after the satellite?"

"What else, the silverware?"

"Plans, drawings, models, documentation. Something a lone operator could walk off with easier than a rocket or its payload."

"Thanks for the help, Carroll, but I think we've got this under control."

"You do, huh? Look at this kid—what is he, twenty? Must've been his first run. And he got this far before somebody nailed him."

"Both satellite and plans are all present and accounted for," Kendrick said evenly.

"You can steal plans without putting them in your pocket. Did he have a camera?"

"Yes."

"All right then. Let's develop the film and see what he got."

"One of my men exposed the film, just to be on the safe side."

Jespers's head snapped around, and he and Mallory stared at Kendrick together. Even Kost looked up in surprise.

"One of your . . ." Mallory let his voice trail off.

"He was a new man," Kendrick said stolidly. "He's been spoken to."

Mallory was shaking his head. "A new man. How about the goon who beat the kid's face in so no one'll ever be able to ID him? Was he a new man, too?"

"Maybe you ought to be happy about that, Mallory. My people spotted you in Monaco talking to someone of this boy's approximate size, build, and complexion at about 0625 Friday morning on the Avenue d'Ostende."

"His approximate *size* . . ." Mallory said pityingly.

He broke off as Jespers strode around the table, eyes bulging, and slapped Kendrick across the face with all his strength.

Kendrick blinked as the blow landed. His head did not move, and his expression did not alter.

"I've heard enough," Jespers spat. "I have heard *quite* enough from you, Kendrick. I thought you were a competent man, and now I see you acting in this, this *childish* manner. I see you attempt to blame your own shortcomings, your own *failure* on my friend, on a man who has won my *trust*. This man understands me, Kendrick. He understands the *spirit* of this organization. He has a clarity of sight, he has capabilities you lack—he sees what is *essential*. And all you can think of is how to shift the blame you yourself deserve onto *him*. Perhaps twenty-three hours remain until launch time, and there is no time for your bungling or your childish jealousy. And so I am forced to act." He turned to Mallory. "Jack, I apologize. I see now that I need your services more than I had thought."

Mallory said, "I don't need an apology, Arne. Kendrick's right. The kid might not've had a man inside, but it's likely he did. Everybody here needs to account for themselves, including me and Lil. Including Kendrick. And including the crew that showed up last night. Just about when the kid did, as I'm sure you noticed. Kendrick's right to be considering all the angles. I just think he's a little too eager to think it was me."

"You are generous, Jack. But we have no time for generosity, either." Jespers turned to Kendrick. "From now until you hear otherwise from me, Mr. Carroll is in charge of security for this operation. Complete your survey of the grounds and then report to him for instructions. And make sure none of the staff give our guests, our bidders, the *slightest* sign that there has been any untoward occurrence this morning. Do you understand?"

"Dane—" Kendrick began.

"You have your *instructions*, Kendrick," Jespers hissed. "When we have further instructions for you, you will be *notified*."

"All right," Kendrick said neutrally. He turned to the remaining guard. "Robles, keep Dr. Kost secure until you're relieved. Stand guard outside. I think Mr. Jespers and Mr. Carroll will want to, ah." His jaw tightened slightly. "Will want to talk to Dr. Kost in privacy. And please note that from here on, Mr. Carroll's orders supersede mine. Let's go."

He left the room, followed by the hulking Robles, without a backward glance.

When the door closed, Jespers sighed. "It is very weary—wear-*some*? Wear-*y*-some?"

"It tires your ass," Mallory said.

"Yes, Jack. It tires my ass." He smiled bleakly. "But if it was always easy, I suppose that this would come to tire one's ass as well." He turned to the man in the corner. "Dr. Kost, please let me present Jack Carroll, who will be assisting us in making this operation run a bit more *smoothly*. Jack, this is Dr. Walther Kost. Doctor, would you be so very kind and tell Mr. Carroll about your interview with our intruder earlier this morning?"

"That's not where we start," Mallory said.

"No?"

"No. We start at the beginning. We start by telling me what the hell Archangel is. I don't intend to go on working in the goddamn dark."

Kost looked inquiringly at Jespers. Jespers nodded.

"He knows nothing?" Kost said. He turned to Mallory. "From the beginning?"

The old man's voice was light and precise, and his accent faint. His eyes held a look Mallory had seen in certain Special Forces men who'd spent a long time in deep jungle. They seemed to register the smallest detail that passed before them without any particular effort. Though Kost's shoulders were narrow, his carriage was erect without stiffness and his white-maned head sat lightly on his neck. According to the briefing packet, he'd been a commando in his youth. Old as he was, Mallory figured he'd still make a pretty fair one.

"I know it's a spy satellite," Mallory said. "I know Hitler put you to work on it and that he thought it was something special. And I know the Russians thought the same thing. But I don't know what makes it worth all this hullabaloo."

"Yes," Kost said. "Sometimes I wonder myself. There has been a great deal of hullabaloo, hasn't there? A great deal of money, a great deal of blood, a great deal of ambition." He glanced dully at Jespers, then back at Mallory. "All right, then. Archangel was inscribed in the docket of the Supreme Technical Command early in November of 1943. As you say, the original ambition was Herr Hitler's. He saw, quite correctly, that the future of war was in the upper atmosphere and above. That quite soon men would be killing their fellow men from outer space. He brought us, as you know, into the age of the missile. If we are for some reason inclined to give thanks for this, such thanks must be due to him. The original V-1s, of course, were extremely crude, no more than stones flung over a fence. He pointed them in the general direction of England. When they ran out of fuel, they fell. I suppose you have heard the old jest, that they killed more laborers at Peenemunde than Londoners. I am confident that this is quite literally accurate. To give Herr Hitler his due, this result dissatisfied him, and the V-2s had a rudimentary guidance system. He became obsessed with the idea that if he could only aim these V-2s accurately enough, that lasting supremacy would be his, in spite of a depleted Army, ruined factories, and an increasingly erratic military strategy."

"Doesn't sound like you're Hitler's number-one fan," Mallory said.

"Herr Hitler," Kost said very slowly, "brought complete destruction and utter disgrace upon my—upon my country. Twenty years ago, Mr. Carroll, I was proud to be a German. This is no longer possible. It will not be possible a century from now. Herr Hitler—" Kost squeezed his eyes shut. "He made an obscene mockery of my country's highest, its *purest* ideals. No, Mr. Carroll, I am not Herr Hitler's number-one fan."

"Time is short, Doctor," Jespers remarked.

Kost's eyes opened again and regarded Jespers almost curiously. "My apologies for the digression, Mr. Jespers. Well, as I was saying. Hitler assigned me the task of providing precise targeting information for ballistic missiles from low earth orbit. All this is relatively simple, and primarily a problem in mechanical engineering, but I was able to convince Der Führer that it was desirable for Archangel to meet an additional requirement. The satellite should, I felt, be able to communicate targeting information to the V-2 directly. To control the missile's guidance system, to watch over the missile as it rose and to carefully direct and adjust its path until it reached its proper target. Hitler greeted this proposal with enthusiasm, and I was given all the resources I required to proceed, so that by the end of the war, we had attained a measure of success. After the project's subsequent, ah, changes of *venue*," Kost said dryly, "I was able to refine the device further, and now I believe that I can say the first Archangel is complete and ready for deployment. Tomorrow morning it will be launched into orbit. And though the world is full of spy satellites and spy planes that can read matchbook covers from five miles up and so forth, these speak only to men on the ground, while Archangel can speak to rockets in flight. And so in this sense it remains unique."

"Yeah," Mallory said slowly. "I guess I can see why it'd be something special. Especially the midcourse-correction part. Would your gadget help a missile take evasive action if it was threatened by ABMs?"

"You are an intelligent young man," Kost said. "That is correct. And so a small array of such satellites would triple the effectiveness of any existing atomic arsenal. But this does not fully represent Archangel's value."

"No?"

"No. When I began the project in 1943, I of course studied, and even helped to refine, the guidance system of the V-2. In Murmansk I was given a thorough knowledge of Soviet guidance systems, in addition to such information as they were able to obtain about American and Chinese systems. And since coming here, I have studied British and French systems as well. My intention was merely to understand the fundamental features that must exist in any missile guidance system so that I could provide a very strong, robust communications link from *any* missile to Archangel, a link that would be clear and strong even as the missiles' guidance systems inevitably evolved and changed over time. But in pursuing this objective, something quite unusual began to happen. Archangel became, you might say, multilingual. It became versatile enough to guide, not only one's own missiles, but those of one's neighbors, as well."

"You're telling me—" Mallory said.

Jespers could contain himself no longer. "With a fully deployed network of Archangels," he said delightedly, "one controls all the world's guided missiles. Do you understand what I am saying, Jack? *All.* One can't launch them, of course, because this is done electrically on the ground, but once they are in the air, one can abort them in flight, deflect them from their targets, or redirect them to a target of one's own choosing. One can turn Country X's missiles upon its own capital. When it shoots off antimissiles to defend itself, one can turn these upon the capital city as well. One can direct missiles launched from SubMarine Y to sink SubMarine Y. One can destroy alliances by directing the allies' missiles at each other. Wouldn't you say, Jack, that such a technology would be worth five hundred million dollars? Wouldn't you say this is actually quite a good *deal*, that for a fraction of the cost of a major nuclear arsenal, one can hold in one's hands *all* the world's nuclear arsenals?"

"Yeah," Mallory said. "I guess it does sound like a pretty good deal when you put it like that. 'Course, I can also see why somebody's trying to lay hands on the gadget without paying the tab."

"Of course," Jespers said.

Jespers had, Mallory noticed, completely forgotten the grisly bundle at his elbow. He might have been standing beside a shelf full of books or a vase full of flowers.

"All right," Mallory said to Kost. "This thing goes up tomorrow morning at—"

"Five o'clock," Kost said.

"Good. When are you supposed to be in the launch room or block-house or whatever you call it?"

"I should have been in the control center twenty-six minutes ago."

"Take me with you," Mallory said. "I don't need the whole guided tour. I just need to know how to keep this thing from coming unwound until it's in the air tomorrow at 0500. I need to see how you got your lines secured, what frequencies you're running, how you got the missile and the gizmo itself secured—I'm guessing Kendrick'll have to fill me in there. I need to see how you enter the launch codes and the target coordinates, and who's got access when. I'll need to take a quick look at the bird. Can you fix that up for me? Arne?"

"Give him what he asks, Doctor, if you please," Jespers said.

"All right," Kost said. "But I warn you, I will have no time to repeat myself. And some of my technicians speak only German."

"My German's pretty good, and so's my hearing. I think we'll be all right."

"Very well, then." Kost rose and gave a tug at his trouser seams to straighten them. It seemed a habitual gesture. He took a last look at the bundle at the table. It was the look, Mallory thought, of an old soldier who'd seen too many corpses.

Mallory didn't think he could risk a last look at Billy himself. Not and stay as cool as he needed to be for the next few hours. It would be hard enough to get through those hours as it was. It was already hard. It was sick-hard.

Well, there wasn't much left of Billy on that table anyway. He'd say good-bye to Billy later. He'd say good-bye properly, when the time was right.

At 0500 the next morning.

It was past three o'clock that afternoon when Mallory got back to his room. He stepped briskly through the door, his face set and lightly preoccupied, like a man who's working out a chess problem he expects to solve. His iron-gray hair was dusted with snow, and so was the borrowed fur coat. Beneath the coat, his shoulders were square, as always, and held no more than the mild tension of a working professional in the middle of a busy day. Laura looked past him for an accompanying guard. There was none. *He's brought it off,* she thought. *He's cut Kendrick out somehow. Jespers has put him in charge.*

When the door clacked shut behind him, the look of busy alertness left Mallory's face.

His shoulders did not actually sag—she'd never seen them sag—but the strength seemed to go out of them, and the firmness left his mouth. He looked like a man who'd been struck in the stomach, in that still, breathless moment before pain takes hold. He glanced at her, muttered, "'Lo, hon," and scanned the room until he caught sight of the armchair by the bed. He made his way to it and sat down. He had not removed his coat. "How've you been," he said lifelessly. "Avery didn't give you any trouble, did he?"

"Avery—? Oh, the guard. No, Avery didn't give me any trouble. Quite the reverse, in fact. Since there didn't seem to be anything else useful to do, I went to work on him a bit. Asked him to stay with me because I was frightened, let my coat fall open and so on." She grimaced. "He was pretty rattled by the time he left. I didn't get any useful information, but for what it's worth, the next time Avery's assigned to us, his mind won't be on his job."

"Thanks, hon," Mallory said. "I know how you hate that."

He sat there in the damp fur coat, looking vacantly at his hands.

"You're a bit snowy," she said. "And you ought to take off your coat. Getting pneumonia won't help." He did not respond. She went into the bathroom, came out with a towel, and offered it to him. It took a moment for him to focus on it, and then he took it, dabbed at his face, and sat holding the towel on one knee as snowmelt began to trickle from his shoulders and hair. "I see you've been out," she said. "Had a look at the rocket?"

"Yeah," Mallory said. "I got the guided tour. They, ah—"

He reached into his pocket and pulled out a massive ring of keys. Laura recognized the two matching circular keys that Kendrick had used to deactivate the electric-eye barrier that morning. There were at least a dozen others she didn't recognize. The sight of the keys seemed to distract Mallory. He swallowed and lapsed into thought.

She said, "Jack. There's nothing you could have done."

"I could've done my job," he said, running his thumb over the keys. "I could've done that. Gray gave me Billy to take care of. He knew he didn't have good sense. He knew he needed taking care of. And I didn't do it. Didn't send him home. Knew in Monaco Billy wasn't ready for the field. Goddamn obvious. And if I'd sent him home, I wouldn't've heard any backchat from Gray. 'Stead I brought him here and gave him the trickiest part of the job first thing. He was my partner and he annoyed me and I let him die."

"No. That's wrong. It's wrong and it's stupid, and we can't afford it."

"He was my partner and I let him die. It's just as if I . . ." Mallory paused to think. "Don't believe Kendrick did it himself, actually. Got the hands for it, but he's no psycho. 'Sides, you saw his knuckles. They aren't puffy like they'd be. Dunno who did it." He shrugged. "Gonna have to kill him anyhow 'fore I leave. Kendrick." Abruptly, Mallory yawned, widely and unself-consciously, as a child yawns. "Bushed. Need a little sleep. Little sleep and I'll be all right. Ready t'get some-body else killed. You, maybe."

Laura dropped to her knees before him, took hold of his arms, and shook him. The keys slipped from Mallory's hands to the floor. "Oops," he said.

"Jack," she said. "You have to stop. Please. You have to stop now."

"I'm fine, Laurie," Mallory said, his eyes steady and dead. "I just screwed up, that's all. I'm just tired."

"*Jack*," she said. "Please. You're just being—"

"What?"

She knew what Jack was being, all right. She'd understood for a long time the melancholy that underlay her partner's drinking and woman-chasing, that permitted him to risk death on a regular basis with something like boredom. She knew Mallory's life was a black ocean that he crossed like a swimmer, exerting himself constantly to stay above the surface. Between assignments, he couldn't always see the point of all that work, and after a while he'd start to sink. What kept him from doing it while on a job was the knowledge that he had to take care of his partners. That was why Gray no longer let Mallory work solo: looking out for his partners kept Mallory alive. And now Harmon had died, and Mallory was sinking from sight as she watched, but that wasn't the sort of thing you could tell someone. "What'm I being?" Mallory asked.

"Self-indulgent," she said.

"I'm being goddamn sloppy. If I hadn't been sloppy, Billy'd be safe at home."

She released his arms and stood.

"Jack," she said. "We can't just—"

"Sure we can. Why not?"

"We've got *work* to do," she cried.

This seemed to surprise Mallory.

"Work, huh?" he said.

Then he chuckled, and his eyes fractionally brightened. "Work to do. That's what I told Kendrick. He didn't like hearing it, either."

"But it's true."

"Yep. I guess it's true, all right," Mallory said slowly. "If you come right down to it, I suppose you could say it's the only goddamn thing that's true." He sighed. "All right. All righty, then. Let's get started."

He rubbed his face again, then looked at his dripping fingers in puzzlement.

"Jesus," he said exhaustedly. "I'm wet."

The Bowl of the Sage

She was looking for someone whose face had been smashed in, who had been beaten so badly that he seemed to have been burned or flayed, but he didn't seem to be anywhere, and time was short. She was walking down the aisles of a darkened jewelry store on the Ku'damm, a store where once she'd spent twenty minutes on business in April of 1959. Sometimes she was Laura and sometimes Jack. When she was Jack, she felt awful, as if she'd been poisoned. Finally she put her hands to her face to wipe away what she thought were tears, and instead felt mangled flesh and bits of crushed bone, and then she was somehow looking down at herself from a high window. From up there she could see that her face was gone. Her jaw had been mashed in. Her shattered cheekbones jutted through her pulped skin. *Oh, it's only me,* she thought with relief, and turned and dove down to a deeper, dreamless level of sleep.

She awoke promptly at midnight with no memory of having

dreamed and reached a slim arm out to the bedside clock to check the time. She was alone and appeared to be naked. In spite of the moaning cold outside, the blankets were down around her waist, and her skin bore the sheen of incipient sweat. She took three cleansing breaths, turned back the blankets, and got gracefully to her feet, and now she seemed to be some sort of outlandish hybrid: from the waist up, a young blonde with a Malibu tan; from the waist down, a black silhouette—a shadow. She bent and made a scooping gesture with each arm, then straightened and passed two fingers up her body from groin to throat, and then she was a shadow to the chin. The Arctic Ops thermal suit was a bit of gear she particularly disliked. It was made of some elaborate blend of silk, wool, latex, and glass fiber, was extremely warm and somewhat itchy, and clung to her body like a coat of black greasepaint, throwing into high relief her collarbones, the dimples behind her knees, and everything in between. She was certain it had been designed by a particularly dirty-minded man. It always took a while to wriggle into the suit, so she'd gone to bed in it to save time, but the damn thing had been too hot and she'd wriggled half-out again.

In the bathroom, she switched on the light and did her hair up in a tight chignon, then dipped two fingers into a small jar and began to paint her face shadow-black as well. She seemed to be demolishing it stroke by stroke. For a moment she half remembered her dream. But there was no time for dreams now, and she dismissed it. She pulled a snug black skullcap over her blonde hair. A nude bald shadow with glaring blue eyes examined her from the mirror as she tucked away a few last golden strands. She washed and dried her hands, slipped on skintight black gloves, and turned out the light again.

From the bedside table she took a heavy Rolex Navigator and strapped it to her wrist. From the wardrobe she pulled a white one-piece ski suit, trimmed with white fur at collar and cuffs. In the daylight, it looked a bit little-girlish. Against the snow, it would look like snow. She zipped it on, then donned white boots, white gloves, and a white ski mask: the shadow became a slim snowwoman. She took out a small white knapsack, a pair of white-painted aluminum Head Eiger VSs, broad for powder skiing, and clipped one to the other. She did not look inside the bag. All that had been triple-checked before she slept. She slipped her arms into the straps, tightened them, and moved her arms and shoulders through two fluid figure eights, testing her freedom of movement. She looked at her watch, then went to the window and, with no noticeable transition, was crouching in the deep stone sill. She opened the window, slipped through, and swung it shut behind her, leaving it unlatched. Then she hunkered on the ledge like a gargoyle and waited.

It was a near-vertical drop of almost thirty feet from the ledge on which she perched to the base of the monastery wall. From the base of the wall, the snow sloped upward to the foot of an icy cliff, which rose before her into the dark sky. For the hundredth time, she traced it with her eyes: the complex runnels of ice to the left, the vertiginous sweep of powder snow to the right. From the top of the cliff, she knew, one could look down into the deep cleft that split the summit of Mont Saint-Séverin. From the top of the cliff, one could look down onto Archangel's launchpad.

She watched the snow intently, one eye on her Rolex. It took four minutes and thirty-three seconds for the perimeter guard to appear, trudging into view around the uphill corner of the building. On Mallory's instructions, they were circling the monastery in heavily armed threes instead of in twos. He had shifted manpower from the mountaintop launchpad to the peak's upper slopes, pointing out, reasonably enough, that it was better to prevent intruders from ascending the peak than to muster an Army to meet them when they arrived. The launchpad, he'd explained, was comparatively small, and could be easily controlled by a single guard. The two time clocks already installed at opposite sides of the pad provided added assurance: if more than one hundred seconds passed between turns of the sentry's key, the main alarm would sound and the full strength of Saint-Séverin's security forces would converge on the intruder.

The guards below carried powerful flashlights and flicked them around as they walked, sending flares of light up the monastery walls and the icy cliff before her. "Those flashlights aren't purses," Mallory had told them. "Don't hold 'em down by your sides like you were looking for a lost nickel. Keep 'em moving around, like this." This was almost sound advice. In fact, though, a flashlight beam in constant motion creates flicker and dazzle that makes it easier to miss, say, a white-clad climber clinging to an ice-white cliff.

Laura noted with satisfaction that, though they'd been circling the monastery all night, the guard seemed to be trudging through virgin snow. By the time they vanished around the downhill corner, the wind had nearly erased the prints they'd left at the uphill corner.

She paused for a moment to make sure they were out of sight.

Then she seemed to flow down the rough-hewn stone wall to the moonlit slope.

Twenty-eight seconds later she was across the narrow snowfield and tucked inside a yard-wide vertical runnel of ice extending two-thirds of the way up the cliff. She'd spent the afternoon gazing at the cliff and plotting her ascent. The slope was dominated by an expanse of plate-steel ice that was unclimbable without pitons, bolts, and a lot of noisy hammering. The ice beside it was badly chandeliered. Between, though, was a useful-looking dihedral that at seventy feet petered out into a narrow ledge of bare stone, which in turn dropped back into a twenty-five-foot granite chimney. It would take her at least twenty minutes to get to the upper ledge, during which time at least one convoy of guards would pass by, flicking their flashes over the cliff face. When that happened, all she could do was wedge herself into the dihedral, hold still, and hope that, in her all-white kit, she looked as icy as she'd often been accused of being.

From her pack she drew a pair of double-pointed steel crampons and strapped them to her boots. She pulled out two aluminum ice axes. They too had been painted white, but aside from that were simple, classic designs with fixed heads and straight shafts. A curved shaft was supposed to keep you from smashing your knuckles on the ice, but Laura thought that was nonsense. If your form was correct, you didn't need a curved shaft, and if you swung wrong, you'd bash your knuckles no matter what. The adze was a supremely versatile instrument, and could be used to dry-tool on rock. Before turning in, she'd sharpened the tips with a few strokes of a flat file and touched up the teeth with a round one. Lily Prentice's steamer trunks had been capacious not just because she was a girl who liked her clothes, but because Logistics had had no idea where Archangel might be hidden and had therefore been compelled to equip Laura Morse for terrain ranging from the Alps to the bottom of the Caribbean. They'd provided a full set of mountaineering ropes, harnesses, and hardware. She'd left most of this behind. It would be too loud to hammer in pitons; all the noise she could afford was the occasional crack of the ice axe, which she hoped would pass for the natural snapping and popping of Alpine ice. Besides, she'd be climbing solo, without a second to belay her from below, and there was no time to self-belay. If she fell, she fell.

She found a crevice above her, stretched up, and hooked the left-hand axe into it; she hoped to ascend mostly by hooking instead of hammering.

She braced her barbed right foot and began to climb.

A mountain is a very large thing, best seen from far off, but one ascends it by means of small details that are often close enough to be misted by one's breath. Laura covered the first ten yards in a single sprint. It was bad technique, starting off at top speed like that instead of conserving one's wind, but she wanted to be well above the guards' eye level when they rounded the corner again. She was not as good a climber as Harmon had been, and lacked his nonchalance about heights. In fact, heights frightened her. She'd hated skiing as a child, and had become a first-rate skiier only because Morses were expected to do things well or not at all. And she'd learned to climb because Gray thought it was a nice thing for a girl to know. For a while, the search for usable crannies and cracks distracted her from her fear, and then the flaring pain in her arms and back did. But every few yards she had to look back and down for the telltale glow of the guards' flashlights, and nothing helped her then. At fifty feet, when she'd been climbing for almost eight minutes, the canted glass roof of the control center came into view. At sixty feet, Laura could see the rows of desks, each with its own arrays of dials and recessed TV screen. A lone guard strolled down the aisles. He seemed infinitely fortunate to be warm and indoors, with his feet on firm ground. When she'd ascended two yards more, the perimeter guards reappeared, and she stopped still. Her arms, legs, and head were tucked well into the dihedral, but she knew her pack and rear end were protruding. The flashlight beams were swarming below her, darting and circling, and finally one flicked directly across her back. It seemed to lick at her like flame. She closed her eyes and silently recited a sutra for dispelling fear:

> *The bowl of the sage may be broken*
> *but the emptiness within can never be broken.*

That, Laura thought dryly, *is a great comfort.*

Her right knee was nearly tucked into her armpit and her left leg stuck out at right angles in the opposite direction. She was splayed, as a climber so often is, like a frog, and the pain in her spine and thighs was excruciating. For a period impossible to measure, she held herself still anyway, even slowing her breaths so that her heaving back would not draw a sentry's eye. The beam of light did not return. There was no rattle of automatic gunfire. Laura knew from sad experience that one often seemed to hear oneself being shot before feeling the impact of the bullet. At last she let herself look down.

The guards were gone. Nothing remained but a faint glow around the far corner.

She eased herself up and jammed her left foot into a lateral notch, moving up another eighteen inches and shifting the load on her tortured muscles. Relief swept up through her body from calves to nape. She thought she'd swoon.

She was on the ledge two and a half minutes later, unstrapping her crampons and tucking away one of her axes. Four minutes later, she slithered out the top of the chimney and was crouching at the summit of Mont Saint-Sévérin.

The mountain's cleft peak was shaped something like a vast mitten. Laura was perched on the mitten's fingertips, facing the broad thumb. Nestled between fingers and thumb, a dozen yards below her, a lance-like white rocket stood on a quadrangular concrete slab, supported by a steel gantry that seemed black as iron. To Laura's right was the wedge-shaped glass roof of the control center. The desks beneath the glass roof rose tier upon tier, like an immense amphitheater. The rocket stood before them like a lone soprano on an empty stage, surrounded by floodlights casting dagger-shaped shadows.

Directly below her was a long corrugated-metal roof of the kind

that shelters train-station platforms. Beneath it, she knew, was a row
of wheeled carts containing the equipment and instruments needed to
ready the rocket for flight. In another two hours, the launchpad would
host a swarming Army of technicians, while another brigade would fill
the empty desks below.

Now the vast eerie prospect was deserted except for the tiny sentry beneath the glass roof, patrolling the aisles of the control center,
and another one, endlessly circling the concrete apron below her, a
black ski mask concealing his face and hair, a Kalashnikov AKM in his
arms.

The snowwoman unstrapped her white pack and skis and nestled
them into a snow-filled crevice. She drew a white hand down her
belly, split in two, and dwindled into a small white heap of snow. The
slim black shadow rose from the heap, paused, then poured herself
smoothly down the steep incline and disappeared into the shadows
under the metal roof of the shed.

Crouching among the wheeled carts, she checked her watch again.
About six and one quarter minutes ahead of schedule.

Close enough. As previously agreed, she did not wait.

The four floodlights stood atop delicate pylons at each of the
four corners of the launchpad, and the sentry cast four shadows as he
walked. The next time he passed the far end of the row of equipment,
he seemed to gather a fifth. Then Laura had fallen noiselessly into step
behind him, following so close that the guard in the control center below, had he glanced up at his colleague, would have seen only a single
marching figure.

There was a key clipped to the sentry's belt, hexagonal in section,
with irregular circular dimples stamped into each of the long faces of
the shaft. She reached forward and, with the delicacy of a pickpocket,
unclipped it.

The guard's broad shoulders stirred. He reached up a lean arm and
lifted the canvas strap of the heavy assault rifle from his shoulder.

Without looking around, he handed it back to her, and Laura
slipped it over her own shoulder. In spite of the icy air, the strap was
faintly perfumed with sweat.

Jespers is right, she thought. *Jack does smell wolfish.*

Moving in unison, the two operatives proceeded to the next time clock, and Mallory watched as Laura reached around him, inserted the key, and twisted it three quarters of a turn counterclockwise, then a half-turn clockwise. He nodded imperceptibly.

The doubled figure left the time clock and marched toward the gantry. As it passed the gantry, it seemed to dwindle. The marching figure that emerged on the other side was single.

Laura had taken Mallory's place, circling the launchpad, pausing twice each circuit to insert key in time clock. And Mallory had begun to climb the gantry's steel fretwork.

After that, all Laura had to do was play toy soldier while Jack worked. It was an absurdly simple task. So she executed it with particular care, doing her best to mimic Mallory's gangling, loose-limbed walk and concentrating hard each time she used the hexagonal key. Overconfidence kills far more agents than fear. By the time she'd made a full circuit of the launchpad, Mallory had reached the top of the gantry. By the time she'd made three and a half circuits, he'd teased open a hatch on the side of the missile and was hard at work. She'd completed seventeen circuits before Mallory descended the gantry, fell into step behind her, and smoothly relieved her of key and gun. The next time they passed the rows of wheeled carts, she slipped away and rejoined the shadows.

Mallory was still marching around the launchpad when Laura reappeared between the mitten's snowy knuckles, a dozen yards above him. She'd garbed herself in white once more and had fixed the white aluminum skis to her boots. In her hands were a pair of telescoping white ski poles.

She turned back toward the monastery. Below and to her right were the stone chimney and long spill of ice she'd climbed. Below and to her left lay a steep plane of snow; from her vantage point, it seemed vertical. And directly beneath her, the trio of guards were plodding through the drifts.

She squatted motionless until the wavering swarm of flashlight beams faded from view.

Then she flung herself forward into empty air.

Laura let out a tight cough of pain as her skis struck the slope and the impact flashed up through her aching knees and thighs. Then she was gliding left into a broad traverse, gathering speed, skis hissing through the powder beneath her, invisible in a blurring cloud of white. Not being able to see your skis was one of the things she disliked about powder skiing. She tucked her head a bit tighter, her hands well up and forward. It made her feel oddly childish to assume the racing stance her father had taught her long ago. He would not have approved of the unladylike ten inches between her skis, but just now she was not concerned with style, and she eased into the second traverse, knees juddering beneath her. By that time, the pitch of the slope had eased enough to permit a single straight schuss down to the base of the monastery's stone walls, her slim body curled into a near cannonball and the icy wind raking at her eyes. It had taken her nearly thirty strenuous minutes to ascend the cliff. She descended in less than thirty seconds, swooping downward like a falcon.

At the bottom she braked with a wrenching jet turn and was at once unlatching her bindings and snapping her skis to the back of her pack, then flowing up the monastery's wall again, climbing it almost as fluidly as the guards' flashlights had done minutes before.

And then she was in the window, panting with the ache in her legs and back, tears of pain freezing to her cheeks, watching the wind erase her tracks.

Laura Morse latched the window shut behind her and climbed down from the sill like a rickety old woman. "Ah," she said aloud. "Oh dear." She stripped to the skin, hurled the catsuit into the farthest corner, and vigorously scratched her legs and buttocks. "Um," she said. She took a small swig of brandy from the steel flask on the bedside table. "Uff." Then she picked up Mallory's Browning .32 automatic and limped, naked and black-faced, into the bathroom.

When she emerged, her face was clean and she was dressed in the old flannel nightgown and still carrying the automatic. She looked out the window: the tracks of her skis were gone. If the guards had heard the quiet slithering of her descent, which they really ought to have done, they'd dismissed it as settling snow, as she'd gambled they'd do. She waited another five minutes, gun in hand, then put it in the bedside drawer, tidied the room, mopped up the puddles of slush, and cursorily dried her boots and clothes before tucking them away. There was no way to get things properly dry before morning. If they examined her room, she was done for. But by the time they got around to doing that, the matter would have been decided, one way or the other. She climbed back into bed and stretched out a hand to her clock: 1:25 a.m. It seemed impossible that only an hour and a half had gone by. She closed her eyes.

Twenty-six minutes later, Mallory walked quietly but not stealthily into the room. He went to the bathroom and closed the door, and she saw a seam of light appear beneath it. The water ran for a long time. He wouldn't want his hands to smell of oil in the morning.

When he emerged, he wore pajama bottoms, and his hair stuck to his damp face. He crossed the room and climbed into the other side of the bed. He smelled now like soap and icy rock.

"Go all right?" she whispered.

"We'll see," he said.

The moan of the wind rose, then fell again. Laura thought of guards still circling through the snow outside.

"You smell cold," she said.

He grunted.

They went to sleep.

5

Zero Hour

Two hours later, Mallory let out a sigh and sat up in bed, waking her. She smelled the dry, wolfish smell again. Even before she saw his face, she knew from the set of his shoulders and the curve of his spine that he was better. He was exhausted now, but not sick. He'd come back from wherever he'd gone the previous afternoon. "Morning," he said, looking around at her.

The eyes were the familiar attentive, slightly sardonic gray eyes.

"Good morning," she said.

"How you feeling?"

"Good."

"I talked a lot of slop yesterday afternoon. Thanks for putting up with me."

"It was all right. You just needed some sleep."

"I needed my teeth kicked in. I was feeling damn sorry for my-self."

"You weren't so bad. You've been a lot worse when you thought you were fine."

"Probably, but I was damn bad, and I apologize."

"Don't mention it," she said.

For a woman who had an excellent chance of dying by violence before noon, Laura felt unreasonably happy. Of course, there was that tightness in the center of her gut, that going-into-battle tightness, but you didn't stay in her line of work long if you minded that. You even got to like it after a while. It felt as if the spring that drove you was fully wound up. Laura had slept briefly but well, and now she could see that Jack was all right again. She stretched luxuriously. Mallory watched her with a touch of sadness. *Damn*, he thought. *If Laurie ever decides she likes some guy, that'll be one fortunate son of a bitch.*

She sat up and said, "Well, I promise to kick your teeth in first thing, if we get home. You still need sleep."

"No, I grabbed a gear and I feel fine. No, no, stay in bed," he said, swinging his feet to the floor. "Get a little more sleep if you can. I figure things couldn't start hotting up before"—he looked at the clock—"well, I guess it could be as early as 0520, if we're really un-lucky. Maybe you ought to get up pretty soon at that."

"I don't want to sleep. I want to do a quick kata and drink a big cup of really hot coffee."

"You must be sore as hell."

"I am sore as hell, but I still feel good. That was a ridiculous plan of yours, by the way. We had no right to get away with it, assuming we did."

"It was pretty goofy, all right. You worried?"

"No. I'm . . ." She considered.

"Ready," he suggested.

"Yes. That's what it is. I'm ready. Even if we don't make it, we'll give them something to think about. We're not going to waste what Billy gave us. How are we doing, by the way? You went so fast yester-day that I'm still not sure I got all the details."

"We're done. I had all the time in the world up there, and I checked my work five, count 'em, five times. And unless I'm blind or crazy, the job's basically all done except for one part."

"The getting-out-of-here-alive part," she said.

Mallory scrubbed his hands through his rumpled gray hair, yawned, and walked stiffly toward the bathroom. "Yeah," he said over his shoulder. "That."

It was the best coffee Mallory had ever tasted. He hoped the stuff Laurie was drinking was half as good.

He was at the top tier of the control center, on the highest level of the glassed-in amphitheater, sitting at a vast oval table of stainless steel and polished ebony. Beside him sat Jespers, Milena, and Kendrick. Jespers gazed musingly up at the white rocket before them. Kendrick gazed musingly at Mallory. And Milena pillowed a smooth cheek on a big hand and gazed drowsily at nothing at all.

On the other side of the table sat the bidders: Melnikov, Halprin, and Xiong. The Laotian and the Argentine sipped their coffee and ignored each other, their eyes on the laboring technicians below. The Russian was buttering a roll.

At the head of the table, facing the rocket, sat Walther Kost in a white tunic and aviator's headset. Before him was a canted row of television screens, set into the polished black wood, and a constellation of dials and switches across which his bony fingers danced. Now and then he murmured a word or two into his headset, directing the ranks of technicians lining the curving rows of consoles below them, each with his own headset and television screen.

In the front of the control center, standing before the bottom row of technicians, was a huge world map etched into a single curving sheet of glass. A lone red light blinked upon it in the center of northern Europe.

Along the back of the control center was an uneven row of heavily armed guards: Jespers's, Melnikov's, Halprin's, and Xiong's.

On a cord around Mallory's neck were a pair of smoked-glass welder's goggles. An identical pair hung around the neck of each person in the huge room.

On the table in front of him was a little silver pot of the best damn coffee he'd ever had. He freshened up his cup. He felt all right, considering.

"You look pretty perky, Mr. Carroll," Kendrick said. "For a man who's had such a busy night."

"Caught my second wind," Mallory agreed. "How about you? You been pretty busy yourself. Freshen up your coffee?"

"Final disconnect," Kost murmured into his headset.

Before them, the last of the hoses and cables detached itself from the white rocket and sank gracefully to earth. Xiong watched them fall, his brown hands folded before him. Halprin glanced at his wristwatch. Melnikov began buttering another roll.

"Something tells me," Kendrick said, "that none of us have been quite as busy as you have, Mr. Carroll."

"Say when," Mallory said, pouring more coffee into Kendrick's cup.

"That's plenty," Kendrick said, staring at Mallory. "That's more than enough."

"Be quiet," Jespers said very softly, eyes on the rocket. "This is a moment for silence. Be silent."

The Argentine with the narrow German face smiled meaninglessly, then stopped.

"Retract gantry," Kost said. "Gentlemen, Miss Swierczy, would you all please put on your goggles."

Halprin was the first to don his goggles. Mallory was the last. The room became a gray sea in which odd black creatures floated. A hundred squarish lenses filled with light: the television screens all over the room had brightened so that they could be read through the welder's goggles. The glow of the screens lit the strict lines of Kost's jaw and nose, and made his black glasses gleam. Mallory felt the friendly weight of the Browning against his leg.

"Final electrical . . ." Kost said softly. "Check. Final mechanical . . . Check. Final instrument . . . Check. Final visual . . . Check. Clearing blast area. Clearing pad personnel. Sealing access corridors. And . . .

thank you. Gentlemen, we shall initiate countdown in five seconds, retract in ten seconds, and launch in fifteen. On my count . . . *Ten.*"

Kendrick regarded Mallory through two black disks.

"Nine. Eight. Seven."

Jespers showed his stained dentures. The black gantry opened its jaws.

"Six. Five."

With startling suddenness, the gantry fell away from the rocket.

"Four."

The gantry bounced gently on its fulcrum, twenty degrees from the vertical.

"Three. Two. One."

Kendrick smiled broadly at Mallory.

"Liftoff," Kost said dispassionately, and the base of the rocket dissolved in a dazzling disk of white light. And then the disk swelled monstrously into a roiling blot of whiteness, almost painful to see, even through the smoked goggles, forcing the gleaming shaft upward as it grew. And then the rocket was sliding slowly and then more quickly into the air, and then it was a brilliant, dwindling star in the morning sky.

Below, the light on the vast glass map blazed a steady flame-blue.

"Phase Two is complete, gentlemen," Kost said matter-of-factly. "Archangel is in the air."

A cheer rose up from the ranks of technicians below, and a smattering of applause from all those whose hands were not busy, and Milena ascended from her chair, almost as impressively as the rocket had, scooped Jespers from his, and hugged him, grinning, Mallory thought, like a fourteen-year-old girl whose field hockey team had just won the state championship. Jespers freed himself with difficulty and stood beaming and adjusting his crooked spectacles. Two guards rolled out silver ice buckets of Taittinger and began filling and handing around crystal flutes. Down at the base of the amphitheater, the blue dot on the big glass map had become a slowly lengthening blue arc.

Jespers pulled off his black goggles and stood blinking and raising his champagne glass high. "A toast," he said. "To the long-awaited, brilliant, and quite richly deserved—"

"Don't," Mallory said.

"My goodness, you startled me," Jespers said. "What is it? Jack, you're not raising your glass. Why, Mr. Kendrick, Dr. Kost— Why aren't you gentlemen raising your glasses?"

"Carroll's right," Kendrick said. "It's too early to toast anybody's success."

"This is quite true, I'm afraid," Kost said. "Far too early."

"Well," Jespers said. "Well. I am—chastised. I stand corrected. Yes, *corrected*. Very well, a new toast! To the, ah, hard work, talent, and fiery, ah, *caution*—" There were scattered chuckles from the guards. "Of my wonderful Team Archangel."

Mallory picked up his glass. Through the black glass, the champagne looked like muddy water.

"To you, Arne," he said, and drained it.

"Ah, this is a nice moment," Jespers said.

"I imagine it is quite gratifying to you," Xiong said. "Of course, all we have witnessed so far is the correctly executed launch of an ordinary, commercially available booster rocket of conventional design."

"I've always liked fireworks," Melnikov said. "But they're more fun after a full night's sleep, you know."

"Indeed, gentlemen," Jespers said. "I did not mean to suggest that we had seen anything more than a sort of prologue, the *overture*, to the great *symphony* to come. By midmorning Archangel will have left its vehicle and be in orbit. By eleven o'clock we shall have seen it fully *engaged* with our own earthbound computer via radio and television link. Such tests are highly technical and perhaps not of compelling interest to non-scientists, and so I have arranged a light luncheon and a bit of entertainment in our refectory, where I hope you will all join me. We shall return here at noon for a more substantial demonstration: the launch of an American weather satellite from Cape Canaveral in Florida. It is this launch that has determined the date of our little gathering. The satellite itself is of no consequence to us, of course, and indeed is of only modest consequence to its owners. However, it will serve as an admirable test subject upon which to demonstrate Archangel's capabilities. You will observe with your own eyes, gentlemen, as

Archangel takes charge of the American rocket. You will observe as it beckons it off course. And lastly, you will observe as Archangel aborts it in space. A fairly conclusive exhibition, I hope you'll agree."

"Hardly," Halprin said. "For all we know, you employ clandestine operatives in Cape Canaveral who have arranged the entire thing beforehand."

"But how could this be, gentlemen," Jespers said, "when you yourselves will choose the American rocket's new trajectory, with no interference from me, as well as the precise moment of its destruction?"

"There are three of us," Xiong said. "How are we to choose a single compass heading?"

"Through discussion among yourselves, Mr. Xiong. A discussion in which I and my associates will not join."

"One of us may in fact not be a legitimate bidder, but a shill—suborned by you, effectively in your employ, and charged with decisively influencing the course of this discussion in return for some financial or other consideration. I shall not be convinced unless I see the rocket set off on a course which I myself have chosen."

"I admire the critical *rigor* of your thinking, Mr. Xiong. I respect your skepticism. Shall we say that each of you will select a compass heading, and that Dr. Kost will steer our test subject in each of the three directions in turn before demolishing it?"

Halprin said, "Better, Mr. Jespers, but still not satisfactory. You say all this will happen 'before our eyes.' But in fact, we must rely upon the evidence of instruments and"—he gestured at the vast glass map below—"pretty colored lights, all of which are under your direct control. How can we assure ourselves that we have not been party to an elaborately staged hoax?"

"By reading the papers, my stern young friend," Melnikov said. "By having your colleagues at home spend a few coins on tomorrow's paper. You logical fellows always forget the obvious thing. A launch like this isn't a military secret. When the rocket goes off course, when America's much-admired technology goes ka-blooey, it will make a small amusing story in newspapers around the world, and the serious ones will report the matter in detail. You all talk too much, and too little of it is interesting."

"Thank you, Sergei," Jespers said. "You are as eloquent as ever. Mr. Halprin, Mr. Xiong, does this satisfy you?"

"It seems sufficient," Xiong said. "As far as I am concerned, you may proceed."

Halprin nodded grudgingly.

"Excellent. Dr. Kost, when can we next . . ."

Jespers broke off as a faint commotion broke out in the amphitheater below. Two technicians had gotten up from their consoles and were bending over a third, all peering at the same screen and muttering together.

The blue arc on the great curving glass map was blinking orange.

Sweet, merciful— It was too soon. Much too soon. Mallory just managed to keep from looking at his watch.

He said, "What is it, Kost? What's going on down there?"

By now the commotion among the technicians was general. Kost alone seemed composed. He gazed through his goggles at the screens before him and said, "We have a deviation, Mr. Carroll. No more than an eighth of a degree, but a deviation nonetheless."

Jespers set down his glass.

"What does that mean?" Mallory said. "In short words."

Kost frowned. "It means Archangel has been tampered with. Not the satellite itself, but the booster. Someone has— It could only be that someone has manually set new coordinates. A new trajectory."

A babble of angry voices rose around the table. Mallory's was clearest.

"Correct it," he said.

"Impossible," Kost replied. "Such coordinates are entered mechanically into a unit on board the missile. This process incapacitates our guidance systems. The missile is no longer, in any meaningful sense, guided." He smiled joylessly. "It is an interesting irony. Even if we had an array of Archangels waiting in the sky, we could not gain control of our own missile now. It has in essence become a large artillery shell."

"Where's it aimed?"

"It would take time to calculate this. Perhaps another orbit from the desired one. Or perhaps the missile is set to splash down— Who knows? In mid-Atlantic, perhaps. Or to crash in Canada somewhere. Or perhaps even farther on, in Siberia."

"Siberia, huh?" Mallory said, staring at Melnikov. "Can you still abort this thing, Doctor?"

"Yes."

"Do it," he snapped.

It was pure bedlam then.

He was the first one to make himself heard. "I said abort it. Arne, tell him."

"Jack, you're suggesting a most—"

"Goddamnit, Arne, wake up. This isn't sabotage," Mallory said. "This is theft. If all somebody wanted was to keep Archangel from getting deployed, simplest thing would've been to rig it to blow on launch, or just cross a wire so it wouldn't work when it got up there. What somebody wanted was for Archangel to go off course, for it to land someplace where they could go scoop it up themselves. Maybe somebody's already out there, waiting with a big net. Somebody's stealing Archangel, *now,* while we watch 'em do it, while we sit here goddamn *talking.* Let's blow it before they finish the job."

"You're a bit free and easy with Mr. Jespers's money," Kendrick observed.

"Jesus, Kendrick," Mallory snapped. "I know it cost a few million to build this thing, and maybe a couple hundred grand for the booster. Nobody likes spending that kind of money twice, but it can't be helped. A few million isn't half a billion, and if we wait for this thing to land, we won't have anything to sell. Do you know what'll happen if—"

Abruptly, the world went black.

Mallory whipped off his smoked goggles and was on his feet, his Browning in his fist. The vast room was dark but for the daylight streaming down through the glass roof. The rows of TV screens were black mouths; the dials were empty gray eyes; the technicians and guards black wraiths. The only thing clearly visible was a towering plume of white smoke before them, still drifting slowly heavenward from the blackened launchpad.

"Well," Mallory said, and spoke truthfully one last time: "I guess somebody doesn't want us to abort Archangel."

There was no pandemonium now. There was silence.

Then a series of clicking noises as Jespers's men all drew powerful flashlights from their belts, flicked them on, and, moving composedly, fixed them to the barrels of their machine guns like telescopic sights. The gloom was filled with glaring yellow eyes. It was nothing Mallory had told them to do, and he felt a moment of ungrudging admiration for Kendrick.

Xiong recovered first. The cool flat voice came out of the shadows: "It is regrettable that our time has been wasted in this fashion. However, I see no reason to suspect you, Mr. Jespers, of deliberate malfeasance. You have been too plainly embarrassed. I shall return at once to Samneua. I withdraw our bid for Archangel. And in view of the situation, I believe I am entitled to expect an early repayment of the one million dollars we have advanced your organization in earnest money."

"He's right, Arne," Melnikov said, nodding. "We have paid our three million for a look at the merchandise. And where is the merchandise? Flown away. Never mind, Arnushka, such things happen, and we've had a nice visit, but let's see the money soon, hm?"

"Gentlemen, I'm sure there will be no need—" Jespers began.

"There is *every* need—" Halprin snapped.

"All right, that's enough," Mallory said, his voice cutting through the babble. "I'm gonna guess two of you deserve your million back. And one of you owes us half a billion bucks."

"I am afraid I don't understand," Halprin said coolly.

"We were penetrated last night," Mallory said. Jespers sighed in exasperation. Melnikov raised his eyebrows and clucked his tongue; Halprin and Xiong glanced at him, then at each other. "We killed the operative, but whoever it was must have somehow gimmicked the rocket's controls before he was discovered. And he couldn't have done it without an inside man." Mallory raised his voice over a burst of outraged voices. "You all want this gadget. And none of you would mind getting it without paying. Melnikov, it looks like it's headed up toward your neck of the woods."

"You are a young ass," Melnikov said, pouring himself more coffee.

"I have been. I'm about ready to stop. We've all been taken, all but one of us, and that one of us is the taker. Most likely somebody at this table. Maybe everybody here ought to retire to their rooms while we get this sorted out."

"Maybe you should, too," Kendrick said.

"Kendrick, there's no time for this."

"You're trying to—"

"Arne?" Mallory said. "Am I working for you? Then call off your dog."

"Where is Dr. Kost?" Jespers said grimly. "I have not seen him for several minutes. Has anyone?"

There was a short, stunned pause.

"All right," Mallory said in the tones of a drill instructor being very patient with an especially dense batch of recruits. "We'll sort this out." He turned to three guards. "Cordero. Balashov. Houghton. Please escort Mr. Xiong and his—"

"I must particularly object to this—"

"You'll have to object later, gentlemen. I'm afraid that's just the way it is right now. You three take Xiong. Menzies and you two, take Halprin. Avery, Yamada, Bauer, and you over there, you're assigned to Mr. Melnikov's party. Our guests are to be shown all possible courtesy, but they are not to leave their suites for any reason until you hear from me."

"I am going to take a nap," Melnikov announced.

"Good. Meanwhile, gentlemen, there's the matter of your bodyguards. You've all three got enough armed men in here to make this place a shooting gallery. Unless you want a free-for-all—"

"Now you are a little more intelligent," Melnikov said. "I don't like noise when I sleep. *Grishka*," he called. "We keep our weapons, but otherwise we cooperate and are nice fellows until"—he glanced at his heavy gold watch—"1800 tonight. Then we go home, and shoot anyone who asks us to stay. All right?"

"Twelve hours seems to be a reasonable interval," Xiong said. "We shall do similarly."

Halprin looked at his three bodyguards, nodded once, and returned his furious gaze to Mallory.

"Thanks." Mallory went to the railing and called down among the tiers of consoles. "Gentlemen, I see thirty-one technicians down there and nine guards. I expect to see precisely those numbers when I return. Nobody leaves this room till you get an all-clear from me directly. Guards, watch the technicians. Technicians, watch the guards. Anybody see anything they don't like, you tell it to Mr. Kendrick. Mr. Kendrick, please keep this room sealed and orderly. Huffman and Cho, go down to the power plant and get these damn lights on. You see anyone who shouldn't be there, bring him to Kendrick. If he objects, shoot his legs out and carry him. And you two, Parmenter and Branzi, come with me. We're going to find Kost. We'll start with his drafting room." He turned to Jespers. "All right, Arne?"

"All right, Jack," Jespers said quietly.

"Good." He turned to the waiting guards. "Let's move."

The two men on the doors pulled them open, revealing another row of waiting guards in the dark hall, each like a straddle-legged cyclops with a single glowing eye at chest level. As they had in the Hôtel Hermitage in Monaco, the bidders left separately with their minders, taking care not to pass too close to each other. As in Monaco, Melnikov waddled out last, looking amused. Mallory followed Melnikov's guards, and Branzi and Parmenter padded obediently after him, lighting his way with the flashlights fixed to their guns.

Until the moment the heavy steel doors swung shut behind him, Mallory was waiting for some word from Jespers. Some question or admonition, or even a simple "Not so fast, Jack." It never came.

But it would. Mallory had bought himself some time, no more.

And now he needed to buy himself some luck.

The corridors outside were already dissolving into chaos. Halprin's bodyguards were arguing with the escort Mallory had assigned them. The rest of Jespers's Army, who hadn't heard Mallory's briefing in the control room, were milling around wondering what their orders were. Mallory observed the growing confusion with grim gladness. It bothered him as a professional, but as a man who wanted to live until lunchtime, he was glad to see it. He had not quite reached the whispering gallery when the crowd of guards parted to reveal Laura, sprinting toward him in bare feet, her slate-blue eyes wide with fright and her fur coat gaping open to reveal one of Lily Prentice's more immodest nighties. Parmenter and Branzi fell back respectfully as she flung herself into his arms. "Jack, I'm so *frightened*," she cried. "What are they all doing? Jack, what's *happened*?"

Mallory held her narrow body against his and gently stroked her sleep-tousled hair. Tenderly, his lips almost brushing her ear, he whispered: "0540 at the chopper."

"And if you're not there?" she whispered back. Her eyes were squeezed shut, but her voice was cool and level.

He kissed her cheek and pulled his head back a bit so she could read his lips. *"Give me until 0545,"* he said silently. *"Then leave."*

Back in the control center, there was a long silence. The vast, gleaming, oval table was empty but for Milena, Kendrick, and Jespers. The Dane's nicotine-stained hands lay flat on the polished wood. He stared at them as if he couldn't imagine how they'd gotten there. Finally he nodded, raised his head, and looked at Kendrick. "Mr. Kendrick," he said, his voice slightly unsteady. "It appears that you have been correct after all. About Mr. Carroll, and, I think, about his lady friend as well. It appears that I owe you quite an apology."

"You don't owe me anything but my pay, Dane."

Jespers seemed not to hear. "And now . . ." he said, then sighed. "And now."

He turned to Milena, his face damp and gray in the gray dimness. He told her, "First Carroll. And then, *liebchen*, you can have the girl."

Milena drew the iron ring from her pocket and, smiling tranquilly, slipped it onto her finger.

Branzi had been a mistake, Mallory decided. The boy had seemed agreeably thick-witted when he'd picked him out of the crowd behind the oval table. Like Parmenter, he had big, empty cow-eyes above a monstrously muscular body, and in addition boasted a slack mouth that moved inconclusively when people talked. But mouth-breather or not, Branzi had seemed unpleasantly alert while Laurie whispered in his arms, and now that she'd gone, was showing unwelcome signs of intelligence. "Sir," he said as they crossed the whispering gallery. The monosyllable became a rushing of wind and flew about the long room. "About the Signorina Prentice . . ."

"She'll be all right, son," Mallory said. He tucked the Browning into his belt, pulled out the two cylindrical keys, and deactivated the electric-eye barrier. "Up the stairs, Mr. Branzi. I'll follow. Parmenter, you trail."

At the top of the stairs, Branzi tried again. "Excuse me, sir, but when you was speaking to the—"

"Keep it down, soldier," Mallory said, dialing in the door lock's combination. "When I open this door, you two move in fast, Parmenter first, and search the suite. Take down anyone who isn't Kost, but don't shoot to kill unless you've got to. You know the layout? Right. On three."

The two boys knew their business, Mallory had to admit. He watched from behind as they traded the lead efficiently, taking turns covering each other while they methodically swept the darkened workroom, conference room, and sleeping quarters. It took very little time for them to return, shaking their heads. But by then he'd eased the door shut behind him and had sorted through the ring of keys for the one to the heavy oak door of the closet where Mallory guessed the plans were kept. It was the next best thing to Kost himself.

"Clean, sir," Parmenter said. "What's next?"

But Branzi was eyeing the key in Mallory's hand with disapproval. "Signor," he said, "I must—"

"Closer," Mallory said. "Branzi, give me your light."

Branzi hesitated, then reached forward to disengage the flashlight from the barrel of his AKM.

As if impatiently, Mallory took hold of it himself and tried to wrench it free, twisting it deliberately in the wrong direction.

"Let me—" Branzi muttered in exasperation, shifting his hand away from the trigger to prevent a mishap. Parmenter had moved in to watch, swinging his machine gun down and away from the two of them. The room was dim, Parmenter's eyes were on the recalcitrant flashlight, and he never saw the swiftly rising boot that smashed into his solar plexus just as Mallory, reversing direction, whipped the heavy flashlight free and swung it through a whistling half-circle and into Branzi's left temple.

Branzi dropped, and Mallory released the flashlight to drop after him, bringing the stiffened edge of his palm with crushing force down on the nerve cluster beside Parmenter's thick neck.

Parmenter sprawled diagonally forward and collapsed across his comrade's body, and the room was silent except for the rough snoring sound of the unconscious Parmenter fighting for breath.

Crude work, Mallory thought, retrieving the flash. *Goddamn slapstick comedy.* He tucked the Browning more securely into his belt, tried to fit the key into the closet's lock, and swore softly: wrong one. Things were smelling a little sour. The lights had gone out on time, all right, but not quick enough to keep Kost from figuring that Archangel had been diddled. Mallory'd had to use a bunch of reverse-psychology monkeyshines to keep Jespers from aborting it there and then, and now everyone was a lot more riled up than he'd wanted them, and getting home with a whole skin would be a lot tougher. And Kost wasn't where he was goddamn supposed to be.

It was 0528:16. In a shade under twelve minutes, he was supposed to meet Laurie at the chopper. He'd give the closet until 0530 and no longer. If the next key wasn't the ticket, he'd forget it and leave before that.

The next key slipped smoothly in, and Mallory swung the door open. Inside was a nasty little slot in the stone wall, the kind of coffin-like space Mallory didn't even like looking at, lined with enameled-steel shelves. The shelves were stacked high with battered notebooks and rolled blueprints. The opening door made more noise than he'd thought it would.

When the door stopped moving, the soft creak continued. A third of a second too late, Mallory realized that the door to the workroom was swinging open behind him.

He spun, his Browning in his hand, to meet the blinding glare of two flashlights and the muzzles of two guns.

He went still.

"That's right," Kendrick's voice said. "We can see you, and you can't see us. But you do see the guns, right? You can see that much."

"Yeah," Mallory said. "I see 'em."

"Good. All right, Carroll. You know the drill."

Moving smoothly and very slowly, keeping both hands in view, Mallory set the Browning on the stone floor and rose again.

He heard a sharp whistle. The lights came on.

Kendrick was in the lead, with a flashlight in one hand and a .44 in the other. At his shoulder, submachine gun ready to fire, stood the guard named Avery, whom Laurie had vamped the previous day and whom Mallory had sent to babysit Melnikov. It had all come unwound, all right. Behind him stood Arne Jespers, hands in pockets, looking pensively at the two unconscious mercenaries at Mallory's feet. Behind Jespers towered Milena, her white hands on his shoulders as if steadying a fretful child. On Milena's ring finger shone a thick iron ring. Mallory didn't have to come any closer to know it would be shaped like three twined serpents, each holding the next in its jaws.

"At least tell me this's the right closet," he said very quietly. "At least tell me I'm not gonna be shot for burgling the wrong closet."

Kendrick had drawn nearer, keeping well out of Avery's line of fire, and was examining the fallen guards.

"Yes, Jack," Jespers said. "This is the right closet."

"Still breathing," Kendrick said. "When they wake up, I'm gonna give them cause to regret that."

He sighed, took a short length of nylon rope from his pocket, and began securing Mallory's hands behind his back.

"You've made me sad, Jack," Jespers said. "You've made me very sad. And now I'm going to make you sad."

"Well, I guess I'll be pretty sad when you shoot me," Mallory said.

Having checked the rope around Mallory's wrists, Kendrick hunkered down to bind his ankles. "There you go," he grunted, rising.

Jespers said, "No, not with a bullet, Jack. Nothing so quick. Nothing so pleasant. We'll have to give a bit of thought to this. We'll have to think hard about how we can make you properly sad. Milena, dumpling, would you help Mr. Kendrick to— Oh, perhaps we'll just tuck him away in that cubby there. Nice thick stone walls, and just enough space, I think, to squeeze in a skinny fellow like Jack. We'll close him

up there for the moment and then see to him properly when we've
done a bit of tidying."

Mallory couldn't help himself: his eyes darted to the dark, narrow
closet with its massive black oak door. *Easy,* he told himself. *Easy.*

Milena moved smoothly around Jespers and Avery and slipped her
massive hands beneath his arms again. He felt himself rising weight-
lessly into the air. He willed himself to breathe normally. He willed his
body to relax.

Jespers cried, "Stop!"

Jespers's large nose was quivering. His wet brown eyes were bulging from their sockets.

He took a step forward and sniffed again.

Slowly he said, "Fear. Yes, no doubt of it—he absolutely reeks of
fear."

"Not surprised," Kendrick said.

"*Quiet,*" Jespers said. "We . . . Let me think. We threatened to
shoot him, and that didn't . . ." He stopped and chewed his lower lip.
"But the sight of that little, small . . . and it lacks windows, as well. And
the very *sight* . . ."

A smile spread over Jespers's homely face.

"Gentlemen," he said, "I believe I understand now. Our friend
Jack Carroll is a—a claustro, claustrophobi . . . *ac.* Claustro-*phobe*? He
doesn't like to be shut into little small spaces, you see. He doesn't like
that at all. Didn't I say, Jack, didn't I say that one day we'd find what
you were afraid of?" Jespers was beaming now, like an uncle getting
ready to propose a treat for his favorite nephew. "You know, I believe
that we can, after all, conclude this matter right now, immediately, in a
very *satisfactory* way. I believe we can arrange something a bit better
for our friend Jack than that closet."

The forklift's engine was roaring, but the casket's stone walls were dull-
ing the noise. There were still five or six inches between the lid of the
sarcophagus and the edges of the casket. The inside of the lid was
concave, so there were maybe eight inches between the smoothly fash-
ioned stone and Mallory's face. He stared up at it. When the lid closed,

it would be flush against his mouth, the way the sides of the sarcophagus were already mashed tight against his shoulders. Mallory twisted his head and peered out through the bright gap between the lid and the sides. A bit of a stained-glass window: golden rods shooting out of a cloud, striking some saint in the forehead. The saint looked surprised. The corner of the Edwardian crapper, just a worn oaken corner and the edge of a frayed leather strap. Milena's huge white arm, still crushing him flat against the casket's stone bottom. Her hand with its iron ring on his chest. The yellow steel prongs of the forklift, scraped bare of paint in patches and the bare patches starting to rust, running under the lid just over his chest and hips. He could see a bit of Kendrick's gray lapel and gray shoulder. They were the last things he'd ever see. He'd managed not to scream when he saw what they were going to do to him. He'd managed not to ask to be shot, to beg for it, but there was nothing Mallory could do about the heaving of his chest or about the shrilling voices beginning to fill his head, *anything but this anything else but you don't get to pick how you die you don't get to pick it just don't—it'll end soon it'll end sometime it has to end you won't mind it when you're dead just don't cry. Just don't cry so they can hear.*

Jespers's protuberant eyes appeared in the gap. "Well, there you still are. Still awake? Still with us? You've been so quiet, Jack, I thought you might have fainted, and this would never do. We'd never get to say a proper good-bye." Mallory stared at him. He did not even hate Jespers. He was too terrified. It was too precious to see a human face. He'd never get to do that again. It had been so hard not to struggle when they'd put him in, not to give them the satisfaction. He found himself wanting to tell Jespers how hard it'd been. He was silent, and he knew his face was dead and still, that was one thing they taught you, but his chest was going and there was no helping that. "Well," Jespers said, "I suppose we're all done here and can turn our attentions now to Miss Prentice. Maybe you'll have a bit of luck, Jack, and smother quickly. But this lid, it isn't airtight, in my opinion. To me, it doesn't really look airtight. And so maybe you'll lie in there a long time. I don't suppose anyone will come here when we've gone. Not for a year or so while we are cleaning up the muddle you've made and getting our affairs back in order. If you don't smother, you'll have plenty of time to think about how very foolish you have been. Well, good-bye to you, Jack. It's a pity we don't have another sarcophagus for the lovely Lily, but we'll manage. And that's that, I suppose. You've caused me a great deal of trouble, you know." The eyes vanished, then reappeared. "It's a shame the way things have turned out." They vanished again, and Mallory heard him say, "All right, Avery, kindly lower it down."

The grinding of the forklift's engine grew a little louder, and Milena's arm slithered away like a startled snake. The last human being who'd ever touch him. The bright gap dwindled to a line. And then the deafening grating as they dragged the prongs of the fork out, and a huge clank, and then black. Nothing but black. The stone crushing in on him, pressing against his shoulders, his knees, his feet, his bound hands trapped behind him under his buttocks, his head mashed down crookedly against one shoulder. A thin noise escaped him before he could choke it off. If he could only straighten his head, if he could only lie straight and dignified, he could take it, maybe he could take it, if— He heard his own hoarse breathing. The air already seemed thick and dead. *"Take it,"* he whispered aloud. He could feel his mind unraveling into tiny wet animal-voices, into shrieking scurrying flocks of wet, toothed thoughts that tore at him *not like this not like there must be there isn't there won't be ever anymore if I could just straighten my I can't take it take it you better take it. You better figure out how. You better figure out how to take it. Take it. Take it.*

6

Queen of the Mountain

When she looked at it again, Laura's watch still read 5:46. She lifted her head carefully. From where she crouched, behind the pilot's seat of the big Sikorsky, she could just see the heavy sliding glass doors that led into the monastery's east gallery, glittering coolly in the hard mountain morning light. She waited a minute or two, then looked at her watch again. Still 5:46. The fourth time she looked, it read 5:47. Jack's instructions had been to leave two minutes ago, whether he was there or not.

Laura's breathing was even and disciplined, her pulse strictly regulated. She was holding panic at bay. But if Jack didn't come through those doors in the next minute or so, with or without Kost, she doubted she could keep it up.

He must know she hadn't left yet, no matter what the schedule said; he'd have heard the chopper. Everyone would hear when the twin Allison turbines got going. She'd gathered a little arsenal of guards' weapons in case the first people through the glass doors weren't friends: the Luger in her hand and two heavy AKMs in the hold behind her. If that wasn't enough, nothing would be.

She rose, glanced back at the guard outside—still unconscious, still tucked away in the snow behind the chopper's big right sponson—and slipped into the pilot's seat. She swung open the hatch. A gust of snowy wind swirled in. She was a fat target now, but if Jack made it through those glass doors, it was better to have the rotors turning and the door waiting open.

The face of the left instrument panel was hanging by a single bolt. She set the Luger on the floorboards, reached inside the console, and located the red and blue ignition wires she'd painstakingly traced to their sources. She twisted them together with her gloved fingertips and heard a dismal grinding noise, then a low hum and a rising whine as the turbines came to life. Slow as the second hand of a clock, then more quickly, the heavy five-bladed rotor began to turn overhead. Laura double-checked the angle of the rotor blades: still flat level. It wouldn't do to take off just yet. She turned back to the glass doors, reaching down for the Luger on the floorboards, and saw an immense white hand wearing a thick iron ring, inches from her eyes, closing on her arm.

And she was in the air.

She struck the snow-dusted concrete of the helipad as gracefully as a champion swimmer striking the surface of a pool, rolled, and flung herself skyward again, landing balletically on the balls of her feet just in time to see Milena squeeze back through the narrow hatch of the helicopter, step out onto the snowy helipad, and rise to her full seven feet one.

"Hello there," the huge girl said.

Milena's hands were empty. She made no effort to pick up Laura's Luger or the two heavy assault rifles lying ready behind her.

"Arne gave you to me," she said. "Do you know that? He did. He said I could do what I like with you."

The tiny bestial eyes in the lovely face were serene.

She began to walk toward Laura, the monstrous braid swinging slowly behind her.

"I am going to like this very much," she said.

Laura took two quick steps, whipped a long leg forward, and drove the side of her tensed right foot into the soft cup between Milena's collarbones. It was a lethal blow.

If it had landed, but somehow it didn't. And she was flying again.

She twisted in midair like a cat as the giantess flung her skyward, then savagely straightened, sending the point of her left elbow into Milena's right temple with murderous force and snapping the sleek head around in a quarter circle.

This time, Laura landed in a Hawk stance. Arms outspread, she waited for the huge girl to fall. Milena blinked twice, openmouthed, eyes empty.

Then she smiled beatifically.

She said, "It's better. It's better than I even hoped. You will give me fun before you die."

The young Pole sank backward into a lopsided fighting stance: right leg flexed, left straight, left hand hooked as if ready to draw a bow, right hand loose, and Laura recognized the Bent Spear stance of the Iron Bowl style. Too late, she realized what Milena was. A graduate of the so-called Assassin Factories of Shantou, where young toughs were trained by renegade masters to be empty-handed killers, sparring and exercising for eighteen hours a day, living on iron bowls full of raw chicken entrails and cold rice and sleeping each night in a shallow pool of iced water. Those whom the regimen did not kill were very difficult to kill indeed, and matchless at the killing arts.

And this one was a giantess with bones like steel.

For a full minute and a half, the two women stood motionless as the snow danced around them and the rotors of the helicopter passed rhythmically over their heads, slowing and slowing but not quite stopping.

Then, simultaneously, they struck.

The vast Milena seemed to levitate, to billow upward like a sheet blown by the wind, her vast braid hooking through the air behind her, and her cannon-thick leg sweeping forward toward Laura's jaw, just as Laura seemed to dematerialize, to spill down along the ground like roiling water and then shoot up beneath Milena like a geyser, hooking both feet hard into the girl's abdomen.

And it was Milena's turn to fly, in a lazy arc through the open glass doors and onto a heavy wooden trestle table that had served the monastery for over four hundred years, and which now split down the middle and collapsed.

The impact would have killed most ordinary men and incapacitated the strongest, but Laura Morse was a quick learner, and she didn't need to be shown twice that her opponent couldn't quite be judged by human standards. She leapt forward to deliver a final killing blow—or two, or three, or however many this huge creature might require—and was driven back by a cyclone of flying, churning legs. And then Milena had righted herself and was rumbling forward.

And then they were trading feints and blows, and the contest was on in earnest.

The exchange was too swift for any observer to follow. They themselves scarcely knew what blow, block, feint, or kick they were applying until it was done and they were midway through the next. Their arms and legs whistled through the air; they emitted brief, sharp cries; now and then a blow went home with a deep thud. Their faces were twisted with a kind of stylized fury, but their eyes were blank as the eyes of sleepwalkers. What passed between them was not a studied application of technique but an impersonal frenzy like a hurricane, as if their masters and their masters' masters were fighting through them, pouring out centuries of fighting lore through the conduits of two superbly trained young bodies to meet in a swirling maelstrom of fists and feet.

For a minute it lasted, for two, for an impossible third, as they drove each other from one end of the terrace to the other, circling the thrumming military helicopter and the fallen guard, skirting the icy stone parapet and the plunging depths below. Four times Laura delivered killing or crippling blows to Milena with her full weight behind them; four times they were shaken off. And she understood perfectly that if even one of Milena's slashing punches or kicks was to land, she herself would die.

Laura Morse was accustomed to fighting opponents larger and more powerful than herself. She'd met a few who were as skilled as she, and even a few who were nearly as fast. But she had never faced an opponent who combined the highest level of lethal skill with impossible speed and inhuman strength.

"You can't . . ." Milena panted as she fought. "Can't . . . win . . ."

"I know," said Laura Morse.

Pivoting elegantly, she flung herself over the stone wall and into the abyss.

For a long moment she dropped through the air, arms and legs windmilling. Then her left foot struck the steep, snowy slope, and she was bounding downhill, bouncing impossibly high with each enormous, plunging step, as if she were on the moon. With the third step, she struck the slates of the lower roof, just where Billy's map said it would be, and then she was scrambling over the rooftree. Then she was sliding down the far slope of the roof, scrabbling madly to slow herself. She was still scrabbling as she tumbled over the far edge.

And landed in the massed snow of a waiting balcony.

In the next moment, she was up again and running along one of the narrow parapets that twined ribbonlike around the ancient structure. Rounding a corner, she found herself at the front gate, facing, across another snowy terrace, the empty gondola of the cable railway. Behind her, she heard the laboring of massive lungs and the loudening thud of boots on snow.

She dove across the terrace into the gondola and slammed the door, and the sleek scarlet pod coasted off on its downhill journey.

Wrong. She regretted her choice as soon as she'd made it. She'd hoped for a strategic withdrawal, not a full retreat—had hoped to fall back until she found *something*: some weapon, some kink in the terrain, something to give her some tiny advantage against an inexorable and seemingly invulnerable opponent. Even just a few moments to regroup. The last thing she wanted was to save her own skin at the cost of any chance of saving Jack's. But now, for precious minutes, she'd be speeding directly away from where she needed to be, with no plausible way of getting back but riding the same damn gondola right up to the front door again. Laura's regrets took perhaps three-fifths of a second, much of which time she spent spinning around and grasping the door latch. Maybe if she opened the door again, this damn thing would stop.

She turned to meet an immense white fist swinging toward her face.

She threw herself back across the car and, as the window burst inward, scattering pebbly bits of automotive glass, Laura's boot shot up and demolished the window opposite. The crushed safety glass flew lazily through the air. She seemed to hear herself placidly commenting: *"They don't open."* Then, as Milena's massive legs slid through the window, Laura scrambled out the opposite one and up onto the sleek, slippery red roof.

She was on her belly, gasping, trying to pull her legs up away from the window so that Milena couldn't reach up and grab them and fling Laura down the mountain. She hitched herself forward on elbows and belly across the car, wriggling like a worm, grunting with fear, hitched forward and then forward again. The gondola was suspended from the slanting cable by a single steel strut in the center of the roof. She closed her fingers around it and dragged herself inward.

And then Milena's tiny eyes rose over the horizon of the car's roof before her, full of merriment.

Laura scrambled to her feet, and Milena reached out her arms, wedged her fingers into the seams in the steel body of the gondola, and heaved herself forward. In a moment, the two were standing on opposite sides of the swaying roof, legs akimbo, facing each other.

Blood dripped slowly from their gashed hands.

"You ran away," Milena commented.

Laura gazed at her, getting used to the feel of the curved, swaying roof beneath her. It was a bit like getting one's sea legs. Only you had just a few seconds to do it in, and if you couldn't manage it, you died.

"You left," Milena said, "and I wasn't finished."

The car was picking up speed. The growing wind tugged at Laura's hair and stirred Milena's long braid. From the monastery above them, she could hear the sporadic cracking and rattling of gunfire.

"Do you hear?" Milena said. "Do you hear these silly boys?"

The rising howl of the wind almost drowned out the noise.

"They all shoot each other now, each thinking the other has betrayed them, and all shooting at Arne's men. The Russian men shooting the German, the German shooting the Chinamans."

"Laotians," Laura said.

"All the stupid men shooting each other. All this trouble you make, you and Jack."

"Don't mention it."

"You don't like this. I see you don't like it, being up so high. I like it. I like it when you will fall."

Her big hand snaked out and almost closed around the central strut. Laura's booted foot swept past, and Milena pulled back just in time to keep her knuckles from being crushed.

She grinned.

She said, "Do you ever go to Japan? Arne take me to Sapporo, and we watch sumo there. Two huge big fat men in a little small circle, and each one try to make the other fall out of the circle. When a man is pushed the other man out, he wins. I liked the sumo very much. But sumo is for the big and strong, not for skinny little girls."

Laura was unzipping her coat. She shrugged out of it and let it fall. The chill wind bit at her through her heavy sweater. Milena hadn't bothered to wear more than a wool cardigan. It was decorated with pearl beading and absurd little pink bows.

A merry light danced in Milena's tiny eyes. "Don't fall," she said.

Very slowly, their eyes on each other's hands, feet, centers of gravity, the two women eased into shallow crouches and undid their boots. Then they rose, just as slowly, and kicked them off, one by one. The boots spiraled away through the rushing winds to disappear with tiny white puffs into the snow-loaded trees and the white slopes speeding past below them. They were in their stocking feet now, their toes gripping the curving roof, the wind rippling their sweaters.

"Don't fall," Milena said. "Don't fall until I make you fall."

"You can fall any time you like," Laura said. "Don't mind me."

She feinted left and then kicked right. Milena twisted out of the way, then untwisted again, letting the momentum carry her clockwise around the central strut and toward Laura, who fell back just before a big arm swept her over the edge. They were facing each other again, but now they stood at the fore and aft of the gondola's roof, Milena ducking her head slightly to keep her hair from tangling with the cable. She surged forward again and Laura oozed out of her way, hooking a vicious fist into the girl's ribs as she passed, then backed off again as Milena's fingers nearly closed on her arm. It would be death to let the huge girl get a good grip on her, and nearly as bad to let her get a good grip on the central strut.

The lower gondola tore past them on its way up the mountain, and the entire car jolted and wobbled in its wake. For a moment, both women fought to keep their balance.

"We forget!" Milena cried, amused. "We forget the other car. We're two pretty silly girls, huh?"

Laura scuttled sideways and lashed her left foot forward. It glanced off Milena's hip, and she followed up with a straight jab with the heel of her right hand. Milena took this straight in the chin. It did not appear to impress her, but the impact jolted painfully up Laura's arm, and she backpedaled and got her balance again. Her shoulders were ablaze now with the effort of keeping her guard up. The endless series of futile blows had drained her strength. Milena looked fresh and at ease. Her big braid swung jauntily behind her.

"Silly enough," Laura panted.

She parried a roundhouse kick and fell back clockwise again. Enough blood had dripped from their hands that she had to watch where she stepped on the gondola's roof.

"I don't like you," Milena said. "You are cold, a cold little bug-girl. You are like an insect. Even fighting you is not a pleasure. You are not a good woman for Jack. He needs a woman with warm blood."

An arm like a railroad tie flashed before Laurie's face, nearly erasing her nose. Her counterstrike was weak and unfocused.

Milena smiled reminiscently. "He was not so bad, for a little thin man. He was not weak like most men. He was glad to get a girl who is not thin and cold. I liked him. I will miss him a little, maybe. Everyone will miss him now."

Lunge, parry, strike. Laura was exhausted and falling into a rhythm, as if she were drilling in the dojo. That was fatal. She mustn't let that happen. She feinted, feinted again, and then feinted a third time before raking a low cyclone kick across Milena's knees. The big girl deflected without much trouble. Laura was losing her concentration. She was getting sloppy, letting herself be distracted by schoolyard taunts. She had to tighten up again somehow.

"Yes, he is gone. He has gone now. What, you don't know where he is? You don't know where your little man is?"

Don't listen. Tighten up. Laura shuffled in on aching legs, launched another punch, and had it deflected.

"We put him away," Milena said.

Tighten up. Fight.

"We put him away in a box," she crooned. "In a little stone box, where he doesn't make any trouble anymore."

For a moment, Laura simply stared.

And then she understood.

The sound that rose from Laura's lips then was like nothing Milena had ever heard. It was an inhuman noise, like the shriek of rending metal. And the dry, thin, careful woman Milena had been fighting was gone.

In her place was a yellow-haired demon with bloody fists and twisted white slits for eyes.

Milena fell back, and fell back again, and then again as the creature swarmed forward, clawed hands and hooked feet slashing at her, dealing blow after blow with sickening force. She parried as best she could, but there were too many now, and coming too quickly. A Returning Crane kick slipped under her arm and knocked the wind from her. A palm strike to the forehead rattled her, and she lost a second and a half reorienting herself and finding the roof's edge again, and before she'd regained her footing, she felt two of her ribs crack, and then a collarbone. She felt smashed teeth rolling loose under her tongue. A black limb struck snakelike at her eyes and she flinched, but it was only her own braid, whipping through the air with each of Laura's blows. An awful mistake had been made. She'd been sent out to kill a devil. She'd been trying to kill what was already dead. God was angry with Milena. He'd sent her an angel of death, a flame of pure rage risen from hell, and she was trapped up here in the sky with it and no escape anywhere.

The car was slowing again, the wind howling in a lower key. The trees were speeding past them. Milena was surrounded by branches and demon's claws. She could see the corrugated steel roof of the little terminus swinging up to meet them. She could see the huge orange bull wheel spinning, hauling the car closer and closer. They were gliding up to the station, and she was ready to leap down and flee, but the yellow-haired demon would not stop, and Milena saw the world dimming, a blackening world full of fists and feet that snapped her head endlessly from side to side and swung her braid at her own face like a flail. The gondola was slowing and leveling off, the dark steel roof was sliding over their heads, and still there was nowhere to hide from the killing swarm of kicks and blows and, in the corners of her eyes, the angry lashing of her own braid. And abruptly there was a monstrous wrench at her neck as if God had snatched her up and shaken her.

And she knew that her braid, her beautiful braid had caught between the cable and the huge orange wheel, and God was yanking her up into the sky.

Milena's scream could be heard all the way up the mountain. And then a wet, crackling rending only Laura heard, and two soft, heavy thumps as something fell in halves to the snowy platform.

The giantess had been dragged up into the cable car's mechanism by the hair, and the steel cable, meeting the iron wheel with the force of many tons, had split her down the middle like a game hen on a chopping block.

The car had stopped. For a moment, everything was still.

Laura picked her way over the blood-spattered roof and leapt lightly down. She did not look at the huge cleft thing lying to either side of the bull wheel. She did not seem relieved or triumphant. On her face there was no hint of human expression. She opened the door of the gondola, leaving dark red smears on the scarlet enamel, and climbed inside. She slid the door shut.

The cable car set off on its journey again, gliding up through the trees along the mountainside, and Laura turned her eyes upward to the peak.

Jack was up there. Dead or dying, shut up in that hideous smirking stone thing. In the worst place in the world. They must have found out somehow that it was the worst place in the world for him, and they'd stuck him in there. They'd put him in the worst place in the world and left him there to die.

And they were going to die for it.

Now that the shooting had quieted down a little, Avery was in a pensive mood. Kendrick had sent him to patrol the front corridor, from the door to the big fireplace, and though he could still hear the occasional snap of a distant pistol, his own area was quiet, thank God, and he had a little time to think. Not even breakfast-time yet, and it had already been a hell of a day. Avery had served as a mercenary in seven countries, and had been through a lot of damn peculiar kinds of action, but this morning's shoot-'em-up had been the stupidest waste of people and ammo he'd ever seen. Everybody popping off at anything that moved. At least four guys he knew down, and probably two of 'em for good. What was the point of all that? Well, he guessed he saw the point of it for Carroll. Carroll's orders had sounded good when you heard 'em, and it was only when things actually started happening that you saw how little sense they made—how little sense they were supposed to make, Avery guessed—and how you should've stuck to Kendrick, who'd always kept things wrapped tight. He'd liked Carroll, too. He could've sworn the man was solid. They'd all been conned pretty good, all right. It had been one big old sloppy mess. Then all that stuff with the stone coffin, that creepy stuff you always had with a creep like Jespers. Avery didn't like even thinking about it, but what the hell did Carroll expect? He'd known what he was signing on for, trying to con a man like Jespers. It wasn't something Avery would ever be eager to try himself.

No, the one Avery felt bad about was the Prentice girl. Looking at it logically, she must have been in it with Carroll. She had to've been, but Avery couldn't believe she was really cut out for that kind of crap. She was too sensitive. They'd gotten to talking the other day when he'd escorted her back to her room, really gotten to talking, sort of heart-to-heart, and Avery could tell. You could always tell what kind of people belonged in the business and who'd been sort of talked into it because they thought it sounded exciting or something. Avery had no doubt in his mind that Carroll had told her some tale. He'd probably made it sound like her part of it would be easy and glamorous. And what happened? She wound up getting fed to Milena. There wasn't anybody Avery'd ever hated bad enough that he'd wish that big Polish freak on them. Boy, Lily had been pretty. He'd spent the whole day after meeting her having these sort of daydreams about taking care of her and protecting her. Though, to be honest, there'd also been another daydream, involving a pair of pulleys and a knotted silk scarf. He'd seen that done once in a Bangkok brothel and thought it'd cripple the girl for life, though afterward she'd been all smiles.

When Avery first caught sight of Laura, he, like Milena, thought he was seeing a vengeful ghost. He'd just reached the fireplace and was turning around, his Luger in its hip holster, his AKM at present arms, and there she was, shooting down the hall toward him, no coat or shoes, scarcely seeming to touch the floor with her flying feet, completely silent, her eyes all wrong and her long teeth bared. She didn't look like a sensitive girl who needed protecting. She didn't even look human. It was the worst thing Avery ever saw.

And it was the last thing he ever saw. An instant later, his neck snapped as the side of Laura's left foot smashed into his jaw. She vaulted over his toppling corpse without breaking stride and was around the corner before it struck the ground.

His Luger was in her hand.

The guard Melnikov had called Grishka had been shooting anything that moved all morning, and when Laura sprinted around the corner he saw no reason to vary his policy. His bullet trimmed a lock of pale hair from over her ear. Hers pierced his breastbone and knocked him backward into an illuminated vitrine full of tiles. His comrade got off a single shot at her retreating back before she disappeared up a short flight of spiral stairs, but only struck chips from the stone wall behind her. In the upper gallery Laura met two of Jespers's guards. As they raised their guns in unison, she rose into the air. The ball of her left foot smashed an AKM from its owner's hands, shattering his right ulna in the process, and the stiffened edge of her right hand struck the other guard squarely in the center of his forehead. From the end of the gallery, Howie, in his stained plaid blazer, watched with his assault rifle poised as one guard dropped cursing to his knees and the other flopped lifeless to the flagstones. And then as Laura shot down the hallway toward him, her narrow face distorted with something like madness.

He dropped his gun, turned, and ran heavily away.

The whispering gallery was deserted when Laura got there, and so was the chapel. The forklift was beside the sarcophagus, thank God. She jammed the Luger into the waist of her slacks and was able to start the engine up without much trouble, but the lid fit snugly, horrifyingly snugly, and it took several scraping lunges with the steel forks before, sobbing with frustration, she managed to wedge the tips into the seam between lid and casket. She almost let the lid drop back on Mallory before she managed to grind through the forklift's gears and find forward so she could lever the mammoth stone thing up and over the casket's back edge. It struck the stone floor with a report like a mortar explosion and split in two. Inside the casket, Mallory was letting out great roaring groans for breath, writhing spastically in the narrow stone slot, eyes squeezed shut, his head mashed down against his left shoulder. She leapt from the seat of the forklift, snatched a jeweled scimitar from the wall, and slashed the ropes binding his ankles. He jerked a foot free and almost kicked her in the face. She slipped an arm behind his shoulders, helped him sit up, and sliced through the ropes binding his wrists. He clutched at her blindly and they half climbed, half fell to the floor. She flung the scimitar away and gripped his shoulders with her bloody hands. "*Jack,*" she shouted. "*Jack.*"

He glared in her direction but did not seem to recognize her. His face was spit-gray and shining with sweat or tears. He could barely stand. His eyes roamed crazily all over the room. She wondered if he'd had a stroke. At last they seemed to focus on her, or at a point just beside her ear, and widened with horror. She felt a tug and looked down to see that he'd snatched the Luger from her belt and was swinging it up toward her nose. She barely had time to twist out of the way before he fired, and fired again.

She spun to see Howie swaying in the doorway behind them, the muzzle of his assault rifle wavering in her direction, two reddening holes in his stained plaid blazer.

Then the rifle fell to the floor. And then Howie did.

Mallory was swaying a bit, too. He rubbed his wet face with his free hand.

"Let's find Kost and go home," he muttered. "This is getting to be no fun anymore."

7

A Long Time Coming

"Leggo," Mallory said. "Leggo me, hon. I'm all right."

She released him, and he tucked the Luger into his belt and walked fairly steadily over to Howie's corpse. He bent, gripped its hands, and dragged it into the door and out of view of the hall. It left a thin smear of blood across the flagstones, leading into the chapel like a signpost. He tried to scuff it away with his shoe. "Close enough for government work," he decided. He picked up the dead man's AKM and silently closed the door. "You all right? What happened to your hands?"

"I had to punch out a window."

"Hoo. Hoo boy. That wasn't too pleasant. Mmph. I don't like the looks of those hands of yours. You okay? Can you handle a gun? Where're your shoes?" he said, and handed her the assault rifle. "Here."

"Long story. No offense, Jack, but wouldn't it make more sense if I kept the Luger and you took the big gun?"

"I'm not going to fire that thing. I got a headache. You make it to the helicopter?"

"Milena jumped me there."

"Where's she now?"

"That's a theological question."

"Good. Seen Kost?"

"No, nor Jespers or Kendrick."

"Guess the chopper's off the board."

"Kendrick'll have it bottled up tight by now," Laura agreed. "You must be the only one on the mountain who didn't hear the turbines kick over."

"Cable car's no good either. They can probably stop it from the house. That leaves skis."

"You're not that good a skier, Jack. Kendrick'll have men on staff who can move. I might have a chance to outrun them, but you haven't."

"That's why I'm shooting Kendrick before we go. Son of a bitch's too good at his job. With him gone, I'm not worried about anything these big clowns can think up to do. Huh," he said, examining the Luger's clip. "Five rounds left. Oughta do it." He snapped the clip back in. "Hoo. Still little shaky. How's it look out there?"

"Quiet," she said. "I'm guessing everyone's holed up in their rooms trying to figure out what happened."

"But Kendrick'll be on the move, picking up pieces. Good. I want you to get back to our room, grab our skis and sticks—and some shoes for you, for God's sake—and meet me, ah . . ."

"I killed the man on the front door. They might have resecured it by now, but I doubt they'll bother securing the slope directly beneath the front terrace. They'll be too busy making sure we don't try for the gondola above."

"Nice. Meet you there at 0742?"

"Fine."

"Kill Kendrick if you see him first, but don't expose yourself by coming after him. Try to pick up a couple more pistols so we got something light to shoot with on the way down. If we make the village—"

"We'll figure something out," she said.

"Right." They moved together to the door, and Mallory set a hand on the knob. "Good luck," he said. "And thanks."

"For what? Oh," Laura said. "Well, you're welcome."

It took Mallory three and a half minutes to work his way down to the front hall and find it deserted except for Avery's corpse. That was a good sign. It meant Kendrick's men were stretched thin enough that they didn't know right off when one of them was down. Encouraged, Mallory was a little more aggressive moving from the fireplace near the front entrance to the end of the east gallery leading to the helipad. There were plenty of men around the doors to the helipad, all right, but no Kendrick he could see, unless he was out on the terrace himself—Mallory couldn't see around that corner, and was disinclined to linger long enough to be sure. Everyone thought Mallory was still in the sarcophagus, which gave him a little bit of an edge, but he doubted it was one you could push very far. He turned and began working his way back toward the whispering gallery. He was just approaching the entrance when he heard the shot and felt the sting of flying stone chips against his cheek.

Mallory was already diving forward into a barrel roll, letting off two rounds back along the bullet's path to discourage follow-up shots. Three-quarters of a second later he was in the dimness of the torch-lit gallery, and half a second after that he was crouched behind one of the massive twisted columns. From the corner of his eye, he'd seen his attacker following him in, and knew he was now ensconced behind one of the columns of the gallery's other side. Which one, he didn't know. All Mallory had seen was a fleeting silhouette. But, short, blocky, and impossibly wide at the shoulders, it was not the sort of silhouette you forgot after you'd seen it once.

"Not bad," he heard Kendrick say. "Being buried alive didn't slow you up any."

Mallory scanned the dim oval hall, waiting for his eyes to adjust and trying to get his breathing under control. He didn't know exactly how far the whispering gallery would throw the sound of his ragged breath. He was squatting down on the balls of his feet, steadying himself with a light left hand against the clammy column. Instinctively, he'd made himself into the smallest target possible. He wanted to use the column's shelter to rise to a marksman's crouch: more stable, more mobile. But he didn't know where Kendrick was, and didn't want to betray himself by moving. There were eight columns on each side of the hall. Mallory was behind the northern colonnade, the second column from the door. Across the hall, on the southern side, it seemed like the shadow behind the third column from the door was just the least bit wider and paler. As if it contained a motionless, broad-shouldered man in a gray suit.

"If you aren't the hardest-to-pin-down little bugger I ever saw," Kendrick said. "Like trying to trap a mouse under a coffee cup."

Mallory leveled the Luger at the pale center of the shadow and fired. The echo of the shot clamored in his ears and took a long time to die.

"Uh-uh," Kendrick said easily. "But that's the spirit."

Stupid. A bullet gone to no good purpose. He needed to bear down and get serious before he fired again. But he couldn't afford to wait Kendrick out, either. He remembered how silently the man could move. He might be on the move right now, bringing Mallory's flank into view.

Kendrick laughed quietly, and the laughter rose spiraling into the air and seemed to branch endlessly like the stone columns above them. "You've balled things up pretty good all right, you and your little pal. I've got to hand it to you. Lost five of my men that I know of. Maybe six: haven't heard from Avery for a while. Halprin's dead. Xiong's down with a bullet in the hip. You know who got clean away, though? Melnikov. Right down the mountain, zippity-do. Who knew that fatty was such a skier? And Milena's down the mountain, too. Busted in two. I've got to say, that kind of impresses me. I figure there's maybe half a dozen people in the world who could go up against our Milena and live, and only one of 'em's a skinny little blondie with a snotty Boston accent. And if she's Laura Morse, well, I guess that makes you Jack Mallory. Doesn't it?"

Mallory was in motion again, sprinting toward the glass doors at the gallery's end and glancing over his shoulder to see a wide pale blur let loose a spark of orange light. The bullet dug a chunk from the column behind him, and Mallory spun and tried to put a bullet directly into the orange spark, then dove and rolled to rest behind two columns down. He listened hard.

"Wish you'd hold still," Kendrick said.

Another round wasted.

"I mean, for your own sake. You just showed me where you are. And all I showed you is where I used to be. And I guarantee you, Mallory, I'm not there now."

Mallory held his own breath and heard, as if it were next to his ear, the quiet breathing of a weary man. But he still couldn't tell which direction it was coming from.

"Like I say, son, you did a job. Hell, it'll take us weeks to get things back on track. And you've put a dent in our reputation it'll take years to hammer out. It was pretty damn cute, the way you played the old man. I didn't like it, but I sort of had to admire it. You came in here with no plan I could see and no backup except some poor dumb smoke I wouldn't hire to mow my lawn, and damn if you didn't get your hand in the cookie jar anyway. You and the girl can die knowing you did better than you had any right to. You had a good run, Mallory. It is Mallory, isn't it?"

The voice was coming from nowhere in particular, like a ringing in Mallory's own ears. The shadows along the colonnade writhed and shimmered in the flickering firelight. The longer he listened, the less he knew which way to shoot next.

"You're getting the idea, now, aren't you? You're figuring out why I keep on talking. And why there's no sense firing at the sound of my voice. 'Cause my voice comes from *everywhere*. That's the trick of our little whispering gallery. Voices, footsteps, breathing—none of that helps you. It's all a matter of knowing the terrain. And you don't seem to know it too well, do you?"

The shot ruffled his trouser legs, and Mallory was rolling and scuttling again. How many bullets did he have left? One. One goddamn bullet, and no idea where to put it.

"Now, that, you'll have to admit, was pretty close. In all fairness, you've got to admit I nearly had you there. C'mon, buddy, say something. Tell me your goddamn name. Let me at least know I guessed right. Let me know I did at least one goddamn thing right since you first walked in the door."

Mallory brought the Luger near to his face and studied it. His nostrils filled with the sharp, harsh stench of cordite. He tried to remember the last time he'd used one on the range and how the clip unlatched.

"This has been a long time coming. I always knew we'd wind up like this. I don't hold it against you, Jack. You're just doing your job. And your job was to make a monkey of me. And now I'm gonna do mine. It's not just a matter of my self-respect, or even me being mad at you. It's Jespers. He might like to play the fool, but he's no fool. And I've got to show him I'm not a guy anyone can waltz in and make a monkey of. 'Cause if he decides I am, well, there goes my job. And like he says, Mallory, Arne doesn't fire people."

There it was. He set his thumb on the latch, covered it with his free hand, and squeezed tight. For a moment, his mind flicked back to the bathroom on the Boulevard Albert, Kirsten asleep in the next room, him jamming the towel against the bathroom tap and easing the faucet silently open. Slowly, slowly he eased the Luger's clip open, the flesh of his palm deadening the *snick*.

"Right? Mallory? Don't you answer to your name, boy? Isn't that your name?"

With the clip protruding an inch from the bottom of the grip, Mallory raised the gun, took a breath, and pulled the trigger.

The whispering gallery echoed with the sound every professional knows well. The sound of a hammer snapping on empty chamber.

"Ah," Kendrick said fondly. "Finally you got something to say."

Mallory heard the faintest hiss of boot leather on stone. Kendrick had left the shelter of the colonnade and was coming after him.

"That you're out of ammo at last," Kendrick said.

Mallory slammed the clip home as he rose to meet Kendrick, five yards away and moving in fast, his gun rising. He took aim at the middle stripe of the man's necktie and fired his last round.

And missed. The bullet meant for Kendrick's heart smashed into his shoulder instead. The rising gun flew from Kendrick's hand and skittered across the floor, and the squarish face wrinkled with pain, but the short broad man did not slow.

A moment later Kendrick had slammed into Mallory and the enormous left hand was closing around his throat.

It was like being garroted with the anchor chain of a tugboat. There was no human warmth or softness in the great fingers; they were as unyielding as iron. Mallory sent his fist into Kendrick's stomach, and again, but the fingers continued to close. In a moment, Mallory's windpipe would collapse. The eyes close to his were feral now, bright with pain. "Who are you," Kendrick grated. "Tell me your name."

Mallory smashed the empty Luger against the man's temple. The iron grip did not loosen.

"Tell me," Kendrick said.

Mallory brought the Luger down on Kendrick's temple again.

"Tell me," Kendrick said, his mouth loosening. *"Tell me your name."*

Mallory smashed the gun against the squarish skull one last time and heard the crunch of disintegrating bone.

"Mallory," Mallory said, his voice a creak. *"I'm Mallory."*

Kendrick nodded and died.

The big hand opened, and Mallory staggered back and dragged in air with a mewling noise as the heavy corpse slumped to the ground. It was all he could do not to follow. His hand was on his chest, just beneath his tortured throat. His throat was too sore to touch. He forced down a breath, and then another. He was freezing cold. *Don't pass out,* he told himself.

But he wasn't cold because he was passing out: the glass doors at the end of the gallery had slid silently open. Beyond them, a smallish figure stood silhouetted against the freezing rock, swathed in sable, a pistol in one nicotine-stained hand. The muzzle was fixed unwaveringly on Mallory's chest.

"Closer," Jespers said in clear, cold German. "Closer, Jack. I don't want to shout."

8

A Man Like That

Mallory stared blankly at Jespers. Then he took a few steps forward.

"That's enough," Jespers said.

His quiet voice seemed to fill the long gallery, seemed to grow wings and flutter around Mallory's ears.

Mallory stopped.

"The gun?" Jespers said.

Mallory looked down at the bloody pistol hanging from his hand. "It's empty," he croaked.

"Nevertheless."

Mallory let it fall. The clack reverberated endlessly. Icy air was pouring in from the open door. It felt good on his sweaty face. From force of habit, he counted the steps between himself and Jespers, checked the angles, swept the room and balcony for anything he could use as a distraction, even mentally choreographed a few feints and gambits that might give him a slim chance at taking Jespers's gun out of play without incurring an immediately fatal wound. But it was all idle, mechanical, no more purposeful than doodles on a legal pad. Mallory had led enough men in the field to know the moment when all the fight goes out of a man, when he will quietly let himself be killed because it's too damn much trouble to try and save himself, and he knew that he had reached that point.

"Thank you," Jespers said.

"Sure," Mallory said, and coughed.

Jespers chuckled softly. "You know, it's a funny thing. When I came through the door just now and saw you, for a moment I must admit that I was glad. Even though you were killing my Mr. Kendrick. Even though I very much want you dead, I was glad to see you, Jack. Because, you see, I had missed you. We could have done great things together. And I was sorry that this would never happen. I was sorry that we'd never get to have another of our nice talks."

"Uh-huh?" Mallory began coughing again.

"Throat a bit sore, Jack? Never mind. I promise you I can cure this quite easily. Ah, me," Jespers sighed. "What an awful day it's been. Kendrick gone, poor funny Milena gone, Kost— You haven't seen Kost anywhere, have you?"

"No. 'Fact, I was looking for him."

"Kost gone. And Archangel gone. Where is Archangel, by the way? Where did you send my pretty little rocket?"

"Hudson Bay."

"Why?"

"My boss's got a Canadian trawler there waiting to scoop it up."

"Your boss, the mysterious Gray. Who is no doubt working for the Americans. And you are Jack Mallory of the Consultancy. And you are not gone at all, but continuing to cause me all kinds of sorrow."

"Not as much as I'd like."

"Quite enough, I think. Quite enough for me. Well, Jack, I admit I underestimated you once again. I should have shot you right away. Your partner came and let you out? Yes? Where is the talented Miss Laura Morse?"

"Around."

"This time I will shoot you both."

"Well, me, anyhow."

"And then I will go and begin to tidy up this mess you have made."

"Go on and try. We got your technology, Arne. Or we will once it splashes down. You got nothing to sell now."

"Oh, I disagree, Jack. I shall find something. There is always something to sell for a man like me. I shall even find a way to sell the little bits you've left of Archangel."

Mallory coughed again. It still hurt. He wished he didn't have to die with such a damn sore throat.

"It's you, Jack," Jespers said, "who has nothing to sell. All you ever had to sell was your nerve, your wits, and your luck. And I am afraid you have run out of all three."

"Looks like."

"And so it's time to say good-bye once again. And this time, I think, for good."

The mouth of the gun was an unwavering black dot.

"Good-bye, Jack," Jespers said.

"Uh-huh," Mallory said, and closed his eyes.

Mallory's body jolted as the little automatic spoke. He felt no pain. This didn't surprise him; like Laura, he'd learned that one often hears a gunshot wound before one feels it. He waited for the pain to come, or perhaps just the darkness, but a moment passed, and then another. And then he began to feel silly, standing there with his eyes closed. And so he opened them.

Jespers was swaying before him, openmouthed and vacant-eyed, his gun arm beginning to droop. A scarlet stain was spreading across his mink-clad upper chest. He peered down at it, confused, and, with his good hand, tried to brush it away.

And Walther Kost was striding out of the shadows, Kendrick's pistol in his hand.

"Yes," Kost murmured, filling the long chamber with murmuring. "Yes, Mr. Jespers, it's time to say good-bye. For three years you have shut me up like an animal in a cage. For six months you have offered me around to the scum of the world's nations like a slave on an auction block. You have perverted my life's work to fill your filthy pockets, and you have seen your plans collapse of your own disgusting greed. And now it is time for our good-byes."

"I—" Jespers whispered.

"Good-bye," Kost said, and shot Jespers again. "Good-bye." And again. "Good-bye." Yet again. With each *good-bye*, another red stain blossomed on Jespers's breast, and he staggered another step backward. And then, with a cry like a frightened infant, he toppled backward over the stone parapet and was gone.

There was a moment of silence. Mallory breathed again. He wondered whether he was going to start shaking. Sometimes you did.

He decided he was too tired.

"Well, that's that," Kost said in English. "An unpleasant and ultimately trivial man."

He raised a hand to rub his weary eyes, realized he still held a gun in it, and glanced at it with annoyance. "Here. I don't want this anymore," he said, and handed the pistol to Mallory. "My God, what these peasants have put me through. Have put us both through."

"Thanks," Mallory said hoarsely, taking the gun. "I'm kind of glad you came along, Doctor. We'd gotten to one of those awkward pauses."

"So I saw. You're all right, young man? You don't look well."

"I'm all right."

"I have had some medical training, young man, and I would say you are most certainly not all right."

"I'll do."

"Yes, I suppose you will. We both will. My God, what a time I've had. These miserable— Ach."

"How'd you manage to get free this morning?"

"Ah, it's not worth talking about. It's all very stupid and sordid."

"I thought they were watching you pretty close."

"Indeed they were. But I'm afraid, Mr.—Mallory, is it? I'm afraid I recently earned myself a degree of freedom by pretending to—what is the American phrase? Play along. I'm sorry to say I have been playing along."

"Playing along?"

"Yes. I had been trying to convince them for some time, you see, that I had joined their—their cause, I suppose you could say, and that they need not fear I would try to escape. But it was not until yesterday that I was actually able to persuade them. Early Monday morning one of the parties to this auction sent a young fool to my workroom. It was the most extraordinary thing. He said that his colleagues intended to abduct me the next day. He seemed to want to *discuss* the matter, as if we were planning an outing. He was young and obviously untrained, and apparently improvising on the spur of the moment, and I saw at once that if I fell in with him he was likely to get us both killed. And so I, ah, permitted his presence to come to Mr. Kendrick's notice. I told the young man that the rooms were not bugged—they were, of course, as any professional would have known—and that he could speak freely. And he"—Kost spread his hands—"did. And so he was eliminated sooner rather than later, and, reassured by my apparent *cooperation*, Jespers permitted me somewhat greater freedom of movement today than usually. And so—here we are. All very shameful and unpleasant, you see, just like this entire business."

Mallory was silent. Then he said, "His name was Billy."

"Pardon me?"

"His name was Billy Harmon."

"Who? The— Ah, he was one of yours? I am surprised to hear this."

"Yeah."

"Surprised and, of course, very sorry."

"You're very sorry."

"Naturally. I apologize—well, it's a bit late for that now. But I do apologize. I regret the error deeply."

Mallory was silent.

"In my own defense," Kost said, "I must point out that the young man's impulsiveness made him a bit of a menace, not only to me, but to himself, and by extension, to your own operation. Good intentions are all very—"

"Let me see if I got this," Mallory said slowly. "Let me try and get this straight. You been locked up here for three years. Cooped up like an animal, like you been saying, for three years. And a guy comes along and tries to spring you . . . A guy risks his *life* trying to spring you. And you, you just . . ."

"Once again, I apologize," Kost said with a touch of impatience. "I didn't know he was one of yours. But for heaven's sake, you know the fellow would have gotten us both killed, don't you? A man like that— Couldn't you do any better than a man like that?"

"A man like what?"

"A *schvartze*," Kost said. "A black savage, a very degraded type. Couldn't you tell that the man was of mixed blood?"

"Yeah," Mallory said after a brief pause. "I guess I could tell that."

"Forgive me for speaking bluntly. I suppose I have, during my long captivity, lost the habit of diplomacy. But an impure—"

"You said you hated Hitler, Kost. Why'd you build Archangel for him?"

"What? Why, I hoped it might help restore Germany's glory. Why else? I'm aware that this is not a goal that stirs every American's heart, but surely a fellow Aryan like yourself can, to some degree, understand? I hoped for a return to purity, to the highest ideals of my race. Instead, I found myself working for crossbred imbeciles, for a clubfoot like Goebbels and a fat clown like Göring and for Hitler himself, a mongrel if ever I saw one. Well, inferior types produce inferior results. It is not surprising that we were defeated. It is only surprising that so many young men of unpolluted blood were willing to sacrifice themselves for those . . . *ach*. And then I was carted off to Murmansk to work for a gang of Lysenkoist tractor mechanics, and then dragged off to Switzerland and obliged to slave for this degenerate *pimp*. This is my life's tale, Mr. Mallory: sent here, sent there, and never able to call my soul my own. And now," Kost sighed, "I suppose you're going to send me to America."

"Now," Mallory said, "I'm going to send you where you belong."

When Laurie loped out onto the balcony, she found Mallory standing alone by the parapet, gazing down into the ravine below, an unfamiliar gun dangling from his hand. *"There* you are," she said. "Thank God. Where's Jespers? Where's Kost?"

Mallory seemed not to hear. Then he opened his hand and let the gun drop over the edge. His eyes followed it down until it disappeared into the snowy crevasse.

He turned and took Laura's elbow.

"Tell you what, hon," he said. "Let's not wait around for them."

EPILOGUE

All You Can Ever Do

The fender of the silver Jaguar was warm under Laura's legs. The sun was warm on her face. Above her head, frail breaths of cloud were slowly revolving in the deep blue sky. It was a beautiful day. Morristown seemed a nice enough place. Even the houses closest to the train station were fairly nice, and the cars streaming past the station parking lot were nice without exception. She could hear the whispery rattle of a rotary mower as a boy down the street trimmed his family's lawn. He was tiny in the distance, his shirt a dab of red, his face a pale gold glint. Across the street from him, a small girl in a pink bathing suit did a solemn, private dance into and out of a round inflatable swimming pool. Laura could smell cut grass and heated asphalt, and hear the faint music of a far-off ice cream truck, monotonously clinking through its childish melody. She was not religious, but she felt it was somehow sinful not to enjoy a day like this when you had the chance, to enjoy being alive.

The first thing Laura generally did when she got home from a job was to sleep the clock around. This time, she'd had to stop off at Doc Chaudhury's consulting room to have a few stitches put into the palms of her gashed hands and some salve applied to her frostbitten feet. But after that, she'd gone straight home and crawled into bed, not even bothering to shower, and slept until the following afternoon. When she rose, she bathed as thoroughly as her wounds would allow, made a pot of very strong Constant Comment tea, and set it on her coffee table with a mug, a plate of crackers, and a pot of jam. She stretched out on her living-room sofa to finish reading her rumpled paperback Nero Wolfe, which she'd managed to retrieve from her luggage before leaving Switzerland. It was called *Champagne for One,* and she'd read it two or three times before. She'd read all of Stout's books two or three times before. After she turned the last page, she lay for a short while with the book on her chest and stared at the ceiling. Then, rising, she did up her face, brushed her hair, and put on a dress she particularly liked in spite of its peculiar color and awkward cut. She called a youngish, tallish midlevel attaché at the British embassy, with whom she'd had a brief and careful interlude some three years back, and ascertained he was not engaged either for the evening or for the longer term. The next morning at 8:30 she fed him scrambled eggs and overdone sausages and politely turned him out again.

When she'd done all this, Laura Morse felt recovered enough in body, mind, and heart to resume her civilian life.

She wished she could say the same about Jack.

Laura had been sitting on the fender of her Jaguar for nearly two hours when Mallory came into view, walking steadily down the sunlit street past the boy with the mower and the child in the inflatable pool. He was wearing a suit and looked, even from that distance, vaguely official. Mallory was good at looking official, in spite of being the least official man she'd ever known. She tried and failed to detect the moment when he caught sight of her. She presumed it had been almost as soon as he came into view of the train station parking lot. His gait and expression did not alter as he drew closer; both could best be described as patient. His weathered face was grayish beneath its perpetual tan. His throat, she could now see, was mottled with blue and purple bruises. When he was close enough to speak without shouting, he said, "Tracked me down, huh?"

She shrugged. "You didn't make it difficult."

He boosted himself up on the fender beside her. For a moment, they sat and watched the cars swish gently by.

"You look pretty beat," she said.

"I'm all right," he said. "Been having a little trouble sleeping. Chaudhury said I might for a while. Gave me some pills to take if I felt like I needed 'em."

Laura didn't answer at once. Then she sighed and said, "No."

"What do you mean, no?"

"I mean, no, that's not what Chaudhury said."

"It isn't, huh?"

"No. Dr. Chaudhury," Laura said, "told me you haven't been eating. And that you've been sleeping no more than three hours a night. And that you can only do it sitting up in an armchair, with the lights on and the doors and windows open. Otherwise, you can't breathe. He said your blood pressure's elevated and your resting pulse is above ninety. He said you're about as bad a case of nervous exhaustion and acute traumatic shock as he's seen, and he makes a living treating them, and that he'd tried to send you to a specialist in battle fatigue, but that you wouldn't talk to her, and that he'd begged you to take sedatives, or even just something to let you sleep, but that you'd rather just drink." She straightened the crease of her slacks, and then refolded her hands neatly in her lap. "*That's* what Chaudhury said."

"He's a gossipy little son of a bitch, isn't he?"

"He's worried as hell, and you won't give him a straight answer. So he came to me. And I told him if he wanted me to answer his questions, he'd have to answer some of mine."

"You been checking up on me."

"Spying. It's what I do. I was worried, too. I thought you might do something like this."

"Something like what?"

"Something like go see Billy's parents."

He sighed, and for a moment was quiet again.

"You're worried it was insecure," he said.

"I don't give a damn whether it was insecure or not."

He kicked a heel against the Jaguar's front tire.

"I guess it wasn't the smartest move. And I know it's not the kind of thing Gray'd ever give a crap about."

She waited.

"But I figured somebody ought to do it. If Billy was still in the Marines, there'd be somebody to do it. Somebody to go and sit with them, and, you know, do right. Even if you couldn't tell any of the details. I wanted to tell 'em . . ."

"Something," she said sadly.

"That's right, something. I didn't want us to, you know, just pull down the blinds. I gave 'em the idea we were CIA but couldn't say so. I told 'em their son was a good man. I told 'em he helped keep some pretty high-powered weaponry out of the wrong hands. I said we couldn't have done it without him. I guess I tried to make them feel like he didn't die in vain or however you want to say it." He grimaced. "*Didn't die in vain*—that's the kind of crap I wound up talking." Mallory shook his head disgustedly. "I wasted their time. I kept talking, and talking, and the more I kept talking— They were trying to make *me* feel better about things. They'd just lost their son, and now they had to sit there and listen to me."

"There's never anything to say, Jack. You know that."

"Well, I sure said it anyway." He stared down at the white line separating Laura's parking spot from the next. "They were nice people. They were awful nice, especially considering what'd just happened. His mom's the one, you know."

"The one what?"

"The colored one. Negro, I mean. She's pretty pale, about like Billy, and I guess that's how they got to buy a nice house here and so on before the neighbors got things figured out. But they've figured it out by now, boy. They put up big fences on both sides, the neighbors did, those big redwood ones that're kind of woven, like a basket, and I don't get the impression that anyone out there's too friendly. And I can just sort of imagine Billy growing up. Looking at his dad, looking at his mom, and those big fences up around the house, and just knowing that nothing in life was going to be easy or smooth."

"I'm sure they were happy you'd come, Jack, even if there wasn't anything you could say or do. They must have appreciated it, that somebody else was sorry. That somebody came around to say so."

"He was their only boy, you know that? Their only kid. I don't know what they're going to do now. They're a little long in the tooth to try and make some more. They kept trying to get me to eat lunch with them. They must have offered me shepherd's pie and creamed corn about half a dozen times, and finally I sat down with them and had some shepherd's pie and creamed corn and root beer, and peach pie with ice cream after that. So you're wrong about me not eating, 'cause I just ate about six pounds of pie. It was the only thing I could do that seemed to make them feel a little better. Eat their pie. Well, thanks for tracking me down, I guess. You saved me another train ride, anyway."

"You tried to do what's right, Jack," Laura said. "That's all you can ever do."

"If that's all you can ever do then I don't see the goddamn point of bothering."

"Well, I'm still glad you did."

"And don't goddamn look at me like that," Mallory said violently. "Don't look at me like poor Jack can't help it. I don't remember putting out a call for a social worker. I don't remember sticking a sign up in my front yard saying please come spy on me, 'cause I don't have good sense myself."

"I can't help worrying, Jack."

"You can goddamn try a little harder."

"I'm sorry."

"Everybody's sorry."

"I guess we are."

"I was a damn fool to come out here."

"Well, get in and I'll run you back home."

"I'll drive," Mallory snapped.

"All right," she said, and dug in her purse for the keys.

She handed them over, then hopped down from the fender and walked around to the passenger door.

Mallory stood motionless, staring at the keys in his palm. He poked them with a forefinger, as if counting them.

Then he closed them in his fist, shook his head, and smiled shame-facedly.

"Aw," he said. "Aw, hell. Somebody oughta take me out behind the barn and shoot me. I'm awful sorry, Laurie. I really am. Here I am barking at you, when all you're doing is trying to take care of me. Just like you did back in Jo'burg. Just like you always do."

"You said that very charmingly," Laura snapped, angry for the first time. "But sometimes, Jack, your charm wears a little thin."

"But you don't ever buy my charm, Laurie. That's what I'm talking about. You think I'm a drunk and a pouter and a big old pain in the ass, and you take care of me anyhow."

She was silent.

Mallory walked back around the car and held out the keys. Laura took them wordlessly. He eased into the passenger seat, and she climbed in behind the wheel. The big engine started up with a gentle roar, and he let his head sink back and his eyes half close. The bruises on his throat gleamed, dusky and faintly metallic. She said, "Why don't you try to get a little sleep on the way home?"

He opened his eyes. "That's an idea. I might try that."

"Sure," Laura said. "Give it a try."

He closed his eyes.

She put the silver car into gear, and they slipped out into the endless stream of traffic.